This book was judged Best Self-Published Novel by the James River Writers Club (Virginia) in 2016.

HEAVEN WILL PROTECT THE WORKING GIRL

A NOVEL OF SUSPENSE

JO ALLISON

Copyright © **2016 by Jo Allison**, TX 8-287-397
Re-issue: 2021

ISBN-13: 978-0-9973145-4-0
Printed in the United States of America

Design by Rebecca Sharkey, rebeccasharkey.weebly.com
Editing by MS Editing, mandyschoenedits.com

Please visit:

joallisonauthor.com
1910-stlouis-by-jallison.com

*To Angelia Denise Stanley, first reader, steadfast
encourager, and proponent extraordinaire
of double-entry bookkeeping*

1

*From **The St. Louis Globe-Democrat**, Tuesday, October 11, 1910*

> *Plans have been completed and all of St. Louis is ready for the visit tomorrow by former President Theodore Roosevelt. Colonel Roosevelt will be joined by Governor Hadley in speeches promoting Republican candidates.*
>
> *Some ten thousand St. Louis school children will spend time Columbus Day hearing from the Colonel at the Fairgrounds.*

Something's floating on the black surface a few feet from me. I'd hit water on the third step from the bottom. By the time I gain the last step, moving gingerly on water-slick wood, the floating mass is waving tendrils at me. Does it reflect my motion? Or a will of some sort?

Silly of me. There shouldn't be anything alive—other than the woman I'm seeking—in this flooded basement. Of course, the woman might not be alive. Might not even be here. We have only the word of a prostitute upstairs, who whispered a name and this dark location to a passing officer.

Hair? Maybe the floating mass is hair. All I have to do is get the lantern closer, and I'll have the answer.

"What is it, Miss Nye? Why are you stopping?"

Captain Mike Messerton likely thinks that's a stage whisper, but it's certainly too loud for our purposes. We want to show as little official presence as possible to anyone in distress. The last victim found confined to a basement in this neighborhood panicked when confronted with a squad of St. Louis police, rescue notwithstanding, and darted outside into the path of a moving auto. So Chief Micah Wright recruited his typist, me, to wade in rescue tonight—and make a good first impression.

I don't look back up the stairs where I left the Captain and the sporting house's madam, standing with arms akimbo and frowning. Instead, I wave my free hand to reassure him and, more importantly, shush him. Of course, his question means I should commence moving. One step onto the basement floor and two more into the chamber, and I'll be out of their view. And into contact with the floating fiend.

Only two steps give me enough light to see a stick attached to the stringy mass. The mop simply floated to the surface as the water rose. I'm immediately grateful to Captain Messerton that I moved when I did. Had I hesitated longer, I'd have cops on my heels, and I'd never live down the monster mop episode.

The possibility is nearly enough to distract me from the cold water that soaks my boots and stockings and wicks its way up my bloomers. Good thing I insisted on dashing upstairs at home to change. The thought of this coal-dust-thickened water, carrying smells of mildew and worse, soaking a long skirt and petticoats is too dismal.

All of which does not sidetrack me from my mission. I ignore other floating items. I tell myself that anything bumping against my legs under the water is rightly there. I peer into every corner my lantern's light offers. The boiler sits on a platform, and the fire isn't threatened. Neither is the coal supply in its bin. Everything else is a shimmering, sloshing, black bath, hitting just below my knees.

"Hello?" My voice is flat, as if its echo is lost in a dark corner. "Is anyone down here?" Sergeant Witherspoon wasn't too sure about the name he'd been offered, but I'll try it. "Marian?"

Maybe movement. Ahead and slightly to my left. "Marian?" I call again.

Nothing. Oddly, I'm getting to higher ground. The flooding from our incredible run of rain, early ice, more rain, seems to pool only around the stairs. I clear the water just as something crunches under my left foot.

I shift to my right. A swing of the lantern catches the glint of glass. I poke at it, but it's just glass, already broken, now in small pieces. The piece I pick up is unusual only in its thinness. Maybe there's a bit of a curve to it. I'm trying to reckon it out when movement ahead catches my eye.

The movement bursts into sound: painful coughing fading into a moan suggesting more than ill health. I press forward, trying to see into the shadows at the end of the cellar. What little light there is constitutes a distraction, reflecting on the water to each side of me and rolling off to my left.

"Marian?" I try again.

"No."

No? How many women are down here?

"Who's here?" That seems a reasonable question on my part.

"Only me. Who are you?" A reasonable question on not-Marian's part.

I commence explaining that there was a raid upstairs when the woman breaks into another fit of coughing. I declare it lasts two minutes, as I move my lantern about and wonder one more time why a raid tonight. The police do occasionally raid sporting houses but not on nights when half the force is guarding a visitor as important as former President Roosevelt or when the city is crowded with political visitors and tourists. I have a whole store of questions to ask the cops upstairs. Later. The lantern finally locates movement—on the wall.

The woman seems to be curled up on a shelf.

The coughing ends this time in a sigh of exhaustion, and it will be a wonder if she can respond to my next attempt. "My name's Julia Nye, and I work for the police department. They raided this place, and a woman upstairs said someone named . . . well . . . that someone was down here. If you're hiding, it's safe to come upstairs."

No answer.

"We'll get you dry and warm and do something for that cough."

Her voice is also flat. "Did they arrest the man who runs it?"

Unfortunately, I'm not sure how to answer. I wasn't privy to the original raid. Chief Wright didn't call me in until he thought my youth and energy and concern were needed. I should have a card printed: "Typing and messy odd jobs for the St. Louis Police Department."

And now I need to say the right thing. "I'm sure they arrested anyone upstairs who seemed to be running things. There are some women up there still, and one of them told us about you."

The woman coughs again, and the lantern and I move closer. Ah. Not on a shelf. The basement doesn't extend the full length of the first floor. A crawl space was dug into this end, and the woman has climbed into it, above the damp floor but wedged against what must be a wet wall.

"Please come with me. No one will arrest you. We only want to help."

She isn't screaming, and that's good. But I can see her face now, and her chin is trembling. Big blue eyes reflect my light.

"Who are you?" she asks again.

"My name's Julia, and I want to help. Please. It's cold down here. Let's go upstairs."

Nothing. The lantern light catches more movement and more of the woman. She's trying to slither back into the slot, pulling a long, once-white garment around her.

"Really, I can help. Did you get trapped by the flood?" I move closer, and she rolls her eyes before she turns her back and tries to wiggle away, deeper into the crawl space. A coughing spell catches her, though, and she doubles up, lying on her side, her back to me, quivering.

I take advantage of her momentary incapacity and reach for her. Her back is wet. I can't say if it's mud from the wall or something more worrisome. But I grasp her shoulder and pull.

The round blue eyes turn on me, and she crawls into my arms.

Logically, I wouldn't know what to do with a full-grown woman clinging to me. Luckily, instinct takes over. I wrap one arm around her upper body, put the lantern on the ledge, scoop my right arm under her legs, and retrieve the lantern. I don't know if I can carry her weight, but I'm going to try.

2

When I reach the stairs, Captain Messerton clatters down to take the lantern. Marian, or whoever she is, clings to me even tighter and murmurs my name. I'm so glad I don't have to raise a skirt to get up the steps. The woman's long dress, heavy with caked dirt, is enough of a burden.

"Julia, miss, Julia, please don't leave me," she's saying. I doubt anyone else can hear her, although the captain's trying.

We emerge into the kitchen, and the warmth is immediate. It's as if the light and the heat and the chatter are embracing me as firmly as I'm holding the woman. A ring of faces watches us. One is the painted resident who'd been standing just the same way when I went down the stairs: hands on her hips in impatience, disapproval on her face as she took in my bloomers. And something else on her face now. Maybe satisfaction.

Beyond her Sergeant Red Witherspoon, the one who got the tip, is talking to Chief Micah Wright, who's staring at me. Usually, I spend my days smiling and bantering with officers and typing away outside the chief's door in my unconventional job downtown. Now the chief is seeing me be even more unconventional, wet and bothered, in St. Louis' red-light district.

I glimpse another man standing in the background: the police reporter for the *St. Louis Globe-Democrat*—and my beau. William McConnell doesn't usually cover raids. Someone at Headquarters must have told him I'm here, and he's covering this piece of police news personally. Maybe he's why the room feels comforting. I can't get my mouth past the nest of blonde hair to smile at him.

I'd thought to put the woman on the big oak table, but I don't want her to turn and see the men. The captain tries to get her to raise her head with the result that the woman tightens her grip and starts breathing hard again. Every breath ends in a whimper and a shiver.

"Can you get us a blanket?" I ask. The madam huffs but turns to give an order. I maneuver a chair with my foot and sit so that Marian faces back toward the basement door. I wish someone would close the darn thing. Damp is wafting up the stairs.

I'm managing to hold the woman because she's tiny. And, of course, it helps that she clings to me instead of being limp weight. I put my mouth close to her ear. "What's your name?" She shakes her head, and that sets off more coughing.

A blanket arrives, and the madam says, "It won't matter if she gets blood on this." I try to look over the woman's shoulder at her back and can tell it likely *is* blood coming through the filthy white dress. And soaking my sleeve.

The woman shudders in my arms, and I try again. "What should I call you?"

"Don't leave me."

So, I hold her. I tell her it'll be O.K. I have no idea what happened in the first place, meaning my reassurance is a hollow promise, but she starts to relax.

Then ambulance workers come in with a stretcher, and the woman turns to look without loosening her grip. I jerk forward.

The ambulance chaps must think I'll drop her, because one of them grabs for her arm. She screams, a straight scream right in my ear that makes me jerk back again. Then she's screaming my name. I try to keep hold of her, but the men pry her arms from my neck.

They want to tie her to the stretcher, but she's hardly cooperating. I move around them, hoping to take her hand. She starts to reach out but pulls her hand back to cover her bosom. After I glimpse more blood, thin lines of it indicating scratches beneath the sheer fabric, I throw a corner of the blanket over her.

Captain Messerton's talking, trying to reassure the woman. The ambulance guys are talking between themselves, loudly, and Sergeant Witherspoon is now talking noisily to the brothel lady.

William looks sympathetic. I reach out and grip his hand briefly as I pass. At the least, I want to see the screaming, struggling woman into the ambulance.

The sporting house was once a nice home with a deep porch and wide steps, a steep half dozen of them. About half way down, gravity comes to the woman's aid, and she slides under the restraint.

Men yell, and I yell louder. The woman lands on her hands and knees, and the ambulance attendants stand there with the stretcher as if they expect her to jump back on it. I lean over the railing and see the woman crawling along the foundation. The bushes that once bloomed there are sticks now, and the woman's dress hangs up. She manages to stand and is tugging at it when I get to her.

"C'mon, gal, we gotta get you to the hospital." The voice comes from behind me. "We'll get you warm, let's go now."

But the woman is clinging to me, and I'm holding her by the arms and trying to think how to help. "Don't let them touch me, please," she whispers.

"C'mon now." The deeper voice tries again, and an arm snakes around me to grab at her.

I let go as the woman pulls back and turn to say, "Give us a minute. You're scaring her."

I'm interrupted by another scream, and I turn back to find the poor woman on the ground again, rolling back to her left into a bush. The captain moves to the edge of the porch with a lantern.

The woman writhes in my arms and reaches for her leg where a short-handled garden claw is embedded in her right knee. It looks as if one prong has wedged itself in above the kneecap, maybe after she tripped over the filthy handle.

One attendant pulls it out, and the other slaps a folded cloth on the joint. The woman screams again, but I think she's running out of breath fast.

"I'm riding with her." I take a good grip. "Help me pick her up."

"You can't do that, ma'am," the older attendant says. "There's no room."

"Then leave him here." I gesture at the younger man as I manage to lift the woman, who's clinging again and gasping.

I put her down on the floor of the ambulance and then have to crawl in myself while she holds onto my neck. A snicker sounds behind me.

Once in the ambulance I can't quite stand. So, I waddle and scoot to the bench. We both sit rather heavily. The man who fetched the stretcher chuckles as he shoves it onto the floor beside us.

Having gotten the woman this far, I can't get her to lie down. I tell the men to let us sit for the ride to City Hospital. They don't like it, but they give in. One of them hands me the same folded cloth, now wet and dirty, and the blanket that slipped to the damp ground. Then he joins the driver up front. There's room after all.

From the back window, I see the chief with his hands on his hips, sure sign he doesn't like the way things have worked out. And William is saying something as he heads down the steps. He has my jacket, the one that I'd made to match the bloomers back when I was a teener. The younger attendant opens the door a crack and tosses the jacket on the floor. I yell, "Thank you, Will."

I don't know that he heard me, or if he'll follow us. I also don't know that I need another man around just now. Or if this sobbing, clinging, hurting woman needs one, more to the point.

I put my jacket around her shoulders. It's old, after all, and I can clean dirt and a bit of blood out of the lining. She clutches at me, and I try again. "Please tell me your name."

Three audible, difficult breaths later, she says, "Meredith."

It's half a minute before she adds, "He'll come after me."

3

The glimpse I get of City Hospital through the slit of a side window is enough to be a welcome sight. We pull around to a back entrance. The wagon is still, so someone must have appeared to hold a bridle. The city's going to change over to automobile ambulances, but it hasn't happened yet. Of course, an automobile might have backfired and bucked. Maybe the newest isn't always the best, although it runs against my inclinations and politics to admit it.

The minute the door opens, I know my inclinations and politics are about to be exercised further.

The hatless man who should be helping Meredith stares at my outfit.

"You can't come in the hospital dressed like that, miss," is his opening line. No questions about the woman coughing and bleeding in my arms.

But Meredith certainly hears him and starts begging again. "Don't let him touch me, Julia."

I've given up patting her on the back, because I can't tell exactly where her wounds are. Instead, I press my hand against the back of her head and try to sound civil for her sake.

"She needs me, sir, and I don't think you'll be able to help her unless I stay with her."

"You work at the brothel—like that?" Maybe I'm seeing the hint of a smile.

"No, sir. I work for the St. Louis Police, and I wear clothes like this when I'm wading through flooded basements. Trying to get this woman some medical assistance. Would you care to help us down?"

The man's clearly going to question the police part, but one of the ambulance drivers is saying something about "officers around front." I don't get the other details because Meredith is coughing up a storm in my ear. I decide not to sit there any longer and take a better grip on her.

As I get to the back, the first gentlemen kindly takes his hands off his hips and lowers a set of steps I hadn't noticed before. A nurse has come out along with two younger men pushing a stretcher on wheels, and she's the first one there to actually lay hands on Meredith.

Meredith jerks and holds me tighter, but she looks at the nurse and doesn't scream. Between me and the nurse, we get her to lie down, mostly by promising to get out of the wind and damp.

It's more than obvious that she doesn't want anyone male touching her and equally obvious that the male doctors intend to do just that. I try explaining that she was hiding from someone at the brothel. That she's obviously been beaten. That she needs medical help, but she needs it from the nurses. The nurse looks at me as if I'm mad.

We get her to a large room, and another nurse appears to draw a curtain around us. The doctor who met us is back to standing there with his hands on his hips.

"O.K., miss, we'll take care of her now. The nurses will help." My doubts must show, because he puts a firm hand on my shoulder. "Your police friends are waiting for you. Jones here will show you back out, and you can catch up with them around front."

He's saying I'm supposed to walk around the sprawling building, instead of going through it, wearing very wet wool pants. I'm almost distracted from Meredith's protests and her grip on my hand.

While I try to think of something to say to the smug little doctor, one of the nurses pulls Meredith's hand from mine and moves between us. Another tosses my jacket to me, and the doctor pulls me, with some difficulty, outside the curtain. Meredith's calling my name, each iteration decreasing in volume.

The doctor lowers his voice. "We'll patch her up. She won't last long with that cough, but we'll patch her up and keep her here, in case the police have questions." I'm sputtering, and he looks the slightest bit sympathetic. "She needs our help now, not yours. We'll take care of her, regardless of where you found her. Go on now."

Regardless of where I found her? Meaning they'll waste a few bandages on a whore on a slow night?

I have a whole women's rights lecture, but I decide not to waste it. "You better help her. The Chief of Police is the one waiting out there." Threats. That's what men understand.

I can't see her for the nurses between us. I can't hear her call me for the coughing. I hurry out the way I came in, hoping to heck the doctor doesn't check to find out who's really waiting in front.

◆ ◆ ◆

To my surprise, Chief Wright is indeed waiting just inside the door, along with William, Captain Messerton, and Sergeant Witherspoon. It's too late at night for me to shock more than a few people by opening the big front door and walking right up to them.

The hospital is imposing with its columns and dome on the

outside but, when you step inside, the building gets down to business. A large sign points to various floors and functions. Hospital smells flow toward the door. A dozen chairs await anxious visitors, but only one is occupied. An elderly man sits with elbows on his knees and head in his hands. He doesn't look up.

I'm more angry than shaken. But William holds out a hand, and I take it. All three of the city's finest notice and smile. I wouldn't normally grip his fingers so tightly, and Will surely knows it, even if the cops don't.

I explain that our brothel escapee is being helped and that a doctor says they'll keep her here, presumably overnight. At least he didn't ask who's paying, but then this is City Hospital, not one of the private hospitals in St. Louis. The chief nods.

Oddly, it's Captain Messerton who asks if she'll be O.K. Messerton commands one of the nastier districts in the city and has a tough reputation. Usually, his smallish brown eyes just hover, dull and too close together for good looks, and wait for someone to say something incriminating. Tonight, his eyes are bright.

I'm curious to see his reaction, even if I don't like my answer. "The doctor says that cough is bad. I guess they can fix all the scratches and bleeding." I hope her knee doesn't go bad, but I don't say that to Messerton because he might take off after the ambulance attendants.

The chief and William and Red Witherspoon make sounds that add up to "too bad." Messerton says, "Damn," and distracts a passing nurse who's staring at me. "Did you get her name?"

"Only Meredith. Nothing else at all, except she's afraid of whoever runs the place." I turn to the chief. "I'd like to come back tomorrow."

He smiles. I take my job as typist seriously, being the first person and certainly the first woman to hold the position. And on those occasions when I've detected without the chief's permission, I've been careful to do it on my time, not the department's. But I'll be on holiday tomorrow anyway, for Columbus Day. Meaning I'm suggesting doing police work on my day off.

"That's a good idea, good to hear what she knows." The chief turns the whole group to head outside. "I thought you'd want to see the aeroplane exhibition."

I look at William, and he says, "I think you should at least check on her."

William's giving me an excuse. He has to know that coming back to see Meredith is important to me, but it means I can't watch the big event. Because it isn't only that Teddy Roosevelt is going to greet the aviators at the air show. The St. Louis news corps was offered a ride in an aeroplane for one lucky reporter. I don't know that all that many men in the city's large reporter pool put their names in the hat, but William didn't hesitate. He's excited to be chosen. I'm excited, too, and worried in a way that my politics and personality don't allow me to express. I don't know how he understands that I'm hesitant to watch.

I squeeze his hand and change the subject to include the cops. "It's a good thing for the woman you decided on the raid tonight." Tonight is totally inconvenient. The chief has fewer men to spare than usual and a long day tomorrow on top of today's efforts. In fact, I can't imagine why the chief of police would show up at a sporting house raid anytime, let alone tonight.

Messerton doesn't answer. He starts walking faster. "I'll check with you after you see her tomorrow, Miss Nye. A little before noon, maybe, at your boarding house?"

"Yes, that would be good," I answer to his back. He nods and walks off into the clearing night.

Witherspoon gives me a smile. "Nice work tonight, Miss Nye." He starts after his boss. Then he turns back to say, "Be careful up there, Mac."

Chief Wright gestures toward an automobile I recognize. It isn't his department vehicle, a Darby, made in St. Louis. It's his personal, new Buick Model 10. I've ridden with him once in the slower Darby. Makes me wish the streetcar would appear.

"You heard about the first raid," the chief says as William graciously moves to the front of the Buick to man the crank. The chief gets in to fiddle with something. Someday I'll figure out what all the fiddling is about. Meanwhile, neither helps me in because I've trained them not to. In this case, negotiating the running board and tiny half-door is so much easier minus my skirts I have to smile.

I perch on the edge of the back seat, staying on the right so I can talk to the chief close to his ear. "I heard there was a raid a week ago and that a woman ran out naked. I typed some of the details, but I have a feeling the squad room had a different take on it."

William is cranking away, and the engine catches fast. He joins me in the back seat, as I hoped he would, although most men would crowd up front with the chief.

"The thing is," the chief says loudly, looking back over his shoulder, "some woman who was obviously trying to get away from the brothel—a block or so down from the one tonight—ran out in the street. I also heard she wasn't wearing much."

The chief turns onto Broadway in a wide sweep, and I'm grateful it's after midnight. Because he also keeps talking.

"The boys must have been having trouble with her. I'm betting they didn't much want to take hold of her, and she got away. She was running along Eugenia when Messerton showed up, driving the Darby we keep over at the Eighth. And the woman veered and ran into his path. Practically ran right at the car, he said. Hit hard and rolled over the hood."

The chief seems to slow down just thinking about the collision. We pass a streetlamp, and William is frowning, eyebrows drawn down in the center over dark blue eyes. It's getting to the point where looking at him distracts me.

"Messerton was really troubled," Chief Wright continues. "Whatever the madam back there told him, he insisted on that raid tonight. I think he's afraid there's something going on other than business as usual. But I'll have to press him for his thoughts when all these politicians get out of town."

It could be a while. There's no presidential race this year, but the state races and some city ones are particularly contentious, and then there's the state vote on prohibition. I'm not sure how the newspapers find room for police news with all the advertisements pro and con.

Which makes me turn to William. "You aren't going to try to get this story in tonight, are you?"

"No." He finds my hand in the dark and squeezes it. "There's no time and no room. But I'm betting the *Post* won't have any room tomorrow either." The *Globe* is second in circulation to the *Post-Dispatch*, and they compete wildly. The *Globe* might have an edge on the week's events what with William's first-hand account of an aeroplane flight.

We agree William needs to get home, and his boarding house is closer than mine, so the chief drops him off first. I have no idea how to tell William to be careful. He's going to sit up there on flimsy wood, on a board balanced between struts. The only way to be careful is by not going. And I certainly wouldn't suggest that because I'd take the chance in a heartbeat. Most likely.

I swallow hard as William climbs down. "Maybe you can find a telephone and call the house when . . . you're on land."

William gives me his usual smile, a gentle stretch of lips that forms deep creases, vertical dimples. "I will." He tips his hat to us both.

I sigh as the chief bounces us forward. I'll spend the night worrying about a beau I can't shelter and about a stranger I can't save.

4

*From **The St. Louis Globe-Democrat**, Wednesday, October 12, 1910*

Former President Roosevelt is expected to join Columbus Day crowds at Kinloch Field today to watch top aviators at the aeroplane meet. Among the pilots performing will be Arch Hoxsey, in a Wright biplane, according to Aero Club president Albert B. Lambert. Hoxsey set a time record in flying over a hundred miles from Springfield, Ill., to St. Louis, Sunday.

Carl Schroeder paces in front of the crowd that fills the aviation field at Kinloch. Folks in the grandstand strain to see the three aeroplanes currently aloft; Carl's only interested in seeing that the Wright biplane carrying William McConnell is still in the air.

Carl put his name in the hat for the ride, assuring the promoters that his piece would run in both the *Westliche Post*, the German paper he gets paid to write for, and its sister paper, the English-language *St. Louis Times*. That wasn't a problem. The *Times* reporters all thought he was out of his mind.

He's been telling himself he's disappointed not to be chosen. Not that it's the total truth. He wants the experience. For one thing, Julia Nye and Fran Collier and their suffragist friends would be impressed as all get out. But he can't quite imagine himself getting in the fragile little craft. He was beside himself today when Will crawled into the narrow space.

There's nothing he can do if the aeroplane gets in trouble. But he was happier a few minutes ago when the pilot was simply circling the airfield. After two passes, the machine rises and joins the French pilot in a Bleriot monoplane and a pilot who's going for an endurance record in another Wright biplane. The three move east toward the city. Will's going to see downtown St. Louis from the air.

Carl paces, scanning the sky, wanting the aeroplanes to reappear. Two do. Carl curses and grabs the sleeve of the Aero Club official standing nearby. "Why are only two of those damn things coming back?"

The man sighs and pulls his arm loose. "Let me see, Mr. Schroeder. And kindly be calm."

The man fiddles with his binoculars. Probably hard to focus and sight in on the moving vehicles. But Carl bounces with anxiety anyway. Will would be so cool in his place.

"Uh-huh," the man says. "It's your friend in Arch Hoxsey's biplane and Monsieur LeBlanc. I'm betting Welch is circling back east, putting in the time."

Words of relief back up in Carl's throat. The gentleman laughs and strolls back toward the the grandstand where ten-thousand people start to applaud when they catch sight of the craft. There'll be more folks at the field this afternoon, when Colonel Roosevelt's supposed to visit the exhibition, but this might be the high point of Carl's day.

LeBlanc comes in high and begins to show off over the east end of the field. Will's chauffeur, the flying ace named Arch Hoxsey, heads west. Hoxsey set some sort of best himself, getting to St. Louis, but Carl has lost track of the records set and broken by these fools. All he wants from Arch Hoxsey is what he gets: a graceful turn and a landing as smooth as any Carl has seen. Carl's off and running to the spot where the plane should roll to its stop.

5

I pop out of bed early on this Columbus Day, without an alarm, waking from a dream of flight. Maybe I dreamed darker dreams, about subterranean mud and cold, but I don't remember that. I do remember Meredith.

Because I'm up and around, I decide to go into Headquarters and get some of the night reports done before I visit her. I type furiously in the quiet second floor that houses a squad room, administrative offices including Chief Wright's, and my desk in its open reception area near the chief's door. Normally, I'd have said hello to at least a dozen cops and be ready to greet detectives, some of whom wouldn't even bother with handwritten reports. They'd just dictate to me. Today they're all out on the streets for the holiday and Colonel Roosevelt.

I've done half a day's work before mid-morning. William is somewhere in the sky over St. Louis, and our friend Carl Schroeder is undoubtedly watching out for him, covering the story as well. In the quiet of the Headquarters, I think I hear the drone of an engine. I've seen an aeroplane in flight once, and it thrilled me.

Normally, I'd be having a wonderful day, even if I was nervous about William covering the story quite so intimately. I'd rejoice in the modernness of it all. I keep telling my friends and family this new century is going to produce unimaginable change, beget new ways of doing things, usher in new and enlightened attitudes. And here I am, having moved to the big city, agitating for the suffrage, earning my own living however meager the pay, making a small but significant difference working with the police—and hearing aeroplanes race overhead as I work.

And instead of reveling, I'm hurrying so I can visit a woman who undoubtedly cares nothing about any of that. Her world has indeed changed in ways she couldn't have imagined.

When I realize I'm making typing errors thinking of Meredith, I quit. I cover the 'writer, grab my bag, hat, and sweater, and hurry off to the streetcar.

Apparently, not everyone is watching the air show from Kinloch Field. The crowd at Twelfth and Clark is looking at the western horizon, where two birdlike shapes are gliding. I wish I knew which one William's in so I could say I'd seen him.

I shake my head and dodge both horse-drawn vehicles and automobiles, crossing the street to wait for my streetcar. I have to have seen him. I look up again, and the craft are smaller.

It's early for visiting hours at City Hospital, but that gives me the opportunity to use my new identification card. It says I work for the St. Louis Police Department and Chief Micah Wright appreciates any courtesies extended to me while I'm on official police business. I can hardly wait to show it to my father the next time he visits.

The hospital staff isn't as impressed with the card as I hope Dad will be. But they also don't seem to care if I'm early, whoever I am, once they find out who I want to see. A nurse outside Meredith's curtained cubicle smiles and hurries off in a white rustle of petticoats and starch.

I hope Meredith will be sitting up, irritated because she doesn't like hospitals. Maybe she'll be angry I left her last night. That's O.K., too. Anger is sometimes good medicine. I worry when sick people don't care about much.

I'm ready, therefore, for irritation when I part the curtain.

It isn't that Meredith isn't angry. She is. She's also hurting and scared, I judge. And tied to the bed. On her face.

She looks around at me as I approach from the foot, and she tries to say my name but starts coughing. The sheet that already has slid aways down her back slides further. The binding cloth runs around her chest, above her breasts and under her armpits, and disappears under the bed. I raise the sheet, without thinking, to see another binding across her buttocks. Her back is bandaged, I can tell, under the worn hospital gown. She strains to take weight off the heavily wrapped knee.

"Julia, can you help me?" She's whispering and trying to free a hand to reach out, and I realize she's jammed her hands under her body, probably to take the weight off her breasts.

I take her hand. "Why are you tied?" I whisper, as well. The nearest occupied bed is no more than ten feet away, and a nurse could be right outside the curtain which I'd let fall behind me.

Tears start running down her face. "I can't stay here. And they won't let me go. He'll find me. They won't keep him in jail, I know they won't."

Drat. I don't even know if a man was arrested, so I can't reassure her on that count. Instead, I make a more basic decision. I let go of her hand and open my bag to dig out the folding knife I carry. Of course, anyone looking in my bag would see the revolver first, but I'm not ready to shoot anyone yet.

Crawling under the bed isn't my first choice although the hospital staff might prefer me to do that, to untie the restraining cloths. I cut through the top restraint easily, and Meredith gets her hand back under her body. I move even faster on the lower one, and she immediately turns to lift the weight from her knee.

I see the staff's dilemma. Her back is obviously damaged. Could they have tied her on her side?

Meredith rolls back to her left, closing her eyes in pain.

"What hurts the most?"

"My knee." She gasps for breath.

The blanket has slid off the bed. I roll it into a pillow and put it under her knee, adjusting as she bends the leg slightly, looking for the least painful position. Then I hold her and the blanket as she begins coughing violently. I don't like that cough at all.

When she finishes, she doesn't seem to have the energy to move. I spread my sweater over her, sit carefully on the bed, and take her top hand, draping her arm across my leg. I see a bit of blood coming through the gown from a scratch on her breast. I can't tell if she has bandages there as well.

With my other hand, I push damp blonde curls off her face. There are bruises, but I can tell she's very pretty. Doll-like. Nothing like me.

So much I want to know. And I'm not sure I have much time.

I brush her hair with my hand and try to keep my voice soft, reassuring, non-official. "Meredith, what's your last name?"

She keeps her eyes shut tight. After a few moments, she swallows and says, "No."

"O.K. But why won't you tell me?"

She turns her head into the pillow, and I have to lean in to hear.

"Don't want anyone to tell my parents. They thought we'd all come to the city and make a good living."

It's a longer speech than she has breath for, and she seems to sag into the bed.

I digest that and stroke her hair some more.

"Who's 'all'? Do you have brothers or sisters here?"

Slight nod.

"Don't you want them to come see you? Take you home?"

That makes her stir. She looks at me directly. "No, please, Julia."

Fine. Whatever the reason. She can rest now. Being tied has left her to fight the restraint all night, I suppose. I would have. Now I'll sit here and hold her hand and smooth her curls over and over.

Occasionally, I ask a question. I spend the time between questions and whispered answers planning the next query. Sometimes she won't answer, and I wait awhile, try to justify my question, ask again. It takes an hour to find out she moved to St. Louis with two brothers and a sister. There are younger children at home, and the four are supposed to send money back. She remains silent about the location of home. She and her sister had decent jobs at a waist manufacturer, and then she got a chance at a job with higher pay in what she calls the new factory.

I gather she's lost that job somehow, and her brothers pressured her to go to work in the brothel. Only sewing, she says.

Meredith goes into a coughing spell that lasts way too long. My mother died of pneumonia, and I know. After Meredith stops and rests a bit, she manages to look me in the eye again. "I didn't . . . Julia. He insisted, but I said, 'no'."

I'm pretty sure I know what she means. I squeeze her hand and lean in again. "Who is this man?"

She's suddenly terrified. She pulls loose and looks like she's going to get up and run. I try to restrain her and know I'm hurting her. I have more sympathy for the hospital staff.

"You arrested him," she pants.

"Probably." Well, maybe. "But I didn't stop to get his name. I just went downstairs looking for you."

"If the police don't have him, he'll come after me." She claws at my hands for help getting up.

"Meredith, Meredith, calm down. Promise you'll stay here, and I'll go telephone the police. They can send someone to stay outside your door." Silly thing to say. She's obviously not a paying customer, and the hospital staff won't have thought to find her a real room.

"We'll get you a room." Somehow.

She lies back down, but it's likely because she can't move much more. I wish she'd cough, because I don't like the limpness.

"He'll come."

"The police'll be here."

"He's the boss." I can barely hear her.

"Meredith, tell me your last name. I need it for the police."

"No."

"Then just tell me. I won't pass it on to the police."

Nothing.

"I promise. Tell me. Because I care."

She almost smiles, and her eyes twitch but don't open. "No," she mouths.

◆ ◆ ◆

It takes a while to get a hospital employee to let me use a telephone. And then the man stands close by to make sure I don't ask for a long-distance exchange or tie up the line. So he says.

He's just curious. And no doubt enjoys hearing me beg the desk sergeant at Headquarters to send someone out on a protection detail for the woman from the brothel. And beg I do, but it isn't working.

Sergeant Spencer is harried and probably right when he tells me he can't spare anyone. "Really now, Miss Nye, I shouldn't even be entertaining the thought without word from the chief or a captain or some such, but if they was to order it, I don't know who I'd find. Colonel Roosevelt has a motorcade stretched out to Kinloch, and the governor is ariding with him, and there must be a hundred cops just out there, and the Jefferson Hotel is crawling with bigwigs. The mayor wants everyone else out on the street, looking spiffy and doing about nothing, Miss Nye."

"O.K., I understand, Sergeant. Thank you."

I smile at the hospital clerk and say, "Sorry, one more call," and start to make the connection while he objects.

I get hold of the Eighth District over on Laclede and pray Captain Messerton is in. He isn't. All the senior officers are out on what Sergeant Cott calls "political duty." The patrolmen who haven't been diverted to downtown are trying to control pickpockets and fights as the crowds around Union Station spread out for a good time.

There's no one to do guard duty, it seems. But before I let Cott disconnect, I have him check the arrest record and see who was taken in the raid last night.

The answer is no one. No one? No, ma'am. He heard Messerton say they missed the big cheese, and the ladies aren't the problem.

Well, I think as I head back to Meredith, you can say that again, Sergeant. The ladies aren't the problem.

◆   ◆   ◆

When I finally get back to the cubicle, I've decided I'll stay and try

Messerton again this evening. Meanwhile, I have a gun with me. I've used a gun before on the department's behalf. But the deal is, I'm supposed to act only on the chief's orders. I have no legal protection if I act on my own. Maybe I can talk my way through a situation and hope Messerton comes looking for me. He was supposed to call me before noon and it's past noon now, past one o'clock, according to my timepiece. I'm looking down at the little watch I wear on a slender brown ribbon around my neck as I get close. And that probably helps me notice the trouser legs standing next to the bed.

I freeze. A nurse coming toward me slows, and I motion for her to be quiet. She puts her tray on the empty bed across the way and leans on the foot rail to see what I'm up to.

The man's voice rises about then, and Meredith responds with a whimper.

"Now you stop talking back and get out of that bed. We need to vamoose. He's expecting you."

Meredith's whimper says, "No," convincingly.

The nurse tilts her head. She seems almost as curious as I am.

"You bitch. The man said fetch you, and that's what I'm going to do."

The legs start moving, and so do the nurse and I. I suspect she'll go the official route, so I try something different.

"Meredith!" I pull the curtains apart and peer in, trying to smile. "You've got company! How nice."

The man lets go of Meredith's arm, and she falls back with a moan. He turns to me, and the glare, the jutting chin, the widened stance, say "bully." His big blue eyes in an otherwise hopeless face say "brother," or at least close kin.

"You must be Meredith's brother." I want to speak before he can say something aggressive. I stick out my hand, which surprises him even more than my words.

"I'm Julia Nye, a friend of Meredith's. How do you do, Mr. . . . ?" Luckily, he's too surprised to ask how come I know Meredith and don't know their last name.

"Alfred Magruder." He stares at my hand. It must give him time to think because his belligerence rushes back.

"You work at that house?"

"No." My tone stops short of "No, silly."

"I'm with the police." I give up on the handshake.

The belligerence melts some as he frowns at me, more uncomprehending than concerned, I think.

The nurse steps forward. She's almost my height, tall for a woman, but heavily built. "Please be quiet, sir. You're disturbing the other patients."

Meredith chooses that moment to begin coughing. Dear Alfred whirls to tell her to shut up. The nurse says, "Sir, please." I move around the bed and settle on it, turning Meredith toward me.

You can tell Alfred doesn't intend to take orders from women. Our only hope lies in the fact he doesn't have any of his cronies around. He wouldn't back down otherwise.

He ignores the nurse and glares at Meredith. "I'll be back, gal. You get yourself ready."

"She isn't well enough to go anywhere, sir," the nurse puts in.

"She'll go where I say." His voice rises again, and the nurse puts her hands on her hips, sure sign of her authority.

Then Alfred has a real thought. "I'll get my own doctor," he yells and brushes past us.

The nurse sighs, probably hoping he'll return on someone else's shift. Then she looks at me. "Are you really from the police?"

"Yes." Maybe a bit of explanation is in order.

"I helped Meredith out of the basement of the house where she . . . well, during a raid last night. I came back to check on her today."

Meredith has curled on her right side, holding on to me. I know her knee must be throbbing.

The nurse studies us. "Did you untie her or did he?"

Meredith is alert enough to try to say something, but she chokes and starts coughing again. I decide not to lie.

"I did. She was balanced on that bad knee. Maybe she'd rolled over."

"We couldn't let her leave, and that's what she wanted to do."

"Well, she certainly didn't want to leave with that gentleman. Or maybe she didn't want to be here when he came."

I'm in the mood to trust the nurse. Maybe it's the realization I can't stay here indefinitely.

"I'm trying to get hold of an officer to stand guard. She was afraid, earlier, of someone coming to get her. But you can imagine the shortage of officers just now. T.R. and all."

Lordy, I'm name-dropping.

"Can we get her to a room where she'll be safer?"

The nurse looks at me for several moments. She's taken in my bachelor-girl uniform: white waist, a serge skirt less full and several inches shorter than appropriate, the sensible sweater now wadded beside Meredith, and the convention-defying braid down my back. She looks at Meredith, who's breathing heavily and holding on to me for all she's worth.

"O.K. A room. But I'm not sure how that will help unless you can get your police friends in here.

I'm not sure, either, to tell the truth. But I have to do something.

6

Carl notes a rare event: Will smiles, showing teeth. Will's one of those men who usually widens his mouth without opening it, in his case creating dimples from deep vertical creases. People with bad teeth don't smile much, but that isn't the case with Will, whose teeth are neat—like the rest of him. Carl offers his own full, oft-exercised grin.

Will's talking with the pilot Hoxsey, and other reporters and photographers mill about. Carl hopes someone's gotten a good photo. The National Guardsmen who help with the aeroplanes and with crowd control are pushing the machine back to its take-off point.

Someone asks how the ride was, and William replies, "Check the *Globe* in the morning." That gets a laugh and some groans. Will and the pilot shake hands again, thanking each other. Lord, but Will has a way with people, quiet, calm, always in control. Carl admires that, maybe envies it.

Will's back to a wide grin as he claps Carl on the shoulder, then folds the sporting cap he wore in flight into a pocket. Will's thick, dark blonde hair ruffles in the breeze, and Carl thinks to hand his friend his homburg.

"Well?"

Will laughs. "I don't know. I've got to find the words. Soon."

"I guess so. When you going to write it?"

"I thought I'd beg the use of a telephone first. Maybe the club will let me use one in return for the publicity. I told Julia I'd call when I'm back on land. Then I'll get something to drink." William gestures toward the food vendors setting up behind the grandstand. "And find someplace to hide out and write before the politicians get here."

Now this is the part Carl would really like: calling Julia to casually say it'd been a great ride and he'd tell her about it later. But to be honest, he's all but given up on that particular fantasy. Will and Julia have gotten a lot closer since their last detecting adventure. And Carl's concluded that he and Julia will never be more than friends. They'd probably have argued each other to death after a couple of dates anyway. Some days, Carl regrets introducing Julia and William, but those days are fewer and fewer, and today isn't one of them.

Carl's trying to make up his mind among the food stalls when Will returns, no longer smiling.

"How about a Falstaff?" Carl wouldn't consider a non-German beer, but then, there aren't many of those offered. Will shakes him off, and Carl asks, "Problem?" as he pays for his drink. Will chooses coffee.

"Not sure. Just that Julia isn't at the house or at her desk. I got hold of Spencer, and he says she's at the hospital with some woman." Will considers the Frenchman's aerial antics for a moment. "Must be that the woman from the sporting house isn't doing too well."

Sporting house? What the hell is Julia up to now? Will offers Carl a few details, but the whole thing seems odd. Why a raid last night? Frankly, the police don't raid brothels all that often and why bother on a busy night? And why call Julia in? See, Carl tells himself, this is why you and Julia would never make it. She was crawling around in a basement after a prostitute. Carl glances at Will and decides not to say what he's thinking: that it's Will's job to make her stop that sort of thing, to say no to Chief Wright, if not to Julia herself. He doesn't say it because Will would laugh at him.

Will finds a chair and situates it close to the grandstand, takes out a memo book, and gets busy. Carl wanders back to the reporter corps to talk shop. The moving film photographers arrive, set up equipment, and join in the waiting.

It's almost half past three when a racket and a cloud of dust announce that Theodore Roosevelt has arrived. Carl met the president when he campaigned in St. Louis in 1904 and Carl was a youngster, new to the job. Roosevelt had impressed him then and impresses him now. You have to hand it to the man: he's an original. No pomp and circumstance for Teddy. He's running an hour late, and it's probably because he stopped a procession of twenty-odd autos to shake hands with someone along the road. And then he must have had his driver try to outrun the aeroplanes getting here. The dust might extend all the way back to downtown St. Louis.

Both a *Times* and another *Westliche Post* reporter are among the newspapermen following T.R. They're covered with dust and are more interested in shaking their coats and hats—and finding a brew—than seeing what the colonel's up to. Fairly funny until Carl realizes he's planning on traveling back into the city with them. They wave him off to go make sure the colonel doesn't say anything outrageous and quotable to the pilot who's just landed.

Carl joins Will following Roosevelt as he heads down to the little biplane. Governor Hadley's hurrying to keep up and frantically trying to say something. The moving camera crews guessed right and are able to follow the colonel's progress.

Suddenly, everyone's moving faster. Roosevelt hands Hadley his hat and is trying to negotiate the wires. In the midst of all the words flying about, Carl notes that Will got into the narrow confines of the passenger seat much more gracefully.

The colonel's aides are insisting to him that he can't really fly; he'd said it was out of the question. The New York reporters are insisting to everyone else that they can't believe their eyes. The engine's running when Will steps forward and offers T.R. the cap he wore earlier. The pilot, Hoxsey as it turns out, smiles at his less illustrious passenger and starts inching the machine forward.

The crowd noise is so loud that Carl glances back. The grandstand is jiggling from people jumping and clapping. Then the aeroplane rises. Slowly. Even with Will beside Hoxsey, the craft gained altitude more slowly. And T.R. outweighs William by more than a few pounds.

But Hoxsey arches the aeroplane gracefully over the trees and begins to circle the field. The crowd, which seems to have held its collective breath as the machine lifted off, is roaring again and waving. Carl's torn between watching them, watching the craft, and stealing a glance at Governor Hadley and the colonel's New Yorkers. Hadley's about to crush T.R's trademark slouch hat.

Then Hoxsey gets playful and takes a couple of dives. Carl edges close to Will to hear him say, "Damn. Be careful."

Everyone around gasps, and one of the New Yorkers asks what the problem is.

"He needs to watch out for the wires." Will's shaking his head. "Waving his arms like that isn't good."

The politicians groan, but they obviously can't do anything.

Luckily, Hoxsey isn't cowed by his famous passenger. Even from the ground, Carl can tell he's partially turned, presumably asking the colonel to restrain his joyful waving to the crowd. T.R. settles down a bit, and the governor looks faint, and Hoxsey clearly is going to land at the end of the second turn around the field. When he does, Carl rushes forward with everyone else. The National Guard wisely took up positions between the landing spot and the grandstand, but the reporters alone form a small stampede toward the ex-President. They run beside the craft until it stops.

Colonel Roosevelt's shaking hands with everyone he can reach—including Hoxsey, who looks as relieved as Carl can imagine a man being. The flight took all of four minutes, Carl noted.

The colonel keeps saying "Bully," over and over, and telling everyone that it was "fine, just fine." He grabs his hat from a smiling Governor Hadley, who's trying to act as if he masterminded the whole thing. Then T.R. locates Will in the crowd, hands him the well-traveled cap, and motions him to the motorcade. Carl joins Will, crowding into a Darby meant to hold fewer people, and the motorcade moves out.

Less than a mile and it's obvious that flying above the earth isn't the only way to travel dangerously.

7

It took time and talk, but we got Meredith into a real hospital room with a door. No windows, end of a hall, basement level, but it will be easy to guard. If I only had a guard.

But I don't. I ask the nurse, whose name is Irene, to stay a bit. I dash upstairs and telephone Sergeant Spencer to give Chief Wright a note explaining my predicament. I telephone Sergeant Cott, asking him to get word to Captain Messerton as soon as possible. I want to leave a message someplace for William, but I don't know where to start. I resist the urge to ask if there are any injuries from the air show.

So, I relieve Irene and settle in to wait. The room is a white cave. Make that an off-white cave. Everything in it is a dirty white or a worn white. Meredith doesn't add much color. The blonde curls are matted close to her head, stringy down her back. She lies on her side and has pulled the nubby blanket up to her neck. One pale hand snakes out to latch onto mine. I stare at the contrast between my healthy, if fading, summer blush, strong, blunt fingers, nails I keep well-manicured, and Meredith's white hand with its broken nails and scratched knuckles. I hesitantly push up her sleeve to investigate the hint of a scratch. There's color after all, color I hadn't noticed last night: the purple shading into green of bruises on her wrist.

Irene made Meredith as comfortable as possible. Her knee is supported, and Irene said she'd put a fresh bandage on it. "That's a nasty puncture wound. Do you know how it happened?" So, I told her. She nodded her head as if it confirmed something for her, maybe the notion that Meredith is a victim and is therefore due more sympathy than a mere prostitute. Irene didn't put that into words, so I didn't have to respond. Meredith and I will take all the sympathy she can get. Her brother irritated me. Her fears have made me afraid of whoever she's afraid of.

The afternoon passes slowly. Meredith wakes, almost always unsure where she is and frightened. I'm pleased to be here for her, but I worry what will happen when I leave. I try to keep her awake by talking, which never works for more than a quarter hour or so.

But, along the way, she tells me she's a good seamstress and "likes to make pretty things," when she sews for herself. I say, "Pretty things for a pretty lady," and that makes her cry. She nods her head and cries and buries her face in the pillow. Because she's pretty? I'd never thought of being pretty as a curse since it isn't an issue for me personally. But maybe it's a problem if it's led to this.

The crying seems to trigger yet another episode of hacking and gasping for air. Meredith's hand convulses in mine as she fights for breath and finally gets enough air to relax a bit.

I turn my new realization over and around. I guess I envied the pretty girls, although I was never willing to try to look like them. I was a tomboy from the start, my mother's despair, my father's joy, my brother's pal. My mother complained about my thinness, my long face, my thick chestnut hair always braided to control the tight waves and keep the mass out of my way. When I was young, I wondered why she didn't like tall, thin, and long-faced. After all, I looked like her husband, the man she clearly loved.

I might have been attractive if I'd tried. But it became an issue between my mother and me, and I was a lot more stubborn than vain. Now I ignore fashion for good political reasons, choosing not to bow to men's notions of beauty. I abhor makeup, which some modern women are choosing, because it's too much trouble. And I tell myself that my clean complexion, grey-green eyes, and full mouth are fine as they are. Maybe I'm right, I conclude as I assess Meredith's pretty, abused features.

As the afternoon wears on, I tell Meredith about myself, explain that I live in a boarding house of "new women," women who seek the vote and independence and respect. She must think she's dreaming, to judge by the look on her face. I do a lot of sewing myself, I tell her, it being my designated chore in the household. I don't really love to sew, but I'm good at it, and it surely does suit me better than cooking. She falls asleep instead of smiling.

I don't explain that one of the New Woman's Union's current concerns is reports of white slavery, of brothel owners whose recruitment techniques cross the line, go even beyond ensnaring women who have no other option. That's what I really want to know about her situation. Why would a woman who can make a living otherwise end up beaten in a sporting house? We've heard that white slavers are moving out of Chicago because of the uproar about it there. And, we're hoping to create an uproar of our own here. Meredith might be the first evidence we need.

Irene's shift ends in the late afternoon. She comes to check on us and brings food. We try to get Meredith to eat, but that seems to require too much of her available breathing capacity. Irene tells me to go ahead and finish up the soup, and I do. I'll find Meredith more food if she needs it. It's early evening when Irene leaves, and I hate to see her go.

I try more questions, but Meredith won't answer. Once, she repeats the fact that she said "No," to someone. That heightens my suspicions and I want to identify the someone. Meredith is too frightened and too weak to tell me, though. I stop asking. It distresses her, and I'm confident I can find out. I have to, one way or another.

◆　◆　◆

I escape while Meredith is sleeping to call the boarding house. If Fran's surprised I've spent the day sitting at a hospital with a woman I carried out of a brothel, she doesn't let it show in her voice. My housemates are getting used to my police activities. Such good stories for rainy evenings.

I also pick up a cup of coffee. The staff is becoming more sympathetic by the hour. I sit back and watch Meredith and sip away. She's pale, breathing shallowly and frowning in her sleep.

A knock on the door surprises me, and I almost spill the remains of my coffee. I hurriedly put it down and say, "Yes?" as I reach for my bag. I should have had the revolver out by now.

"Messerton." The voice is gruff. "And friends."

Friends? Has the relief shift arrived?

Meredith stirs, and I take her hand as I say, "Come in."

She starts coughing and tries to sit up, as if to let the congestion settle lower in her lungs. She gasps out my name—or tries to: "Jule" is as far as she can get.

She sees Messerton and panics, grabbing at my hands even as she sags backwards into my arms.

Her efforts subside, and I turn to him, as far as I can turn and still hold her upright.

"I got your message," Messerton says. "Crandall is here, and he can stay the night."

Meredith pulls on my hand.

"Outside, of course," the captain says.

I hope my smile tells him how much that pleases me. But when I turn back to Meredith, my smile fades. She knows. She knows I'm leaving and, even if no one comes through the door, she'll be alone. And she might not make it until morning. The cough isn't getting worse, but she can't get enough breath.

"Meredith." I help her lie down and lean close. "I'll be back first thing in the morning. Early. You can rest safely now, because there'll be an officer outside. And tomorrow, we'll figure out a way to get you out of here."

I say it before I think it through. Can I move her? What can I do for her that the hospital isn't doing? I make up my mind. "I'm thinking you can come home with me tomorrow. No one will know where you are, and I may as well miss work there as here." I smile at that, and she follows my example, weakly.

"Thank you . . . Jule—" She chokes on my name, closes her eyes, and lets go of my hand. I know she hasn't fallen asleep that fast because she's still fighting for breath. But she's releasing me.

I gather my things and dodge around Captain Messerton. And stop abruptly.

William is leaning against the doorframe. He grins, offering sympathy, I judge. I'm so glad to see him I'd be embarrassed if I thought it showed.

A young cop I haven't met is standing in the hall, smiling a different smile.

Messerton nods me and William on our way. As we leave, I hear the captain giving the officer he calls Crandall his orders.

What to say first. I decide to comment on how filthy William's clothes are. He never appears in public like this. Neither his sense of style nor his vanity allows it. But he beats me to the conversation opener before I can frame a question.

"Jule? I like that. Good nickname: Jule." He sobers a bit. "Did she make up a nickname for you or was she out of breath?"

"Out of breath, I'm afraid. But you can try it out if you want to." I smile despite my worry. "I like it better than Julie."

My Dad and brother call me Julie, and they're the only ones who can get away with it.

William smiles, and it's my turn. "I'm glad to see you safe on earth. Sorry I wasn't where I could hear from you." Had he called? Of course: he said he would.

"Spencer explained where you were. I imagine you'd rather have been at work, all in all."

"I'm really worried about her. But I'm glad she has a guard." I lower my voice. "She's afraid of someone coming after her. I met her brother this morning, and he was trying to drag her out of the hospital. But he didn't come back." I've pondered it, but I don't know what to make of Alfred Magruder and his visit.

William's frown says he's thinking about the threat, but I sincerely want to know about his day.

"So, tell me about it. How was flying? And how did you get so dirty?"

William laughs as we head down the steps of the hospital. It sounds better out here than it would in the sterile halls.

"You could say I flew twice. Once in the air and once on the road from Kinloch to the Fairgrounds—which is a lot less smooth than gliding through the air. I asked T.R.'s driver: he hit seventy miles an hour on the way back. And needless to say, I wasn't in the lead car."

We're waiting for a streetcar on Lafayette, and I can see him clearly in the globe lamp. He must have washed his face lately. He smiles as I stare. "I may have a few bruises under the dirt. I know Schroeder does."

"And to think I was worried about you in the aeroplane. Seventy miles an hour?" I try to imagine it on that road. I'm not sure a train can move that fast.

Will shakes his head. "You should have seen Chief Wright. He was red under the dust. Governor Hadley, on the other hand, was still pale. He'd had a pretty exciting day already."

"How's that?"

"You haven't heard?"

"I haven't heard anything but coughing, William."

"Well, the big news of the day is that Colonel Roosevelt decided, on a whim, to go for an aeroplane ride. The pilot had asked him to go up, but Hoxsey was nervous as all get out when the colonel took him up on it."

I laugh at the image.

"My account of flying in the morning is going to be 'what the colonel saw'."

"Does that bother you? That it's not your story, but the colonel's?"

William lets me precede him onto the platform of the streetcar. He doesn't help me, although I suppose he'd catch me if I missed a step. We've gotten non-chivalry down to a routine.

"Not at all. In some ways, it'll get more readership."

Reporters. "So how was it? Or will you make me read about it?"

We settle in and hold hands in the dark of the streetcar while he tells me about the incredible sensation of leaving the earth, seeing the tops of trees and watching the crowd shrink to toy-size. He had a much longer flight than T.R. got, going east over the city. He describes seeing the rooftops of the tallest buildings, the spires of churches, the dome of the old Courthouse and the Mississippi River looking like a strip of blue grosgrain. I try to imagine tiny horses, tiny carriages, tiny autos, crossing the Eads Bridge.

I squeeze his hand. "I thought I might have seen you."

"Really? When we were flying over downtown?"

"Yes. I was on my way to the hospital. I went to work early and typed until I was making mistakes, worrying about Meredith, worrying about you. At the corner, the crowd was pointing. There were these two small machines, moving west."

"That's when Hoxsey and the French pilot, LeBlanc, headed back." William squeezes my hand in turn. "Why were you worried about me?"

I twist to see him better in the evening gloom. "Why would I be worried? Because you're sitting up there, hundreds of feet above the earth, on next to nothing. And the whole thing is held together with a few wires. And . . . well, don't you suppose the governor was worried about Colonel Roosevelt?"

"He was, but that's because he didn't want the negative publicity if T.R. fell overboard. Which he almost did, by the way." William chuckles. "But my point is, you're always irritated if I say I'm concerned about you. The odds of my getting hurt in an aeroplane are a lot less than you getting shot by some maniac trying to start a riot."

That was a little scare from August. But beside the point.

"I don't like it, Will, that you get all worried about me when I can take care of myself. How do you take care of yourself in an aeroplane?"

"By knowing not to rattle those wires, for one thing."

I sigh and put my head back against the closed window. William seems content to let the issue go. I'm so bad at these kinds of things. I can argue for suffrage on street corners. I can explain society's biases against women quite well. But when it's me and William, I just get defensive. I don't think I've ever managed to make him understand that I don't want concern because he's a man and I'm a woman. Concern because we've gotten so fond of each other is something else, but I'm not always sure which is which. And I have no idea why I hadn't wanted to watch him today.

William is asking about Meredith again, and we talk about her situation until we're on the porch of the boarding house. I need to be up early in the morning, and William looks ready to head for a bed as well. But he takes time for a last comment. "I really don't mind if you worry about me, Julia. Jule." We've learned to stand away from the lights from the parlor, and William kisses me gently. "Worry about me if you want to, Jule."

I get that tingle in my gut that signals William's close. Luckily, he can't see it. What he can see is my very best smile in return. "Worrying" about him seems easy at the moment.

8

*From **The Kansas City Times**, Thursday, October 13, 1910*

> *Special Dispatch from St. Louis, Missouri – Crowds in St. Louis were treated to an historic event Wednesday when former President Theodore Roosevelt took a brief aeroplane flight. Arch Hoxsey, who pilots a Wright biplane in competitions and exhibitions, offered Colonel Roosevelt a flight during his appearance at an air meet at Kinloch, just outside St. Louis City.*

Kansas City Police Officer Elias Higginbotham jumps when the telephone rings. Although, the interruption's fine with him because he was laboring over this story about Colonel Roosevelt going up in an aeroplane over St. Louis. The dangdest thing. But then the dangdest things go on in St. Louis. Likely where this call is from. From the new boss.

Hig puts the newspaper down on the kitchen table as if he's peeved to be interrupted, as if he's somehow obliged to listen in on this end of the conversation. Anna Henry, who used to own this place but now manages it, is saying, "Yessir," a lot.

"Yessir, that'll be fine. Everything can keep until tonight, sir." Her slanty brown eyes say otherwise, but she adds, "We'll look forward to seeing you then, sir. Good-bye, sir."

"What?" Hig asks. He doesn't wait any, shouldn't have to. But Anna gives him a look that says it's her conversation and she'll slam the earpiece down and push the instrument back into its spot before she'll bother to explain. Hig wonders again why the boss put the new telephone in the kitchen, anyway, and is reminded as Anna straightens things around in her new four-foot by four-foot office spot. Isn't too bright, the boss said, to conduct business discussions in the parlor of a sporting house. It has other uses.

Hig's getting hot under the collar waiting for Anna's explanation. She's a contrary woman, no doubt about it. Finally, she says, "You could have saved yourself getting up early to come see the boss. He has to do something last minute in St. Loo, and he won't be here 'til tonight when you'd come around anyway." She smirks and gets up to deal with the laundry she abandoned.

"Fine. That's fine by me. All I wanted to know was, who was calling."

"Right, Sergeant. Now you can go back to your reading. Don't get a headache."

She laughs softly, and Hig flushes. Maybe he'd been scanning along with his finger as he sometimes does. Not that he reads anything often. It's a habit from school, one the lady teacher tried to break him of.

Hig's glad Anna doesn't actually own the brothel anymore. He likes the idea that the new boss is a man, one he can talk to, feel comfortable with. Women owning businesses makes no sense anyway, even this kind of business. Look at all the boss has done. Look at all he does.

The boss owns a big business in St. Louis, a factory. Employs a lot of women there, he'd said, with a wink for Hig. And he's bought a couple of brothels there and this one here and is changing things O.K. The whole top floor, which had been dusty storage rooms, has been cleaned out. There's a big open space where three rooms have been put together, and the windows are new, larger than the old ones, to let in lots of light. The boss is a photographer and says you can't have too much good light. Of course, Hig noticed right away that the boss takes a lot of pictures at night. When the women are at their best, maybe.

And the boss keeps mighty busy, making lots of trips back and forth. Hig joked that the boss kept those train rails right hot, and the boss laughed and said that was too true and, by the way, maybe Hig can come along some time, when he's off-duty, of course, and help out. Hig takes a deep breath, just remembering. He doesn't get out of Kansas City much.

And as for off-duty, that's mostly a blur. Officially, according to the chief, if Chief Benson cares, Hig works the night shift in the West Bottoms and Ward One, a beat that involves sporting houses and bars and more houses. Hig lets his fellow officers take care of the other residents of the Bottoms, the stock yards, even Union Depot. Wouldn't they be surprised to see him and the boss come strolling out of the Depot some afternoon?

But Hig checks out the brothels in the daytime, too, and sometimes on his day off. Always in uniform. Makes him official. Makes him welcome most of the time because the customers don't cause trouble with a Kansas City police sergeant lounging in the parlor. Of course, they have to get used to the idea, some of the out-of-town ones, that he isn't there to arrest anyone. Locals know that. Anyway, it's his job, and he's done it off and on for years.

And even the people who know better call him Sergeant or Sergeant Hig. Although he certainly isn't a sergeant and doesn't particularly want to be one. They mostly work at the stations. Hig doesn't want to be anywhere except where he is, waiting for the boss.

9

I gather my seven housemates around for a quick discussion after William leaves. We agree this is the perfect chance to make a difference. We're very fond of that phrase, "make a difference." I think taking care of a woman who's probably dying of pneumonia, linked to one or two men who aren't exactly coming around to offer sympathy, goes a bit beyond making a difference in the political sense. But I'm not happy leaving Meredith in City Hospital. Crandall looked so young. Younger than me, and I'm not going to be twenty-one until the end of the month.

We figure we can get Meredith settled in by afternoon, and Mary and Fran will come home on their lunch hours and stay. When you get right down to it, we all earn around twelve cents an hour, so it doesn't really matter who's earning and who isn't, and I'm less likely to get fired than the others. But I'm not happy getting so far behind in my work.

I plan to be at the hospital well before six in the morning, thinking that, because Meredith isn't a paying customer, the hospital might let me walk out with her provided no one official is there to notice.

And maybe Crandall will be willing to help me with her, get her into a taxi, perhaps, in return for being able to head home early. Planning is my antidote to worry. I worry about Meredith's cough. I worry about her fear. I worry about her being alone in that room, even if nurses are checking on her every few minutes. And I'm not sure anyone will have checked on her at all.

So, I make my way in the dark October morning that causes me to shiver aside from my mission. Coal smoke shrouds landmarks and mixes with the mist off the Mississippi to remind me of the early winter. The few people hurrying to work or hurrying home from night duty huddle in on themselves and disappear into the gloom. I walk so fast I'm almost running. I've pulled a shawl over my sweater and around my crossed arms, hunching against the morning. My bag, slung by its strap over my left wrist and weighted by the .32 caliber police positive pistol inside, slaps against my tummy.

I sigh in relief when I step into City Hospital, unwinding the shawl a bit to free up my arms. Unfortunately, the lobby is hardly warm and inviting. What it is, is silent. I count three nurses on my way downstairs and each of them might be floating just above the floor.

I hear noise as soon as I push through the door to the basement hallway. Irene is there, along with another nurse, one whose erect bearing exudes authority. A man who looks a bit like Meredith and a lot more like Alfred is arguing, with Crandall mostly, although the nurses are trying to add their piece. Crandall looks glad to see me.

"Here she is," he says, as if everyone is expecting me to arrive at half past five.

"What is it?" I want to get past them into the room. The door is ajar, and Meredith must be disturbed by all this talk. Is anyone in there with her?

"Miss Nye, I'm so sorry." Crandall sounds more than sincere and, when I turn to him, his face says the same thing. "I watched all night. I don't know when she died."

Died.

Damn.

The Alfred-look-a-like stares at me. "Why are we waiting for her anyway? I'm going to take my sister's body and go."

My tummy tightens, but I put the shock of her death in a back drawer of my mind and open the drawer for anger.

I don't like the callous tone, the impatience in the squinty blue eyes, when I turn on him. He has Meredith's beautiful hair, which unfortunately doesn't cover a pockmarked face. I shake my head and move into the room, ignoring whatever else he's saying, the tightness in my body almost painful.

I'm not surprised to see Meredith dead, of course. I am surprised to see another, equally small woman standing at the foot of the bed. I shake my head again, this time to vanquish the thought: she looks like Meredith's bad twin.

She's small and fine-boned. I look at her wrists as though I expect bruises. The resemblance is that strong. The features are eerily the same, just different in impact. Ugly where Meredith was beautiful, sour where Meredith—even abused and dying—was gracious. I want to study this woman, figure out the effect, but the male voices outside tell me I don't have the time.

I have to have a name, though. "Hello. You must be Meredith's sister."

"Ida," she says shortly. "Why are we waiting?"

"The police investigate murders."

"I don't know why you'd think it murder. She just died, that's all. And there's a policeman outside already. My brother told him it's no murder. Who'd murder a dying prostitute?" She says the last word with as much distaste as a Lucas Place matron could have mustered.

I consider her for another second and turn to the bed. Meredith looks weary. It could have been the fight to breathe, but I doubt it. Particularly because there's a hint of bruises around her mouth.

I raise the blanket that's neatly laid over her body. She hadn't been able to manage neatness before. Her twisting had left the covers in enough disarray that I'd been constantly straightening.

She's again tied to the bed, by two bindings. Tied on her back this time.

Ida's saying, "Leave her be. Who are you, anyway? We want to get her out of here, get her buried."

I bet you do, I mutter, replacing the blanket and turning to the door.

Ida starts whining to the brother she calls Leonard, saying he needs to get "her" out of here. I step around Ida to ask Crandall if he's called Messerton, and he says he asked Mrs. Kline to do it, gesturing at the older nurse.

"Said he'd be right here, not to move her." It's obviously not the first time the nurse has explained that. "Surprised me. I thought he'd be more than a little put-out that I'd telephoned at five in the morning."

"When did you realize she was dead?" I ask.

Crandall hesitates and looks at me for a split second as if to say we might leave this for the real detectives. But guilt has him, and he replies, "I didn't. Mrs. Kline came in and saw her . . . because her folks were coming to check on her."

I digest the fact that Meredith's siblings arrived at 5 a.m. after having ignored her all day yesterday.

I don't get to ask them about that because I turn to the noise currently coming down the corridor.

Messerton might not be angry at being awakened, but he's

certainly angry at the reason. His questions balloon out in front of him as he hits the hallway.

Everyone recognizes his authority, and everyone but me jumps in to say their piece, explain their presence and their need to get on with it.

Messerton takes it all in and turns to me. "When did you get here?"

"Maybe ten minutes ago. Can you step in here with me?"

He may think I'm afraid to go see a dead person without him. And then again, maybe not.

He nods, but I don't hear him moving behind me. I glance around to see him staring at Ida just as I had.

Ida's saying, "You shouldn't be looking around at my sister's body." She looks as if she'll stand there in the doorway and defend it.

And, of course, Messerton says, "I'm police, Miss. It's my job."

He comes into the room with me and regards the still figure for a second. He looks at me, and I raise an eyebrow.

"If you'll excuse us, Miss," he says to Ida Magruder. He pushes and talks her out of the room, along with Leonard, who's crowded in.

He closes the door and turns to me. Not to the body.

"What?" He's angry. Without thinking, I put my hand up to shush him, as if he'll bother Meredith with his ugly tone. I feel foolish immediately, but it softens his tough features.

In my fantasies, I want to be a police detective. It'll never happen, but when the opportunity presents itself, even informally, I'm determined to be professional.

"Look at this, please, Captain." I turn to Meredith and fold back the covers. He goes around the other side of the bed, and I can tell he's put his tough face back on.

"This bothers me. First of all, she's lying on her back. I don't think the hospital staff would do that. She was restrained when I came in yesterday, on her side. It was too hard for her to breathe, lying on her back. Furthermore, the covers are too neat. She kept twisting, struggling to breathe."

"Why was she restrained in the first place?"

"Apparently, she tried to get away, leave the hospital. You saw she didn't want to come here. She told me someone would come after her, someone she was afraid of. Wouldn't give me a name. She was scared of her brother, but I think there's someone else."

Messerton pulls out a notebook and scratches for a few moments.

"Someone she hoped you'd arrested Tuesday night."

Messerton looks up and growls softly. "What else?"

"I don't like the way she's tied. Her other injuries were cuts on her breasts and back, and the knee that she hurt trying to get away from the ambulance crew. Both of these bindings must have hurt." I point to the one over her breasts, tight enough to look painful, even as it holds her upper arms down. I run a finger over the bruise nestled up against the binding on the arm nearest me. The bindings over her knees are tight enough to make her lower legs seem to angle up from the plane of the bed.

Messerton's getting angry, I think. And not at me.

"Do you know any more of her story?"

I gently pull up the covers and tell Messerton what I know. He scratches at his pad some more.

"Let's find out if Crandall saw anyone."

Messerton orders a nervous Officer Crandall into the room and closes the door on everyone else. Leonard Magruder is shrill.

"I'm sorry, Captain. I only went upstairs to the lavatory twice, just after midnight and then again about five."

"I told you not to sit here and drink coffee all night. How did you know anything was wrong when you got back?"

Messerton isn't tall, but he bounces up on the balls of his feet when he talks, particularly when he asks questions. I've heard his officers don't like those questions any more than the difficult citizenry of Mill Creek Valley.

Crandall swallows. "I didn't drink any more coffee than I had to so as to stay awake, Captain. I paced up and down the hall and didn't bother anyone. Ever once in a while a nurse would come down and offer me some coffee, and I only took it when I had to." His chin comes up a little, and I'm sympathetic. What a miserable night. I hadn't thought of the boredom part.

"When I came out of the lavatory this morning, I met the nurses and the family, arguing about seeing her." He motions at Meredith, and doesn't look at the body closely. "Mrs. Kline hurried down ahead of me. When we all got down here, she told me Miss Magruder was dead."

"You didn't hear her coughing?" I jump in.

"No, ma'am, she hadn't been coughing for hours, ma'am."

Aside from the fact I'm not old enough to be "ma'am" to Officer Crandall, that bothers me.

"She was coughing every few minutes all day." I argue that with Messerton, who puts a hand to her face.

"Well. I don't think your last trip to the toilet was the occasion of Miss Magruder's death, Crandall. Because she's been dead longer than an hour." He's talking to me now. "Feel how cold she is. She has a bit of body heat left but if she'd died within the hour, she'd be warm as life."

I obligingly feel her face again and duly note what he's pointed out. One part of my brain snorts at me: here's a murdered woman, Julia, and you're pleased with yourself because the captain is explaining this to you instead of poor Crandall. Lordy.

I shake off my silly reflections. "How long?" I ask. For some reason, I reach under the cover for Meredith's hand. I push the cover back and look at what I feel: a hand clinched into a fist too cold and tight for me to open.

Messerton nods and studies me closely when I look up at him. I can hear Crandall breathing again.

"I'd guess about midnight, although the coroner's office can say better. That's when you left the first time." He barks at Crandall.

"When did they tie her like this?" I add.

Crandall wisely answers his captain first. "The doctor was here when I came back from the toilet, just going in the room. He was in here a while, maybe as long as ten minutes." Crandall looks at me. "Maybe he tied her then."

He seems to think about it. "But surely she was tied before. I heard her begging the nurses to let her go, earlier," he says. His frown says Crandall was bothered.

That bothers me, too. Despite the police protection, despite my plan to move her out, she wanted to leave. More than it bothers me, it saddens me. Particularly because she'd been right.

I turn on the young officer. "Are you sure he was a doctor?"

Crandall actually takes a step back in the face of my anger. "Well, he looked like one. Wore a white coat. Sort of distinguished-looking. When he left, he said she was resting quietly and he'd check on her in the morning."

Crandall fidgets with a tunic button. He thought he'd erred by leaving for an understandable couple of minutes. Instead, he'd let the killer in and sat outside while his charge was murdered. I'm sure of it, and my anger makes Crandall sure of it too.

Messerton comes to his rescue. "O.K., we've got the pieces here. We interview nurses, check out the mysterious doctor . . . and get an autopsy." He turns to look at Meredith again. "If he suffocated her, an autopsy will show that." He heads for the door. "Besides, it will irritate these people." He almost grins when he looks back at me. "I'll bet she wasn't depending on her brothers for help."

He stops with his hand on the doorknob. "Wait a minute. When did the brother and sister get here, Crandall?"

"A little bit ago, quarter past five or so."

"Did they say why they appeared at this hour of the morning?" Messerton asks.

"No, sir. The nurses said they'd have to come back later, but the men insisted they were getting ready to leave town and had to see her now. Mrs. Kline said they could come down after she checked on Miss Magruder's condition. They followed me downstairs, Mrs. Kline told me Miss Magruder was deceased, and they heard. There was a lot of talk about taking her right on out of here, but the nurses insisted the police had to clear that. Both ladies seemed right suspicious and insisted there had to be some kind of investigation, not only my word they could go."

I have to say it. "Were they surprised she was dead?" I tilt my head toward the hall, where the noise level is rising. "They don't seem to be grieving now." Messerton raises an eyebrow at me and opens the door.

Leonard Magruder is saying, "She's dead, and you gotta let us take her home. She don't need a doctor now."

The doctor in question pushes his way in the room, with Mrs. Kline on his heels, and closes the door. Ah. My little friend from two nights ago, the doctor who met us at the ambulance. The room is small, and there're suddenly too many of us in here. The Magruders wouldn't have fit if they wanted to.

The doctor, for some reason, decides to stare at me. "What are you doing here?"

Mrs. Kline answers for me. "Irene says she stayed with the poor woman all day yesterday and was coming back this morning to do the same. She's the one who got the woman moved down here so she could be guarded, Irene said."

Messerton offers his answer. "Miss Nye works for the police, Doctor. She's been the one to interview the woman and stayed because we couldn't free up a police guard with all the politicians in town."

The doctor hesitates as if he'd like to know why a woman works for the police but instead, he says, "At least she's dressed," and turns his attention to Meredith.

Messerton says, "My officer here says a man he took to be one of your staff came in right after midnight and supposedly checked on her. He could hear movement in here earlier, but after the man left, there was nothing from her, no more coughing or movement."

"No, no," the doctor says, pulling the covers back. "Good Lord," is his next opinion. He turns to Mrs. Kline, who steps forward.

"Oh my." She and the doctor exchange looks.

"Did you step in here earlier?"

"Yes, I did, Dr. Herndon, but I only noted that she'd expired. I didn't turn the blanket back. I did think it strange she was on her back."

The little physician straightens up and puts his hands on his hips. Again. "Well, Captain, this woman was not restrained like this by our staff. She had pneumonia and would have died, drowned from the fluid in her lungs, lying like this. I wouldn't be surprised, mind you, if she'd died naturally during the night, but you'd have heard coughing, and so on. She wouldn't have died quietly. Rales, you'd have heard. She could've called out, at least once or twice."

He checks her face again and shakes his head.

"Furthermore, I don't know what doctor would've been down here. Nurses would have been the ones to check. If anyone. It's been a busy night with lots of travelers in town. There's me and Dr. Banyon upstairs at night for emergencies. But we wouldn't have been down here. We all knew it was just a matter of making her comfortable—and seeing that she didn't leave."

"Well, we've pretty much figured this is a murder, Doctor. An autopsy can tell us more. Maybe Mrs. Kline can find out if any nurses checked on her—along with serving up coffee." Messerton nods at her and looks ready to herd everyone out of the room, which is getting warm and unpleasant. My inner tightness has shifted to a vague nausea.

"Wait a minute, Captain," the doctor says. "Maybe I can tell you more. Are you thinking this mysterious caregiver came in here and strangled her or suffocated her or some such thing?"

Messerton growls again. "A pillow on the face is my guess."

Dr. Herndon makes a "humph" sound and props one hand beside the pillow that's now under Meredith's head. He's muttering about laying a woman on her back with a pillow as he forces an eyelid up. I breathe in sharply but manage not to gasp. I don't like the blue eye suddenly peering at us.

For one thing, I'm close enough to see what the doctor sees. It looks as if the blue part of her eye is floating in a pale red pool. My first thought is that the man beat her.

As I watch, a tear flows from her eye toward her hair. It's only a bit of liquid, I tell myself, trapped by her eyelid and released now. I compose my own face and look up. Everyone else has seen it as well.

Thankfully the doctor closes the eyelid and then catches the teardrop on his index finger. His sigh washes through the room.

The doctor stands. "Definitely suffocated. You can have the coroner confirm it, but the broken blood vessels in her eyes are all he'll need."

Messerton nods and leads us outside. He gets a few feet into the hallway and stops, backing us up behind him.

It's quiet. No one's arguing, no one's pacing. No one's here.

10

Officer Crandall tentatively offers me his name. John, it is. But I can call him Johnny. My pleasure, Johnny.

Johnny doesn't seem to notice my lack of interest. He trails me upstairs, saying, "I can't believe she was dead the whole time I was sitting there."

I don't reply. I only want to get to the telephone. Addie answers at the boarding house, and I give her the news. Fran and Mary will presumably readjust their plans and proceed on to their jobs. For some reason, Addie says, "I'm really sorry, Julia." I snort and tell her I'll be home late.

Instead of wanting sympathy, I want to get to work and type every report in sight. I'll make detectives sit down and dictate reports that aren't in the basket yet. I want to be busy. And then, when I'm too worn out to do anything else, I'll open that little box where I keep sorrow and regret, in my room, in the dark, exhausted.

Captain Messerton follows us upstairs and rounds up Irene. I hear her saying she followed the Magruders, but Leonard pulled his sister up the stairs and out of the building. Ida stopped protesting about halfway out, and they ignored Irene.

I say, "Thank you for your help," to Irene and head out, fast. Messerton says that he'll be by Headquarters later. Fine. He can explain to Chief Wright how Meredith Magruder died within yards of her police guard.

It's only six in the morning. I won't be more than a quarter hour late to work and, frankly, no one's there to know. More people are on the street now, and it's lighter, although still dim. In fact, the mist has turned to a very light drizzle. That's fine, too. I don't ask the weather to cooperate or to lighten my mood. I don't want to lighten the guilt. Guilt will drive me to make it up to Meredith quicker than grief.

The streetcar isn't cooperating, and I don't wait. I walk down Lafayette to the next stop, almost running on the uneven sidewalk. People scatter out of my way.

At Headquarters, I uncover my neglected typewriter, adjust the lamps I use in the darker hours, straighten reports cops have dropped into—and near—the basket on my desk. Why they can't hit the basket or put the reports in straight instead of sideways, whopper-jawed, upside down, I'll never understand.

I situate the first handwritten report beside the typewriter and sandwich fresh carbon paper between two report forms before I take time for my first step in unraveling the Meredith mystery. I can't wait any longer. I pull a City Directory from its spot on the bottom shelf of the telephone table behind my desk.

And find the family.

Meredith Magruder lived in what might be a tenement house, almost certainly an old building of some sort, in the seedy neighborhood north of downtown, not far west of the river. It's a neighborhood crowded with factories of all kinds. Alfred works on the wharfs. Leonard makes tiles. Between the four, they should have been able to save enough to send a nice sum home. Wherever home is.

I grab a business directory and rush into the squad room, hoping it's vacant at this hour. It isn't. Officer Aaron Jamison must have come up the back stair, and I hadn't heard him. He's taking off his hat and heading toward the coffee pot in the same move.

He smiles. "May I pour you a cup, Miss Nye?"

For a change, I decline. Maybe he reads something, because he frowns. "Is anything wrong?"

I like Aaron Jamison. He's been my assigned escort on occasion, and he's thorough, even if he's probably no more than my age. He's going to rise fast through the ranks, unlike Johnny Crandall. And I can't very well start going over the map without explaining what I'm doing.

So, I tell him I'm trying to locate waist factories near Second Street. Meredith and Ida wouldn't have had to live close to work, but with both of them at one job site, it would make sense to locate there in the first place. Save fare. I'd live closer to work if I could.

Aaron puts his coffee cup down and comes over to run a finger to each of the garment factories I read out of the directory. We locate several garment factories in the neighborhood, but only one is a waist factory. Hancock Garments is the name, but the caption says, "Specializing in Fine Shirtwaists." It's two blocks from the Magruder flat. The other waist factories are west and south, strung out along Washington Avenue.

I thank Aaron, explaining that I've been trying to help a young woman and she hadn't said where she worked, precisely. He nods but is too polite to ask more. I smile at him and hurry back to my desk, having noted the address of Hancock Garments. Maybe I'll take a lunch break today after all.

Having something concrete to do spurs me toward noon. I've made a dent in the stack of reports when Messerton appears about ten o'clock. Sergeant Witherspoon is with him, and they both look at me for several beats. I nod them into Chief Wright's office.

To be honest, there aren't as many reports as usual. Crime suspends itself for the likes of Teddy Roosevelt. How can you even issue a speeding violation when the law says ten miles an hour and the Colonel's driver managed seventy miles an hour?

No more than a quarter of an hour later, Chief Wright, Captain Messerton, and Sergeant Witherspoon step out of the chief's office to invite me to join them in the conference room. I don't know what my look says, but the chief feels obliged to ask twice. "Really, my dear, you surely have gotten a lot done already, and we need your help on this." Then he chews his mustache a bit. That tells me the case bothers him. The "my dear" tells me he's feeling paternal. He's an old friend of my father, and he goes into that mode when he thinks I might be bothered myself.

He hurries into the Conference Room ahead of us and gets the lights on. The shiny table is meant for a dozen or more people, and we huddle at one end.

"My dear, I'd like to hear what you found out about Miss Magruder."

I cross one arm at my waist, balance the other elbow on it, and start fingering my watch.

"The four Magruder siblings moved to St. Louis to help support their family. From off in the countryside. I don't know where. In fact, she didn't want to tell me her last name. I got it when Alfred Magruder appeared, yesterday morning. She said she—"

"Wait," Messerton says. "How did you get him to tell you the family name?"

"I just said, 'I'm glad to meet you, Mr. . . .' and waited until he gave me his name."

"Oh." Messerton smiles.

The chief, who's trying not to smile, asks about Alfred Magruder. I tell him about the brief conversation and give him my impression that Magruder is a bully, used to telling his sisters what to do. Messerton gives him a similar assessment of the relationship between Leonard and Ida Magruder.

"That fits," I say.

"Fits what?" the chief asks. Messerton leans forward on his elbows.

"Meredith told me that she worked at one waist factory and then went to work at what she called the 'new one' for higher pay. Somehow, she lost that job, and her brothers were so angry they insisted she go to work in the brothel. As a seamstress."

I roll my eyes, and the men nod.

"Apparently the job turned into a bit more." That's Sergeant Witherspoon. Red. I'd met him before the raid but with his helmet on. The only impression I had was full lips and a sincere smile. Today I can appreciate the tousled red locks, as red as any hair I've ever seen. And very blue eyes.

"I'm not sure what the job turned into." I consider the engraved arches on my watchcase. It's a wonder I haven't worn the thing smooth over the last couple of years. "She insisted she hadn't cooperated, hadn't done what he wanted her to do."

Messerton moves abruptly. "Did she mean she wouldn't prostitute herself?"

I look at him seriously enough to match the intensity in the little brown eyes. "I assume so. What else would he want her to do?"

"He? Who do you think that is?" Chief Wright jumps back into the conversation.

"The man she was afraid of, Chief." I lean forward myself. "She asked me at the brothel and at the hospital if we'd arrested the man who ran the place. She wouldn't give me his name, but she was terrified of him. She said he'd be after her. And her brother, Alfred, told her the man had ordered him to fetch her."

"And how do you know that?" The chief doesn't miss much.

"I was coming up to her bed yesterday morning. I'd been off calling, trying to get a guard for her." I cock an eyebrow, and the chief sighs. "When I came back, her brother was standing next to her bed, inside the curtain. I couldn't help but hear."

The chief sighs even louder, but Messerton and Witherspoon are smiling.

"She also referred to him as 'the boss,' as if he had authority, maybe beyond the house."

That sobers everyone up.

The chief drums stubby fingers on the polished table top. "I think we need to know who owns that brothel operation." He turns to Messerton. "And the other one. Did you say it was going to change hands?"

Messerton nods and makes notes in the memo book I saw before.

"And we need to know where she worked, both places," the chief adds.

Ah, decision time. I suppose I should tell the chief what I've figured out already, what I intend to do.

"She may have worked at Hancock Garments on Second Street. Then moved on to the new factory. I don't know that for sure . . . but Hancock's the closest factory to their flat, and since both sisters worked there . . ." I shrug and decide to continue. "I thought I'd go there and ask around about her at lunch, try to find out if anyone knew her and where she moved on to."

I don't look up. I open my watch. Close to eleven. I hope I'm still on with Hancock Garments in an hour.

The chief leans forward, and the lecture is coming. "Julia, I have told you before that's not your job."

"It's my lunch break."

"You're meddling in police business."

"It's meddling when I ask a simple question but not when I wade into a basement on your orders?"

"I want to keep you safe, my dear. You have no business going into that part of town. What if the 'boss' works there?"

"What if he does? Maybe he'd give me a job. I'm a good seamstress."

The chief slams both hands on the table, and Messerton steps in. "How do you know she worked for Hancock Garments? Did you think to ask her that?"

"No." I subside back into my own chair. I hadn't realized I've been leaning my hands on the table. My palms have left moist spots.

"I don't know for sure. I looked the Magruders up in the City Directory. And I checked the map."

That freezes the chief momentarily. I don't understand the man sometimes. I like him, like working for him. In my calmer moments, I realize he only reflects the general view on women's abilities— until he needs a woman to wade into a basement after another woman or shoot a man from a distance. Following his orders. When I evidence any initiative, he falls back on his conventional image.

"Honest to God, Julia."

"Are you telling me I can't go check at Hancock Garments?"

"We have detectives for this kind of thing, Julia, as I've said to you—and Mr. Schroeder and Mr. McConnell—before. I'm assigning Irwin Edwards to the case, and he can go ask that question."

I assume Messerton has recommended Edwards because he's a

detective who works out of the Eighth. Messerton says, "I think I'll go with Edwards. It's been a while since I was in that part of town. Maybe we'll locate a new factory just looking around."

The chief's eyebrows go up. "Sure."

Messerton looks at me. "I'll have Edwards meet me, we'll check the neighborhood, and get back here as soon as possible. Maybe we can continue this discussion by noon."

That's good. I'm not exactly happy, but I'll work until then and think of something else to do. I'll think of Meredith and maybe my thoughts will suggest how to unearth the truth behind her words.

11

Carl has no more than settled in at his desk, shaking the first newspaper in the stack to unfold it, when City Editor Erich Zimmerman waves the mouthpiece of the city room's telephone at him. The machine has an extra-long cord, and reporters usually grab the device and head for a small desk tucked against the wall. It isn't truly private, but you can hope the clatter of typewriters and the chatter of their operators gives you some privacy.

Will McConnell greets him. "May be a change in our lunch plans, Schroeder."

"How's that?"

"Well, I expected Julia to be at the boarding house this morning and at work this afternoon. But I stopped by Miller's, and she's not there. No one's home. I need to run her down. She's probably either at City Hospital or at Headquarters."

"Whoa. Back up. Why would she be at home? Or at City?"

"You remember she helped that woman from the brothel. Then she ended up spending the day at the hospital with her yesterday. She planned to try to bring her home early this morning." William stops to sigh. "Either she couldn't get the woman out of the hospital . . . or worse."

"Good Lord, Will."

"I rang Headquarters and her exchange, but there's no answer either place. Someone usually picks up, but maybe all the cops are sleeping off their day with Teddy."

"I'd say that's a better idea than babysitting a prostitute."

Will groans. "Don't say that in front of Julia. She doesn't think the woman was there voluntarily. Neither does Mike Messerton, from what I can tell."

Carl's turn to groan.

"Anyway," William continued, "I'm at the office, so I think I'll go to Headquarters and see what they know. Do you want me to call you from there?"

"No, for Christ's sake. I'll meet you there. That woman—"

"Save it. It'll probably get better." William rings off without saying good-bye.

Carl breaks a string of German curses to tell Zimmerman he's headed to check on what's probably nothing, but you never know. Zimmerman nods him on his way, the tilt of his eyebrows saying he noted the aborted comment about "that woman."

Carl slaps on his derby and whips the scarf around his neck. This might be his opportunity, he decides as he scampers down three flights, his chance to make it clear to Will that Julia's edging out of control. Woman's suffrage is fine, one of many social causes Carl feels strongly about, and he approves of Julia's activities along those lines.

But if she and Will are going to start getting serious, Will needs to rein her in. Nursing prostitutes? Where does that fit in her job description? Or a wife's? What's she thinking? What's Chief Wright thinking? And it isn't as if Carl can just walk in and straighten everyone out. No. He'll have to wait for the right moment to bring it up. Some moment when Julia's stubbornness—and propensity to walk into danger—is obvious to everyone. Maybe today, maybe not.

◆   ◆   ◆

Carl bounds up the steps of the combined Headquarters and Central District on Twelfth. The double front doors squeak in the new cold of approaching winter. He nods to Sergeant Spencer at the desk and to two other officers who're chatting, draped across the big counter. One is Irwin Edwards, a detective who normally works out of the Eighth. Odd. Carl dismisses the matter, though, when he reaches the second floor. Will sits in the chair Julia keeps precisely at a right angle to the front of her desk.

Carl's arrival gets their attention, and he wishes he'd been a little less obvious so he might have picked up something from the tone of the conversation. The content isn't in much doubt.

"Julia. Is there bad news about your . . . patient?" Carl asks.

Julia looks at him as if she's considering his word choice. "Yes. There's bad news. She's dead."

"Will said she was in pretty bad shape when you found her." Carl glances at William, who shuts his eyes briefly.

"She was in bad shape, all right. She might have died of the abuse she'd taken. But she didn't. She was suffocated in her hospital bed instead."

Julia tosses that little bomb and looks at her typewriter as if she'd like to get back to work, maybe wouldn't mind both of them leaving.

Carl isn't budging. "Suffocated? In City Hospital? Good Lord." He glances at Will again, this time getting a raised eyebrow that warns him to be careful.

"That's news!" Carl responds as much to Will's restraint as to Julia's mood.

Julia sighs and starts typing, hard and fast. Carl tries Will, who says, "Yes, but we might know more if we wait on the story. Messerton and Edwards are checking on the woman's employment, hoping to turn up something."

"Employment? Didn't she work at the sporting house?"

William begins an answer that starts with, "No," when Julia says, "Drat," and pounds her right fist on the metal casing of the typewriter.

Will bends over the machine. Julia balls her left hand into a fist as well and leans her forehead on it.

"A jam," Will says. "I'll get it."

"No."

Will pulls back.

"I'll get it in a minute. When I get back. Just leave it." As Julia rises, she pushes her roller-footed chair hard enough for it to hit the table behind her desk and rock the telephone that resides there. She grabs her coffee cup and heads for the squad room.

Carl's staring at Julia when the doors that close off the stairs from the first floor open. Captain Messerton walks in, and Julia stops in her tracks.

"What did you find out?" she demands.

Messerton smiles, at the lack of preliminaries no doubt. "You were right, it was Hancock. And we got a name for the 'new' factory. Although it took some hard asking. You'd probably have had an easier time of it, if you'd been there."

Julia's eyes widen, and Carl groans inside. *Lord, Messerton's encouraging her.*

"A woman was headed in to work, late, obviously. We stopped her and asked about Meredith Magruder, if she knew where Magruder worked now. The woman didn't want to tell us, but I think it was because she was afraid of us, didn't want to get Miss Magruder in trouble. I guess cops have that problem sometime." He looks down at his uniform, and Julia follows his gaze.

"Well, you got the information anyway." Julia sounds pleased and a lot calmer, as if something in Messerton's story has struck a positive note.

The captain turns her to head back to the chief's office and her desk. He nods to Carl and William but keeps talking to Julia.

Julia stands by her desk, worrying the coffee cup. "Where? Where's the new place?"

Messerton pulls out a memo book but, instead of consulting it, starts writing in it. "I let Edwards do the note taking, but I want to make sure I have it down. Justice. Justice Waists. She seemed to think I'd recognize the name."

Julia goes for the City Directory and whips through pages, with Messerton crowding close.

Carl glances at Will, who's shifting. And frowning slightly. "You know, I think I've seen that sign," Will says. "Over on Locust, one of the new buildings. Maybe between 11th and 12th. Maybe too new to be in this year's directory."

Julia closes the book, apparently finding nothing, and looks at William more kindly.

"It caught my eye because the name fits the owner's intent, at least his stated intent. We had a story about it."

"The owner?" Julia pounces on the word. "As in the boss?"

"I suppose so," Will says. "Does that mean something?"

Julia nods unevenly, clearly agitated. Messerton says, "She was afraid of the boss, didn't you say?"

"But that would be the man who ran the house, not the waist factory," Will says.

Julia jerks her head, maybe in disagreement. More likely in impatience. "What did your story say? What does a waist factory have to do with justice?"

"It seems he pays the women who work for him rather well. A matter of justice he says."

The intensity of the conversation fascinates Carl, and he's swiveling from one speaker to another when something prickles his memory. "I've heard about the factory owner, too. A German. Moved here last winter. A young friend of my family is his new bookkeeper. He was practically bragging about the salaries. Thought it was quite progressive of the man to pay more, and it seems the guy gets good work out of his girls. Turns a nice profit even with the higher wages."

Julia's now staring at Carl. "So why did this particular one of his girls end up in a sporting house?"

"I don't know. Maybe she didn't work hard enough." *How would I know?* Carl stares back.

Julia shoots him a look that makes Carl—and the other two men—draw back a bit. But she has nothing to say. She moves behind her desk, puts the coffee cup precisely on its pad, and starts to jiggle the two jammed key arms. They disengage under the pressure and fall back into place. Julia pulls a handkerchief from a side drawer and begins to wipe the ink from her hands, absently.

Messerton and William watch intently. But Messerton doesn't get distracted. "So, Schroeder, what's the factory owner's name?"

Really. "I don't remember. There were a lot of people around, and I as much overheard the conversation as partook of it. Do you want me to find out, from my cousin's friend?"

Messerton goes back to staring at the notes in his little book, then snaps it closed. "I think we can find out easily enough. We need to know more about Justice Waists."

"Why?" Carl doesn't see the connection. "She must have gotten fired from there."

"Well, Schroeder, I intend to find out."

Messerton turns and heads for the stairs and then stops to look back at Julia. "Of course, what are they going to tell a cop?" He glances down at his uniform again and then considers Julia, taking her in, head to toe. "Maybe there's a better way."

Carl's sigh is unusually loud, and he realizes Will sighed at the same time.

12

I work hard all morning and make progress. I'm not any more behind than I'd be on a morning when lots of cops stop by to talk.

William arrives at Headquarters to check on me, and he must have said something to Carl, because he arrives a bit later, his negative reaction to my day's activities showing. Messerton arrives as well, back by the time Chief Wright comes hurrying down the hall from an office he'd retreated to half an hour ago. He isn't hurrying just to find the captain and two reporters outside his office. He always hurries.

He must know the topic of conversation.

"Captain Messerton. Do you have something already? Is Edwards on the case?"

"We have the name of the second factory where Miss Magruder worked. And I'd like to talk to you about our next move."

"Sure, sure. Come on in, Mike."

Messerton smiles at me as he follows the chief into his office. I don't know Mike Messerton well but, given his reputation, he must be using up his quota of smiles for the month.

I turn back to find Carl with his hands on his hips, as if I've irritated him instead of the other way around. William stands.

"Carl and I are going to lunch. Can you take time to go with us?"

I could get all teary with William's sympathy. I could get more irritable with Carl's comments about prostitutes and sporting houses. I'm not sure I need either. What's more, I want to be here when Messerton leaves the office.

"I need to keep working. I'm behind." I gesture to the reports, although there are barely enough to justify my refusal. William glances at them. One eyebrow takes note.

"Do you want us to bring you something?" He's correctly deduced that I didn't pack a lunch.

I can't resist his concern. He gets a good smile. "That would be wonderful. Thank you."

I get a nice smile in return, but Carl's shaking his head as they leave.

◆　◆　◆

Detective Irwin Edwards comes through the doors at an amble. I don't know him except through his reports, which are neatly written and complete. Depressing content, because he works the nastier districts. The tone of those reports suggests that he holds himself emotionally aloof from both criminals and victims. The entire Eighth District has a similar reputation.

He stops maybe twelve feet or so from my desk and stares. I decide to stare back. He has brown hair and blue eyes that are unexceptional, but he's exceptionally slender. And maybe an inch under my five-foot-nine.

"Are you looking for the chief—or Captain Messerton?"

"And good-morning to you, Miss Nye. I hear you're back from nursing duty. Nursing. Typing. What a well-rounded woman."

He's still looking me over, at what he can see above the desk at least, and a little smile opens over crooked teeth. Honestly. Cops comment gratuitously, flirt mildly, act like a squad of big brothers, but they seldom leer. I'm so tempted . . . what the heck.

"You left out shooting, Detective." I don't bother to check his reaction. I get back to the report at hand and indicate the door with my head. "The captain's with the chief."

Edwards skirts my territory to knock on the door.

Captain Messerton opens it. "Enjoy your visit downstairs?"

Detective Edwards suddenly isn't grinning. "Yessir. I didn't know you needed me."

"Maybe I don't." This is the everyday tone I remember from Messerton: something close to a growl. I smile into the typewriter.

"What we need is Miss Nye. Could you come in, Miss Nye?"

Oh, jolly. How demure can I be? Not very. I sail right past the good detective, as Messerton steps out to talk to him.

I immediately lose the smile as the door closes. Chief Wright is agitated.

Everyone knows when the chief is mildly bothered. He combs his mustache with his lower teeth. That drives me crazy. Other times he plays with his paperweight, a round worry stone. Or he paces. All of this in a man who is usually good-humored to a fault.

Just now, he's combing the mustache, worrying the stone, and pacing in the small area behind his desk, in front of windows that reveal gray fog rolling off the river.

"Please have a seat, my dear."

I do, and so does Captain Messerton, as he slips back in. The chief paces while he talks.

"Captain Messerton and I are worried about these women and whatever the connection is between a waist factory and the houses. We want your thinking first—and maybe your help."

The chief turns, spins the stone down, and leans on his fists on the desk. "Now, before we say anything, I want you to know that this is totally outside any obligation you have to this department. Your commission says you might do more than type if called upon. But I'm not calling on you as I was before."

Yes, the sharpshooting.

"Really, my dear, we only need your help thinking this through. Mike thinks we might need more, but I can't quite imagine how it would work and keep you safe. And we might not need to try this anyway."

My goodness. I hope I look impatient and not scared. Because I'm not scared. I'm eager. What I need is to go slow and get around their silly safety thing.

The chief looks so . . . fatherly. I try Messerton. The little brown eyes are assessing my reaction.

"Well, I'm happy to talk about the case. I feel involved already, you know."

The chief sighs, collapses into his chair, and grabs the worry stone again. "Tell her everything," he directs the captain.

Storytelling does not come naturally to Captain Mike Messerton. His mouth moves silently as he orders his narrative.

"One of the madams in Mill Creek, the one you met the other night, wanted to talk to me, to complain, I guess, but not about the police. We pretty much let 'em alone, you know, until we hear that something unusual, something nasty is happening. And I guess Ellie thought that was the case. Someone has come in and bought her out, her and Mabe two blocks over."

I want to get all this straight. "You mean Ellie and Mabe owned those houses, those businesses, themselves, and someone offered them enough money for them to sell the operations?"

"Right, the prostitution businesses. He wanted both of them to stay on, to manage the operation, day-to-day. Night-to-night." Messerton doesn't stop to see if I appreciate the humor. Maybe it isn't humor to him.

"But Ellie doesn't like the way things are going. She said he . . . he 'treated the girls like they was property.' That's exactly what she said. She also said something about one business at a time, but I couldn't get her to tell me what she meant. She doesn't like the man, so she talked. But she's scared. Scared of him."

Messerton looks at his hands while he explains, but he glances up to see my reaction. I'm wide-eyed. I certainly don't think women are property, but it surprises me to hear the phrase from a brothel's madam.

"Ellie's a good one," he says.

Oh.

"Anyway, that's why we did the raids. We missed our man both times. But I wouldn't put it past either woman to have warned him. They're really scared, playing both sides." He pauses to make sure he has my attention, I guess. As if I wouldn't be hanging on every word. "And I don't blame them, especially now."

"You mean after Meredith was suffocated?"

"Before that. I carved out time yesterday to go see Ellie. Before I went to the office and got your message. She immediately said she didn't have anything to say to me. As if I was the problem. All the women were looking at me like that, and they all disappeared quick. Only Ellie held her ground, and she out-and-out asked me to leave. Said I was going to get them all beat up. I pushed and pushed and all but begged, and all she'd say was that Betsy was on her way home."

"Who's Betsy?"

"A girl who works there. Home. Meaning she's through at the house. I kept insisting that Betsy hadn't said a word, and Ellie kept saying, well, she's gone. Finally, El lost patience and said, 'He had to beat someone, didn't matter who, I guess.' I got her to say that Betsy had finally been able to move around and get her things together. Left early in the evening. She was limping and wearing a veil, Ellie said. She wouldn't tell me who took her to the station or anything."

He looks at the Chief. "We can send Edwards to ask if anyone saw who put a veiled woman on a train, but the Station must've been wild, everyone who'd come to see T.R. and all. And we don't know where she was headed. Ellie wouldn't say. Maybe doesn't know."

Messerton draws an audible breath. "So, it looks as if a man has bought up the brothels and is either beating the women himself or letting customers do it. But I don't think it's that. Takes time to build up that kind of clientele."

I want to shudder, but instead I think of Meredith. "I agree. Meredith Magruder told me several times that she refused to cooperate. She wouldn't give me specifics, but she didn't voluntarily go with men who hurt her. It was only 'the boss' she was afraid of."

Messerton nods. "As I figure it, both Meredith and Hannah worked at Justice Waists, both ended up in the brothels recently, maybe weren't even selling, just ended up being fodder for the boss, whoever he is."

"Hannah?"

"The woman . . . I hit. All the girls at Mabe's would tell me is that she's from the new factory."

That shuts me up. Justice Waists does need investigating.

"The question is," Chief Wright says, "whether the boss is someone who recruits women from there, in particular, or whether the owner of Justice Waists is actually the one who's bought the brothels."

"Won't that show up in the real estate records?"

"No, my dear, it doesn't work that way."

Messerton takes up the explanation. "The houses are always owned by someone innocent-seeming, usually an absentee landlord. When I say this new guy bought the houses, I mean the prostitution businesses. He paid Ellie and Mabe good money so he has claims to the profits. But ownership of the building won't have changed."

I have a lot to learn. And maybe a lot to do. Nothing said so far is causing the chief to rock in his seat.

"How can I help?"

Messerton and Chief Wright exchange looks. The chief sighs and clearly thinks it's his responsibility to respond. He leans forward.

"Well, my dear, Captain Messerton told me he had a hard time today, he and Detective Edwards, getting the woman at Hancock Garments to talk to them. We think they'll have a harder time at Justice Waists. We don't know what's going on there with the women workers. Maybe it's all innocent at the factory, but they're a lot more likely to talk to another woman." He stops and sighs again.

"I'd ask you to go and just ask questions, but we're not sure that will work either." The chief exhales loudly, looks at each of us closely, glances out the window, examines the worry stone again. He puts it down and slams his palms on the desk. "This won't work, Mike. We can't pull this off."

Messerton scoots forward in his chair and leans on the opposite side of the desk. "It's our best chance, Chief. She's not going to get hurt in broad daylight in a factory."

The chief is shaking his head like a stubborn child. I look from one to the other, the idea forming in my head. They're beyond wanting me to investigate. They might want me to pose as a factory worker. The silence stretches as Messerton stares at the chief, who retrieves the worry stone and gives it a work-out.

"Chief Wright, please. I'm very concerned about all this. We—I mean the New Woman's Union—are worried about this."

That gets him to look at me. "We've heard the exposés of white slavery in Chicago, how it works and all. And it doesn't take a genius—or a man—to figure out that if the State of Illinois is cracking down, the slavers will move their operations elsewhere. St. Louis is obvious."

They both stare at me, as if they think we don't . . . think. I shake my head at them and keep talking.

"Sometimes I'm bothered by our attitude myself. It's easy for us to say that women shouldn't be pushed around by . . . bosses . . . and the men in their families. But almost all the women in the movement are better off. I mean, we have families and fathers who'd happily support us. Most of us could get married if we wanted to."

Could we? Could I? Thoughts of William are a distraction.

"We don't really know the pressures factory women work under. I'll bet lots of them have fathers and brothers pushing them to bring home every penny. And that opens up all sorts of opportunities for them to be taken advantage of, even to fall into the brothels."

Messerton's left eyebrow goes up.

"I know, that's not how all the women end up there, Captain. But we're concerned. I'm concerned. And now there's Meredith." I've moved up in my chair, close to the desk. I lean back and sigh.

"I should've arranged to take her home, to the boarding house, last night, when I thought of it. She didn't want me to leave her. She kept saying he'd come." I try to breathe through my tight throat.

"She lay there, restrained to keep her from hobbling out into a cold night, knowing that he, whoever he is, could talk his way through, past Crandall. Knowing he wouldn't believe she hadn't told us anything. Knowing he'd just kill her."

Neither man is moving.

"I'm willing to try a lot more than you might think. Tell me, please, Chief Wright. What exactly do you want me to do?"

His voice is soft enough to indicate that he's picked up on my emotion. "Go work in the factory. Justice Waists. Listen. Watch. See who disappears."

Good grief. They're serious. I've wanted to do this kind of thing since I can remember. Be a cop. Be like my Dad. Make a difference. Messerton leans back in his chair but keeps watching me as he continues explaining his scheme. "It's only that I don't think we can do it half way. That would be the most dangerous thing. I don't think we can send you to ask questions and then, when you don't get answers, go ask for a job. In fact, I think we need to make sure you get the job and have a good cover story. Maybe move you out of your boarding house into . . . someplace not so better off."

"Maybe we won't need any of this." The chief indicates the door with his head. "You sent Edwards out, didn't you?"

Messerton nods without saying anything.

"Edwards is going to try to find the Magruder family," the chief explains. "I understand they might know something about this boss. Maybe they'll tell us all we need to know. Maybe even confirm Crandall's description, what little he had."

Messerton shakes his head and doesn't look at either of us. He simply considers his hands. "All they have to say is that they showed up this morning to check on their sister. They'll deny everything else."

"Well, we'll see. This factory work may not be necessary." The chief works at his worry stone doggedly.

I consider Mike Messerton. Mid-or-late forties. The gray slight but obvious at his temples. I hadn't noticed it before. He's justly skeptical of help from the Magruders, but, mostly, Messerton is bothered. If I'm bothered about Meredith, he's bothered about the mysterious Hannah.

"Do you know Hannah's last name?"

Messerton jumps in his seat. But he tightens his jaw. "No. I really don't think any of the girls at Mabe's ever got to know her. They thought her name was Hannah, but they weren't even sure of that." He looks at his hands again. "It's as if she never lived, as if she ended it all, nameless, in the street in front of Mabe's brothel."

O.K. We have a cause here, Captain Mike Messerton and I. We will avenge Hannah and Meredith and whoever else we've lost and don't know about. I have the men I need on my side, and I will, by God, make a difference.

Chief Wright says, "I can't tell you to do this, Julia. I wish you'd call your father and ask his permission." He looks at me a second. "Ask his advice," he amends. As if the Sheriff of Callaway County routinely sends his typist into big city factories on the sly and would have some nuggets of wisdom. As if he has a typist. As if he'd send his daughter to a factory. I raise my chin.

"O.K., but promise me, Julia, you'll be careful. I know that sounds pointless, because it's not a careful thing to do. But within the situation, you can be careful. Do you see what I mean?"

He's going to say more, when a knock on the door stops him.

Messerton jumps for the door as if he welcomes the interruption.

"McConnell," he says.

13

I hear only William's name, but I imagine all sorts of things that might be going through Messerton's head. Will Mac try to stop this new incognita officer from taking her assignment? And what will happen to McConnell-and-Nye if he does?

Then I remember that William's bringing me lunch, not checking up on me. I stand quickly. "Oh, William. I'm sorry. We got to talking. I should have left you a note. Did you just get here?"

William steps into the room, and all his reporter instincts must be tingling. He looks at the two men and nods to me. "Actually, I've been waiting. I got us each a sandwich—and sent Carl on his way." He offers the sandwich in his hand. "I got hungry and ate mine, but here's yours."

"I'm sorry, William. I thought you and Carl were going to eat and then drop it off for me."

He smiles and takes a newspaper from under his arm. "Actually, I made a detour to my desk at the *Globe*. I interrupted just now because I have something for Captain Messerton." He offers the paper, which is folded to an inside page. "This is a month old and has a picture of the man we were talking about."

Messerton grabs the paper, and the chief rushes around his desk to look. William's expressive eyebrows rise. I clutch the sandwich, which is a bad idea, I can tell through the paper wrapping. But the name of the enemy might be forthcoming.

"Oscar Renke." Messerton holds the paper close as he reads. "Owner of the sparkling new Justice Waists Factory, Locust Street, has created a stir in the city's garment industry by paying higher than normal wages to his employees. He was invited to offer his progressive views to Chamber of Commerce faithful at the weekly roundtable discussion Thursday noon."

Oscar Renke. The boss? Or the unknowing provider of desperate women to the real enemy? I have to see the picture.

The men let me look. It isn't the best photo the *Globe*'s ever published. William's hand appears to point Renke out among the four posed men. Blond. Middling height. Big dark eyes behind tiny round lenses. Sturdy build. Rich-looking clothing, current style, I think, although I can never quite pick out the little differences that signal fashion-consciousness among men. I only know that William has it and none of the cops do.

"Doesn't look much like Crandall's description of the doctor," Messerton says. "Of course, a disguise would have worked, little as Crandall saw him."

"I've met this man." We all look at the chief, who sighs and retreats behind his desk. "I go to some Chamber events. The Commissioners' idea, but it's probably a good one. And this man was at the Chamber banquet last night. To hear Colonel Roosevelt. We talked a bit. He struck me as one of those men who likes to think he's on good social terms with the police chief."

The chief and Messerton look at each other as if that says a lot. William's calm, as usual, but I can tell by the slant of his eyebrows that he wants badly to ask me what's going on.

Messerton turns to him. "Thanks, McConnell. This is a big help. Saves us all sorts of time." He turns to the chief and then changes his mind and looks at me. "We need to start planning. There's no reason to wait. And maybe there are reasons to hurry."

Lordy, maybe there are. I swallow and, for reasons beyond me, take William's nearest hand with my free one.

◆   ◆   ◆

Chief Wright offers the Conference Room for me to eat lunch. I could eat at my desk, but that wouldn't allow for a private conversation with William.

Still, I'm not sure how to invite him to stay. We stare at each other a moment.

"Coffee?" William's expression tells me he chooses to hear the story instead of getting on to work. What a position he has. What a position I have, given the new possibility.

I smile and nod. He heads off to the squad room, where there's always coffee brewing. I pull a clean handkerchief from my desk and head down the hall. William comes up behind, and I hold the conference room door. He's bummed an extra cup for himself. The smell of coffee fills the room.

We settle at one end of the big table at right angles to each other. Close.

"You look pretty excited." William sips and grimaces at the heat.

I nod and open the sandwich. Ham and mayonnaise run off one side, and I tidy it up before I begin on half of it. Hunger takes over.

William's smiling when I look up from two satisfying bites.

"I am excited." I finish another bite before I look William in the eye. "The chief and Captain Messerton want me to go . . . incognita, I guess you'd say. They want me to work at Justice Waists and find out what the connection is."

William doesn't move. In fact, he goes very still. "Incognita. You'd do that?"

William's voice is colder, somehow. I've heard him ask questions of news sources in that voice, particularly when he's suspicious of their answers. It lends a chill to my response, but I soldier on.

"Of course. Because there seems to be some connection with the two dead women. We can't keep raiding brothels, hoping to find everyone before he harms them."

William hasn't moved, I swear. "So, you assume this Renke is behind the brothel incidents. Maybe Meredith's death."

"He wouldn't have to be. I'm betting the chief doesn't think so, but then he doesn't want to think he's sending me into contact with a killer. Messerton is more likely thinking there's a connection, I'd guess."

William's eyebrows rise from the inside, near the bridge of his nose, instead of at the top of the curve as mine do. He has the most expressive eyebrows I've ever seen. Right now, they're saying, "He may be a killer, so you'll go to work for him." He doesn't even have to voice it.

"Lots of women work for him without ending up in brothels. Messerton thinks it wouldn't do any good to simply ask questions. The women will be afraid, and the men won't talk. Going inside, working there, might give us more information."

"I see."

Does he? I want him to and fear he doesn't.

"And when would you begin?"

I wipe my mouth. "They're making some plans in there now. Messerton and I are afraid there might be other women."

I leave it, and he nods.

William opens his mouth and then closes it, gives me a smile, and reaches out a hand. When I take it, he puts my hand to his mouth and kisses the knuckles. Then he puts my hand back on the table and stands. To leave.

I jump to my feet. "William, thank you for the sandwich." Then I can't think what else to say. *I won't be able to see you when I'm playing factory girl? I'll miss you?* I don't want to say those things. I don't even want to think them. He comes closer to voicing them.

"Will you keep me informed? Where you'll be?"

"Of course, Will. I mean it won't be tonight. Or tomorrow. I don't even know how I'll get a job there."

"You'll manage." He picks up his hat, a brown homburg. No derbies for William. "Do you mind if I continue my own investigation? I'd like to interview the man, follow up on that Chamber story."

"That would be great. We'd get his official, public story. You never know what he might say." Because you're good. "Thank you."

William looks pleased—that I haven't told him to back out? He runs a hand over my shoulder, his dark blonde hair shifting as he tilts his head to look at me. An inside piece of me trills.

"I'll be back late this afternoon." And he's gone. I hold the door open and watch him down the hall, watch his graceful walk, the rhythm of slender hips and broad shoulders, all magnified by that air of self-confidence that surrounds him. I sigh and wish I could read him as well as he seems to read me.

I start on the other half of the huge sandwich. It's from a delicatessen near the *Globe* office where William eats probably half his meals and is warming, as well as filling. I'm excited as all get-out. I finish the food and head for the chief's office, eager for danger. I'll have plenty of time to sort out Will's response, reassure him.

14

I knock on the door of the Chief Wright's office, and Messerton lets me in. I swear the chief has aged while I ate.

But they've been busy. The chief has notes.

"How would you like to have a brother? Maybe a cousin, too?" Messerton's tone is light, but he isn't playing at this.

I think a moment. "Why? And who?"

The chief answers. "The story we're working on is that you and two male relatives have moved to town, maybe following the death of the last family member. There's no one out in the countryside to come looking for you. And these two guys want you to help support them. Maybe one of them's an invalid or at least recovering from some injury. That would leave him free during the day to check on you or contact us."

They're creating this story out of whole cloth. It's a creative side of the chief I've never seen. Too bad he isn't enjoying it more.

Messerton takes up the newly-minted tale. "Your only contact, your family's contact, in town is someone on the force. We'll use someone's wife or some such angle. And whoever it is will ask the chief to write to this Renke on your behalf. You'll have a letter of introduction from the chief of police, even though you've never met him." Messerton looks pleased with himself. I can't help but smile.

Then I sober. "Am I supposed to live with two police officers?" If

William doesn't object, my father will.

The chief slams down a pen. "This won't work, Mike. We can't ask her to do this."

"Wait, please. I guess I can do that. I mean, I trust anyone you'd choose."

But I'm feeling the first flutters of fear—or more accurately, the warning that this isn't going to be a lark of any kind. I'll have to sort out the risk to my reputation. And I'll have to determine whose opinions on my reputation really matter.

The chief and Messerton watch me. Messerton is quiet when he continues.

"You could probably live at the YWCA for a while, but it would look strange if you didn't have a cheap flat somewhere when one of the guys gets a job. And you'll have contact with officers, their protection. You wouldn't have that if you stayed at the Y or some boarding house."

True, but I want to back up a bit. "An officer is actually going to work another job to make this credible?"

"If we're doing this, we're doing it right. The whole story has to be in place, my dear. Otherwise, we're risking your safety, and that's not going to happen." The chief turns the worry stone with both hands. "We've got to find the right men. Actors, really. Cops who can act. They need to act like bullies, in public."

Lordy, this is getting complicated. "Why bullies?"

"It fits the pattern we know for Meredith, maybe Hannah," Messerton explains.

"But we're not looking for me to end up in a brothel, are we?"

"No!" The chief slams the stone on the desk and probably damages the surface.

"No, but if he asked you—or more likely, asked your brother—to move to one, we'd really have something." Messerton is trying to convince me, maybe to reassure me at the same time.

I do need to know the options. "Chief Wright, you know I want to help, but . . . what about a normal investigation?"

The chief closes his eyes in a gesture of weariness I've never seen in him before. Messerton jumps in.

"It's not a normal situation. The women won't talk, certainly not at the brothels and probably not at the factories. The only men we might pressure are the Magruder brothers, and I'm betting they've left town. If we just wait and hope to rescue women, we'll have trouble proving anything—and we might lose another."

"I see." And I do. This isn't a matter of surveillance or fingerprints or interviewing witnesses—since the witnesses won't or can't talk. And I certainly appreciate the urgency. It's as if Meredith is reaching for my hand, still asking me to help her.

I try to picture it. A factory girl. With two male relatives who'll be bossing me about, at least in public. Only in public. I'll make that clear. Cooking for them. Would I have to cook for them? After ten or eleven hours bent over a sewing machine? Wearing a corset? Good Lord.

I glance out at grayness. *Just think, Julia, how gray your days will be. And your evenings.* Will I manage to see William at all?

"I don't cook."

"You don't?" That's Messerton. The chief almost smiles.

"How do you eat?" Messerton asks.

"My housemates and I share chores. I sew."

"Oh. Well, that's good, maybe." Messerton turns to the chief. "Maybe she could show Renke something she's made. It would help . . . in addition to the letter."

I shake my head. "It'd have to be a waist and that'll take me a day or two. I usually don't sew waists. And the skirts and jackets I make are . . . not conventional enough."

Both men smile. And almost immediately sober. I beat them to it.

"I'll need a more ordinary wardrobe, at least a couple of longer skirts."

They nod and try to hide any further thoughts about my usual style.

I stand. "You know, Chief, I need to get busy on all this. Do you think I could just leave now? What about the reports?" Oh-oh. What will the cops say? Can an entire metropolitan police force keep mum?

Messerton moves to the edge of his seat, looking at the chief, "How about you telling the men she was so bothered by the woman's death that she's taking time off? That you're sending her home to . . . Fulton, isn't it? . . . and we'll resume typing the reports when and if she returns." He looks at me, and I suppose I seem shocked.

"Or we could hire someone else to type while she's off recovering from the experience. Couldn't we?" Messerton looks doggedly at the chief as if he doesn't want to risk looking at me again.

The chief sighs. "I'll work that out. Take the afternoon to work on clothes if you want, my dear. And think again if you want to do this. If you say no, there'll be no questions here. You have nothing to prove to me or to my men."

I head for the door. "None of your men can do this, Chief Wright. I can."

◆　◆　◆

I hurry out to my desk, neatly corral all the untyped reports in their basket, and put the few typed ones in another basket in the adjoining file room. Reporters can check them there. It bothers me to think of the conversations, smirking remarks along the lines that they knew a woman couldn't handle working for the police, would need to take a break. And then the newsmen will sit there and try to decipher the cops' handwriting. They'll compare guesses and some of them will say it's still better than having a woman around . . . can't talk free with a woman sitting out there . . . it's a wonder the cops ever manage to say a thing to each other. Well, I'll be back.

The chief meets me in the door to the file room, looks about, and hands me a five-dollar bill. It's almost a week's wages.

He whispers, here in his own building. "If you decide to do this, Julia, you'll need new clothes and so on. And you'll have to make that new waist. If you decide not to do it, keep it as a . . . isn't your birthday soon?"

I smile at him and take the bill because I really don't want to spend my own money on things like corsets. Or make-up. He looks so bothered, though. I resist the urge to pat his hand.

"I'll think it through, and I'll be careful. This is a smart thing to do. Really, it is."

We're almost the same height, so we're looking right at each other. I need to be honest.

"I've got to decide about living with two cops. Maybe the Y is better. If they have room. And I'm worried about my job." I gesture toward the files I just left. "I thought it was important."

The chief squeezes my hand. "It is important, my dear. We may arrange temporary help, as soon as you get the factory job. If you decide to."

I have to smile. How long will he continue to offer me the

option?

"Good. Thank you. I'm on my way, then." I say that a bit more loudly because peripheral vision tells me a couple of cops are stopped outside the squad room, watching us. The chief looks at them and then back at me. He says, to me, not them, "Perhaps I need to talk to Officer Jamison."

Chief Wright likes Aaron, too, and trusts him. Aaron's tall and slender and has brown hair that waves on top and around his ears where it's longest. Maybe he favors me enough to look like my brother.

Lordy. This won't be easy.

15

Actually, I don't shop for new clothes because I'm really careful with a dollar. O.K.—with a nickel. I don't want to buy more traditional clothing my roommates might already have stashed away, either at the boarding house or at home. Because five of the other seven women actually have families living in St. Louis, they can raid a number of closets quickly.

Aside from the frugality of the idea, it occurs to me that walking in in new clothes might not be wise, so borrowing is good. A corset is another matter. I stop by a lingerie shop to look at one of the horrible things. Metal stays in white lace. As if I have anything to hold in or up. In fact, the clerk takes one look at me and suggests a wonderful new product: an "enhancer."

It looks like the kind of bust support I make on my own, except that it's lined with ruffles. Layers of ruffles. To fill in what nature has left out, the clerk says, with an understanding smile.

At first, I laugh and shake my head at the work someone has gone to, the lengths some women will go to. Then a darker thought occurs to me. If the "boss" at Justice Waists is our sporting house owner, he might well hire women based on looks. Or some combination of sewing ability and looks. I can sew. But I'm quite sure no one would hire me on looks.

The clerk mistakes my contemplation for temptation.

"Oh, dear, do try it. It won't make you large you know. It will just fill out the waist ever so nicely."

My waists, bought from a store, made by the very ranks of women I'm seeking to join, do tend to hang a bit. I head for the fitting room, with a tight feeling in my gut and a happy clerk on my heels.

I don't know what she thinks about my current undergarments, but she tactfully says nothing as I reach for the corset.

Like most of the stupid things, it fastens in front and then has to be laced in back. I tighten the laces as much as I can, remembering that one has to do it evenly, not pulling too hard on the left or right. The woman is muttering, "Good, good," as if she thinks I might never have worn one. I frown at her and slip into the ruffled corset cover, hooking it in front, realizing that there's elastic under the ruffles to pull it taut against the corset. I quickly button my waist, thinking it will be tight because of the extra layers, but the constricting forces of the corset and the enhancer make the waist fit as it's supposed to.

I fasten the waistband of my skirt. To my surprise, it hangs loose. The corset has indeed managed to make my skinny waist tiny. The clerk is cooing. She steps in with a handy pin or two to take up the waistband.

I concentrate on not falling forward. That's what corsets do: tilt your bust forward and your tummy back, to emphasize your backside. Instead of allowing a woman to stand up straight, a corset manages to highlight a big bust, a tiny waist, and a shapely backside through the simple coercion of metal stays and suffocating laces. I'm less likely to faint than most women wearing one, but I'm certainly not comfortable.

Then I look in the mirror. Lordy. In one move, I've reverted to conventionality. In fact, I've never been this conventional because I've never used padding before, even at my sister's urging. Now I have that shape considered fashionable, and suddenly my skirt really is too short and my hair really does need to be wound on top of my head. Nothing else will do with the S-shape my body has assumed. Amazing.

The clerk's beaming. And waiting for an answer.

I know myself well enough to be sure that if I spend money, even the chief's money, on a corset and a cover that "enhances" me, I'll go through with the whole plan. I wouldn't do this to myself otherwise.

The clerk clearly doesn't understand my hesitation. She thinks I'm merely making the decision to look either fashionable or unaccountably dowdy. The corset could make me think twice, but there's really no doubt. I have to avenge Meredith. I have to stop this man. I have to make a difference. I'm lucky to be in the position to do so, I tell myself. This is what I've wanted, I tell myself. I tell the clerk I'll take the corset and two covers. With pink ribbon through the eyelets.

◆　◆　◆

I hurry home to the empty boarding house. None of my housemates will be there so early. Ruth and Susan and I get to work early and back early. But early is between five and half past. Dark already on a day like this.

I start coffee and hurry upstairs to find what I need: a fine white batiste for the waist and a pattern I'd drawn. I also find two skirts, one I haven't hemmed yet and one that can be let down, and several petticoats. They're too short for a conventional-length skirt, but I can add a ruffle. I'll have to wear at least another petticoat a day with the fuller skirts. Lordy, the laundry alone will keep me busy at nights. Maybe I won't have time to miss . . . this.

I look around my room, realizing how important it is that everything here is mine. Dad helped with a new sofa bed, and I'd gotten a new Burdick sewing machine for my last birthday. The art work on the walls is modern. The dresser sports a fan with the St. Louis Browns symbol and a program from a recent evening at the St. Louis Symphony. William loves music and baseball. And me. What will he think when he gets to Headquarters to hear the rumors I'm leaving?

He'll telephone or come by here, I tell myself. I'd thought to put on the corset, to practice walking awkwardly. But I'm shy to look so different in front of William. Maybe he'll like me like that.

Silliness. I grab the pattern, the fabric, pins, and my best fabric scissors and head downstairs for the dining room table. Good thing. The coffee needs attention.

By half past six, all my housemates are home. They've all heard about Meredith, and that alone would keep us standing around the kitchen speculating. I asked Fran about skirts when she came in. She has an older sister who's almost my height and uninterested in social issues. Fran can find several skirts.

Therefore, she isn't too surprised when I explain the situation. The others are open-mouthed and wide-eyed.

"But, Julia, that's so dangerous." Elizabeth also doesn't like to stand about and debate suffrage issues if it's getting dark.

"I don't think it's dangerous in that way, Elizabeth," Mary puts in. "It's the part about living with the two police officers. Are you sure about that, Julia?"

"No, I'm not." Maybe I can figure this out if I hear their opinions.

"I see the point. I need bossy male relatives, to duplicate what we know about Meredith. We need to be seen together so they can do their bossy routine. If I'm living at the Y, it ruins that whole angle."

"Are you hoping he'll suggest you go to a brothel?" That's Susan, and she's having trouble generating enough breath for me to hear her. But then, it's a breathtaking notion.

"All he'd have to do is suggest it—to my brother, I guess. I don't think he, whoever he is, would suggest it to me."

Mary's nodding. "Well, I see the value of seeming to have male relatives. And if you have them, why wouldn't you live with them?"

"Isn't there someone else, Julia, a police matron, or someone, who can work at a factory?" That's Addie, Susan's sister. I appreciate her concern, but that's a funny image.

"They're old, Addie. I mean, they're thirty-five at the youngest. No one's going to recruit them for a sporting house."

"But they could work in a waist factory. They could see if anyone disappears."

She's right about that, and I nod to her. "I guess Captain Messerton and Chief Wright think I can do it better. Maybe because I care more."

They all get quiet.

"I should have brought her here last night. She had to lie there and wait for someone she knew might kill her. Would kill her. She had no choices, Addie. Her brothers are . . . bullies, assholes."

There are gasps. Mary rolls her eyes, and I try again.

"Her brothers wanted all the wages she could give them. Maybe they didn't think she'd die. Maybe they thought she'd go work for whoever and then come back and find another factory job. Maybe they didn't know she'd run into this monster. But we do."

They aren't convinced. I share what I've been seeing all day, when the vision pulled me away from typing or sewing.

"She would've heard. She would've heard his voice outside the room where she was awake with fear and gasping for breath. She knew Crandall—the young officer—couldn't stop the boss. And then there he was."

Every eye is on me, and I look at each of them in turn. "I'm betting he stuffed something in her mouth first thing, so she couldn't scream with what little breath she had. Maybe he tied her arms then with something he brought. He'd cut her breasts before, and there was a long cloth holding her arms to her body and pressing tight against her. There were already restraints on the bed because the nurses were trying to keep her from leaving. So, he could have used those to tie her on her back. She'd immediately have trouble breathing. Seeing her damaged knee, he apparently tied another cloth tight around it, too, to increase the pain."

Several women are having trouble breathing themselves. I worry about Elizabeth passing out, and Mary puts a hand on her shoulder as I continue.

"Maybe he was doing bedside doctor talk all the while, so Crandall was less likely to be suspicious. Maybe the man whispered a few taunts. Asked what she told the cops. Then picked up the pillow from the floor and put it on her face. She could hardly fight, but she tried. I know it."

I let my gaze travel around the kitchen, warm and familiar and safe. I look back at my friends, women who think they'll be warm and safe forever. Ruthie's crying, and Fran has a fist jammed against her mouth.

"Do we make a difference or not?"

Heads nod in frightened agreement. I look back and forth between Addie and Susan. If I can convince the Llewellyn sisters, I can convince myself. Susan answers.

"Yes. And we should do all we can to help you."

"We'll know it's . . . O.K. . . . if you live with those officers," Addie puts in.

"And we'll help you look attractive," Susan says. She breaks into a smile she can't hide, and I break out of my dark imaginings, laughing.

Soon enough, Elizabeth has dried her tears and is making a list of clothes, Claire's working on my hair, and Mary's giving me pointers on what she's doing as she cooks. Fran has actually left, making the streetcar trip west to the Central West End where her sister lives. The others laugh at odd moments. When I ask why, they point to the corset cover, which hangs wrong side out on the back of a chair, showing off its layers of ruffles. There's a nervous note in their jokes and questions, though.

We eat Mary's stew sitting about the back parlor, as if we want to be closer than the dining table's ordered space allows. Claire is explaining the easiest way for me to pull off the Gibson girl hair. Every morning. At least ten minutes doing my hair. Ruthie has plans to try some make-up as soon as we finish eating. Probably another five minutes for make-up every morning. Lordy.

I'm moaning about the whole idea and getting laughs when the telephone rings. Fran has just come in the front door and picks it up, juggling skirts over one arm.

"Hello, William. Sure, she's here." Fran hands me the phone, and I plop in the chair next to its table.

"Hello, William." I speak softly, although I'm fairly sure my housemates won't listen in.

"Hello. I missed you at work, thought I'd see what you're up to."

"I'm sorry. I left early to go shopping, and now the girls are all trying to help me put together a new wardrobe. And hairdo. You'll be delighted to know that I'm going to have to wear it up."

William laughs. "I look forward to seeing that."

He says it lightly, but I'm shy about him seeing me in my new style. He had said, in the midst of one of our few arguments, he disapproved of my hair hanging down my back in its usual braid. When I asked why, he'd glared at me and refused to answer. It still bothers me. Maybe I'm afraid he'll say he prefers me to look conventional—and then I'll be the one glaring.

On the other hand, he might just be trying to keep things light.

"Well, I'm not looking forward to it. I can't figure out, at least so far, how to do the hair and the corset and maybe some make-up and not lose half an hour's sleep."

He laughs again. And then pauses. "I hope that's the most you have to worry about."

Hmm. I could say he's worrying about me unnecessarily—but not and be honest. "I hope so, too, William. I'm worried about several things. How I look is one of them, I guess. I don't want to tip the man off—if he's the one."

"That's a good idea. He might be dangerous. Or not. I called there today, to try to set up an interview, but he's out of town."

"Out of town? Does that mean he couldn't be the one who was at the hospital late last night?" Maybe in disguise?

"Not really. The office manager said he'd left this morning and probably won't be back until Sunday evening."

I sigh, and William continues, "But I expect I'll see him then. The manager seemed pretty excited about an interview in the *Globe*. That's nerve—if Renke's the man."

"Overconfidence, maybe."

"I'd say so, if he sat through a banquet with T.R., chatted with

Chief Wright, and then headed out to kill a woman in City Hospital." We both worry that one for a moment.

William sighs in turn. "Maybe Carl and I can judge that. We're meeting with his bookkeeper, that young friend of someone in Carl's family. Promised to see us tomorrow evening before dinner."

"That's great, William. Maybe you two can figure out something, and I can go back to work. And hang up the corset."

William laughs again. At least I'm enjoying the freedom to discuss underthings with a man. How modern. "I'd love to wrap it up," he says. "Cops are starting to gossip already, saying the chief is sending you home. Or maybe you asked to go home after you found the woman at the hospital."

Drat. "I hate that. But I guess it's got to happen. I hope all this is over soon, and I can correct the impression."

"Absolutely. By the way, Wright called several of us in, told us about Miss Magruder, and asked us not to report it. He wants the man who did it to think the hospital is calling it a natural death."

"And reporters are going along with that?"

"They all agreed. But it means there's going to be some pressure on the chief to come up with something. Nobody's going to forget."

That might shorten the whole experience. I can hope.

"Oh, and the chief asked me to give you a message if I talked to you. He wanted you to know the Magruders were located and weren't talking. In fact, they told Edwards they're headed home."

"Well, I expected that. It does tell us that even her brothers are afraid of the boss. Whoever that is."

"Right."

We're silent a second, both of us thinking how nice, if unlikely, it would have been if the Magruders had cooperated. Maybe. Maybe that's what we're both thinking.

I want to say something else to William, to somehow let him know I'm going to miss him. Judge how he'll react to my living with two officers. Meanwhile, it's getting to be a long conversation, and my housemates are wandering in with skirts and make-up in hand, signaling their readiness to get down to work.

"William, I'm going to miss seeing you. I don't think we should try to meet up if you're going to interview him. He'd recognize you if he were to see you in the neighborhood. Wherever that turns out to be."

"I agree, although it's odd to hear you be the one to say that." More humor. William insisted on something similar in our last little escapade, and I'd objected.

"Well, Jule, I'll miss you too. And worry like mad. Maybe we can figure out a way to send messages."

Jule. New nickname. And I like it. Honestly. It would be nice to be beside him, sharing a kiss. As it is, thoughts of intimacy make me air my other concern.

"The plan, at the moment, Will, is to have me live on the north side with two officers. They'll pose as brother and cousin." I stop because I can't say, "Will that bother you?" Won't say it. My breath bounces off the mouthpiece.

There's a pause. "I think that's good. It means you'll have protection when you're not actually in the factory."

Lordy, how have I found a man like this? My throat tightens again. When I can, I explain that one of them might feign an injury so as to have time to make contact with Messerton.

"That might be our way to exchange notes," Will says.
I hope he can hear the smile. "Let's work on that." I ignore, for the moment, all my other fears and concerns.

16

*From **The St. Louis Globe-Democrat**, Friday, October 14, 1910*

Vital Statistics
Burial permits
Meredith L. Magruder, 20, 520 North Second Str.,
pneumonia.

It feels strange to stay home Friday morning. I sleep until six, which is when I usually arrive at work. I make breakfast for several housemates: coffee, which I do perfectly; oatmeal, which I do adequately; and eggs. There're not enough mornings left to learn to do eggs, I conclude as I consider the runny mess on my plate. Mary says I can work on scrambling eggs for supper this evening.

As Ruthie and Susan, then Mary, Addie, and Elizabeth, and finally Claire and Fran, leave, I wander the house with yet another cup of coffee. It's the oddest feeling, something like the sensation when I left my father's house in Fulton. I'd decided then I probably wouldn't return to the house I'd once shared with my parents, sister, and brother. My mother is dead, my sister long married with her own family, my brother newly married and starting his family. I'd thought the lonely feeling was for my father, who hadn't lived on his own for years, if ever.

The pointless nostalgia does remind me that I need to arrange to pay my part of the monthly expenses, in case I'm not back by the first of the month. November 1. The day after my twenty-first birthday. Drat. It's just one sentimental thing after another.

I sit down and write Dad. Explain what I'm going to do and why I have to do it. Tell him we don't know how long it might take to catch our man. That's supposed to head off a surprise birthday visit.

I'll mail it when I figure out the timing. I want Dad to know what I'm doing soon, just not soon enough to stop me. Although if he does throw a fit, we can wait a couple of weeks, and I'll be old enough to ignore any of his objections.

I get busy on the new waist. It will have lots of pleats because I don't like frills. It will have a stand-up collar, but instead of buttoning all the way up, it will be slit in the front and the corners will turn back, making a little "V" to emphasize a slender neck. I planned it because I like my own slender neck, and I don't show it off with upswept hair—until now. After I work for a couple of hours, I go upstairs and fiddle with my hair. Half an hour later it's up. It looks good, but we'll have to see how long it stays like this.

I'm distracted as I sew. And restless. Luckily, the telephone rings about noon. The Chief asks me to meet him for an evening meal with Aaron Jamison, Red Witherspoon, Mike Messerton and Irwin Edwards at the Edwards' house. Mrs. Edwards is going to be my contact through my lost family back . . . wherever.

◆　◆　◆

The Edwards live in a nice house, small but nice, on Russell Boulevard. The outside is neat, neater than the rest in the neighborhood, but also distinctive. There're little touches. The flower boxes boast boughs instead of bare winter dirt. A woven rug graces the porch outside the door—and matches the one just inside.

I'm taken by Mrs. Edwards. She mirrors the house: she's neat and distinctive at the same time. Slender, like her husband. In fact, she also has blue eyes and brown hair. But she's lively. She wouldn't be detached about anything, let alone crime. I figure I've guessed correctly when she takes my hand and begins talking immediately about plans to ferret out a murderer. She's excited to help, she says, ushering me into the dining room, where the men are scheming my immediate future.

Marta's her name, and she keeps talking as she walks me to the table, asking if I want coffee. I agree to that, as always.

Marta turns to pick up the carafe on the table and stops in mid-motion. She looks around the table, and I follow her eyes. Every man is gaping.

Marta Edwards puts down the carafe and drives her fists into her slender hips.

"Why are you gentlemen staring?" When she gets no answer, she directs the question to her husband and tries again. "What's wrong, Irwin?"

I'm as curious about the relationship between Irwin and Marta Edwards as I am about his answer, wondering how this seemingly self-assured woman meshes with the leering man I snubbed yesterday. Maybe I misread him.

I come back to the moment when Chief Wright clears his throat. "Sorry, Mrs. Edwards. We're not used to seeing Miss Nye dressed up."

"Well, she looks quite appropriate, I think."

She turns to consider my outfit. "Is this the kind of thing you'll wear to work?"

Marta Edwards is rightly puzzled. I'm hardly dressed up. That would imply I'm wearing something special. I'm simply practicing what I'll wear on a daily basis. And the cops are reacting—to my long, full skirt, corseted waist, new hair, conventional silhouette. A bit of make-up.

I pat Marta on the shoulder. I like her, and I hadn't really expected to like Irwin Edwards's wife. "They've never seen me with my hair up. I usually wear it down in a braid."

She nods, but I doubt I've said enough to make her understand. All the cops at the table suddenly are holding out their cups for more coffee or checking notes. Marta looks at them, up at me, and goes back to pouring coffee. I take a seat and smile at the chief, who's still staring.

"Will this do, do you think?" When he doesn't answer, I try Messerton. The captain looks up from his notes and smiles ever so slightly. "I think it's perfect."

Mrs. Edwards starts to serve the meal, and I rise to help, although I don't always play these roles properly, on principle. Good practice, I tell myself. Strangely enough, Detective Edwards suggests I sit.

He disappears into the kitchen and returns after a few minutes with a platter of pork loin and a bowl of mashed potatoes. Marta follows with a tureen of beans and a basket of bread and a new look on her face. Whatever Edwards told her about me has made her more curious.

We talk as we eat. Sure enough, Aaron Jamison is to be my brother. Red Witherspoon is to be our cousin and the bully of the story. Aaron will pretend an injury. That will leave him free to hobble off on his crutches every day to make contact someplace with an officer, Messerton or Edwards. They're debating the likelihood of someone recognizing the sergeant. In fact, the talk shifts to Red's hair. If anyone we come in contact with ever frequents the sporting houses of Mill Creek Valley, they might recognize the flame-headed sergeant of the Eighth District.

"Well." I'm serious. "You could dye it black."

For some reason, that breaks up the table. Marta Edwards catches my eye and shakes her head. "Or blonde," she volunteers.

"Blondine," she and I say in unison. It's the standard bleach if you want to be a towhead, and I find it moderately funny. The men start laughing again.

"I think it's a good idea." Messerton sobers up. "Decide whether you want to be a blond or brunet while we finish up here."

Red seems dazed. His very blue eyes—under red eyebrows—are wide. I smile at him, maybe a bit on the coy side at first and then more sincerely. I'm guessing that being "red" is part of his personality. Maybe this will be a challenging exercise for him as well as for me.

We settle several other things. Messerton has found us an apartment on Third. He says it's furnished and has some pots and pans. More humor. Red and Aaron allow as how they might be able to put something together for supper and blame me for it in public. Both are single and occasionally cook for themselves at their boarding houses.

Edwards and Aaron have located a likely bar.

"A bar?" Really? "This exercise requires a bar?"

"Sure," Red explains. "Every working guy in that neighborhood has a bar."

"For that matter, cops have a bar or two." Aaron's eager to educate me. "What we'll do is use The Parrot to meet up with someone and pass messages. It's just down the street from Deem's where some of the downtown officers . . . visit." He looks at the chief without missing a beat. "Who's going to meet me? Or us?"

And what am I going to do? Sit home evenings while they hang out in a bar? Well, at least that'll be some private time.

"You're assuming I'll get this job Monday. What if I don't?"

Messerton keeps looking down at his notes as he answers. "I'm less worried about that than I was."

Because he sees I'm willing to dress appropriately? Why wouldn't I? Strange reaction.

I'm to meet the boys at the Third Street address on Sunday around noon. To move in. Bring whatever I want. Do I need help? Well, yes. So, Red, or whatever his name and hair color will be by then, will stop by to help me carry things. We'll take a streetcar to someplace close and make our way to our new home. Aaron, or whatever his name will be by then, will be waiting, on crutches or a cane. On Monday, Red will take me to Justice Waists and make the case for Oscar Renke to hire me. Then he'll look for work himself, while Aaron bides his time and makes clandestine police contact. At Deem's and The Green Parrot.

As people get up to leave, the chief asks if I'll come by the office Saturday afternoon to type the letter to Renke on department letterhead. The official department secretary could do it, but then he'd be one more person in on the deception. Fine. I can do that.

Then the chief says, "And you should know your names." I'd wondered if he'd mention it or if leave it up to our little family. I'm nervous and don't know why.

"Armstrong. Family name is Armstrong. I think Aaron can use . . . Aaron, and I'd planned on Red being Red. Maybe Blondie or Blackie." That gets him a laugh, and Red starts blushing. I'm amazed.

"What's your real name, again?" the chief asks.

Red blushes even more, if that's possible. "Enos."

The cops are chuckling, and I feel sorry for the sergeant. So, I lie. "I like Enos. Can we use that?" I ask him directly, not the chief.

He smiles at me through the blush and says, "Why not?"

"Great." The chief might not be happy about me doing this, but the whole thing appeals to him on some level.

"So, we have your little family. Cousin Enos, Aaron, and Nancy."

Nancy?

"Nance," Red says.

I sigh. "Why not?"

17

Carl does the introductions inside the front door of the Planters' House Hotel. "Will, this is Arnold Bauer. Arnold, William McConnell, ace reporter for the *Globe-Democrat.*"

"Glad to meet you, sir." Arnold pumps Will's hand, and Carl arches an eyebrow at Will over the shorter man's head in note of Arnold's enthusiasm. Will simply acknowledges the younger man's greeting and leads the way toward the Planters' smoking room.

Actually, Arnold Bauer is probably no more than a year younger than Carl himself, which would make him four years younger than Will. Arnold has a youthfulness about him. He's short and slender. His hair waves as much as Carl's own, but it's light brown and wispy, not substantial like Carl's thick red mop. Arnold's equally-wispy eyebrows move up and down as he speaks. Carl shakes his head: if Arnold were a puppy, he'd be peeing at their feet by now.

Will eases himself back in one of the leather chairs, but Arnold bounces on the edge of his. Carl pulls a leather wingback discreetly close and pulls out a cigar, eager to watch Will do his routine.

"Carl says you work the police beat. So why are you interested in Justice Waists?" It's probably the only intelligent question the guy will ask. Carl lights the cigar and turns to Will to hear his excuse.

"I do run the police beat, but we all do feature stories when our own work is slow. We're expected to come up with assignments sometimes, and I'd put back the article where Mr. Renke spoke to the Chamber of Commerce for a dry spell."

"I see." Arnold looks as if he's storing the information for later use in impressing his friends. The fact that it's barely true is no problem for Carl. Some reporters do features off their beats. Just not Will. Not unless he wants to.

"Of course, you just got through with that big story about Colonel Roosevelt and the aeroplane. Your name was on that one."

William smiles and nods. Arnold leans back with a thump. "I hope to go up in an aeroplane someday."

"Well, I'm sure you'll enjoy it. It's a remarkable experience. But I understand you're busy enjoying your new position. Head bookkeeper for a manufacturing firm is quite a feat for a young man."

Oh good, Will. I bet he doesn't correct you and point out he's the only bookkeeper. Carl nods as if he agrees.

Arnold shrugs. "I've been training for years, actually. My uncles are both bookkeepers, so I've been doing this for a long time now. And Mr. Renke gave me the chance to start from scratch, develop my own system according to the rules."

William tilts his head as if he's thinking about that. "Did he not do things by the rules before?"

"Oh, Mr. Renke did, of course. It's just that I only had a few notes and a couple of ledgers from the bookkeeper in Chicago, and they were pitiful."

"How can accounts be pitiful?"

"Well, I mean they were old-fashioned. You know, single entry—which boils down to recording a transaction, not analyzing it, not really reflecting the company's position." Arnold's starting to enjoy himself. Carl exchanges the briefest of glances with Will while

Arnold pulls a cigar from his pocket and leans sideways to clip it into the claw-footed ashtray beside the chair.

"Mr. Renke said to ignore those books. Said the man was old and wouldn't change and his own sons complained about it, but he always kept books as if it were fifty years ago."

Carl leans forward to offer a light and nods encouragement.

Arnold draws on the cigar and grins through the smoke at Will, who now has his memo book out.

"Let's back up. Mr. Renke moved here from Chicago, right? And when was that, Mr. Bauer?"

"Early this year. January or February, I guess. I started working for him the first of March."

"He must have had a lot to do: outfitting that new factory, hiring all new people, getting you started on the books."

"Well, now, Mr. Renke is tireless, you know. Just tireless. The factory is a thing of beauty, always spotless, and cleaned to a spit every night. He brought two cutters with him—they're the best, he says, and he couldn't leave them behind. Then he went out to hire the girls, but of course, that was easy."

"How so, easy?"

"Oh, that's the trick, you see. He pays more than anyone else, so he can skim the cream, so to speak. Hired the best workers from all the waist factories up and down Washington. If a girl works for him, and works hard, she's got a real good paycheck at the end of the week. And of course, they do work hard, because they want that pay. If they make mistakes, they're out of work, pretty much out of work anywhere in the city."

"You mean they can't go back to their old jobs?"

Arnold frowns a moment, thinking about that one.

"Well, no, Mr. McConnell. I mean, Mr. Renke lets it be known that if a girl can't work hard for the kind of pay he offers, then she can't cut it." Arnold starts laughing at himself. "Oh, pardon the pun," he giggles.

Will smiles and lets him finish his giggling spree. Carl forces a smile as well.

Will puts down his book and looks as if he's thinking again. "So, I'd suppose he doesn't have to let many women go . . . because they work so hard."

Arnold pauses to catch his breath. "A few. Some of these girls . . ." He pauses again to shake his head vigorously. "Every once in a while, one of them keeps making mistakes. The flighty ones, I guess. You know how girls can be."

"Indeed." Will doesn't smile this time. Not a hint, and Carl's watching closely. Maybe he thinks Carl will report him to Julia. That thought tugs at the corners of Carl's mouth, and Arnold seems to think that he, at least, is agreeing.

"Yes, that's it. Some of them are good seamstresses, but flighty. They end up out of there in no time flat." Arnold smiles around his cigar.

Will returns to the subject, pencil poised. "So, when Mr. Renke moved here, he hired you and the female staff and . . . perhaps the new office manager?"

"Wilson? Oh, yeah. But Wilson really doesn't manage much." The little man's enjoying this.

"I mean, if Mr. Renke isn't in town, the cutters, Dexter and Mallory, run things. Wilson just keeps track of financial things for me, makes sure the girls clock in, and so on. Dexter and Mallory give the orders, keep the girls in line."

"And where does Mr. Renke go, when he's out of town?"

Arnold's finally thinking about the questions instead of his answers. The young man looks at Will several beats before he answers.

"He sells. They make waists. He sells them. You should ask him about that."

"I will, of course," William replies coolly. "I thought he would stay here and manage and have other people sell. But that shows what I know." Will smiles.

Arnold, the fool, is disarmed. "Well now, he does work the factory, too. He's quite the designer. He does all our patterns. Artistic he is."

Arnold's nodding to himself, happy again. "I tell you the man has more energy than anyone I've ever known. He has a glass-fronted office up on the main sewing floor so he can keep an eye on the girls. He'll come back to the factory at all hours, and I'll go in and find a wad of cash from sales. He's amazing." Arnold beams at Will. "You'll see."

"Well, I'm certainly looking forward to Monday. Your Mr. Renke seems to be a fascinating character."

The two smile at each other, both having gotten what they wanted out of the session.

Will snaps the memo book shut and starts thanking the man. Then he stops as if he'd been silly to forget to ask. He goes thumbing back through the book. "Pardon me, but did I ask what the man's name was, the old bookkeeper in Chicago?"

Arnold's smile freezes. "Why?"

"Background." Will says it as if Arnold should understand. "If I need to ask more about Mr. Renke."

"Oh. I'm sorry, but I don't really know it. I got the impression he was sort of a friend of Mr. Renke's. Maybe. But his name wasn't anywhere on the pages I got. Just a disorganized mess, if you ask me. There should have been a name, a bookkeeping company name, you know." Arnold shakes his head in disapproval.

"Well, not really important." William snaps the book shut again. "I surely do appreciate the help."

William stands and shakes Arnold's hand and makes small talk as they walk among palms through the lobby. The Planters' is one of the older and more elaborate hotels in the City, often used for meetings such as these, situated as it is across from the Courthouse, a gathering place for reporters and politicians. Small wonder Arnold is pleased with himself. He bounces some more, says good-bye, and heads to the streetcar on Market.

Will and Carl watch him go in silence. Carl glances at his friend, just to check: one eyebrow raised, head nodding ever so slightly. Carl wonders if Will knows he does that when he's detecting—as opposed to reporting. And when he's learned something useful. Or troublesome.

18

*From **The Kansas City Times**, Saturday, October 15, 1910*

> *Half way through the month of October finds the*
> *state with record high levels of rain and record low*
> *temperatures. Official temperatures yesterday were all*
> *on the shivery side of 40 degrees, but the first snow of*
> *the season was too slight to measure.*

Hig knows the two men who deliver the boxes, of course. They've been in the neighborhood a long time and so has he. The two Negroes look to him for . . . relief maybe. Hig doesn't think they mind the work, although he nudges one crate and is amazed at how heavy it seems. No, he thinks they're confused by the boss. The man is something else, O.K.

The boss dithers over the crates, clearly not wanting the two Negroes to come inside. As if they don't know it's a sporting house. But it's cold out and starting to sleet. Miserable weather, winter setting in all of a sudden, in October no less.

Hig says, "Well, boss, we could unpack some of them a bit, carry things in, lighten 'em up enough to carry 'em."

The boss is delighted with that suggestion, and he pays the two men, probably not enough from the looks on their faces as they hurry off in the nasty weather, and then insists that he and Hig do a relay so that one of them's with the crates on the porch all the time.

It's a good idea, Hig decides, after he gets a glimpse of a

photograph that has slipped out of a stack. In fact, Hig decides he'll have to stay here and help the boss for as long as he needs.

Besides photographs, the crates hold heavy plates the boss calls "negatives" and lots of wooden picture frames, all ornate and expensive-looking.

They work all night, and it's early Friday morning when they have everything up on the top floor. The boss won't hear of waiting or even slowing down. Hig doesn't mind. He gets enough glimpses to keep him thinking about more while he works.

The negative plates go in the narrow room at the end of the large open space. The boss calls it a "dark room," and it gives Hig the creeps. The room has all sorts of modern-looking equipment, special clocks, running water—which cost a pretty penny in this attic space—great long tables with flat pans, storage cabinets for smelly chemicals. And apparently, the boss is going to work by the light of two candles. The ones hidden behind blood-red glass. The whole room has a reddish-orange glow Hig doesn't like.

Hig thought he might go home to get some sleep Friday morning, although he's supposed to be on duty. But he feels a strange need to guard the photographs and the half-glimpsed women in them. So, he's convinced himself he *is* on duty, helping a citizen, if he sleeps curled up in front of the fire that's going so good. The boss had big panes of glass put into the slope of the ceiling, and the room's cold if you don't keep a fire going. The girls complain all the time about coming up here to watch a fire on cold nights. But the boss has stoked it up good, and Hig takes advantage.

It turns out to be a good move. The boss is up and around early this morning and ready to work. He seems pleased that Hig's here, rolled up in blankets some of the girls gave him. Or maybe the boss is amused. He sends Hig down for breakfast and then has him help move stands and cameras around.

Hig can't figure at first what in the world the boss wants a picture of by the big windows. There's nothing but sky showing, and it's a dull blue. But the boss insists it's good light for enlargements. Together they wrestle the biggest camera Hig's ever seen under the windows and, when Hig dares say how big it is, the boss explains it's two cameras in one, and it's clever of Hig to notice.

That's reward enough for the hard work, more than Hig usually does in a day, to tell the truth, but then he gets to see the photograph the boss is enlarging. There in the candlelit room, Hig watches the woman emerge from the paper as if she's wading out of the water in the huge pan, looking for him. Maybe looking for him to help her. Because she's naked. Framed in a doorway as if she's coming in to find him and ask for help with the chain he can barely see around one slender ankle.

Her big eyes and long dark hair hanging down and tall, slight nakedness take Hig's breath away. The boss is amused this time, right enough.

But he says he's using this negative, whatever a negative is, to test the enlargement camera. He says he's going to make smaller prints of the woman from this and other negatives. He tested with this one because the lighting had been bad when he took the picture. In a basement.

Hig wonders why there'd be a doorway like this in a basement and why the woman was there in the first place, and it makes him want to find the real woman, not just her picture, and get her out of the basement. And then the boss says, "You can have this one, this big picture, if you want it, Hig. Soon as I fix it and it dries."

By Saturday, Hig's tall slender brunette with the chain and the big eyes is ready to take home. The boss has worked hard all day

Friday and all day Saturday and has developed other pictures of the woman, smaller ones, and put some of them in frames. Hig's real worried about where they're going, because the boss says these pictures will sell good. He's also offered Hig pictures of other women, some of them dressed but in gowns you can see through, some of them in corsets that show bosoms bulging over the tops, some of them naked like his woman but lying on a bed, looking like an invite.

Hig doesn't want any of those pictures, just the ones of his woman. He's struggled all weekend, while he listens to the boss explain what he's doing and helps him hang up pictures in the ornate frames on one side of the room, to get up the courage. Finally, he says, "Can I meet her?"

The boss smiles gently and says, "I'm sorry, Hig. She's dead."

"Dead?" All sorts of things run through his head. Maybe it's an old woman, a woman who had her photograph made years ago and is old now. So old she's dead. But the boss is shaking his head. "You know, Sergeant Hig, the police in St. Louis aren't helpful like you are here. They killed that woman."

Hig gasps and picks up the nearest picture of her.

"Why? Why would they do that? Did they chain her up and kill her?"

"No." The boss laughs. "They didn't chain her. I did that to keep her from running away, from getting hurt. When the police came to raid the house, she did run away, and a policeman saw her running and hit her with his automobile."

Hig tears his eyes from the picture to look at the boss, to see if the boss is joking him. "Why would he do that?"

"Well, Hig, I guess he thought she was just a whore, not a beautiful woman for us to photograph and enjoy. Not a piece of art."

Now the boss is standing right next to Hig, one hand on his shoulder, the other holding an edge of the frame, shaking his head. A piece of art. He and the boss have somehow created art, and Hig can carry it with him.

Hig goes with the boss to the train station when he leaves Sunday for St. Louis. Hig's worried about all sorts of things, what the godawful cops in St. Louis are doing, when the boss will be back, when they can create some more art. He has two small pictures of his woman in his coat pocket, and the boss knows it, of course, made them on purpose just for him.

Union Depot's right busy for a Sunday, and Hig stands there in front of the boss, needing to let him go. There's time for one question. "What was her name, the woman they killed?" he whispers.

The boss whispers back, so only Hig will know. "Hattie. Her name was Hattie."

19

The knot's back in my stomach when I walk into Headquarters Saturday. Why I should be nervous walking up the stairs to my own desk, I don't know. I hadn't dressed in my new style. In case any cops see me, I look like my ordinary self. But apparently something more than the clothes is happening.

I type the letter. It simply says Chief Micah Wright would appreciate any consideration that Mr. Oscar Renke could give Miss Nancy Armstrong for a job at Justice Waists, that Miss Armstrong's parents, now deceased, had been friends of the family of Mrs. Irwin Edwards, wife of one of the city detectives.

It seems a pretty tenuous connection, and I tell the chief that when I take the letter and its envelope into his office. He motions me to sit, and I do, more comfortable in here where no cops might see me.

"Well, my dear, it is a slight link but don't underestimate Mr. Renke's desire to do a favor for the chief of police." He signs the letter, seals it up in its envelope, and picks up the silly worry stone. "The problem is, the more a man wants to get in good with the police, the more likely it is that he's doing something illegal."

That's obvious. "Chief Wright, we assume the man has some connection with the houses. So, if he hires me on the basis of your recommendation, that's good. We'll be one step closer to getting him."

The chief nods his head and turns the stone slowly, keeping his thumb and middle finger on either side of it, in the indentations.

"Just so you'll know, my dear, there's been another raid on a brothel over on Chestnut."

Goodness. "Another woman in trouble?"

"No, no. It occurred to us that our man might get spooked if he thought we were targeting him. So, we simply raided another house for form's sake. Didn't find much as you can imagine. Might do another one tonight."

"Oh. Good thinking."

The chief fiddles, hesitates, and continues. "I assume you're going ahead with this. You can still call it off, you know."

I lean forward. "Chief Wright, I can help you find a man who's abusing and murdering women. I want to do that. Who wouldn't?"

The chief looks me in the eye. "Most women wouldn't do this, Julia." He leans back and looks down at the stone he's started worrying again. "You know that. You know that the . . . men in your life don't want you to do it."

The men in my life? What's that supposed to mean? I jerk in the seat, and the Chief can't help but notice my anger.

"I asked some of them, people who care about you. What I heard was that they don't want you to do it. They're worried you're getting in over your head. They won't stop you, but they'd rather you help in some other way."

I breathe out loudly. Unladylike.

He continues, with the regret showing. "I'm thinking I shouldn't have let Mike Messerton talk me into this, my dear. I won't shut it down, but I want to know that you've thought it through."

I stand. "The plan is in place, Chief Wright. And, it's a good plan.

I'll move in with Red Witherspoon's help in the morning."

We look at each other for several heartbeats, and then I fling the door open. The men in my life indeed. Well, the men in my life can just step back and let me live my life. And do whatever it takes to help other women live theirs.

◆　◆　◆

I spent a good while getting ready for my date tonight. I put my hair up, more elaborately than I'm prepared to do on a daily basis. William wants to see my hair up, and he'll see it at its best. Not because I want to please him. No. I'd planned on an up-do earlier when I designed the outfit. And what I'm wearing certainly won't please William.

The suit I just finished making is the very latest fashion. No corset needed. The jacket is a tunic that blouses slightly at the waist instead of cinching in. No petticoats. The skirt is pencil-thin and ends at my ankle bones. Which show because I'm wearing slippers with straps and Louie heels—no high tops tonight—and dark-but-sheer stockings. Everything is dark blue, the suit a dark blue worsted with a blue silk waist so plain I couldn't take it to Renke if I were willing to. I'd found a hat small enough to get lost in the nest of hair, although the feather that trims it is long and sleek enough to get everyone's attention. It's new and challenging . . . and me. William can prefer tradition all he wants. And say whatever he wants.

My housemates all smile sweetly and maybe nervously at William when he arrives. They're no doubt wondering two things: how William feels about the adventure I'm starting and why I'm thrumming with anger. I leave them wondering.

William's another matter. He asks if I'm O.K. when he really wants to ask why I'm angry. I tell him I'm fine, and, apparently, he reads the unspoken part that says I don't care to share the anger. His eyebrows sink into a frown I can see by the globe lights as we ride the streetcar to the Castella supper club. The cold makes the leather seat stiff, and it's neither warm nor comfortable by the time we make the trip from the residential end to the river end.

The Castella is distinctive. No square doors, lots of arches. No palms sitting in pots, but vines draping from wrought-iron balconies set into the walls. Dad brought me here once, and it had made me feel . . . sophisticated. Tonight, I'm dressed for the part. The Castella is distinctive, and so am I.

I can't stride in the skinny skirt, but I can stalk. William stops in the well-lit sidewalk in front of the Castella and looks at me one more time. He shakes his head. It could be in admiration, but I'm not inclined to give him the benefit of the doubt. I'm stalking when I go in the front door. And get the maître d's attention without trying.

He heads toward us, William and I shuffling side by side, when William steps in front of me and stops. I get a hand up between us and say, "What?" just as William says, "Back away and wait for me outside."

I grab the back of his overcoat, an elegant melton number that's fashionably long and full. "Outside? You want me to wait outside in the cold?"

William has stopped the maître d', and I can imagine the look on William's face that backed the man to his post. It no doubt matches the sternness in his voice. "Do what I tell you, now, Julia. Back away from me. I don't want it to look as if we're together."

He starts moving forward. I have to let go of his coat or look like a fool.

"I'll only be a few minutes." He says it as if he's talking to the maître d', although I assume it's meant for me.

I consider stalking after him, but some small instinct involving pride makes me act more casually. I'm behind one of the arch supports and can't see most of the dining area. I don't know who heard or saw the exchange. I turn slowly to find a couple looking at me with disapproval. As if I were annoying the gentleman who left me standing here unaccompanied.

Of course, the streetcar has moved on when I step outside. The chill wind catches the cape I'm wearing over the suit, and I'm shaking with cold as well as anger. I debate walking toward the next streetcar stop to keep warm, but I don't. If William said he'd be a few minutes, he'll be out here soon. I use the time to order my thoughts, prepare my response. Unfortunately, thinking in the cold makes me even angrier than I was inside.

I'm stalking back and forth in front of the door, glancing in as I pass, snorting at two couples who try to get past me to enter, steaming at the couple who dodge me in leaving, when William appears. He'd been coming to the doorway casually enough, continuing his act, I suppose. Once he clears the door, he rushes toward me, holding out his hand. I step back.

"I'm sorry," he begins, but there's no way I'm going to hear him out.

"You don't want it to look like we're together? We can take care of that, William. Why don't you head on to work, and I'll head home. I need to turn in. I start a new job tomorrow." I turn sharply and head down Washington. A streetcar will appear or it won't.

William catches up with me, of course. I brace for him to take my arm. I plan to turn and shove him. But he's too smart to touch me.

He's also angry. "Wouldn't you like to know who I saw back

there? Or are you going to be stubborn?"

We both know I can be stubborn to my own detriment, but I'm not willing to allow as how that's the case now.

"I don't care who you saw. I won't be talked to that way."

"What did you expect me to say? I needed to seem to be alone—and waiting for someone. To protect you."

"I'm sure you enjoyed protecting me. But you know how little I appreciate that, William. Maybe you should have thought faster. If the right person saw us together, we might have to call off the factory job. You'd prefer that, I believe."

William raises a hand, and surely he's going to grab my arm this time. I let him know I see the motion, and he slams the gloved fist into his other palm. "I haven't said you shouldn't go to Justice Waists."

I huff but don't answer.

We both stop because the streetcar is almost even with the corner we've reached. "Julia. Have I said any such thing?"

"No, you haven't had the nerve to say that . . . to my face." I hurry onto the platform, and William's right behind me.

The car's crowded. There are two seats, not together, and I take one, between a man who's staring at my outfit and my attitude and a woman who's too tired to care. William leans against a door frame and glares.

The woman gets off in two stops, but William doesn't take the seat. He's glaring out the door. One man hesitates and then scoots past William as carefully as possible. I do wonder who William saw that shouldn't see me. Renke isn't back in town yet or isn't supposed to be. I'm not going to ask.

There's no transfer, of course, where William and I can part, so we both exit two blocks from the boarding house.

"Would you please explain to me again why the idea of protection bothers you so much?"

I shoot him a look, but he meets my eye steadily. I turn to watch where I'm walking. Stalking.

"I've noticed, William, that men who say they want to protect you really want to control you. It sounds like a noble motive, but it's just a way to make a woman feel vulnerable and willing to take orders—usually orders to stay home and stay safe."

William stops and exhales loudly, adding to the fog. I turn to him, reminded of one of those Bible pictures of an angry prophet, thundering from the clouds.

"You really think the worst of every man, don't you? Couldn't a man honestly care about your safety without having some evil intent?"

"I'm not saying it's evil. It's . . . manipulative."

"Honest to God. No one is trying to manipulate you, Julia. Certainly not me."

I have no answer to that. And I'm cold. So I say, "Good night, William."

His eyebrows react, and he puts his hands on his hips as if he wants to stand here and continue the conversation.

"I can make it home by myself." I start walking. He snorts again and follows.

"We could go someplace else and talk this out."

"I'm not in the mood to talk."

"Well, I want to talk. I want to talk about marriage."

I slow, as if I can't think about marriage and stalk down the street at the same time. I've had the feeling this discussion would be coming up, but I thought we'd both want to wait until after the factory assignment, when we can at least see each other. Maybe he wants to put his bid in now, have me think about it. And maybe not. I think fast enough to realize the negative interpretation of what he's just said.

"If I said I'd marry you, you'd have grounds to keep me from going to the factory."

"Dammit, Julia!" He stops and turns toward the street, fists on his hips, breathing hard again. I stop altogether. We're close to Miller's Boardinghouse, and I need to say my piece before we collect an accidental audience.

When he turns, I read hurt as well as anger on his face. The streetlight shadows his face, and the swirl of the fog makes it that much harder to see. But I know that face well. Some of my anger seeps away into the mists.

"William, I love you. I do. But I can't marry anyone. I won't turn my life over to any man to tell me what to do. Even if you say you won't do that . . . it's what marriage is about."

William simply looks at me. I'm sure he doesn't agree with what I've said, but he isn't arguing. I try again.

"Right now, it's important to me to . . . to make a difference and argue for suffrage . . . and do it alone. I know you want to protect me for the best of reasons, but I can take care of myself. I have to, William."

William stares at me, one eyebrow angled up. It comes down slowly, and he shakes his head. He makes a loud noise, something between a sigh and a snort. "I hope you can take care of yourself, Julia. Please do . . . at Justice Waists and in whatever other adventures you find."

He tips his hat, and I think he's going to walk off, but he doesn't. "Would you indulge me one last time? Let me watch you down the block?"

I swallow hard. "Of course. You be careful, too, William."

He nods shortly, and there's nothing else to do but turn and walk away from him. When I get to the step, I look back. He waves and turns away. I hold up my hand but don't actually wave at him. He wouldn't see it.

◆   ◆   ◆

We can't have been gone more than half an hour. I hate to walk in the door, but there's nothing else to do My housemates are open-mouthed and silent for several seconds. Then they all start asking at once, what happened, where's William, does he have to cover a story, is he coming back.

I shake my head all the way into the kitchen and sit heavily at the table. I shrug the cape off and twist in the chair. The skirt doesn't seem so much fashionable as awkward.

It takes a minute or so until I can get a word in edgewise. "We had a disagreement."

"You fought? Over what?" Fran asks.

"Over . . ." Over what? Over who I am, maybe. "He was going to ask . . . . or talk about . . . marriage. And I . . . I see that as a way to let a man control me."

"You told him no." Claire sits beside me and cranes to look me right in the eye.

"I didn't give him the chance to ask."

"Because of the movement, because of suffrage?" That's Mary. She sounds more curious than reproachful.

"Julia, I thought you really liked William." Elizabeth breaks in before I can answer Mary. So, I have to explain myself to both of them, to all of them.

"I love William. But I can't marry him and do the things we"—my gesture includes all of us—"need to do. I don't want him, or anyone, giving me orders."

"Would William do that?" Mary's curious again. I look at her and know I'm not so sure of my answer.

"Has he said something about you living with the officers?" Mary's pushing.

"He said it might keep me safer. I'm sure he's worried about me."

"Oh." Mary doesn't blink. "Like you worry about him."

Well, yes. As when I was so worried that I couldn't watch him go up in an aeroplane.

"Oh, Julia." Elizabeth actually has tears in her eyes. "Suppose we get the vote, and you don't find someone else you love. I don't think the movement is worth it."

Elizabeth says the most obvious things. Most of the time, we all shake our heads and smile. Maybe this is one of those times. Except that I look around and not one of the women seems to be questioning Elizabeth.

I raise my hands and let them drop. "It has to be worth it now. For me."

The heads are all shaking. I sigh and say I need to pack. I might as well be alone in my room—given that I feel very alone and a little stupid in the midst of my friends. Truth is, I won't do anything for a while other than replay the scene with William and start second-guessing myself. I did what seemed right. But I already miss him.

20

*From **The St. Louis Globe-Democrat**, Sunday, October 16, 1910*

Actress Billie Burke, whose performance in the comedy "Mrs. Dot" at the Olympic is drawing crowds, charmed a different set of fans at Kinloch Field when she visited an aeronaut friend at the balloon races yesterday.

The only other time I've packed like this I was leaving my family home to move into Miller's Boarding House. Everything was mine then. Everything pointed to excitement, opportunity, civic engagement. The things I pack today are ambiguous. My toiletries—plus make-up. Clothes I might conceivably wear—plus the corsets and extra petticoats.

In a large handbag, I stuff books. *The Awakening* is gospel with St. Louis feminists. Its indictment of traditional marriage might help. Then there's the new Harold Bell Wright novel. I borrowed it from William, and I debate taking it. In fact, I debate picking it from my bedside table. How will I get it back to him? The question is physically painful, a tightening of my gut that I worried with all night. I don't have an answer to any questions involving William.

One of Mary's cookbooks has to fit in. It has pages marked at "eggs on toast" and "maccaroni" and the ten different versions of "potato salad" offered by the ladies of the First Baptist Church of somewhere or other. Mary swears by it. I can surely handle some of the simple recipes, she says. I didn't bring a cookbook from Fulton.

Fran offered a journal. She actually cut out her own pages and gave me blank ones, to organize my impressions. I find myself staring at it and imagining words of wisdom about William. I want to curse over my inability to move past the matter, but I don't want to let go. Part of me will soon be standing across the room, watching the rest of me cry, and saying, "You deserve to be miserable." I can see it coming.

On a whim, possibly thinking I might write William, I grab writing paper and envelopes, a couple of stamps. Although I suppose I can pass notes through the cops. And humiliate myself.

The cops and I are each taking linens to the new flat, so I have those to gather up as well: sheets, blankets, a pillow, towels. It all makes an impressive pile near the front door. My housemates stand around staring at it.

When I answer the knock on the door, it's my turn to stare: Red Witherspoon is just barely recognizable.

He took Marta Edwards up on the Blondine by the looks of his hair. He also let her trim it, and his curls are tight against his head, as if they're clinging together in confusion. The problem is his eyebrows. They're still red. I try hard not to laugh.

The combination of the odd-looking hair and a house full of new women seems to be making Sergeant Witherspoon nervous, even though a sergeant from the Eighth District has been in lots of houses full of women.

I sober up as best I can. "Come in, Sergeant. Ladies, this is Sergeant Witherspoon. He's going to pose as my cousin."

My new relative says, "Nice to meet you, ladies."

I debate naming each of the seven women and decide to go ahead because the silence is horrible. All of the women are staring at the odd combination of hair and eyebrows. Finally, I turn to him, so that the staring women are at my back.

"You let Marta Edwards dye your hair. That should certainly keep anyone from recognizing you."

"Do you think so?"

"Yes. But . . . your eyebrows are still red. If anyone thinks you look a little familiar, they might, maybe, make the connection."

The Sergeant sighs. "I didn't want to let her get the stuff close to my eyes. Silly, huh?"

I tilt my head and regard him. I can understand his concern. But the eyebrows are ruining the disguise.

To my surprise, Mary is at my elbow. "If you don't mind my saying so, Sergeant Witherspoon, we can take care of your disguise with a little more dye."

Red Witherspoon stares down at her. He's almost six-foot and Mary's about five-foot.

I turn to Mary. "It won't take long, will it?"

"No, no, no time at all. The trick is to hold a towel under your eyebrow, tight enough that the liquid can't run. We can do it right now." She hesitates. "It really will look better, as disguises go."

Red looks at me, and I nod. "Mary'll make it work. She's good at this sort of thing."

Actually, I've never watched Mary dye eyebrows, but then I've never thought about the possibility of such a thing. Mary's just competent at everything of that sort.

Red sighs loudly and says, "Sure, let's do it then."

No more than half an hour later, a thoroughly blond Red Witherspoon is thanking Mary profusely. Then all the women have to hug me, and Red's smiling instead of looking impatient. Will wonders never cease.

I'm almost off the porch, balancing two bags on a small hand-wagon full of possessions, when Mary says, "Now you've got the cookbook."

Red laughs and smiles at her.

"I've got it," I assure her.

Red picks up the handle of the wagon, and we make our way to the streetcar stop, where we decide it will be easier to walk, even if we're foot-sore when we arrive.

Along the way, Red says, "So Miss Nye, you're going to do all the cooking?"

"Hardly. I've never had to, and I'm not good at it. In fact, being cops, you guys don't get paid enough to eat my cooking."

Red has to stop and laugh. When he can walk again, I sort out names. "And when you're not calling me Nance, Julia will do fine."

"O.K. Make it Red or Enos then." He looks at me carefully. "I've been thinking about it and, when we're in public, I can't imagine that I'll be a very nice guy."

"I know. I've thought about that, too."

"And we're getting close."

"Yes."

We look at each other, and Enos Witherspoon/Armstrong lets his look harden. I go nervous, maybe scared. I glance down and walk faster. Red moves into his act, louder, with a country accent.

"Well, I reckon Aaron can do some cooking and the shopping since he can't get a job. I hope to hell that foot heals up right soon and he can get to work, but until then he can commence helping out instead of clubbing in some bar. I'm betting he's found one by now."

I glance sideways at him, and he isn't looking at me. He's surveying the place as if he's ready to make himself at home in the neighborhood we've just turned into. There's a strut in his walk I haven't seen before.

I nod my head, because I can't think of a response in character. I'm going to have to work on this persona some more.

"You know, maybe you and Aaron together can get the cooking down. I can't believe Aunty Pearl didn't teach you anything. Anyway, I was thinking we could find us a boarder, too. Make some money that way, maybe. We got this big old flat that Mrs. Edwards found. Don't know why she thought we'd need all that room. It's got two bedrooms."

Two bedrooms? Well, I should hope. I assume he's talking for public consumption and not trolling for a roommate. We pass The Green Parrot, and he says, "That's where Aaron'll probably spend his days while you and me are out aworking, Nance."

"Where are you going to be working, Enos?" I have to get in this conversation sometime.

Red stops walking and drops the handle of the wagon. "I'll find something when I'm good and ready, Nance. You see to it you keep your mouth closed and get that job tomorrow."

He picks up the handle and goes striding down the street. I have my hands full and am trying to negotiate the uneven sidewalks of the near north side. Now I have to walk faster to keep up, the longer, fuller, skirt playing around my feet. It's enough to wipe the smile off my face.

As we move north of Washington Avenue, the streets get narrower and dirtier. Some of these buildings are only thirty or forty years old, but they look dingy compared to the skyscrapers and elegant new constructions of downtown St. Louis, only blocks away. People are, of course, dressed less well. They hurry along because of the chill wind, but that purposeful bustle you'd see downtown is missing.

We're getting looks. I glance at Red, who's still strutting. The look on his face may invite men to check out the newcomer. I blush as I catch a look from one young man holding up a doorway.

The flat's in a three-story building and located on the second floor, so we abandon the wagon and carry boxes and bags up the flight. Aaron Jamison has made his way down to the first floor and watches over the goods as we repeat the trip. Make that Aaron Armstrong. He's in character as well, complaining about all the stuff Nance had to bring along, and Enos tells him to shut up 'cause he isn't helping anyway.

The stairs start a third of the way down a hallway in bad need of paint. They're a straight flight up to the second floor, putting us toward the back of the building. There're two doorways in front of us. Another young man stands in the doorway to the right, looking us over, cigarette hanging from his mouth. He puts out enough smoke to match the coal fog outside. Small wonder the hallway needs painting.

Red glances back to see what I'm carrying, then heads into the door on the left. To my surprise, it opens onto the kitchen.

"Close the damn door, Nance." I'm looking around, wondering that the front door opens onto a kitchen dominated by a big stove and a round, scratched, table.

I drop a pillow and a shoulder bag on the table and a suitcase on the floor next to it. Red dumps another bag on the floor, and says, "This way," in a weary voice. Can the man outside hear through these walls?

The kitchen opens onto a bedroom, with one slender bed, a bedside table, and a chair. The bedroom itself opens onto a very small hallway, which has a toilet room to my right, against the outside wall. There're shelves to the left, holding at the moment only a few towels. The door across from the bedroom we left opens onto another bedroom. This one has two beds, each along a wall, the heads at right angles against another small table.

The door out of this room leads to the living area, and I realize it has a door onto the hallway—the front door we could have chosen if we'd walked around the stair well. This room has a table as well, round, jammed into a corner, with two shabby chairs. Two more overstuffed chairs sit in the room, looking lost.

Red's whispering now, momentarily abandoning his world-weary tone. "We thought you might want the back bedroom. It's closer to any heat we generate in the kitchen. Is that O.K.?"

I nod but don't say anything. Not because I'm in character, but because the place is so depressing. The weak sun outside highlights dirt on the window. There're no curtains, just a blind rolled up crookedly at the moment.

Red reaches out and touches my arm. We look at each other a moment. I nod again and say, "It'll do, Enos. I like having two bedrooms."

"Well, I still say we could have us a boarder. We could put a bed in this room."

"But, Enos, I'd like to have a sitting room. We had one back home."

"You had furniture and your ma's things back home. We don't have that stuff and don't need it, Nance. We can sit in the kitchen, for God's sake."

Red turns off the sneer and smiles at me. Then he goes back to character. "Now get down there and get the rest of your things up here before that brother of yours starts selling stuff."

I hurry back through the two bedrooms and into the kitchen, noting this time that there's a third door, one that opens onto a fire escape. Neighbors are in sight across an alley that must be no more than eight feet wide, given the closeness of the metal stairs and stoops. A woman is pouring something from a pot over the edge of the fire escape that clearly extends her living space by thirty square feet. It occurs to me that neighbors the next floor up might choose to do the same, and that I should remember to look up as well as down in case I get near the railing.

My more immediate neighbor gets my brief nod. He looks to be on a second cigarette. Down the stairs, Aaron's leaning against a wall, as well, chatting with a pair of neighbors, one of them female. The male of the pair is poking in the pile of linens in the wagon.

I grab that particular armful, and the man laughs as I head back upstairs and into our kitchen door. Red's leaning on the back door frame via a stiff arm, watching the woman across the way. "Laundry day," he says without turning as I come in.

I drop the linens on my new bed and head back downstairs. It's another two trips before Red decides to help, four before the wagon is empty, because Red doesn't carry enough to make a difference.

But maybe he's stalled for a reason. On his last trip down, the woman of Aaron's acquaintance, who disappeared during our labors, greets us from the stairs leading to the third floor.

"You, know, mister, you look real familiar."

Red immediately puts down a basket that contains a few larger household items I packed. He leans on the newel post, not more than four feet from the woman, and says, "Well, now, I just got to town yesterday, but I'd be right glad to try to figure where we know each other from."

The woman laughs. "Maybe I'm wrong. You look like . . . like a cop I met once. But it's only a little something. I don't know what makes you look like him. Anyway, I'd just as soon forget him and get to know you."

"Now I am flattered. A cop, you say. One of St. Louis's finest, no doubt."

"Oh, no doubt."

"You live upstairs or you just visiting?"

"Just visiting, but I could be back."

Aaron thumps upstairs about then, leaning on his cane, one foot heavily bandaged. He proceeds to introduce Enos to Helen, last name apparently unnecessary.

I clear my throat from the doorway and say, "Enos, I need those things to put up." I try to look irritable instead of worried that we've been identified already.

Enos replies, "Goddamn, woman, I'll bring the damn basket in when I'm ready." Then he walks over and slams the door shut. With me inside and him and Aaron out there chatting with Helen. It's maybe ten minutes later they walk in, obviously bidding Helen adieu as they leave her. I glance out the open door. The male neighbor on our floor hasn't moved. Ashes are obvious at his feet. Lordy. I sternly close the door on him.

We all look at each other and sigh. Red whispers, "Well, I guess the Blondine was a good idea." We decide right then that we'll be in character for normal conversations and whisper, or talk softly, for our private, police conversations.

The rest of the afternoon is a crazy quilt of whispers and curses, reassurances and threats. At one point, I complain to Red that I don't want a boarder in a tone that might get our neighbor's attention, if he's still in the hall. Red yells, "Shut up, Nance," and then whispers, "Put more whine in it, Julia."

I hate whining. I try never to whine.

I look around the dismal kitchen. O.K. I can whine.

21

*From **The St. Louis Globe-Democrat**, Monday, October 17, 1910*

Distressed about the popular response to Governor Hadley's tours of the southern part of the State, the Democratic State Committee has come up with a new strategy as the Governor rolls into St. Louis tomorrow. They will hire a stenographer to take down all the Governor's speeches, study the reports carefully, and try to discover some statement, phrase, or word on which a reply can be based.

My night was uneasy. We're going to arrive at Justice Waists at half past eight so I didn't have to go to bed particularly early. I worked hard all evening setting the flat to rights, as good as I can get it. I'd even hung some curtains I'd brought, heavy ones that will give us some privacy. We decided to put them in the kitchen, covering the window that looks out to the fire escapes.

Being tired should have helped me sleep, but there's nothing restful about the space. I could hear Red and Aaron moving about, using the toilet. In fact, I could hear the gurgle in the pipes when anyone on our side of the building used the toilets. People moved up and down the stairs.

And then, when it did get relatively quiet, my mind decided to relive the scene with William from the night before. I watched it unfold and, sure enough, I wasn't happy with my performance. I tried changing the ending to something at least hopeful if not happy-ever-after. I probably got four hours sleep.

I dress carefully. After seeing the neighborhood, I decide on a skirt that's proper but worn. My waist is modest and conventional and well filled out, thanks to my new undergarment. I'd found a somewhat wider belt than I usually wear, to highlight my waist.

I'm adjusting a mirror to put on makeup and work on my hair, when there's a knock on the inside door. Aaron and Red are ready to start coffee. I'm dressed decently but not completely. This is going to get awkward. They hurry through my bedroom and, when I finally emerge, Red says, "We'll work out a routine, Julia."

By eight we're on our way, and I'm nervous. Red's in character and irritating me, so nervous is good, an appropriate response. When we get to Justice Waists, I'm clutching my newly-made project, and Red's acting nervous himself. I'm happy to follow him by several steps, happy that's my role. Really.

Justice Waists is indeed a bright new building. It isn't as tall as the new skyscrapers nearby, but its five stories are neat with sharp white trim against the red brick. Four large, arched windows highlight the third floor and are echoed on street level by arched doorways.

The door on the left has a sign that says, "Employees only." The one on the right opens beneath an extravagant "JUSTICE" sign that overhangs the sidewalk. Red takes a breath, and I trail him in.

A Mr. Wilson is the office manager, according to a sign on an inside door. He seems to be busy cleaning and straightening the downstairs office space. And irritated that we've bothered him.

"Really, you should come back tomorrow. Mr. Renke is going to be very busy today. He just got back into town, and he has an important meeting this morning. An interview. For the *Globe-Democrat*. Very important."

Lordy. I'm going to run into William. He must have gotten up early to call and set up this interview. And Renke must have jumped at the chance.

Red doesn't seem to react. "Could you ask Mr. Renke what would be a good time? You see, my cousin here has a letter of recommendation from Chief Wright, the police chief, you know, and he'll be waiting to hear if she's got a job or not."

Wilson acts put upon. He's clearly thinking, "What a morning." A newspaper interview and some country girl with a letter from the chief of police.

I look around as if I'm going to let my cousin carry the conversation. The operation obviously makes money, if you can judge by the downstairs office. There're lots of photographs hanging about in ornate frames, and I'd like to look more closely. Through an inside door, I can see the room served by the other, outer door. It features tables and cloak racks along the wall I glimpse. Women's bags sit along a shelf above the coats. There's an orderliness about it that appeals to me, although most women wouldn't care to leave bags in such a public place.

Red has the letter out and waves it about, insisting that the police chief wants Mr. Renke to meet Nance, when Mr. Renke appears in a doorway.

We swivel toward him. Wilson says, "They say they have a letter of introduction from Chief Wright."

Red adds, "She's a real good sew-er, and our family's friends of the chief." Pause. "Chief Wright."

I'm modestly quiet when I speak. "I brought a waist I made, sir." I hold out the package.

Oscar Renke looks from one of us to the other. He's taller than he seemed in the newspaper photo and more handsome. He wears small wireless-rim eyeglasses that make soft brown eyes larger. His blond hair is loaded with some kind of lotion that weighs it into place. Lavender floats across the room. Renke's dressed in the height of fashion, and I find myself admiring the cut of his waistcoat. Surely he hadn't has time to get home and dress for . . . William. Drat.

He circles us. Wilson and Red turn with him, but I stay still and tighten my grip on the waist. He closes in behind me, and I glance at Red. His very blue eyes are squinting in suspicion—and then he catches himself and looks perplexed. Wilson turns away from his boss and considers me, looking a bit perplexed himself.

Renke steps very close, puts a hand on my back and reaches around with his other hand to take the waist, wrapped in its tissue paper.

"Let's not wrinkle this." His voice is musical. He unwraps the package, and the waist unfolds as he shakes it. He hands me the tissue. Then he examines the waist's construction. I'm nervous, and I expected to be nervous about anything but that. I can't keep my hands from all but tearing the thin paper.

We're all holding our breath by the time he stops in front of me, holding the waist as if seeing me in it.

"Clever collar," he says. "Did you design it for yourself, or is it a pattern?"

"I did design it, sir, and I'd like to have it, but I made it to sell. Back home."

He nods, looking at me closely, making me nervous about all those other things I'd planned on worrying about. Without looking away, he wads up the garment in one hand and holds out the other for the letter. Red hands it to him, and he glances at the return address on the envelope.

"You working for the pin money?" he asks me.

Red is gruff. "Nance better not be buying no trinkets. We expect every penny to come home."

Renke nods, walks around me one more time, and tosses the letter to Wilson, unread. He shakes out the waist and hands it to me. "Nance?"

"Yessir. Nance Armstrong."

"Don't sell it, Nance. Wear it to work tomorrow."

Then he's in action, moving unsociably fast. "For now, get upstairs. Report to Farrell."

He's talking as he disappears into his office. Wilson takes my arm, grabs the waist and its tissue, and hands it to Red. Then he grabs the waist back.

"I'll show it to Farrell so he can judge where to put her. She'll be through at half past five. And hungry if she didn't bring a lunch. Pick her up then."

Red's eyes are wide, and he's starting to grin and nod. "Yes sir, Mr. Wilson. I'll be here."

To me he says, "Behave yourself, girl," as I'm hustled through the door to the next room.

I'm pleased, on the one hand, but my stomach flutters unpleasantly. I calm myself and check out details. I'm already hoping this won't go on long, and I need to pick up anything that might be useful.

It looks as if the ground floor has two parts. The part I'd left might be all offices. The part Wilson guides me into is a large room with tables and chairs at angles that make the space busy. But two walls are lined with the coats and bags I'd seen before, all positioned neatly.

"You eat lunch down here." Wilson is curt. "Put your coat on the last peg." I do that and leave my small bag. It feels light: no revolver. The manager directs me to a wide stair at the back of the building, and we bustle on up it.

Once there, he mutters, "Where the heck is Farrell?" It's noticeably warmer up here, and the reason is obvious. Women are seated at ironing tables, pressing the finished products. Across the way, younger women are wrapping waists in tissue paper and boxing them.

Farrell apparently is up another floor. Wilson grabs my arm and pulls me back toward the stairs. Fortunately, I've schooled myself to swallow the comments I'd normally make about rude male behavior.

Farrell must be the man darting from the sewing tables of the third floor to a desk directly in front of us as we finish our climb. I don't know how he can move so fast and write on a clipboard at the same time.

"Who's this?"

"The boss says for you to look at this." Wilson gestures at the waist, not at me. "I gotta get downstairs."

Farrell drops the clipboard on the desk and no more than glances at me as he grabs the waist. He holds it by the shoulders for a second, then tosses it up, and turns the bodice wrong side out as he catches it. The man probably spends his day checking the corners on cuffs, the lay of a facing, the depth of a hem.

"You made this, I suppose." It isn't really a question but I answer politely in the affirmative.

"We need a gal on the sewing lines. Ever use an electric machine?"

Actually, I have. I'd stepped up to one at a World's Fair exhibit and loved it. I was fourteen. To say I'd made anything would be an exaggeration. "No, sir. But I'd surely like to try one."

That gets his attention away from the waist. He looks me over closely, and I check him out. My height, solid build, dark hair, and grey eyes. Sweating on this chilly fall day sufficient to curl the hair around his face. "Did you design this?"

"Yessir."

"Do you work as a seamstress or some such?"

"I do the sewing for my family." Acceptably close to the truth. "I like to create things. I like to finish things." That sounds odd, but I realize it's true. I get a thrill out of seeing a project through to completion. I suppose that won't happen here. But Farrell smiles.

"Well, maybe you're here to sew after all." And what else would he think I'm here for? He can't know—

"Come here." He doesn't grab my arm, and I appreciate that. I manage to follow him without help. He gets the attention of a woman standing half way down the long sewing line.

"Esther, I've maybe got you a new sew-er. Try her out, O.K.?"

Farrell turns back to his desk with my waist but calls over his shoulder, "Enjoy the machine."

As a matter of fact, I do enjoy it. For a while. Esther, who is clearly the supervisor of this table, doesn't waste any time showing me how the Willcox & Gibb works. Our job back here, at the table nearest the alley side, is sewing the bodices of the waists, the easiest sewing job on the floor. The two women closest to me glance up to smile without missing a stitch.

My side of the table is making a pleasant blue lawn number, on the fancy side with lace panels, probably something that will sell as a Christmas gift. Women on the other side of the table are working on a white waist with lots of pleats, which means they have to do some hand work before they can stitch the shoulder seams.

Esther stands back and watches me sort out the appropriate pieces. I find the markings for the darts, stitch on the lace panels, and run up the seams. The machine's drive wheel is attached to an electric line that extends from a cable running above the length of the table. I add little to the noise of clattering needles as I stitch.

I pull the bodice from the machine to check the results, but that's clearly Esther's job. The small, middle-aged woman exudes competence: all her features are neat, business-like. She darts a hand in to relieve me of the bodice, approves my work with a nod, and hands it to a young girl. Who whips over to the next table and lays it on a stack of similar garments.

Esther smoothly moves pieces close to my right hand and says, "Concentrate now. Don't make mistakes. You have to meet a quota of perfect bodices on this table to get your pay."

Which will be? Well, no time to worry about it now. I'm going to do this right and check out Renke's other operations on break, lunch, coming and going.

An hour later, I've lost count of how many bodices I've turned out. I can tell my work is good. I read the expression in Esther's eyebrows, the smile on a sewing mate's face, the energetic response of the runner—who can't be more than thirteen or fourteen.

I'm working fast enough that the girl has some trouble adding me to her routine. In the few seconds before Esther barks and the girl—Susanna, I believe I heard—responds, I glance around the room.

The table next to ours seems to be the one where the waists are assembled. Runners from the two tables nearer the front of the building are delivering sleeves, cuffs and collars to the third table to be joined to the bodices we're turning out. It looks as if everyone on the street sides of the tables is working on the white waists, while everyone on the alley side is sewing up blue waists. I have to admire the speed and efficiency of Justice Waists. Only one thing is out of place.

A woman at the third table, facing me, is standing while everyone else sits. She's bending over the table, maybe setting in sleeves. Why she'd choose such an uncomfortable way to work I can't imagine. And then Miss Susanna arrives with a large stack of bodice pieces, and I ignore the standing worker.

Break is announced by a little bell sounding over the clatter. The machine noise dies off slowly. Each woman apparently finishes the seam she's on, and it takes longer for some than others. Women stand and stretch, most staying close to their stools. A few go dashing off toward the far wall.

"You only have five minutes, at a quarter past ten. If you have to use the toilets, make it fast." The last is a question on Esther's part, and I shake my head. "Good. Lunch is at noon." I nod and turn to meet the two smiling women who work closest to me, Lynn and, across the table, Roberta. They ask easy questions, and five minutes pass quickly.

As I sit, I check on the woman at the next table. She must have spent the break leaning her weight on her hands on either side of the machine. As the break ends, she glances up at her table foreman, a tall, heavy-set woman with arms crossed under a bosom that doesn't need enhancement. The standing woman swallows hard, I can tell from where I sit, and starts in to work again. She better have a strong back.

My work arrives, and I get to it. Esther comes to stand near me. When I look up, she says, "You've got the skill. What you have to do is work hard and not draw attention to yourself." Her head tilts toward the standing woman, and I get the message. Already.

The message is louder and clearer by lunch time. The rest of us troop downstairs, and the standing woman is leaning on her hands again, making no motion to follow us. I want to look back, but Lynn pushes me toward the stairs, as if she doesn't want me to get in trouble by reading the situation.

My lunch is a quarter of three different sandwiches and a sliver of cake. Word seems to have gotten around that I know what I'm doing, and several women are surprised I haven't worked in another factory somewhere. Apparently, my attention to detail when I learned to sew is paying off. I grudgingly offer silent thanks to my mother and sister. As we head back, Lynn explains that everyone benefits, usually by getting to leave early, when the entire floor exceeds its quota. Someone does a lot of counting around here.

During the afternoon break, I try not to stare at the standing woman, but I'm noting features so I can locate her tomorrow. Dark, nice hair. Light eyes. A little under average height. Probably a nice figure, certainly not heavy, but it's hard to judge. In all my moments of observation, she never seems to stand up straight.

That little mystery is answered right before the ending bell. A burly man strides into the room. A wave of tension builds as women notice him. They quickly look away and keep their heads down. He slows and moseys among the tables, checking work, it seems, although I'm careful to keep him in my peripheral vision only. Finally, he ends up behind the standing woman. When the bell sounds, she collapses forward. I'm close enough to note hairy, bare forearms on the man as he unties what I thought was an apron of some sort.

It was, instead, a restraint of some sort. The woman hadn't straightened up because she couldn't.

22

I look away from the woman who's been tied to a table all day and shudder. Esther's in front of me with a raised eyebrow that says, "See what I mean?" What she says out loud is, "You go on down stairs and stand in line. The men have to check you out."

I must look surprised or wary.

"You really haven't worked in a factory, have you?"

"No."

"Well," she turns me toward the stairs. The rest of the women—other than the collapsed brunette—have tidied work areas and are out of the room in nothing flat. "The bosses always check the women to make sure no one is walking out with anything: cloth, lace, buttons, thread, scissors. Some places, the bosses are more thorough than others, and here they'll not take a chance you have anything on you."

"What does that mean, they check us?"

We make it to the stairs and, as we pass the second floor, I see that the women there are still working. Makes sense: any waists finished on the third floor at closing time will be pressed before the doors close for the day.

"Now," Esther's saying, "you don't be afraid. You'll be the last of the floor to go in, but you just step inside the curtain and someone, either Mr. Renke or one of the cutters, will feel around and—"

"Feel around? Feel what?" I come to a stop, and the woman who bumps into me from behind might have said something but for a look from Esther.

"They'll feel around your . . . body . . . to make sure you didn't hide something in your waist." I change the look on my face from outrage to fright.

"And then they'll lift your skirts to make sure you didn't hide anything under your petticoats."

She's serious, so I don't offer the obvious objection.

"They do that in all factories here?"

"Well, some are better. I've heard of some where they let the girls lift their skirts themselves."

She pats me on the shoulder, and that doesn't seem to come naturally to her. "You did good today, Nance. You'll work out real well. Now don't be scared. And—" she gets quieter— "don't look 'em in the eye. That's the way I manage."

With that she hurries to the head of the line. The women around me must've heard and respond by trying to include me in conversations. Some of them complain about the work ahead of them at home. A few have beaus they'll see. The usual talk of working women. I try to join in, but I can't stop considering the two curtained areas at the ends of the lines.

I hadn't noticed before that there are hooks in the ceiling from which circular rings are suspended. The rings hold curtains that remind me of miniature dressing rooms. They're no more than six foot in diameter, and it's going to be tight in there. The cloth moves occasionally as someone brushes against it. They have to pull out a ladder to string up these portable rooms every evening. What a lot of work for such a ridiculous exercise.

There aren't many women still about when it comes my turn, of course, although I notice that Esther's still here, talking to another woman who I recognize as a foreman up at the first table. If Esther's waiting around to make me feel safer, she's made a friend.

Apparently, I'm supposed to part the curtains and move in as soon as the woman in front of me departs. I take a deep breath, open the white flannel, and come face to face with the burly man from upstairs. He's still bare-armed. And huge. Not tall, just heavily built and muscled. He has a huge mustache as well and, somehow, he manages to hide behind it. Little eyes glitter under shaggy eyebrows, and I can't identify a color.

He simply reaches out and pulls me toward him and "feels around" puts it mildly. I fight not to pull away. Outrageous. Not only that someone thinks this is necessary but that he's enjoying it. I follow Esther's advice and keep my eyes off his face after the initial glance.

Unfortunately, that leaves me looking at a wide leather belt and a holster displaying a pair of slightly curved cutting knifes. They're probably eight inches long in the blade, have padded handles, and gleam with sharpness. A cutter, for sure. I've heard of the men who cut the fabric, combining strength to cut through multiple layers of cloth and an eye for laying out the pattern in the first place to minimize scrap. It's highly skilled labor. I hadn't known running a finger under my belt was part of the job description.

The burly cutter is getting to the skirt-raising part, and I'm wondering if I can get by closing my eyes when he gets help. Oscar Renke steps into the opening, and the cutter gives way, handing the boss the front of my skirt in the process. Renke holds the fabric in one hand, and feels among my petticoats with the other. He leans over and runs a hand down my calf. As if I've hidden a length of fabric in my stocking.

He stands and drops my skirt and says, "I hear you are indeed accomplished, my dear. To the tune of 20 cents an hour. I look forward to seeing you tomorrow in your quaint little waist."

He and the cutter laugh, and he turns me toward the opening. I all but run to the coat rack, find the waist, quaint little thing that it is, next to my bag, and dart for the door.

I don't know what Red thinks about the look on my face because he's in Enos-mode and a fine mood. He announces that he's found the cheapest way back to the flat. He laughs at his slight humor and grabs me by the elbow. I make a little sound that says I'm not in the mood for that, but either he ignores it or he'll apologize in private. We walk past the stopped streetcar, and it's clear the cheapest way home involves a mile-long walk. As the car pulls away, I recognize two of my workmates near a window. One of them waves.

Red talks continuously, pausing only for an answer to the question about the pay. He chortles—and you so seldom hear people chortle—and tells me he can use the money and that he'll be really well off—Aaron too, of course—if we get a boarder. Of course, I'll have to work on my cooking.

Wrong thing to say. My stomach grumbles so loudly that he jerks my arm and tells me to behave myself. Enos has one admonition for every situation. I pull my arm free, and he acts as if he let me go.

It's full dark and cold when we get to the flat, and our second-floor neighbor is waiting. I hoped he'd have a job during the week.

The neighbor, along with Aaron and anyone else who might live on the floor, knows we're home because Red's urging me to "get in there and get some supper on."

Aaron greets me with, "Hear you're a working girl now, Nance."

He and Red laugh and let the sound die slowly. Both watch as I hit a chair hard. Aaron leans the cane against the wall and nimbly pours a cup of coffee, setting it in front of me and seating himself beside me. I really like Aaron Jamison. I'm not too sure about Aaron Armstrong, but I do like Aaron Jamison.

Red pours his own coffee and sits quietly. "How was it, Julia?" he whispers.

I take a sip and think about that. "Pretty good. If we think Renke is our man, I'd say we made progress. For starters, he doesn't mind mistreating women."

I draw them a verbal picture of the brunette who worked tied to a table all day. Both are immediately angry and try to air their disgust quietly.

Red finally says, "You know, I think that's illegal. There's a law, isn't there, that employers have to provide a seat for female employees? I guess the trick would be what it means to 'provide' one."

"Yeah." Aaron snorts. "Across the room."

I'm well aware of the law. Most suffragists see nothing wrong with it. Others in the movement think it's the type of distinction that makes women second-class workers. I'm too tired to air the debate with the cops.

I move on. "He and his men—and there are very few men who work there—have a lecherous streak I don't like at all." I explain the leave-taking ceremonies. Red curses, and Aaron twists in his seat.

"You mean they actually raised your skirt?" Aaron's almost too loud and Red shushes him.

"I've heard factory workers get searched, but I was thinking bags and pockets. Julia, you don't have to put up with that. We can stop this right now." Red's leaning across the table.

"It doesn't hurt, Red. If he's doing it to any woman, then I can take it." Although the memory makes me angry. Every day, for

Pete's sake.

I clear my throat and continue. "I intend to keep my head down and learn the routine, make friends so they'll talk. And, the actual job went well. My job is sewing, not pressing or packing. So, it pays better. That's good—if we think Renke would ever fire me and proposition us. A woman would have to lose a lot of salary for her family to sell her off to Renke. If a woman didn't make so much, her services would be more valuable at home. Right?"

Red's nodding. "Twenty cents an hour," he tells Aaron.

"Wow. That's good."

"Well." I push myself to my feet. "At least I know I can make better money than typing for the St. Louis Police Department." Red's blond eyebrows are rising as I head for my room.

23

*From **The St. Louis Globe-Democrat**, Tuesday, October 18, 1910*

> *Negroes in the 26ᵗʰ Ward met yesterday to organize a Citizens Defense Committee. They will set up a headquarters and cooperate with other committees, as well as the Negro Waiters Association, to defeat the prohibition amendment.*

I'm at the employee's door just before 7:30 this morning. I used a streetcar, getting off several stops farther away than necessary, eager to tell anyone who asks that my cousin Enos doesn't want me to use the pennies for fare.

I left my watch at the flat. It would be too much affluence . . . and in the way. But I know it isn't 7:30 yet because of the rush. Women are hurrying in, hanging up coats, stacking bags on the top rack, lunches on a side table, and checking in at one of the four tables. Ah, more organization. Each table corresponds to one of the work tables upstairs and is manned by the foreman. Forelady. That has a nice ring to it.

The whole process is watched, however, by the big cutter and another man, taller, strong-looking, also dressed in bare arms and knives. I could swear they're looking at me.

When I get to the table, Esther says, "I forgot to tell you not to be late, but I guess you figured it out. They lock the doors at 7:30. Get on up to your place." She notices me looking about. "The tall one is Mr. Dexter. The one you met yesterday is Mr. Mallory." She raises an eyebrow that tells me to stay away from them. I intend to.

But I also intend to find out today about the standing brunette. As it turns out, I see what everyone else sees. She's standing at her place when I come in, holding her arms crossed tight over her chest, looking as if she's been crying. And sure enough, here comes Mallory. But he's carrying a stool. The woman looks surprised and so relieved the tears are running down her face as she sits.

The reason becomes obvious when Mr. Renke himself walks onto the sewing room floor at about 9:45. A bell rings, and we all stop working in mid-seam. Reactions tell me this is out of the ordinary. Renke glances about in apparent pleasure.

He's a delight to look at—if you don't suspect him of murder. I'm not sure what it is that constitutes fashion, but he has it. Polished hair, the swagger suit, finely coordinated colors on shirt, collar, cuffs, waistcoat—which shows above the V of his buttoned single-breasted—striped trousers and coat, polished shoes, all setting off a trim build. No lout. A murderer, perhaps, but no lout. And again, there's a musical quality to his voice that fascinates me. Do any of the women fancy him? I glance about and decide the answer is no. Curious. Lordy, maybe he's married.

"Ladies. I hope you noticed that the room is particularly clean today." I'd been impressed yesterday. "That's because we have a photographer coming in. Some of you may find your picture in the newspaper this week."

The titter is immediate but not nearly as loud as I'd expect. Too bad, because I need noise to cover the thumping in my chest. I compose my face and smile at Lynn, who grabs my arm in excitement.

Renke's saying he was interviewed by a reporter from the *Globe-Democrat* yesterday, and the paper's photographer will be here soon. He'll set up and shoot pictures during our break. At which time we will, of course, be staging work, not taking a break. No one seems to object.

I tell myself that William won't have to be here to watch his photographer work. Why would he turn out at mid-morning two days in a row? William works afternoons and evenings because the *Globe* is a morning paper.

Well, I answer myself, William's investigating. He'll show up to see if the place sets off any alarms for him. We haven't talked, so he won't know I'm working yet.

Renke's urging us to straighten up our work areas, but there's really little to do. Nothing's in the way of efficiency to start with. He acknowledges that with a smile.

"Fine. It looks fine, ladies. I trust all of you will be serious and courteous, at the same time. You may go back to work until the gentlemen arrive."

Gentlemen? Plural? O.K. William can probably control his reaction. Carl couldn't have kept his composure, but William can. I hadn't wanted him to see me in this garb, but that's the least of my worries now. There's the concern that I'll be identifiable in a photo, but that might be a matter of literally keeping my head down.

The true problem is deeper. I've admitted to myself I was wrong Saturday night, but I've put off analyzing what I did. Not seeing William every day at work means I have time to sort it out. Seeing him now is going to make for a sleepless night at best. And if we hadn't fought, this would be such a lark.

My hands are trembling, which makes it hard to get the seams straight. I slow down, but no one notices.

It seems like no more than a few minutes until the voices coming up the back stairs break the pattern. Darn. That'll put the photography party right next to me.

I hear William, of course. As if I wouldn't know his voice. He's talking to Farrell, standing back behind me. Farrell's explaining that Mr. Renke keeps an additional office up here, on the sewing floor, in the glass enclosed space behind me, because he wants to be in touch with the process. Renke himself is helping the photographer, asking question after question, something about reflex cameras and stopping motion.

After Renke wastes maybe ten minutes on questions, it occurs to me he truly has an interest. Maybe he's the one who took the photographs downstairs, the dramatic landscapes.

We keep working, although we're murmuring to each other. Finally, the photographer says, "Just keep working, ladies. Then freeze. Hold your work, hold your breath when I tell you to."

He does, and we do, and it's fairly painless. The photographer has set up over my right shoulder and aims across the space. I'm not sure I'm in the picture at all and, if so, it's my back anyone will see. William's saying something to Renke as the pictures are taken. And then it seems as if I might have escaped. William's voice retreats behind me, toward Farrell's desk and the stairs.

Renke actually helps the photographer pack up sufficiently to move to another floor. I hear him say the man might need his lights upstairs. And it occurs to me what the glass underfoot, the slightly curved glass in Ellie's basement might have been: the glass of a camera lamp. The more I think about it, the more likely it seems. I'll ask Aaron to suggest it to Captain Messerton.

I'd been more fascinated than repulsed, watching Renke operate today. But now I wonder if he took pictures of women in that basement. Pictures of Meredith.

I'm shaking a bit when I stand. Farrell announced a brief break before we return to work for real. I turn away from my table mates, thinking to pace a few steps, and glance toward the stairs. William's watching me. I catch my breath and stare back, as he lets his gaze drift from my face downward. As if to let him see the whole package, I turn away slowly—before we can look each other in the eye. Then I sit and vow to concentrate on the work for all I'm worth.

24

*From **The Westliche Post**, Wednesday, October 19, 1910*

> *Gefühl ist Gebäude gegen das Verbotmaß, das vor Missouriwählern in zwei Wochen ist. (Sentiment is building against the prohibition measure that will be before Missouri voters in two weeks.) . . . We base this on the number of anti-prohibition advertisements we see in English-language papers, as well the general tone of protests. The Anti-Saloon League advocates are being met with rebuttal at every public appearance.*

Carl's reading the *Westliche Post* in detail. When he gets to work, he'll read through other papers to see what others know, but at home he reads the *Post* front-to-back. For one thing, it's already at the door each morning because it's the only paper his mother and sisters read.

He and the women always divide up the edition and pass portions around as they eat. Sometimes they wave the pages while they finish a bite of egg, to get everyone's attention, and then read a particularly interesting tidbit. Carl generally humors his younger sister and dismisses his older sister. Julia wouldn't put up with either approach, but his sisters work their wills in different ways.

When the telephone rings, his mother drops her section, Marj jumps to her feet to answer it, and Lenna says, "Edgar better not be calling here at this hour of the morning."

Carl gives her a look that says, "Don't worry Mother with silly suggestions," and heads for the phone. His mother has picked up the paper and is fanning herself. He's told her time and again there're no tolls if someone calls you and no tolls period for the calls that aren't long-distance. But she worries about money every time the phone rings. Tells everyone it's an unfortunate necessity of Carl's work, that they have to have the contraption in the house. Marj pouts as she hands him the earpiece.

William McConnell greets him softly.

"Carl, can we meet for lunch today?"

"Sure, Will. Something up?"

"Yeah. I'm leaving tonight for Chicago, looking into the Renke story."

"Chicago? You're kidding. There's something so suspicious about the waist factory that you have to leave tonight?"

"That's a couple of questions, Carl. Maybe I can answer them at lunch."

"O.K., sure. The deli?"

"Yeah, but before the crowd hits."

"I'll be there at 11:30."

"See you then."

And that's that. Carl shrugs at his family as he walks back into the dining room: he doesn't have a single answer to any of their questions.

◆　◆　◆

By the time he gets to Bank's Delicatessen on Pine, Carl has even more questions for Will. Who sits in his preferred booth. Carl knows it's him behind the copy of the day's *Globe* by the way he holds it, so he walks over and hits the back of the page lightly with his derby.

Will's smiling when he emerges and smoothly folds the pages while Carl slips out of his coat and into the booth.

Will raises a cup of coffee in greeting and takes a swig. Carl sighs and looks around for one of the waitresses so he can get his own cup. Sarah's the woman who's already on her way over.

It's early for lunch, but Carl orders the special of the day without much thought. The deli serves breakfast, huge sandwiches in the evening, and a special for lunch every day. It's Wednesday and therefore pork chops.

"Let me get this down now: the *Globe* is paying you to travel to Chicago and look into the background of Oscar Renke."

Will smiles.

Carl twists a bit in his seat. He sometimes wonders if Will McConnell's coolness bothers him because he can't duplicate it or for a more legitimate reason.

"O.K. What exactly about Oscar Renke is worth a trip to Chicago . . . how long will you be gone from work?"

"Which question do you want me to answer?"

Carl flushes. He doesn't question the people he interviews like this, really.

Sarah sits a cup of dark brown coffee down along with a small pitcher of cream. Carl reaches for the sugar and starts in to make a light tan concoction.

"What do you suspect about Renke?"

"The same things the police suspect. Plus, I thought he had an incredible ego."

"Lots of successful people have egos."

"True."

"Well, if all you have is what the police suspect, why aren't the police checking out Chicago?"

Will nods. Which Carl takes as evidence of a good question. "Actually, I think they have done some checking. I had a session with Chief Wright this morning, and he's telephoned a friend of his on the force in Chicago. The man did ask around, and no one knows anything about an Oscar Renke. And there are enough perverts coming and going in the Levee that they haven't missed any."

Well, no doubt. The Levee. Chicago has put all its sexual vice into one neighborhood so some of the unluckiest cops in the world can take a shot at minimizing the crime that flourishes there. Or to look at it another way, get a piece of the pay-off.

Carl snorts. "And what can you do if the cops don't know Renke?"

"Check out bookkeepers. Your friend Bauer said there was an older bookkeeper who worked for Renke. The police wouldn't know that."

Carl stares a moment, and Sarah takes advantage of the lull to say "Here you go, Mr. Schroeder," and slide a plate of pork chops, mashed potatoes, and cabbage in front of him. Carl offers her a wide grin.

But loses it immediately. "O.K. I have two questions and you can answer them in order, if you'd like. Why doesn't the chief ask his friend to check out bookkeepers and why in the world is Forrest letting you go? Are you getting paid for this?"

"That's three. I think Wright is fine with having me do the asking because it's such a long shot. Actually, I mentioned the Chicago police checking around, and he said it's unlikely they'd get around to it anytime soon. Meaning, they have no political reason to do so. And yes, I continue to draw pay. Forrest is buying the train ticket, and I'm paying for my own hotel and board expenses."

"For how long?"

"I have no idea. I'd imagine a week, ten days."

"Ten days? Wait, you didn't answer the question about why Forrest is even letting you do this."

Will's having chicken soup and cornbread, and Carl watches him butter a chunk of the bread.

"I told him I needed to get away."

Carl lowers a forkful of mashed potatoes. "And why do you need to get away?"

"Think and rethink . . . things."

Vague and hesitant and not like William.

"I haven't taken more than a couple of days' holiday to see my folks in ten years. I want to get away from St. Louis, see someplace else."

Carl gives up on the food and rests his elbows on the table. "Julia, Will. Talk about Julia."

Will's silent. But, for a change, it isn't Carl who gives in.

"Julia. Well, she's incognita, you know. Working at Renke's factory. She's doing her bit to solve a murder, and I'm doing mine."

Carl twirls his fork through his fingers.

"She has something to prove—as usual—by doing things her way, and I'm choosing to do things my way. By getting away for a while. I will indeed ask questions in Chicago. And I plan on enjoying the Congress Hotel and taking in some music and the Art Institute. It seems like a reasonable arrangement to me." Will smiles as if he's answered the question.

Carl goes back to his plate and finds the cabbage cold. He works at cutting up a pork chop.

"When was the last time you talked to her?"

Will pauses over the soup bowl but doesn't look up.

"Saturday night. Before she moved in with Witherspoon and Jamison."

"Moved in with two officers?"

"They're posing as her cousin and brother. It gives her police contact while she's living on the north side."

Honest to God. This is what drives Carl crazy about the relationship. Maybe it's getting to Will as well. "I'd say it gives her police contact all right. Do you approve of that?"

Will's frowning when he looks up. "We've hashed this out before, Carl. I don't approve or disapprove of what Julia does. That's not my job."

Carl lets both knife and fork clatter on the plate. "It's your job if you care about her. Are you going to marry her? What then, Will? You'd let your wife go live with two police officers?"

Will pushes his bowl back and leans on the table.

"Well, it would be more appropriate for a married woman to live with two cops incognita than an unmarried one. And if Julia thought the cause were worth it—and the murder of that young woman qualifies—she'd do it regardless. And I'd support her. If she thought it were that important. If I were married to her. Which I'm not going to be."

Carl's started shaking his head, preparing to set William straight. Even if it's Will. Who's too in love with a headstrong woman to oppose her. But it's worse than that.

"Are you saying you've asked her to marry you and she said no? Good Lord, Will."

"No, I haven't asked, and I won't. That's not what she wants. And therefore, it's not what I want. I'm ready to move on, maybe literally."

"You mean you'd move to Chicago because you're not going to

ask Julia to marry you?"

"I'm going to check out Chicago. Maybe I'll like it, maybe I won't. And I'd have to find a position there. Which could take a while. And since I'm there trying to track down Renke's past activities, I might as well look around."

Carl hits the back of the seat, trying to sort all this out. Trying to figure out what he's going to do about losing Will as a friend, losing Will and Julia as a couple. How ironic that he has to worry about that.

A small possibility occurs to him. He leans forward and downs a mouthful of potatoes before he continues.

"I suppose you might as well look around. So how do you start? You're going to call on all the bookkeepers in Chicago?"

Will's eyebrow twitch as if he doesn't think Carl will let the matter go so easily. But he answers.

"That and Chief Wright is writing a letter of introduction to his friend. Captain O'Brien. Of the Twenty-first Precinct."

Christ. Everyone knows about the Twenty-first Precinct. The Bloody Maxwell. Every kind of crime and vice, and more cops injured in one precinct than in all of St. Louis. And Will will end up wandering around there, and in the Levee, doing his investigation, for all the world as if it were the Mill Creek Valley in St. Louis. Christ.

Carl needs to get away and get busy. He has to make up the perfect story for Zimmerman, the perfect story idea in Chicago.

He checks his watch and drops it back in its pocket. "Well, I hope you'll stay in touch. I'm going to worry about you there."

"I'll write. Postcards. Every few days. How about that?"

"Sounds good."

Will moves on to small talk as they pay up and walk out. He

seems a bit curious about Carl's muted reaction. They're splitting up to head to work when Carl asks, "When are you leaving? Do you want me to see you off?"

Does Will look sad? Can't be. "No, you'll be at work or home in bed. I'm taking the midnight limited."

Carl nods, shakes hands, and turns left, headed for Broadway. His plan is to develop a story idea in Chicago by the time he hits his newsroom. There was a time when he worried that Will would ask Julia for a date before he could muster the courage. Now courage consists of keeping his friends together—and safe, of course. He would have thought safe was the harder part.

25

*From **The Chicago Daily News**, Thursday, Oct. 20, 1910*

Representatives of the Anti-Cigarette League and the Anti-Saloon League will appear tomorrow before the Vice Commission's subcommittee on Social Evil and Saloons. It is reported that a number of police officers, including captains, lieutenants, and patrolmen, are meeting individually with the subcommittee on Social Evil and Police.

Carl hates traveling. Mostly, he hates the confinement of the train. He can't read on a train—although he's brought a book in hopes it will be different this time. Reading is something he does in his own chair in his own corner in his mother's living room. He reads a good deal. But not on a moving train.

So, he makes lists, lists that get thrown away once he arrives because he never has reason to consult them. If he writes it, he remembers it. He's often distracted, though, even from that activity, by people sitting near him, moving around him. Stations are a mixed blessing: a chance to get out of the coach, but every stop makes the trip longer.

Carl hustled so to get on a Thursday morning train that he'd thought he might nap. No such luck. Instead, he keeps seeing the look on Will's face and replaying what he told his mother and Zimmerman.

His mother objected loudly to his going to Chicago. She would object under any circumstance, but in this case, she hadn't had time to worry sufficiently. She kept muttering about fools and apes, *alles begaffen*. Just have to look at everything. In this case, it did little good to say it was his job to look at everything.

Zimmerman, now, listened to his idea without expression. At first.

"You see, sir, we have readership all across the country. It seems like a good question to inquire into the health of German communities in other large cities. How does the Chicago German community compare to St. Louis? You see? This is perfect timing. I can catch a turner fest somewhere, ask around the *Staats-Zeitung* staff, check reactions to prohibition. Our readers will love it."

Zimmerman hadn't blinked. Just looked Carl in the eye and said, "Good idea, Schroeder. I could send Berno. Send him to Chicago, Milwaukee, maybe on East."

So, Carl had to give in.

"And, remember, there might be a story brewing over this Renke guy, who has some ties with the German community here. Frankly, it could be a hell of a story even if he weren't German. A police story." Zimm nodded at that.

"On top of that, there's my friend, McConnell, you know, over at the *Globe*. He's headed on up there. I can get in on the story, and we can find out more together. I can look out for him—and get two good stories out of it."

Zimmerman went right to the looking-out-for-William part. "McConnell can't take care of himself in Chicago without your help?"

Carl had paused and finally said, "He's stubborn, and he'll dig into Renke's activities regardless of any danger. And he doesn't have the motivation to be careful he once had."

"Why's that?"

"He and Julia—Miss Nye over at the police department—have sort of . . . ended their relationship." Zimmerman had finally fidgeted a bit. "And that's a mistake. But I intend to work on it."

Lord only knows why he shared so much. He's worked for Zimm for six years, but he wouldn't call him a buddy. Not like Will.

But something in there did it. Zimm leaned on the table in the conference room they'd retreated to and fiddled with a pad and pencil. Another compulsive list-maker. "And Jack Forrest just up and let him go? Is he paying him?"

Carl agreed it was out-of-character for Forrest, and Zimm had chuckled. Then he offered the same deal: continuing pay, a round-trip train ticket, Carl paying for food and a hotel room. Carl had taken a breath and argued that he'd come back with two stories. Zimm had muttered but came up with a spare $30 for food.

Carl works on analyzing Zimm's motivation as the train heads north through the cold-looking Illinois countryside. The only thing he can figure is that the German angle is a good enough story, and Zimm's letting him do it, as opposed to someone else, out of appreciation for his friendship with Will.

That leads Carl to wonder how he's going to find a story among Chicago's masses, a million more people than St. Louis and none known to be particularly friendly to a reporter from the rival city. And that's the other reason Carl doesn't like to travel: why would anyone choose to poke their nose into other people's affairs in other people's worlds? Everyone's business might be his to ask about in St. Louis, but not in Chicago. Meaning his mother might be right. Maybe Will can come up with a suggestion. If Will isn't overcome with irritation that Carl has intruded on his holiday.

It's a long day's ride to Chicago. Will wisely traveled overnight, using a sleeper car no doubt. Carl left midmorning, will arrive well after dark, and then will have to find his way to the Congress Hotel from the Illinois Central terminal. Maybe what he saved on the sleeper car can be spent on a taxi.

And the taxi idea feels even better when Carl steps out of the building. The winter breeze off the Mississippi doesn't compare to the wind coming off Lake Michigan and battering the terminal on its shore. By the time the carriage gets to the Congress Hotel, Carl's eyes are watering and his hands and feet are numb. The lining of his overcoat is cold, and he tries to move in small steps so it won't touch him.

He stops inside the elegant lobby and hovers near a palm to blow his nose. And is shaking his head as he walks stiffly toward the desk. What a miserable place for a city. Please God he'll get Will out of here soon and go back to where winter is just dull winter.

Two clerks at the desk take in Carl's red face and both smile. A telephone rings, and one man nods to the other to take it. Carl can't tell if he's the easier chore. But the man who waits on him wears a name tag that says, "Head Day Clerk." Carl figures he's ready to leave for the evening.

The man's gracious. "Let me guess, sir: you're visiting from points south."

Carl supposes that would be a huge chunk of the country, but he smiles. His usual response. True that it works well professionally, but it's natural and sincere.

"St. Louis," he replies as he signs the guest register. "I thought it was cold there."

The man nods sympathetically. "What brings you to town this time of year?"

"Octoberfests. Turner fests. I hope they have them inside."

"Turner fests? You'd come to Chicago from St. Louis to find a turner fest? You surely don't think ours are better?"

Carl takes in the name in its smaller type above the title. Schugel. C.R. Schugel. He lets his smile widen. "When you say 'ours', Mr. Schugel, do you by chance mean that you'd be going to some sort of German celebration this month?"

The man laughs. "I will indeed."

"Well then, you might be the man I came to find." Carl sticks out a hand. "I'm a reporter from the *Westliche Post*, and I'm here to do a story on the German culture in Chicago."

"The *Post*? I read the *Post* every day!" C.R. Schugel pumps Carl's hand.

In minutes, Carl has a room and is headed there to freshen up before a meeting in the hotel bar with Schugel, who'll be off-duty in under a half hour. Carl did think to ask if a William McConnell had checked in and Schugel said, yes, this morning. So, Carl left a message behind, wondering where Will might be at this hour of the night in Chicago.

◆　◆　◆

Carl finds the room almost as elegant as the lobby but a bit foreign. He isn't used to sleeping away from home. He hangs up clothes but holds off touching the bed, hurrying downstairs instead. By contrast, the Congress Hotel's drinking salon is most comfortable. It isn't any more elegant than the Planters' House or the Jefferson in St. Louis, but it's newer and has intimate—and warm—spaces to talk.

He doesn't have to get far into the conversation with C.R.

Schugel to change his mind about the cordiality of Chicago citizens. Schugel's more than happy to take him to a variety of German functions, introduce him to leaders in the German community, give him impressions of the German culture. It isn't cohesive as in St. Louis. Maybe too big, too split among various constituencies. If Carl wanted to slack on this, he could report Schugel's impressions and have plenty to fill an article.

As it is, Carl can easily get more impressions Saturday at a festival. Schugel's a senior employee and regularly gets off work for community events. This one's sponsored by his church, a Lutheran parish that has been around for more than fifty years.

"Now, here's an example, Carl, of how things are changing. We've always counted on a donation from an older gentleman—he's been 'older' since I've known of him—to add the little extras. He died this year, and his family, which owns one of the big bookkeeping firms in the City, isn't interested in making a contribution."

A tingle goes down Carl's spine. And he's been warm now for some time. "A German bookkeeper, right?"

"Oh, yes. One of the big firms in the City, Rosenblatt and Drescher, been here for years and years. Old man Rosenblatt was one of the first to organize the bookkeepers into an industry of their own, working for a variety of business firms instead of being employed individually."

"Sounds like a character."

"Sure enough." Schugel looks around the room and takes a long drag on his cigar. "There wasn't even much investigation into his death because of . . . the circumstances. The man had unusual tastes."

This probably isn't the face of the German community Schugel started out to talk about, but Carl suspects the man can't resist the gossip. Carl raises his eyebrows and invites him to continue.

"It seems," Schugel lowers his voice, "that he'd enjoyed a night in the Levee, made it home, had a visit from a hooker, and was found dead late the next day."

"Well, it's an unusual circumstance. Is it unusual taste?"

Schugel laughs and motions for Carl to wait while he goes to the bar. Carl figures Schugel's deciding whether to continue the story. The man returns with two fresh brews. St. Louis beers, Carl notices, with approval. And impatience.

Schugel settles on the gossip. "The room Paul Rosenblatt was found in was some sort of retreat. The maid never cleaned it. The old man did that himself. She wouldn't have gone in when she did if he hadn't missed a couple of meals."

"A retreat."

"One full of all his delights, including photographs all over the place."

"Photographs of women, I'd guess."

Schugel nods and smiles. "Who knows how bad they were? The family is supposed to have destroyed them and put out word that the old man had an apoplexy. As if he'd been shocked to death in his own house. I doubt the family had any idea the rumors spread as far they did. Word was the photos were huge and all of them of women naked. And worse."

Carl shakes his head. He's supposed to act amused and worldly-wise. He also needs to cultivate this source. And what he desperately wants is to share it all with Will.

Schugel looks up and smiles, professionally polite. When Carl turns to look, he figures he's conjured William McConnell.

Will has his overcoat slung over his arm and looks thoroughly at ease in the salon, nodding to Schugel. Carl jumps to his feet and grabs Will's hand, relieved to see him safe, relieved he has news that will make his friend less irritated.

When he turns back to introduce Will to C.R. Schugel, the hotel clerk is smiling more broadly, clearly recognizing their friendship.

"It looks as if you have a visitor already, Mr. McConnell."

Will snorts. "Wait till the papers back home run it. Everyone will think you're trailing after a story, Carl."

The St. Louis papers usually run dispatches listing the St. Louis residents who're visiting the finer hotels in Chicago and New York, evidence that the city is full of sophisticated travelers, Carl always supposed.

Carl shrugs, but Will gets serious of a sudden. "You know, it might be best if people don't link us here together. Bauer might say something. Renke might get suspicious."

Schugel looks surprised. "No one in St. Louis knows you're here?"

"My editor does, of course, C.R." Carl drops the first name casually. "But there's a second story William and I need to be more careful about. Can you keep my name away from the papers?"

"Of course. That won't be a problem. I'll do it before I leave, so there won't be a slip." C.R. winks and stands. "We're delighted to help you keep your little secrets." As if we're playing some child's game here. Carl snorts to himself as he shakes hands heartily and thanks the man. C.R. promises to see them tomorrow.

Will shakes his head and sits down. "It'll be more reasonable not to have your name in the paper anyway. No one would think you'd stay in one of the big hotels. Is Zimmerman paying?"

Carl starts to return the sarcasm, although it's true enough. He's interrupted by a waiter, obviously sent by C.R. to clear his glass and offer Will something. The activity proceeds as Carl and Will consider each other across the polished table.

William says the obvious. "O.K., Schroeder, what are you doing here?"

Carl decided beforehand on honesty. "I want to make sure you're careful, make sure you come back to St. Louis to stay, make sure you get back together with Julia, and along the way I think I can pick up a couple of stories. Maybe help you with the Renke story."

The waiter reappears with a beer and a huge City Directory for William, compliments of Mr. Schugel.

"Looking for a bookkeeper?"

William's glance says that's obvious.

"You might try Rosenblatt, Paul Rosenblatt. Although, our man died within the year. I don't know what will show up in this Directory. Maybe C.R. kept last year's."

Carl's enjoying himself now, and he particularly enjoys the acknowledgement on Will's face.

"O.K." Will takes a substantial drink and leans back in his chair. "I welcome your help. I'll look around to my heart's content, and I invite you to join me. The matter of Julia is off-limits. I'm not going to ruin my holiday worrying about what might have been or about things I can't change."

"Are you saying you can't change Julia?"

"I'm saying I don't want to talk about it."

"You can change Julia, just as she can change you, because you love each other."

"You're right about us loving each other. That doesn't take care of the differences. And I don't want to talk about it." William's eyebrows are heading toward the bridge of his nose.

Carl retreats. "Another day. Anyway, you'll be interested in

Rosenblatt's death."

"I'm sure I will. When did you find out about this, and how do you know he had a connection with Renke?"

"A few moments ago, from my new German friend at the desk, and I don't know for sure about the connection. I only know Rosenblatt was elderly, and his death is a matter of some gossip. It seems the last person known to have seen him was a prostitute, and he died in a room full of photographed pornography. Sounds like a possible connection, huh?"

All traces of irritation disappear from Will's face. "It sounds more than possible."

They make their way from the drinking salon to the dining salon and consider the possibilities over a first-rate meal. Finally, Will concludes, "We need to see a police report, see what they know, and see if anyone recognizes Renke. I brought several copies of our newspaper photo."

They're rising to make their way to the elevators, and Carl thinks he has enough capital on the evening to push it a bit. "The sooner we get Renke, the sooner we get Julia away from him."

Will rolls his eyes. "Let it be, Carl. I can worry about her without discussion."

26

*From **The St. Louis Globe-Democrat**, Friday, October 21, 1910*

Personal Mention

Chicago, Oct. 20 – The following from St. Louis are registered at Chicago hotels:

Congress – William R. McConnell

Carl finds Will already at breakfast and examining the *Tribune*. Carl has to order and get his hunger under control before he asks, "Where to first?"

"I was planning on the Art Institute this morning."

"The Art Institute?"

"A holiday, remember, Carl?"

"But we could be checking with Rosenblatt and Drescher, or asking the police—"

"I have asked the police, and we meet with Captain McElroy at two this afternoon."

"Who's that?"

"Simon McElroy, head of the Third Precinct. The Levee District. Robert O'Brien, at the Twenty-first, the Chief's friend, set up the meeting. Seems O'Brien thinks one of the few kinds of vice he has little of in the Twenty-first is white slavery. We should try the Levee for that."

Christ. William walked right into the Bloody Maxwell, named for the street that runs through it and the activities that fill it. As if the letter of introduction from Chief Wright did him any good until he was in this O'Brien's office.

"What about the bookkeeping firm, Rosenblatt's family?"

"I'd rather know what the police know before we talk to them. I'm assuming the family won't want to talk to us."

"We could ask if Renke was a client."

"Oh, excellent."

"Asking if he was a client?"

"The Symphony is playing tomorrow night. Let's see if your German friend can get us tickets."

"Will." Carl jiggles a spoon to relieve his irritation. It works with his sisters most mornings. "I thought we could ask questions today. I'll be doing the German thing tomorrow. C.R. is taking me to a church celebration. Starts in the afternoon and continues until whenever."

"Fine. That's a good start for your story. I'll tell you about the Symphony Sunday."

"I'll tell you about the fest."

"You needn't." Will folds the paper and finishes his coffee. "Care to join me at the Art Institute?"

Why not? Carl, who generally finishes a meal in about half the time Will requires, is ready to brave the cold. Maybe the wind has died.

◆　◆　◆

The wind has not died, not when they leave the Hotel for what should be a short and pleasant stroll to the new Art Institute, nor when they leave there for a diner. Will consents to ride to the offices of the *Daily News* where they check out Paul Rosenblatt's obituary.

Both of them make notes. And then take the Alley L into the Levee. The two-block walk to the Third Precinct headquarters is no more pleasant as far as the weather goes and even less pleasant otherwise.

"The problem as I see it . . ." Will pauses to dodge to the street side around an overflowing trash can at the corner of Twenty-second and State. That leaves Carl close, too close, to a house where a woman's pacing in front of a window. She isn't wearing much to start with, and she raises that when she sees Carl looking. He shivers.

"The problem is that no one lives here in the same way they do in Mill Creek." Will says. Carl pulls up a vision of St. Louis' Mill Creek Valley, and it's suddenly wholesome.

"I mean, women live here," Will gestures back at the pouting harlot, "and their pimps, maybe, but it's only for business purposes. It's no one's home. No one cares if the place is a sink pit. And there's enough tolerated crime to draw all kinds of other criminals. At the Twenty-first, O'Brien told me that some of the cops are experimenting, making their own knife-proof vests, and might share them with patrolmen over here."

Carl's surprised—and the Levee has already surprised him in a two-block walk. "I'd have thought the Chicago cops . . . protect themselves in other ways."

They nod at a group of men passing, possibly tourists. As if he and William aren't.

"They may all be on the take as far as pay-offs from sporting houses go. That's part of the system. But there's another, deeper, criminal class that certainly doesn't pay cops—or not most cops. Including the Black Hand and several gangs that have been around for a couple of generations."

"Good Lord. And men come here after dark for sport? It's amazing."

"There's no place else to go, so to speak. The city really does bottle up most of the sex vice in these dozen square blocks. The laws against prostitution are pretty much enforced elsewhere."

Carl's shaking his head as they enter the Third Precinct. At least two cops give him and Will a second glance, and one seems to recognize Will for some reason. He motions them to a gate and rushes them through it, strong-arming a big man who tries to follow.

"Captain's in his office," the sergeant says and turns to more pressing business, yelling at the man who's now trying to shake the gate open. Carl doesn't envy reporters trying to cover this mess.

Captain Simon McElroy is younger than a captain of a major metropolitan police force has any right to be. Maybe no one with any seniority will take the job. Two even younger officers are in his office, off to one side, arguing loudly. McElroy looks up, sees Will and Carl, and yells at his men to get out.

Captain McElroy stands to shake hands as Will does the introductions. The Captain's hands look plump, but Carl can feel the strength in them. And the self-assurance. Maybe the captain isn't quite so young: just boyish-looking with curly light-brown hair and light blue eyes with long lashes. His rather dainty nose isn't quite on center. The man takes in Carl's appearance with a look that makes Carl wonder what all the captain might be reading. The captain only glances at Will, apparently having already heard O'Brien's assessment. He gestures for them to sit.

"Well, gentlemen, I got this much done after me and O'Brien talked yesterday: headquarters wouldn't mind at all if we can pull together a case against a white slaver. The mayor's ordered a commission to study vice in the city. You gotta imagine nothing will come of it, but it won't hurt to have a real live example. Better yet if we've already run him off to St. Louis."

Aha. Carl hadn't wanted to ask Will what would happen if the Chicago cops decide to stonewall on the matter. Politics seem to have dictated cooperation. The two of them are safer as well as more likely to find something.

"Course, you're going to have to get me started. Who this guy is, where he worked, what you think he did." He opens pudgy hands to invite them to start, and Will responds by offering a photograph the *Globe* staff produced for the feature it'll run on Justice Waists. Along with an oral dossier.

"His name is Oscar Renke or, at least, that's the name he works under now. We suspect him of luring women away from his waist factory to work in his brothels against their will. To be more exact, we think he fires them from the factory, which has by far the best pay in town, blackballs them from working elsewhere in the garment industry, and then offers their menfolk a lump sum payment to bring them in. Once there, in one of two brothels he's bought in St. Louis, he doesn't let them leave."

Carl hasn't imagined all that. He feels himself color because he let himself be impressed with the higher wages. He turns away from Will to see the captain noticing.

"Now, is this your theory, Mr. McConnell, or Micah Wright's?"

"Both, actually. He and an officer named Mike Messerton, captain in our own red-light district, think this might be how it works."

Captain McElroy nods.

"What we know for sure," Will continues, "is that two women who worked at the new waist factory since it started last February were found in Renke's brothels and are dead now."

"Dead how?"

Will explains how one escaped a raid and ran into the path of a police auto and how the other was found in a raid and died within a couple of days at the hands of a mysterious visitor at City Hospital. McElroy's making notes.

"Neither woman would talk—or had time to. Both were clearly scared of something; the second one kept saying the boss would find her. And we think he did. We just can't get a good id."

"Hmm." McElroy finishes his notes and glances up. "Were these pretty ordinary brothels or was there something nasty about them?"

"Ordinary. At least until Renke bought the operations. Messerton thinks it would take more time than's passed to work up that kind of clientele."

Good Lord, one would hope. This really is more than just a political cause on Julia's part. Carl wishes he'd asked more about the woman she nursed.

"Why don't your cops arrest this Renke on operating the brothels?"

"Wouldn't hold him for long, and for that matter it's hard to prove. The women are scared to death of him. The madams, too. They talk a bit to the cops and then deny it. Or tip Renke off. He's beaten one girl badly enough to send her back home to the countryside. Probably as an example."

"Sounds like he could be one of ours. And this picture"—McElroy studies it some more—"looks familiar. Different spectacles, I'd say. The trick is to ask the right people. It may be good that he's been gone a while, if he's violent. More people will talk. Do you think he ran a factory here?"

"I'm sure of it. I interviewed him for an article on Justice Waists, his new operation. He calls it that because he pays the women at least fifteen percent better than any other shop in town. Says he moved there to exploit the market further west. Spends a lot of time on the road doing the selling himself, Kansas City and between, he says. He moved two guys supposed to be expert cutters with him."

Hoping that Will planned to share this, Carl jumps in. "We happen to know, from his St. Louis bookkeeper, that he had a bookkeeper here. We were planning to ask around and thinking that could take a while. But we may have a lead. And you folks may know something about him."

McElroy stares a moment, seeming to mentally review his notes on Carl rather than the case. Then nods for Carl to continue.

"About all our young acquaintance in St. Louis knew was that this guy was old and did things in an old-fashioned way. I heard yesterday that a Paul Rosenblatt, an elderly man, old bookkeeping company, died under mysterious circumstances. We checked the obituaries. It was January. Just before Renke moved. The rumor we heard is that Rosenblatt died in a room full of pornography. Have you heard of that one?"

"Yes indeed." McElroy puts his memo book down. "The pictures were the talk of several precincts. The old man had a house on Prairie Avenue, a strip of homes that used to be top drawer. But businesses, including our businesses"—he gestures outside his window, which has iron bars on it— "got a bit close, and most of the rich folks moved up to the North Shore. Not your man Rosenblatt, though. Be hard, I guess, to move all the goodies without anyone seeing them."

"What exactly did he have? Paintings?" Will asks.

"No sirree. Photographs. All photographs. Everything from the big wall numbers to little stuff you'd have to stand right next to so you could see it. I went in to look, even though the address is over the line in the Fourth precinct. Because of the nature of the work. Sure enough, it looked familiar. The photographer had a distinctive style, downright dramatic."

The captain seems to be remembering the drama. "And because they were photographs, real women, you'd look at them and wonder. Why did they pose that way? Why were they willing to do that? None of them looked as if they enjoyed it. And of course, some of them clearly had no choice. One of the largest was of a woman covered, to the extent she was covered at all, in chains. It caught my eye because I'd seen one like it in one of the better cribs over on Dearborn."

McElroy looks away, and Carl's both curious and fearful about what the man's picturing.

Will starts shaking his head, and it gets McElroy's attention. "This may be nothing at all, but Renke's a photographer. He has landscapes all over the reception area outside his office and inside it, as well. And when our photographer went up to get pictures on the factory floor, Renke was all over him, asking questions about the camera. He knew what he was talking about."

Carl and the captain stare at Will until Carl breaks the silence with a sigh.

McElroy says, "We've left Rosenblatt's death at natural causes. Easy to do because he was, oh, in his late eighties, maybe, and the family didn't want details out. They sent a man in to destroy the photographs." McElroy chuckles. "New décor all over the neighborhood. Naïve folks, the Rosenblatts."

"But," he continues, "we can reopen that case. We know a prostitute of his acquaintance went in the night he died from the maid who opened the door. The maid heard the old man upstairs after that, for a while, and then nothing for the next day and a half. Wasn't easy to determine cause of death, but it could have been foul play. Everyone was too busy uncovering the goodies and then covering them up to do much investigating right away. And then we had a couple of nasty murders in that part of town. We haven't paid much more attention. Or I should say, the Fourth hasn't. Not my problem."

McElroy drums a finger on the closed memo book and then tosses it on the desk, where Carl fears it will be lost shortly.

"We can do two things. We call Carrier over at the Fourth and ask him to start up the investigation again. Since it involves a prostitute, he'll probably ask me to help, and I can move things along. And we can ask around about your Mr. Renke. In fact, I think we cut right to the chase. Have you gentlemen ever heard of the Everleigh Club?"

Carl snorts before he can stop himself. The Levee's famous among red-light districts and the Everleigh Club is its masterpiece. The Everleigh sisters run the most exotic, most expensive, most lavish sporting house in the country. Maybe on the planet. Even William has a small smile on his face as he nods.

"I think we take this picture"—McElroy digs it up—"to Minna Everleigh. Buy a couple of her outrageous cigars, sit back and get an earful, if there's one to be had, on Mr. Oscar Renke. And Mr. Paul Rosenblatt. He surely would've been a long-time customer from everything I heard about him, postmortem."

To Carl's surprise, the captain says he'll try to set something up for Sunday afternoon. McElroy chuckles when he looks at Carl and says, "That's when Minna receives city officials, lets the occasional crusader in, holds court. I can probably get us an audience."

Well, Carl has to hand it to William McConnell. Following the man around makes life a hell of a lot more interesting. Dead bookkeepers, white slavery, the Everleigh Club.

27

*From **The St. Louis Globe-Democrat**, Sunday, October 23, 1910*

High wages yield better productivity and less turnover, and the new Justice Waist factory is proof of that, according to its owner, Mr. Oscar Renke. Mr. Renke moved to St. Louis from Chicago earlier this year to position his operation to the south and west. His higher wages have stirred interest in the City's garment industry.

I thought Saturday night would be the worst. I'd be sitting home by myself while Red and Aaron clubbed at The Green Parrot. Red planned to brag about how much money his little cousin was bringing in and what a swell time the boys were going to have in the big city.

But Saturday night was anticlimactic. Laundry. Housecleaning. A little introspection. I opened the journal but couldn't muster the energy to write anything. I ran a finger over the spine of the Harold Bell Wright novel but didn't open it. I kept the draperies drawn and the light relatively low and was in bed when the boys came home.

It all catches up with me today. I miss my friends at the boarding house, with whom I normally share a leisurely Sunday morning off. I'm doing something more daring than living with other suffragists and typing police reports, but I feel more ordinary. In a week I've already become my incognita persona: I'm another face in the army of factory women. I've worked hard for six days and all I have to show for it is an untold number of waists. And a bit of humiliation at the end of each shift.

And, of course, I'm miserable missing William. By noon, I'd have digested one of Mary's fine breakfasts and be ready for Sunday dinner with him. We'd go to a nice hotel restaurant for a noon meal and on to an art gallery or a musical afternoon, perhaps a church performance late in the day. If the weather were any better than it is today, maybe we'd simply walk in a park. And be together. Perhaps look forward to spring and our regular Sunday afternoon baseball game.

Aaron says William has gone to Chicago. Maybe something Renke said for the article the *Globe* published today triggered some suspicion. And Carl has followed him. I worry about them and am impressed they're working so hard on the case. I wish I'd written to William. I imagine him telling Carl it's over between us. And Carl saying that if William isn't going to control me any better than he does, it's just as well.

I don't want to imagine what William might say to that.

I'm quietly helping Aaron put together something to resemble a noonday meal when Red comes in from their bedroom. He's in character as far as dress goes, disheveled, wearing suspenders over a button front shirt which is open enough to show long underwear underneath. He's rubbing at his curls and greets me by saying, "Julia, do you think this is starting to show red at the roots?"

Red's not a bad-looking man. He has gorgeous blue eyes under nicely arched—blond—brows. High cheekbones and a curving, sensual, mouth. In fact, he's better than not bad-looking. And I'm not offended at his dress, not really. But I'm about to break into tears at the thought of having to deal with him.

Aaron glances at me and moves between us. "Let me see." He pokes a finger in Red's hair and says, "Well, it just looks a bit darker to me."

I turn and raise my chin and check out Red's blond curls. "Some night this week," I decide. "You can't let that go too long, but it will be easier to dye the roots if it grows out just a bit more."

They both nod seriously. Red says, "By the way, we managed to see Irwin Edwards in our bar-clubbing last night. He had a letter for you. I think your father sent it to you through Chief Wright."

Red hands over a letter that's been folded and looks worn from its travels.

I take it and stare a moment. Aaron says, "Go ahead and read your mail, Julia. I can make dinner."

"Thanks."

I open the envelope as I walk. The envelopes. Dad has written on a note card, sealed it in a small envelope, and put the whole thing in a larger one addressed to Chief Wright. That alone tells me he's gotten my letter about the incognita operation.

He didn't write much. The envelope within an envelope makes it look like more than it is.

I read it. And read it again. I sink onto my bed. The one that isn't really my bed. It's a sway-backed mattress in a cold hole of a room. I shiver and drop the note.

Dad wrote—and I can hear the sarcasm through the paper—that he's so glad I let him know about this little adventure. The day before he got the note, "Micah" had telephoned him and told him I'd be working incognita. Working for a man who's likely involved in abducting and torturing women.

Dad does not want me to do it. Since I hadn't asked, he couldn't say no. Ahead of time. But he would appreciate it if I would return to my boarding house. And my senses. He won't force me to do that, mind you. But he does not want me to pursue this nonsense.

I could be angry with him. And I am, on one level. But it's the old anger, the same thing I've put up with from men for years. Even my father, who should know better because he raised me to be like this. Maybe unintentionally.

No, I'm angry with myself. I assumed those words, "I don't want you to, but I won't stop you," were William's. So, I'd been angry at William. I try to remember why. Because I didn't recognize his right to stop me and then I resented his patronizing me by not trying to? I resented his not saying so to my face but to the chief? And it's taken me the week to make up my mind that I don't care. Or to be precise, I care, but I miss William more. I've decided that "not stopping me" is good enough, because I don't want to lose William.

And, of course, I can see now that Will has done none of that. For all I know, he said, "It's Julia's choice." He might even have said, "I understand why she'd want to."

And he's in Chicago, and I have no idea how to reach him. If I try, it'll be days before the cops can arrange it. All I can do is hope he'll stay safe. The irony of that makes me want to weep into my pillow in the middle of the day.

28

Carl feels odd joining C.R. Schugel and his family at church on Sunday. He's used to being in his own church, used to sitting in the choir; he isn't used to thinking that he'll be heading to one of the most notorious sporting houses in the country in a couple of hours, trying to get a story from one of the most notorious harlots in the country. He distracts himself by thinking how pleased Zimm will be with the more mundane story he's putting together.

McElroy suggested they not eat lunch ahead of the visit. Audiences with Minna and Ada Everleigh apparently involve food, and everyone knows there's no better food in the city. Carl therefore turns down a Sunday dinner with his new friends and returns to the Congress to find William enjoying coffee and toast and finishing off his second newspaper.

They meet Captain McElroy at his headquarters. Carl thought the Levee would be deserted on a Sunday afternoon, but there're pimps in doorways and more women in windows. McElroy actually nods to some of them as he strolls with his visitors down Twenty-second toward Dearborn.

"The Everleigh sisters won't know white slavers directly, but they hear about everything that goes on in the district. They're more likely to tell us something about Paul Rosenblatt than about your man Renke." After a turn onto Dearborn, McElroy gestures a couple of doors down. Carl draws a deep breath. He's heard the Club is elegant, but he doesn't expected the elegance to extend out onto the sidewalk.

The south end of the block between Twenty-first and Twenty-second is suddenly neater, the pimps are gone, and the windows feature gold drapes instead of tired, nude women. Two doors lead to what looks like two houses that have been combined into one. The doors themselves announce that no expense was spared in the effort.

Will must be taking in the exterior of the Everleigh Club as well, but he asks, "The sisters wouldn't buy women?"

"Oh no. They don't have to. They have a waiting list of good-looking, young, healthy women, who want to work here. Several of these places," he gestures north along Dearborn, "not only buy women, some of them have their own breaking-in rooms."

Carl's pretty sure what that means and doesn't want to hear details. McElroy pauses on the steps that lead to the first of the two doors to the Everleigh Club. "About three years ago, we went on a campaign of arresting the men and women who rope young lookers into the trade. We ended up finding and freeing over three hundred girls. And everyone we arrested along the way, the ones who prey on factory girls and shop girls, the ones who scam the immigrant girls from the ships arriving on the coast, the professional rapists, the auctioneers, are all out of jail now. Paid their fines, spent their year, back at it."

Well. That dulls the glitter of the Everleigh Club. For a few minutes. But astonishment takes over as the three men stand in the incredible lobby of the club and watch Minna Everleigh approach.

The place is breathtaking. In his reporter role, Carl's been in some of St. Louis's finest homes and clubs, but none holds a candle to this. The warmth of it enfolds him, and Carl has to concentrate for a moment to sort it out. Besides the obvious steam heat, there's incense of some sort, almost visible, shimmering among the trailing gold and red silk hangings, hovering over the rich Oriental rugs. The glow from elaborate lamps reflects in the shine of the polished mahogany tables and in the veins of the marble slabs that top them. Statues of naked women tastefully peer from behind palms that flourish as if it's the tropics instead of Chicago in October. Something about the arrangement of the furniture makes him look up at the two curving mahogany staircases, twin invitations to the boudoirs of the ladies of the Everleigh Club.

And then there's Minna Everleigh. She's the younger of the two sisters and the public face of the Club. Carl thought she'd be as stunning as her bordello, but that's an overstatement. Under the rich and trailing gown she wears, an ordinary figure approaches. Above the diamond dog-collar is an ordinary-enough face, more than plain but less than beautiful. Carl isn't surprised at the intelligence in her round, dark eyes. He guesses her to be somewhat past thirty and business-savvy beyond her years.

A slight Southern accent underlies the professional purr as she greets Captain McElroy. As Simon.

Simon does the introductions, and Carl's incredibly uncomfortable. Minna Everleigh has standards for the men who visit her club, mostly having to do with their ability to lay out a minimum of fifty dollars for an evening's entertainment. Word is that the cheapest service is ten dollars—for a very limited amount of time—but men spend more, on wine, on the shows and dancing, on the "circuses." Carl isn't sure quite why she's inspecting him and Will. Maybe it's habit.

"Let's talk in the library." She turns in a rustle of maroon silk and taffeta and motions to a woman who emerges from the greenery. "Bring wine."

This woman, who much more closely fits Carl's image of an Everleigh Club harlot, smiles pertly to each of them and says, "Hello, Captain McElroy." By the time she returns with a bottle, Carl and Will and the captain have given their hats and coats to an equally chirpy little hussy and are settling into huge, clean-lined, leather easy chairs in what seems to be a well-stocked library. Carl would like to check the titles. Instead, he settles for the cigar Minna offers. He isn't sure about the wine, because he certainly isn't a wine drinker, but he knows cigars and the Tabacalera is one of the best Manilas.

Minna watches them prepare the cigars as she sips the red stuff. When they've each settled into their smokes, she says, "What can I help you gentlemen with?" Purring again.

Simon McElroy looks comfortable but businesslike. Carl had wondered exactly how a police captain in the Levee deals with the district's wealthiest madam.

"We're trying to find out more about two men: Paul Rosenblatt, the late Mr. Rosenblatt, that is, and an Oscar Renke. Can you tell us anything about either?"

Minna gives a little laugh and flutters a hand at the captain. Two diamond bracelets slide up her arm and there's a ring on every finger. She can hide any deficiency in looks behind the glitter.

"Of course I know Paul Rosenblatt. Knew him. And as you are well aware, Simon, I wouldn't be talking about him if he weren't dead. He was a regular customer since Ada and I opened the place. He was . . . maybe 75 . . . then. An incredible man, if you know what I mean." She directs that last at Carl. He can only think to nod.

"Paul was here occasionally with a man named Oscar. But it was

Oscar Ryan. What does this Mr. Renke look like, Simon?"

McElroy feels through an inside pocket in his uniform and glances at Will, who pulls out another photograph.

Minna raises an eyebrow as she considers the photo. She notes the stamp on the back that identifies it as property of the newspaper. Then she considers Will. "Simon says you're a reporter from St. Louis. Do you work for the *Globe-Democrat?*"

William nods politely. "I've worked for the *Globe* for ten years. I cover police news."

Minna nods in return, and seems to approve. McElroy's smiling. And she catches Carl off-guard.

"And you report for?"

For some reason, Carl gives her the name of both the *Westliche Post* and its sister paper, the *St. Louis Times.* Sometimes people don't want to bother with a German paper, but if they know there's the possibility a story might run in the *Times,* they talk freely. Why Minna Everleigh should care is beyond him. And then he adds, "Police beat."

"And you're working together on . . . on this Mr. Renke?"

Will's cool as he replies. Someday Carl will hear the question William McConnell doesn't have a ready answer for.

"We're both concerned because we think he's linked to the deaths of two women in St. Louis. And the *Post* and the *Globe* aren't strictly in competition. As a matter of fact, Mr. Schroeder is here on another story as well, one of German interest."

Minna looks back and forth between them. Carl manages to smile and nod.

But she goes to the heart of William's response.

"You say two women have died. Were they in the trade?"

"That's hard to say. If so, they were recent and unwilling

recruits, we believe. They were too scared to tell the police much before they died."

Minna sobers, her rather heavy brows drawing down. "My guess is it's the same man then. He looks slightly different, but I'm pretty sure this is the man I know as Oscar Ryan. If he's involved in procuring"—she says the word with distaste—"it's almost a sure thing."

After a second, she says, "How long has he been in St. Louis?"

"Maybe February. He opened the waist factory the first of March."

Minna nods and looks again at the picture.

"He had a factory of some sort here, and if he used the name Renke in that work, I wouldn't have known it. Around the Levee, he was Oscar Ryan, procurer, portraitist and occasional guest of old man Rosenblatt. I believe Paul did his books. It was one of many things I heard them argue about, particularly toward the end."

All three men are leaning forward. William has put down the wine glass and is pulling out a memo book. Minna looks pleased and hands him the photo with a flourish.

Simon McElroy seems to think notes are a good idea, as well, and fumbles for his pad. Will beats him to a question.

"What do you mean by portraitist? Did people, women in particular, sit for photographs for him?"

Minna laughs.

" 'Sit for a photograph' is not hardly what I'd say, Mr. McConnell. William, isn't it?"

Will nods.

She rises and says, "Let's take a little tour, William, Carl." She leaves Simon McElroy to follow, but he's still digging in his tunic for something, a memo book or a pencil, shifting items from one pocket to another.

Along the way Minna Everleigh says, "Have you gentlemen had luncheon?" and responds to their murmured "no ma'am's" by telling yet another trailing young lovely that "we" will take light refreshment in the Pullman room.

The downstairs rooms are so overwhelming Carl feels his senses dulling to the wonder. The big spaces are the ballroom and the dining-room. The enormous chandeliers in the ballroom aren't lit, but elaborate wall sconces light the inlaid floor. The paneled dining-room has the largest table he's ever seen.

"Seats fifty," Minna says casually and leads the way to the music room.

Which Will reacts to. Minna notices and asks if he plays. Will could get distracted by the glistening grand piano, but he responds politely. "We both do." Minna says something about how the two would enjoy one of her musical evenings. No doubt.

The art gallery is all paintings. William immediately points out a landscape by someone whose work they saw at the Art Institute Friday. Carl hadn't paid attention to the name then and doesn't now. He's wondering why one needs an art gallery, apparently a decent one, in a bordello. But then, the Everleigh Club almost doesn't fit that description, even if it has the same purpose. If Frederick Vanderbilt would have it in his house, the Everleigh sisters have it here.

Beyond those relatively public rooms, Carl counts a dozen parlors, each decorated to the hilt, everything from the Moorish Room that makes the Planters' House lobby look cheap, to the Japanese Room, done in teakwood and yellow silk. All the rooms have sliding doors and Minna assures them that all are soundproof. Good Lord. They stop in the Blue Room. Carl isn't sure he wants to go past the doorway. The theme is collegiate, complete with college pennants and blue leather pillows on the couches.

"These are the only photographs I ever commissioned from Oscar Ryan. Ada wanted live Gibson Girls, all done up in gymnastic costumes. I believe Ryan designed the outfits himself. I'd say he has an artistic side. What do you think, Carl?"

Carl's going to have to move into the room to answer that question, so he stifles the sigh and goes to stand in front of the nearest photograph.

It *is* artistic in a way. The costume's designed to look as if it could be worn by a fifteen-year-old girl practicing athletics at school. Except that the costume is sheer. He can see the slender, athletic, naked body of the young woman, caught in motion, tennis racket in hand. She does have a Gibson Girl innocence about her, in the lovely upswept hair, blue eyes, upturned nose.

Carl turns to find all three waiting for his judgment. "Artistic. But it would've been better if the model had enjoyed it. Did this Ryan ever work with women who weren't being forced into it?"

Minna nods her head vigorously, her diamond droop ear bobs highlighting the action. She includes Will and the captain in her summation.

"One way or another Oscar Ryan worked with slave labor. I only deal with men and women who enjoy what they do. I didn't like Ryan's work for that reason, I didn't like him personally and, on top of it all, he was cheap. Unless Paul Rosenblatt was paying, Oscar Ryan wasn't welcome here. And I haven't seen him since last winter sometime."

William moves to look at another of the photographs. Carl doesn't bother to get closer, although he can see the girl is riding a bicycle. Hopefully in warm weather. William nods to the party when he turns, but Carl reads his anger.

"I have one other photograph of his, got it after Paul Rosenblatt was found dead. A gentleman offered it to us for free, saying it would be a remembrance. And I must say it's popular. So, I've left it up. In the Pullman room."

She leads the way again, the three men walking far enough behind her to avoid the trailing silk.

The Pullman room does indeed refer to a Pullman train car, a dining car to be exact. The room's designed to the precise proportions of a railroad coach, but it's an extreme version of the grandest Pullman diner Carl can imagine. Mostly mahogany and gold gilt and silk damask on the chairs. Apparently, it's used for light meals. The Ryan photograph isn't immediately obvious, as the party settles at a table set with china and crystal. The curtains beside the table, mimicking the observation window trimmings on the richest Pullmans, frame a painting of a western landscape.

The two harlots who accompany the meal are nodded out of the room by Minna. Thank God.

The meal would be appropriate, if not light, by a seashore in July. Summer fruits and vegetables and seafood finally make Carl forget the Chicago cold snap. Hot houses and fast trains from the coast, he concludes.

During the meal, Minna Everleigh confirms the relationship between Renke and Rosenblatt, to the best of her knowledge. The last night she saw the old man, Renke accompanied him and she wasn't at all sure that had suited Paul Rosenblatt. She'd heard discussion of "books," which she assumed were accounting books.

"They left earlier than you'd expect, and Katie said Ryan had urged the old man to get on home, that he'd have someone pay a house call."

Will's eyebrows move up, and Minna acknowledges the question he doesn't ask. "No, my women don't make house calls. Why would they leave this?"

Good question, Carl thinks, and Will smiles in response.

"Who then?" McElroy asks.

"Laurie, over at the Victoria, I expect. She used to work for me and always enjoyed the old man. Katie said she heard mention of the name, 'though she's too new to have known Laurie."

Will clearly has a question and sets his wine glass down, as if debating how to phrase it. Carl hopes it's the same question he has.

Minna Everleigh seems to enjoy reading their minds. She holds up the other jeweled hand. "Laurie?"

Will nods.

"She got too old. It's a young woman's trade. Laurie's close to thirty and healthy enough still, but she tends to drink. It takes a toll. I had to ask her to move on. She works out of the Victoria on Archer."

McElroy's finally gotten his hands on the memo book and is writing as he says, "We'll check with her. The maid said she let a woman in, a prostitute she thought, presumably the last to see Rosenblatt alive."

That seems to sober Minna. "Laurie wouldn't kill him, I don't think. But she might need the money. Bad habits are starting to get the best of her."

That sobers everyone else. Carl puts down a forkful of strawberry crepe and looks at Will. He nods.

"We certainly have appreciated your hospitality and your information," Will says. "Everything we've heard seems to fit with what we know."

Minna looks to Simon McElroy. "Are you going to open a murder investigation on Paul Rosenblatt?"

"Looks like it, Minna."

"Well." She thinks a moment, takes a sip of wine, and stands. She walks to a wall and pulls back what seemed to be curtains over a "window" toward the end of the car. All three men are at her side quickly.

You might glance out the window of a moving train to see the young woman clinging to the post of a gaslight. On a windy night. Maybe a cold wind blows the woman's long wavy hair out behind her, molds the chemise to her body. And then you'd be haunted by the fear on her face, as if she's forced to wait for someone she really doesn't want to see return. She seems to be debating a dash into the darkness behind her.

How did Renke do it?

William answers the question out loud. "An electric fan, I'd guess, and props. An elaborate studio."

"Maybe you'll need it back as evidence of something or other." Minna Everleigh sounds tired as she speaks to McElroy. She lifts an arm to direct the men out of the room, and Carl, for one, is happy to go. He's uncomfortable for several reasons, but one is the very small desire to have enough money to enjoy this place. So, there's a mix of regret and more guilt, and he can do without either.

They're at the door, having passed several women who seem less than happy to see them go. Carl and McElroy thank Minna Everleigh again. Will has the nerve to say, "And what do we owe you for the fine luncheon, Mrs. Everleigh?"

Carl holds his breath, but that gets her to smile again. "Oh, Mr. McConnell, rest assured that our policy regarding Chicago newsmen applies to you and Mr. Schroeder as well: newspapermen are always welcome here, free of charge. All of our services, Mr. McConnell.

Mr. Schroeder."

Good Lord. Will smiles and tips his hat. Carl escapes ahead of him.

29

*From **The Kansas City Times**, Wednesday, October 26, 1910*

> *Members of churches across the city are joining partisans from the Anti-Saloon League and Women's Christian Temperance Union in patrolling the red-light district in the West Bottoms. On a recent evening, three groups were in evidence, carrying banners, singing hymns, and lecturing gentlemen entering and leaving the sporting houses.*

Sealing wax secures the envelope, and it has a curlicue "R" for the boss's name in the middle of the red circle. Hig runs his finger over the seal again and again, noting the slight edge where the hot wax curled up around the metal head. His mind dashes to one thing after another that the circle reminds him of: frosting spread with his finger or jelly or some such, or a petal torn from a red rose on the best bush, or a drop of blood, dropped from up high, maybe from a chicken she'd just killed. Although his mother would've been angry if he'd messed about in the kitchen. A voice in his head reminds him she was angry for a fact when he'd scattered blood after he'd found a thorn on the rose bush.

Hig doesn't get letters sealed with wax initials often, hardly at all, and he hates to break this one. But Anna's asking what the boss wants. Hig doesn't see that he should share what the boss has written. After all, if the boss wanted Anna to know, he'd have put it in his letter to her. But the problem is, maybe the boss does want him to do something, and he'll never know what it is if he doesn't break the seal.

He tells Anna it's none of her business and goes into her kitchen to work on the table. He pulls his knife out of its sheath inside his jacket and carefully slides it under the seal, working it until it's the paper that tears, and the wax itself is still round, just a little nicked on the edge. Then he puts the knife up and pulls the letter out and looks around to see if Anna or any of the girls is close. Anna's leaning in the doorway, O.K., but she can't see from there, so Hig leans back in the chair and unfolds the note like it's his kitchen and he gets notes from important men every day.

He doesn't stay leaning back for long. He reads the first sentence and then sits up and lays the note on the table and reads more. Then he traces over the message with his finger to make sure he hasn't missed anything, to make sure he's gotten all the words right. The boss writes in a pretty hand, but the words and the lines are close together.

The boss thinks he's found a woman Hig would like, one that's tall and slender and has pretty brown waves. It will take him a while to get her to Kansas City because it takes time, the boss says, to recruit special women for our purposes. But the boss is working on it and meanwhile Hig should make sure it will be O.K. with the police and the Kansas City bosses if he brings a special woman from St. Louis. And he'll write, or maybe telephone, soon, and let Hig know how it's going.

Hig sits back again and leaves the note on the table in front of him, cradled between his hands. He lets his eyes go out of focus, and the writing is a pretty pattern, wavy like the new woman's brown hair.

Hig can't quite think just what the boss is asking him to do. Why wouldn't it be O.K. if he brings a woman to KC from St. Louis? Who would know? Who would care? Hig *is* the police as far as Anna Henry's place is concerned. Other officers stop by sometime, to see a girl maybe, but he's the only one who sits in the kitchen, who Anna talks to, who Anna feeds.

Bosses must mean Mr. Jim Pendergast and Mr. Tom Pendergast, but Mr. Tom doesn't care. Anna pays her money like everyone else, she always has. Hig has a job because of Mr. Tom, and Mr. Tom trusts him to do his job. Mr. Jim, now, is sick, and wouldn't want to be bothered about a new woman at Hig's brothels.

Anna's coming around the table and pulling out a chair. Hig grabs up the note. And the envelope with its blood red seal still round.

"So, what does he want, Hig? Is there something you should do?"

Anna looks worried or maybe just put out that the boss has written him.

"No, it's men-stuff, politics and all."

"Politics?"

"Nothing to worry about, Anna."

Anna fiddles with the edge of the tablecloth. "You know, Hig, Mr. Renke has taken over making payments . . . said it was something he'd take care of."

"Well, that's O.K., Anna. He's the boss now. Probably wants it to be man-to-man, you know."

"I suppose." That's what she says, but then she stares at Hig, and he stares back.

"Don't get in trouble, Hig," she says softly.

Hig laughs. Anna tries to mother him sometimes, and Hig likes that, likes the attention, because, of course, Anna's nothing like his mother, like any mother. She's a madam.

But she looks real worried now, and Hig stands up, frowning a bit himself.

"There's no trouble, Anna. Really. The boss . . ." Hig thinks about the note again and looks down at it in his hand. He doesn't want to say the boss is finding a special woman just for him. Anna might think he doesn't like her girls. And truth be told, what Hig really likes is looking at his woman and sometimes the other women the boss has captured in his art, in his photographs. So, he says, "The boss wants to make sure everything's O.K. upstairs. I'll go up and check the fire, Anna. You and the girls don't have to go up there."

He smiles, and Anna closes her eyes and shakes her head. Hig puts the note in its envelope, real careful, and puts the whole thing in an inside pocket, next to the knife.

30

*From **The St. Louis Globe-Democrat**, Monday, October 31, 1910*

> *Germans in St. Louis who are fighting the state-wide prohibition amendment are inspired by the same ideals and love of freedom that led them to fight against slavery during the civil war, according to key Republican politicians who spoke yesterday at the laying of the corner stone of the new Tower Grove Turn Verein. Mayor Kreismann and Congressman Bartholdt are both members of turner halls in the city.*

The time in Chicago has been fascinating, but Carl's ready to head home by the weekend. Get back home, back to the prohibition fight. Will, however, decides to go with Captain Carrier and one of his detectives to talk to the Rosenblatts on Saturday. Carl's torn between meeting the Rosenblatt family and going off with C.R. to another festival. He decides to have fun. Given all he's heard about Paul Rosenblatt in the last week, he doesn't much want to meet the old man's relatives.

It's been a busy week just past. On Monday afternoon after their visit to Minna Everleigh last Sunday, they'd gone with Simon McElroy over to the Fourth precinct and sat down with the officers there to read over the report on Paul Rosenblatt's death. Murder. The old man had been found half sliding out of a chair in the midst of his pornography and accounting ledgers, in his private rooms.

Those rooms held a bed, and the maid didn't clean them, so no one had checked on him for some time.

Aside from spending most of their time cataloging the artwork, the investigators had found only one item of interest. The old man had been clutching a piece of paper, torn paper, clearly ledger paper because it looked like he'd grabbed one of the page tabs with letters on it. There were other ledger books on the desk, all old. The cops hadn't been able to make anything of them. The family had taken those and ordered the rest of the room's interesting contents destroyed. Too bad it hadn't happened. The ones Carl's seen are plenty.

No one checked for fingerprints, and Carl is reminded of Jimmy Parson, the St. Louis cop who works miracles with prints. St. Louis actually prosecuted a man on fingerprint evidence last month. Parson would've had a good old time in Rosenblatt's room and not because of the pornography.

Carl and Will sat up late that night, trying out theories and deciding the books for Renke's operations might hold the key. They assume Renke and Rosenblatt fought over the books and that, while the family might have them, it's more likely the important books are in the possession of young Arnold Bauer. Another reason to get home.

But the evidence kept pouring in. McElroy told them on Tuesday he'd located Laurie, the prostitute seen at Rosenblatt's the night of his death. Of course, she wasn't talking unless she had some kind of protection. Even though Renke took his goons with him. That's what she'd said, and Carl and Will think that's significant on its own. McElroy said he was working on the protection part and would get back to them.

Tuesday had been a fairly pleasant day, warmer, sunny, and Will had led Carl on a walking tour around the city. By dinner time, back at the Congress, Carl finally managed to say what had been bothering him as they'd surveyed the rising new skyscrapers. "You know, Julia's not only working for Renke, but those two cutters are there as well."

Will hadn't told him to leave it alone. He'd nodded his head without looking up. And Carl hadn't been able to think of anything positive to add, so he'd gotten quiet as well.

On Wednesday, they'd gone with several cops, including McElroy, to the factory Renke had owned on Morgan Street. The new owners were willing to say it had been Oscar Renke they'd bought from, that they'd paid a good price because the machines were top-notch, most of the staff was willing to stay, and everything was efficiently run. It had paid off, they said: business was great. There was a strike in town, but their workers had been happy enough they hadn't walked. They recalled Renke saying he was going to buy all new equipment in St. Louis because it was easier than moving everything. He had enough to move with his photography equipment.

Alert to any suggestions about photography, the cops, Will, and Carl had trooped to the basement and indeed found evidence of a dark-room and a subterranean studio, perhaps, wired for electricity. There were odd pieces of furniture around, but nothing truly suspicious. It was ominous for some reason Carl couldn't put his finger on. And Will wondered out loud why a legitimate operation would run out of a factory basement. The new owners said they'd had the impression it was a hobby on Renke's part. They knew him, they pointed out, as a successful businessman, although they'd wondered why he would move his business instead of just expand it. And why, exactly, were the cops interested now?

The cops had sidestepped that one, and Carl got the impression no one would argue further with them. Neither McElroy nor Carrier seemed to have a particular way with the public outside their districts, but then maybe the owners were impressed that not one but two police captains were out investigating. It had the smell of something the political bosses wanted done, and the factory owners had read that.

McElroy rode back to the Congress with them and said he'd interviewed Katie, the harlot at the Everleigh Club who'd entertained Rosenblatt the night he died. She'd confirmed everything Minna Everleigh had said, including an argument between Rosenblatt and Ryan about the "books."

McElroy was enjoying this investigation. And certainly spending time on it. Carl pointed that out, trying to sound appreciative, and McElroy was entirely forthcoming: the brass thought a conviction on what Illinois called pandering and, secondarily, murder, would be perfect political timing right now.

Friday morning had found Carl weary of sightseeing, but McElroy called early to say he'd gotten Laurie "a new position," and in return she'd had plenty to say about Oscar Ryan and Paul Rosenblatt, and could they come by his office. William apparently had no more desire than Carl did to visit the Levee unless necessary and offered to buy lunch at the Congress. Will would not normally buy lunch for a news source—or take lunch from one, being more fastidious about that aspect of his work than most—but Carl was grateful he'd been willing to suggest it now.

McElroy had wiped the last of the Congress' excellent chowder from his mouth and leaned back in his chair. "Seems Ryan paid Laurie to go to Rosenblatt's house on the night in question. She wasn't supposed to see the old man, just go in the front door, get close enough to his room to fool the maid, head down the backstairs, and open a little-used side door, leaving it blocked open with a brick she'd left outside for that purpose." McElroy seemed to be picturing it.

"So that Ryan could enter at his leisure, you see. She left without seeing Rosenblatt but said she saw Ryan waiting in a shrubbed patch of darkness near the door. Didn't speak to him."

Will and Carl took notes.

"I hurried right on over to the Rosenblatt house and found a brick outside the side door. It's enough to take to the prosecutor's office, and we got an appointment this afternoon. Thought you two could shed some light on what Renke's up to in St. Louis."

Lord. Carl caught himself before he said out loud that there was no imagining what could get done when the motivation was political.

At the Criminal Court Building, a senior Assistant State's Attorney named J.G. Norton had listened carefully. "What we need," he concluded, "is motivation. It would surely be nice to have those books. Otherwise, the evidence could as well point to the woman Laurie." The obvious starting place was the Rosenblatt family, he'd said. Will and Carl had exchanged looks that said Bauer was much more likely. They came to a mutual if silent agreement.

Will explained. "Renke has a new bookkeeper in St. Louis. He might have the books."

Norton considered that. "It's a good back-up possibility, but we should call on the family Saturday anyway. Do either of you want to join me—along with enough cops for us to be intimidating?"

Carl had begged off, because C.R. wanted him to see another celebration. Carl had already written one story that was downright insightful, he thought, regarding the variety of German communities based on when they'd immigrated. But a two-parter would delight Zimm, and Carl was feeling guilty. He telegraphed his boss: "Great stuff. Home Monday." And hoped Zimm would be in a good mood when he finally returned.

Will wasn't too happy when he returned Saturday. The Rosenblatts were defensive and horrified the case was being reopened and simply wouldn't talk about either Oscar Ryan or Oscar Renke at first. When the police got pushy, they'd admitted the old man had done the books for Oscar Renke, the factory owner, but they had no idea where those records would be. After all, Renke would likely have them himself. Was that standard procedure, Will had asked? And the family had assured them it was.

Several hours were wasted looking at the books the police had let the family take from Rosenblatt's house. Will and McElroy and Norton had flipped through pages and pages of dusty old ledgers until they finished the pile, but there was nothing regarding a waist factory nor Renke nor a pornography operation.

"As if they'd have kept such a thing," Will said over yet another fine Sunday luncheon at the Congress. Carl was starting to miss his mother's cooking along with being quite aware of the tab they've run up. "We're probably better off if Renke took the books to St. Louis and Bauer knows where they are," Will added.

Carl agreed, darkly. And further agreed to stay until today when Norton will offer some kind of final decision. They'll head home on the midnight special tonight, arrive in St. Louis Tuesday morning early.

That means they won't do much talking on the train. Sitting in the Congress's comfortable parlor, Carl issues one last try on the matter of Will-and-Julia.

"You know, if you married her, or were even courting her again, you could keep her out of this kind of thing. If you wanted to."

Will snorts, but it's no doubt regarding what Carl's saying, not that he's saying it. Progress.

"Carl, you don't understand. Don't understand Julia or what she wants from a relationship. I thought you'd be on the same page—all these 'new rules for a new century' you two always talk about."

It's Carl's turn to snort. "I believe in women being able to vote, Will. God knows Julia's intelligent enough to exercise the franchise and so are most of her friends. That doesn't mean someone doesn't need to rein her in. The other women in the movement may demonstrate or even get arrested occasionally, but they're not off shooting people or doing detective work. Only Julia. I worry about her. Don't you?"

"Of course I do, Carl. Everything I've learned here makes me more worried. But she worries about me, as well. And about you, for that matter. Can you imagine what she's thinking right now? Surely she's heard we're out of town, and she knows investigating can be dangerous. Turns out not to be, but you never know."

"We can take care of ourselves!"

"So can Julia, at least as much as we can. She's better with a gun than I am. And you don't even carry one."

"She's going to shoot her way out of every situation? She isn't carrying a pistol to Renke's factory, is she?"

"I don't think so. When I saw her, she looked like every other factory worker. And I think they search bags for stray fabric and such."

"You saw her?"

"Yeah." Will gives him a strange look and stops to light a cigar. Will doesn't smoke often, and the fact that he took C.R. up on the offer of a cigar told Carl he might be in an odd enough mood to talk.

"Yeah, yeah. When?"

"I went up with our photographer to get pictures on the floor."

"She's in that picture you ran?" They'd managed to pick up a Sunday *Globe*, and Carl read the story closely, examined the pictures carefully.

"Only her back. I knew it was her, of course, but I didn't see more of her until we were headed out and she stood for their break."

Will goes silent, puffing on the cigar to get it started.

"Christ. She isn't wearing her usual outfit, is she?"

"Of course not. She looked very conventional. All that hair up. Corset. Long skirt." Will pauses. "Tiny waist. Make-up, I thought, from a distance."

Carl works at picturing her. "Pretty?"

"Yes. And that worries me."

"Worries you how?"

"Well, for one thing, Julia doesn't try to be pretty. Normally. So, I'm sure she's uncomfortable. And the other thing is, she might look tempting to Renke. More than pretty, she was . . . willowy. Even in a work outfit, she's tall and graceful. Attractive."

Lord. Carl stares, and Will seems to think it's about Julia's incognita role. "I suppose that could move the investigation along if Renke fires her and makes some kind of proposition," Will says.

Carl has never admitted how attractive he finds Julia. For one thing, he's thought it might just be him. Julia certainly doesn't show off anything womanly. She's attractive in a natural, unintended sort of way. Why shouldn't Will have noticed? Or worse, yet, Oscar Renke.

"And that doesn't bother you. Good Lord, Will."

Will looks up sharply, leaving whatever image he's held as he stared off toward the lobby. "It bothers me for several reasons. But I understand her need to do it. Don't you? Two women, women who may have been in similar circumstances but didn't know what they were getting into, are dead. Have you forgotten that?"

It hits Carl then. Will can be convincingly civilized, but he's as capable as Julia of suspending all sorts of convention, including what Carl considers progressive-but-appropriate men's and women's roles. He's seen William ignore social rules—at least what Carl thought were rules—regarding race relations. Carl just hasn't realized how deep that runs. And how much it plays into Will's relationship with Julia.

The brief meeting he and Will had with Chief Wright before Julia went off to start the factory job comes back to him. The chief asked how they felt about it, and Carl had taken the opportunity to say that Julia will go way beyond acceptable behavior if no one stops her. Wright had looked stricken. But Will had said it isn't up to any of them to stop her from taking chances if she thinks the cause worth it.

"You know, Will, I've changed my mind. About you and Julia."

"Really? You don't think I should try to . . . reestablish the relationship?"

"See, that's what I mean. I'd have said, 'get her back,' but you don't think about it that way. You'll never possess her. If you were married, would you call her 'your wife'?"

"I haven't thought about it. What are you getting at?"

"I'd imagined you getting back together so you could protect her. Instead . . . well, I guess I still think you should get back together. But your job is to convince her you really are different from every other man on earth, every man I know. You'll really let her do these outrageous things and not even think it's a matter of . . .

protection."

Carl has let the ash on his cigar start to drift toward the plush carpet. He quickly finds the ashtray and, along with it, the deeper question.

"When did this happen? When did you decide that a man shouldn't take charge in a relationship? Taking charge is something you're good at, you know."

Will humphs at that and leans forward to put his cigar in the standing ashtray. "I'd never thought about it before I met Julia, never thought that protecting a woman meant limiting her options." He looks Carl in the eye. "If I'd fight for a man's right to 'take charge' of his own affairs, I should argue for a woman's right."

Carl can only shake his head. "Honest to God, Will. You're as crazy as she is."

Will doesn't argue. He just sits there looking at Carl. Considering. Then nodding. After ten days of nagging, Carl has finally gotten Will to listen to him. And he isn't sure he likes what's been said.

Not only will Julia be no safer if she and Will get back together, but now Carl has some thinking to do about his own position. One he was so sure of when he began this mission.

◆　◆　◆

Carl and Will are engaged in yet another luncheon, this one downtown at the Berghoff, when Norton gives them the word.

"Come up with those books in St. Louis, and I'll have a case. I'll file for extradition. And McElroy's put together nasty-looking files on the two cutters, Horace Mallory and Matthew Dexter. We can get them on pandering, assault, and rape. If I can get all three, I'll take 'em." Norton sees them off by saying he'll be waiting to hear. And many thanks.

Will rushes back to the Congress to pack. "We could take an afternoon train," he says.

"But then we'd get home in the middle of the night," Carl points out. "The midnight special is a better idea." And Carl won't have to endure the ride awake. Will agrees, but now they can only sit in the Congress lobby until dark.

Will has a look of anticipation on his face that goes beyond working on the case.

Carl smokes too many cigars.

31

It's an odd sensation, the factory work. I'm going in every day, like before, but I'm losing track of what's happening in the world. If I were in my normal world, I'd be following the campaigns for the state races and the amendments, especially the prohibition vote. Carl and William would be talking to me about everything from Colonel Roosevelt to plans for covering the election. Now, Aaron brought a Sunday paper in yesterday, and I found it . . . remote.

At least my dull work is more productive as far as pay goes. I got a raise Saturday, effective today. If this keeps up for long, I'll actually save a fair amount of money. And so far it's only a job, pleasant enough until quitting time. I'm still offended by the leaving procedure, not only for myself, but for all the women. Behind the chit-chat in line, they hate it, hate getting closer to the curtains.

And Renke makes it in to help, late, almost every day. So that by the time the end of the line walks in—meaning me—Renke's there to put a hand on my back or feel through my petticoats insistently. And yet nothing really happens. The only other thing I can point to is a series of subtle looks I'm not sure I'm interpreting correctly.

Before announcing the raise, two cents an hour, Renke escorted me to a new seat. This one is on the other side of the line, still the back table, and right in front of his door. He can sit in his glassed-in, third-floor office and stare at me. Not that he ever sits still for long. But sometimes he and the cutters gather in the upstairs office and survey their small kingdom.

At least twice in the last week, I've glanced up to see Esther look at them and then at me. And when I leave for the day, she looks at me like she thinks I'm in trouble. But no one complains about my work. I get the occasional compliment, from Renke once, from a couple of co-workers, from Esther herself. I interpret all that to mean I'm not encouraging the men or Esther would warn me. They're interested in me for some reason.

I doubt it's good sewing. They could wait a month or so to give me a raise if they thought I'd be here that long. Maybe they intend to fire me and hope Enos will be so irritated he'll take them up on a compromising offer. The question is why. I'm not pretty enough for them to want me for a sporting house. No enhancer could do that. For that matter, the smiles on their faces tell me both Mallory and Dexter have figured out my little lingerie deception during the checking routine. Skilled workers, indeed.

I can't see any indication, though, that we've been compromised. We've been consistent. Red's been going to work at a building site that hires men by the hour. He comes home genuinely tired and convincingly grouchy. Aaron's foot is healing, we have to admit to anyone that asks, and he'll be looking for a job this week. I'm amazed they're going through with this. I'm amazed it's so futile so far. I can't remember, sometimes, why this will make a difference.

Most of all, it's been another week of being increasingly unhappy and increasingly anxious about William. I've rehearsed over and over the various ways to say, "I'm sorry I was so stupid." And then convince William to at least start seeing me again or, until that's possible, to correspond.

I gave myself a birthday present a day early: yesterday I asked Red and Aaron to help me figure out how to see William when he gets back into town. Which I hope will be anytime now. They agreed they'll work something out. They weren't even surprised. They smiled kindly. Happy birthday, Julia.

I drag myself to work this morning. No one else knows it's my birthday, my majority, so I can ignore it as well. I'm not in the mood.

The work itself interests me for a while because I'm now making a pretty, peach-colored, silk number that requires patience and nimbleness. The silk doesn't hold a crease as the linen did and putting in pleats is difficult. But I've done this kind of work before—preferring pleats to ruffles for myself—and I can tell Esther's pleased with my efforts. I smile at her and reach for another set of bodice pieces, when I hear the telephone ring in the upstairs office. It rings both here and downstairs and, while I admire the technology in general, I don't think much about it.

Renke has a system where the telephone is answered downstairs and a little bell rings in his upstairs office when the call's for him. The telephone stops ringing, and the little bell starts up, but Renke's elsewhere.

Farrell runs for the office and picks up the earpiece. He runs back out, saying to Esther and anyone else listening, "It's long distance, Chicago. Where is he?"

Esther points up the stairs, and Farrell dashes up them. In a few minutes, Renke appears, rushing into the glass enclosure. Leaving the door open.

The electric machines are quiet enough you can hear him, at least from where I'm sitting. My new location's perfect: if Renke can watch me, I can hear him.

"Mr. Rosenblatt?" I try to make note of the name: Rosenblatt, Rosenblatt. "Yessir, a pleasure to hear from you . . . and what's that, sir?"

Renke gets quiet and listens to the speaker. He moves behind the desk and sits slowly.

Finally, he says, "I see. Of course, I have my books. To be honest, they're not too useful because your father's methods were . . . out-of-date . . . according to my new bookkeeper. But then, you know how your father was."

He pauses and listens, picking up a pen and considering it. "Well, sir, I have no idea what the authorities would want my books for. I'd heard your father's passing was due to natural causes . . ." He pauses as if he's been interrupted. I stop my own machine on the premise of straightening the pleats so I can hear that much better. The word "authorities" did it. Rosenblatt. Authorities.

"No, no, no, I have no idea. Yes . . . yes and thank you for letting me know. I hope the matter clears itself up soon . . . yes, thank you."

Renke hangs up the earpiece gently enough. He drums the pen on the blotter, gently enough. And then he explodes in a rage of profanity. Every woman facing him joins me in looking up. The women with their backs to him freeze and look to the rest of us in question. Renke grabs the edge of the blotter and spins it across the desk, scattering papers and desk minutiae across the room. Then he steps out of the room and looks about wildly.

Farrell catches his eye, and Renke screams, "Farrell, dammit, get Dexter and Mallory down here now."

Farrell has just gotten downstairs and is getting his breath at the end of our table while examining one of the silk bodices. But he starts running for the stairs again immediately, tossing the waist generally in the direction of his desk as he passes. He misses.

The foreladies are urging us to keep working, Esther in particular since we're closest. Renke goes back in the office, and this time he slams the door shut. In fact, he slams it so hard it bounces back open aways instead of latching.

I try not to look. And I'm succeeding until I hear him shriek at the operator to get him the number of the *Globe-Democrat*, the news room. When an operator apparently comes up with the number, he yells at her to connect him.

Dexter and Mallory arrive while Renke's screaming into the telephone about that damn reporter and where the hell is he. I start breathing faster, imagining Jack Forrest on the other end of the connection, screaming back. And, of course, I'm wondering where the hell McConnell is, as well. What has he stirred up in Chicago?

Whatever answer Renke gets from the *Globe* makes him even angrier if his language is any indication.

Dexter turns to close the door securely, and I really can't hear anything else. I concentrate on sewing, but it isn't easy. My stomach is knotting. I'd be better off if I knew where William is, here or in Chicago, or on his way home.

The conference seems to last a while, and I only look up when Renke throws something. I can hear voices through the glass walls, although not clearly.

The problem with the two cutters being on the floor is that we'll soon run out of bodice pieces on our side of the table. The silk takes longer to work than the lawn, but it likely takes even longer to cut. The two men cut huge stacks of lawn bodices at one time, and the silk stacks would have to be much smaller. The silk would surely slide from under the knives. It slides under scissors when I make silk garments. Maybe the two cutters, skilled as they are, aren't in a real good mood to start with.

Farrell and Esther are starting to get nervous when Dexter steps out of the office and nods Farrell off to the side. Farrell takes his orders, runs his hand through his dark curls, and goes to his desk to ring the lunch bell. I'd guess it isn't much past eleven. Farrell hurries to the middle of the room and announces we'll have an early lunch break today and everyone should finish the piece they're on and head down to the first floor. We do, although I'd like to stay to watch the scene in the office. I dally a bit but can't help finishing to Esther's satisfaction.

When we return from early lunch and nervous trips to the toilets, there's plenty to watch. Renke yells at the two cutters, and Mallory yells back. But they all three get quiet, watching us settle in.

We start to work, and Mallory hurries upstairs to get more bodices ready. Dexter and Renke stride onto the floor, each with several aprons over an arm. They've decided to work on the other side of the production equation, unfortunately for us.

They start on the far side, against the street windows, pulling two women to their feet, securing them to the tables. I only glance around once and start working faster. Every other woman ducks her head as I do, hoping to escape notice.

The men work methodically, returning to the office once for more of the apron-like restraints. I wonder how many they might have—and worry over the implication that they do this often. Lordy. I glance at Esther, and she's chewing her lower lip.

Two women on each side of four tables. My heart's pounding, now, along with the tightness in my gut. I should be less scared than the other women. I'm concerned about William, but I can afford to lose my job. I've learned the threat: if you're tied, you're slow, and if you're slow, you can get fired.

Renke grabs up a woman down the table from me, and Dexter

moves my way. He actually stops to my right and runs a hand down my arm. I freeze. But he laughs, the bastard, and moves to my left to pull Roberta from her stool. She sobs once, her tension breaking into immediate tears.

He tells her to lean over, and her arms tremble through the table as she braces herself. He takes his time tightening the contraption in back, like a perverse corset. A strap dangles from the front of the apron, and Dexter threads it through a slot on the table and reaches down to attach it to a waiting hook under the edge of the table. He actually slaps Roberta on the backside and moves around the table. She tries to straighten, as much as possible, and then she lifts her hands, groans, and starts to work again. I wonder if this has happened to her before.

Then I get to watch the operation on the other side of the table, two workers down. The damn silk is sliding under my fingers because I'm trembling. I can't help but glance at the slot in front of me. I'd wondered what it's for. Now I wonder if every station has one.

Renke all but pushes Dexter into the office when they're through, telling him to try again to get Laurie. Laurie? Another name to remember. Dexter shoots him a look and settles in at the desk, lifting the telephone. Renke paces.

I glance up, little glances, trying to see what's happening. It looks like Dexter's off the phone and indicating that he's waiting, trying to convince Renke they'll have to wait for the innocent machine to ring. They both gesture at it.

Wilson arrives, carrying folded newspapers. The three of them start going through the pages. After maybe half an hour, they seem happy with whatever they've found, and Wilson looks relieved to scurry back downstairs, his arms now full of disordered newsprint.

Renke comes out after a minute or so and starts prowling around the room, yelling at women individually and as a group, at the foreladies, at Farrell. Dexter goes upstairs to help cut, apparently. Our supply of bodices is running low, even with eight women working more slowly.

I watch Roberta out of the corner of my eye; she can't work smoothly. Standing up means she can't work the silk flat on the table. And she has the wrong angle on the machine. Esther's having to double check the work done by the women who're standing. Everyone is tense and making mistakes, though. I can tell from their reactions and Esther's.

Mallory appears and motions Renke into the office. They confer, and then Mallory takes up the telephone. Renke stands in the doorway while Mallory makes his connection. Long-distance: I hear the word "Chicago."

As I stop my machine to do hand-work on the other side of the bodice, I hear more bits and pieces. Something about a hotel. The Congress. Can William—or Carl—be staying at the Congress Hotel in Chicago?

When Mallory replaces the earpiece, Renke apparently suggests something else. I hear the word "cutter" a couple of times, and assume it refers to the work, but then I hear an order from Renke: "Get ahold of Cutter and tell him the Congress."

A man named "cutter"? I suddenly picture an assassin with a curving blade like the ones Mallory wears. The silk slithers under my fingers, and I mutter as I start the line of pleats again. When I get them under control and under the needle, I glance up. Renke's staring at me.

He turns back into the office and is smiling as he heads around the nearer end of my table with another restraint. I run the seam quickly, hoping to convince him that I'm an efficient cog in the machine and shouldn't be bothered. As if that will work. Although he does let me finish the seam before he puts an arm around my waist and pulls me to my feet. My stool tumbles over behind me.

32

Renke keeps hold of me for what seems a very long time, muttering in my ear about what good work I do, and how much money I could have made here. I try to say, "Please, sir," but I can't draw enough breath to even hear myself. Maybe it's because my heartbeat thuds in my ears along with Renke's words.

He slips the apron around me and starts hooking it. I try to expand my stomach like a horse does, but Renke knows that trick and waits me out. When he has it painfully tight, he whispers in my ear again, "Tiny waist. I like that. I have a friend who'll like it, too." I try to turn to look at him, for any hint of what that might mean, but he's attaching the strap with one hand on my back, forcing me forward. He makes sure it's secure, and I shudder. I'm trembling still when he turns my face sideways and leans close.

"Sew," he says.

I try. It's hard. If the silk was trying to get away from me before, it's much worse now. I want to lean a hand on the table, but I need both of them to work. I try to concentrate, try to figure out what time it is. I've lost all track, and I'll bet there's no afternoon break bell today.

I can tell from Lynn's face, across and down from me, that Renke's taking his time now, scanning faces, picking out victims. Out of the corner of my eye, I see him return at least twice to get more restraints. I should be thinking about someone who does this routinely and still has women who'll work for him. But all I can see is the light peach silk, moving of its own volition, and my fingers chasing it.

And I'm trying, at the same time, to isolate the voices that occasionally come from the office. Mallory is still in there, maybe waiting for the phone to ring. And then it does.

Renke comes running from the front of the room and stops in the doorway, hands on the frame on either side. I can't help but look. Esther catches my eye, and I glance down immediately, but I can still hear. Mallory says, "Tonight. Don't waste time, we don't know when he'll leave. Anytime, we think."

Oh, Lord. Tonight. When tonight and can I get word to William? How will I do that and can I possibly do it in time? After I get loose from the table.

I drop the silk piece I'm working on, but no one seems to notice—or connect it with what I heard. Then I drop it again when Mallory' voice gets louder and closer.

"He's a reporter. He won't say no to meeting Long Gill tonight because Gill'll say he knows something about you. And that should take care of any information heading south out of Chicago."

He and Renke chuckle, and the boss says, "Good work. That's clever, information about me. And if Dexter can get hold of Cutter, that'll be back-up. If that doesn't work," he says, "you'll have to get him here." Mallory heads toward the stairs, and I glare at his back. The three of them have all the time in the world to move on to their deadly tasks, and I'm strapped to this cursed table.

Maybe it isn't William. They haven't used his name, that I could hear. But what other St. Louis reporter would be in Chicago? Well, Carl's there. But Renke called the *Globe*, not the *Westliche Post*.

I try to calm myself and figure out how to escape. If I weren't tied down, I might make a run for it, although I wouldn't put it past Renke to lock the downstairs doors. As it is, I'm going to have to get loose first. A toilet visit seems the most likely. I decide to wait another half hour or so, to make the request more believable.

Unfortunately, Roberta beats me to it. She asks Esther, and I hold my breath. Esther turns to Farrell, who says, "Not today, don't even think about it."

Roberta sobs again. And I have to think of something else. Should I announce I'm quitting, end the whole masquerade here? I'd be willing to do that but I don't think Renke would let me go. And what he said about the tiny waist might indicate he has plans for me, and that might be what we need.

It is, of course, a moot point. Renke won't let me leave, and I can't get away. My back's starting to hurt. And the telephone rings again.

Renke seems hesitant to answer it, and he must have told Wilson not to answer it downstairs because it just keeps ringing while Dexter, who's traded jobs with Mallory and is harassing women, sprints around the tables. Renke urges him on and then stands in the doorway again.

I can hear Dexter making suggestions. "Find out where Gill's meeting him, or follow him from the hotel, the Congress. O.K.? . . . Yes, the Congress. He's been living high on the hog, but not for much longer." There's a pause, during which I strain to hear, and Dexter says, "If it can look like an accident, that's good. If not, just get rid of him. And get away. We don't want this traced back."

I'm cold and shivering and having trouble getting my breath. Just as I always have when William's in danger but heightened to a degree I wouldn't have thought possible. Tears are starting, not crying nor sobbing, just tears of shock.

I should be calm and go through my options again. But I don't have options. I can only choose to work or not work, and not working is worse. I'll be willing to blow my cover when I'm free to run to the police, but there's no point in doing so until then. If Oscar Renke causes William's death, I want to be able to incriminate him. Him and Dexter and Mallory and Long Gill and Cutter. The thought of it leaves me even colder.

Esther comes by to check Roberta's work and then mine. Neither of us is doing too well. Esther pats each of us on the back and advises us to work slowly and try to avoid mistakes. Not to worry about the table's quota. As if I'm worried about that. And she looks at me closely before she says, "Don't let your tears stain the silk, dear."

The party in the office breaks up, and Dexter heads back upstairs, Renke strolling with them. I hear Renke say something about getting rid of the books.

I can't analyze that, though. I try to memorize it, to add to my list of details I'll offer Chief Wright. I'll get out of here as soon as physically possible and head straight for Headquarters. Just in case I'm not too coherent, I'll spit out the details I'm memorizing.

Between now and then I'll try to sew, although it isn't easy. The tears form a kind of screen and images of William flicker across it like a show at the nickelodeon. William smiling, William bleeding, William angry in the cold on Laclede Avenue.

◆   ◆   ◆

By the time the quitting bell rings, I'm trembling so badly I can't pick up the scissors I just dropped. The ache in my back is continuous, and if I weren't shaking with fear for William, standing up straight would be my obsession. I shift from foot to foot, while the seated women work more quickly than usual to get out of here. My feet are numb for some reason, and I have to be able to run. If I can even walk.

Farrell's standing near the stairs and saying, "Just go on out. No check today. Get your bags and go." And the women are rushing down the stairs. I'm stamping my feet in anticipation of doing the same. I look back, behind me, although the twisting hurts, to see Dexter and Mallory unfastening women, one lace at a time. Behind them, the night sky through the large arched windows is dark and hazy. Lord, it's night here and night in Chicago. Dear Lord.

What started as a mild curse changes to a prayer. I lean on my hands, hard, and pray for William's safety. And that I'll take the wisest, quickest path to warn him.

There's crying and moaning and the striking scent of urine at the table behind me, as the tension catches up with a desperate woman. Roberta's gritting her teeth and rocking. Farrell's trying to herd the staggering women down the stairs as if it's an emergency evacuation. Apparently, the boys want to close up early. And have a party, maybe, while they await a confirming phone call.

Mallory appears to start on Roberta's hooks. He doesn't undo the strap first, so as to prolong the pain, maybe. One of the foreladies is helping a woman toward the stairs, and Esther's waiting at the end of our table. Lord, I pray again, let me walk out of here. There's no time to waste on crawling, I lecture Him.

Before Mallory finishes, Dexter appears to free me. Slowly. He does a check as thorough as any downstairs as he works. I stamp my feet again, and my skin squirms where I can feel the heat of his hand through my clothes.

"You want to leave?" He whispers in my ear. When I jerk a nod, he laughs softly. "Maybe we can arrange an easier job for you."

I glance up to see that both Roberta and Mallory heard that. Roberta's wide-eyed. Mallory's look suggests caution. The next minute Roberta collapses on the table, scattering silk and scissors. Mallory pulls her up and pushes her toward Esther. I pull at the front of the apron while Dexter dallies with the last hook. The moment I feel it give, I push away from the table by myself and stumble toward the stairs. I may have surprised the bully; all I hear behind me is his laughter.

I stagger down the two flights. Farrell's handing women their coats and bags, trying to get us out of the building. Wilson's near the door offering a little extra push. A half dozen women are struggling to walk.

I struggle myself, but I'm moving. Farrell may have said something to me but I can't hear it for the pounding in my head.

Out on the street, it's cold and raining, accounting for the haze I'd seen. Doesn't matter, I tell myself, although I slip a bit heading for the streetcar stop. I'm praying again, asking for a streetcar to be there when I make it to the corner of Locust and Twelfth Street. It's the opposite direction than I usually take, but it's the quickest way to the police station. I decided that upstairs while I could still think.

They might have been calling my name, but I hadn't heard Red and Aaron through my focus and my panic. Red catches my arm, saying, "Where're you going, girl?" and I scream, in pain and in relief.

"You're stumbling, like those other women. Did he tie you all to tables today?" Aaron has my other arm and is whispering in my ear.

I nod and, since they're blocking the view back toward Justice Waists, I whisper the situation. "We've got to get word to William in

Chicago. They've got two men trying to kill him."

Red's graceful eyebrows arch higher, and Aaron sucks in air to keep from responding out loud. Red looks up, maybe evaluating the direction I'm heading. He immediately goes into his strut, pulling me along.

"Well, Nance, don't worry about it. We thought we'd eat at a restaurant tonight, celebrate your birthday."

I'm sure he got the message, but I have no interest in keeping up appearances. He must sense it because he whispers, "We'll get to a telephone. Do you know how to find him?"

"The Congress Hotel. They said. But he might leave tonight." I groan and stumble again as Red pulls me faster, racing to the corner for the approaching car, I hope.

We make it to the corner, and Red lifts me on the stopped car. When the car starts and people stop staring, Red hisses to Aaron, "Get to headquarters. The Chief may still be there, but if he isn't, convince Spencer you're on special assignment and have to call that hotel." As the car turns onto Clark, I stand very close to them both, easy given the crowding, and spit out my desperately memorized phrases. Aaron squeezes my shoulder and gets off on Twelfth, to limp the half block to Headquarters and, hopefully, Chief Wright. Red and I get off and wait for a car headed back the other way.

I gasp for air and close my eyes. Pain erupts, first in one place and then in another, up and down my back. Red runs his hand down my spine, and I stiffen. He immediately puts an arm around my shoulders instead and says, "Now, Nance, he'll catch up with us, and we'll head on downtown."

The streetcar headed back along Clark arrives, and I manage to say, "What if the Chief isn't there? Can we call the Chicago police?"

Red can't very well discuss ways to thwart an assassination

attempt on a crowded car. In fact, we're standing on the platform, and if he weren't holding me, I'd fall off. The throbbing in my back is tightening my whole body, and I can't even work out a reply when Red says, "Why didn't you say it was your birthday, girl? Aaron remembered this afternoon." I wonder who really remembered. But I don't care.

I stumble off when the car stops at Pine Street and have to grab a lamppost for more support. I'm not sure why we're stopping here, but at least Red isn't taking us to the flat.

"Who should I talk to at the *Globe*?" I realize we're within a block of William's office. It's a good idea. If the police can't reach William, maybe Jack Forrest will know something. So, I give Red his name and pray the crotchety old so-and-so will be helpful. I explain Forrest knows me and any comments he might make will slow the process. We decide I should wait just inside the door.

It seems forever. I keep my head down because I've met some of William's colleagues and a couple of newsboys. I grit my teeth and try to pray some more. Right now, two men, one of them armed with a cutter's knife, are stalking William. Lord, help him. And Carl. Renke didn't mention him, and I hadn't thought to. Lord, both of them. The tears are streaming down my face when Red pulls me to my feet and out into the chill.

Whatever I'd thought my twenty-first birthday would be, this isn't it.

33

One last meal for Carl and Will at the Congress, because there's no sense in hanging around Central Terminal for hours and eating bad food. Bags are stacked at the desk, and C.R. will stop in the dining room soon, say his good-byes, head on home to his own good dinner.

Will's anxious, ready to head out. Carl's ready, too, but it's refreshing to see Will be the nervous one. When C.R. appears, both of them jump to their feet to shake hands. It's been a productive trip thanks to the man.

C.R. takes his leave but he delivers a note for Will. Carl attends to his meal, which has just arrived. He focuses on mixing his peas and mashed potatoes. It isn't a sophisticated thing to do, but Carl hates chasing the little green beasties around his plate. He looks up to Will's snort.

"Not hardly," is Will's comment as he tosses the note aside. Carl thinks, at first, that Will's noting his table etiquette. But Will's looking at his own plate and hasn't seemed to notice the pea maneuver.

"What is it?" Carl's suddenly and unaccountably anxious.

"Someone wants to meet me to tell me something about Renke."

"Tonight?"

"Yeah. I'm supposed to meet him out by the Lake, across the

Park."

"And you won't?"

"No." William corrals his own peas with a chunk of bread. "We know all we need to know, and I want to get to the station, be ready to leave."

Carl nods. It's a good call, maybe unlike Will, but a good call. It adds to Carl's conclusion that Will's eager to get to St. Louis and see Julia.

He's even more convinced Will is moving to some internal motivation when they finish the meal at the same time. Will leads the way to the desk. The bill's appalling, but Carl's portion is less than Will's and, all in all, worth it. Now that they're leaving.

A taxi is waiting, and a porter starts moving their luggage out. Carl takes one last look around at the elegance that has been home for ten days and heads for the door, trailing Will for a change. They almost make it out, when C.R.'s evening replacement calls for Mr. McConnell.

Will sighs loudly and heads back to the desk. A telephone call, it seems. Carl chats with the doorman. He's made friends with a dozen employees, including Leon. He looks back to see Will frowning as he joins them.

"Leon, we need to hold our baggage here, if you will. We'll be leaving a bit later. Police problem." Will looks to Carl and indicates one of the sitting areas.

Will takes his coat off, a bad sign, and throws it on one chair, throws himself in the chair beside it. The long coat slides off the chair onto the floor, and Will ignores it. The coat's new, and Will usually takes better care of it than that. In fact, he's always neater than that. Carl stands in front of him, hands on his hips, waiting.

"That note C.R. gave me. It's probably from . . . an assassin."

Carl hits the chair the coat vacated with a thump, perching on the edge, peering into his friend's face. Will's eyebrows are drawn down, and he's frowning at a palm and batting his hat on the chair arm.

"What? Who rang you?"

"Captain O'Brien. He just got a call from Chief Wright." Will fans the hat some more and tosses it onto a third chair.

"The chief told him someone working covertly in St. Louis overheard Renke arrange to have a man—or two men—out to kill me this evening. Seems Renke got a call from someone here telling him I've been snooping around."

Good Lord. "Who here would have called St. Louis? Minna Everleigh, maybe?"

"I don't know. O'Brien's headed over here to give us the details, he says. Wanted to make sure that I didn't go out. Dammit."

Carl leans back in the chair and then decides to pick up William's coat and fold it into place next to the hat. He takes off his own coat and drapes it over the chair back and settles in. To listen to his own heart thumping and to watch Will, who's picturing something in the palm again.

"She must have been beside herself."

It had to have been Julia, of course, who overheard the plot, but Carl hasn't given that part much thought, being more concerned with getting the hell out of town in one piece.

Will sighs. "At least, there was no mention of you. You can probably get a police escort to the train and head on out."

"I'm hardly going without you."

William shakes his head and twists in the chair. "Good thing we told C.R. not to use your name." He might be talking to the palm.

Carl's formulating questions when O'Brien arrives, practically on the run. The first thing he says is, "McElroy's on his way over. We've got to come up with a plan."

Will sighs one more time and asks what Chief Wright said.

"Well, it seems he's got someone working in Renke's factory. The guy heard—"

"A woman." Will's face is tight.

"Oh. Right. A waist factory, it would be. Anyway, she heard Renke get a phone call from the younger Rosenblatt."

"Rosenblatt?" Carl can't contain his curse. "*Verdammt.* The damn bookkeeper called Renke?" Surely the Rosenblatt family is above dealing with a pervert like Renke, but maybe they only know him as a factory owner and client.

"That would also explain why it's me and not both of us." Will's voice is calm and analytical again. Although, he's still beating the chair arm softly with his hat.

"Yeah, that's the good part," O'Brien says. "We've only got to worry about one of you. Problem is, the woman heard Renke and his thugs talk about a back-up here and a plan in case you make it home, so we've got to figure out something."

Will winces, and Carl judges it isn't about the immediate crisis. Julia will be beside herself indeed. Even if she said she didn't want to marry William, she'll never rest until she's done all she can to ensure his safety. Carl's seen her in action along those lines before.

There's a bustle in the lobby, and McElroy comes striding over. Thank goodness the Chicago cops are on their side.

The four men move into a more private space and hash out the options. Carl gets more worried as they talk. The problem is, the cops can search out by the Lake and pull in one man, maybe the one they have a name for. "Long Gill" they're saying, for Christ's sake? But then they have another man to find. And if Will survives all that, he'll face another threat at home.

The cops seem to know Long Gill, and McElroy says "Cutter" might be a man named, or nicknamed, Cutter Deem. Carl assumes cutter refers to a job, and McElroy says it does indeed, as well as the man's willingness to wield a blade in his second profession in the Levee. O'Brien and McElroy look at each other for a moment, and O'Brien says, "We wouldn't mind losing Gill from our side of town." And they nod at each other. This can turn into a bloodbath, Carl realizes. They should've left last week.

Will's been quiet during the cops' agreement to get rid of the assassins. He looks away and says, "I think I need a plan for dying."

And he simply sits there, letting the cops think through it and leaving Carl to sputter. "You mean you want the word to go out that you died here, let Renke think you're no threat?"

"Yes. For one thing, if I survive, Renke will think I was warned. I don't know how much it would take for him to finger Julia."

Carl goes cold. He isn't sure he'd have thought of that. Of course, he's worrying about Will at the moment. Will's worrying about Julia.

McElroy and O'Brien are impressed as well. And clearly wondering about this Julia. Will ignores the reactions.

"You could go on home, Carl, see what you can get from Bauer, let a few people know. Phone Bowling Green, if you will, and talk to my folks."

"And you can stay here," O'Brien suggests to Will. "Hole up in Chicago until we get this guy."

"No." Will says it as if he's sure he won't do that, and Carl knows, if the cops don't, that he'll do it his way.

"I need a way to get back to St. Louis," Will says. "If I'm going to hide out, I need to do it in familiar territory."

McElroy considers the situation a moment and says, "Well, we could get you to the baggage area at one of the terminals. You could ride baggage or in a cargo car so no one'd see you on the trip. Have a St. Louis officer pick you up there."

William nods. "That's good. Now, how do we make one or both assassins think the job is done?"

The three start throwing out ideas, and Carl rubs a hand over his forehead, hard. The plan gets more and more elaborate. O'Brien rises to call for back-up and some special equipment. Carl goes out to ask the desk clerk to call C.R. back in. He needs one more favor.

34

Carl watches Leon load his luggage into the back of the auto taxi. Will's bags are back inside the door, and Will himself is headed out across the field that is Grant Park. A monument and a couple of benches are out there, but they aren't slowing the cold wind blowing in from the Lake. Blasted place. Carl's happy to leave. What he doesn't want to do is drive away until he knows what happens in the park. But leaving is his role in this intricate drama of deception.

At Central Terminal, he paces, glancing out a window toward the same restless lake, watching the cargo area. It isn't easy to see much in the gloom, but Carl's so relieved to recognize the police auto when it pulls in that he mutters a prayer in German. A slender, consumptive derelict standing a few yards away turns to consider him. The man nods, for some reason, stands still to light a smoke, and strolls off.

Why the man should be of any interest, Carl can't say. A cadaverous chap smoking a cheap cigarette is common enough. Carl's sure he hadn't seen the man at the Congress, and he tries to think how long the man stood there. Just arrived, he decides. Just arrived at this particular window, watching faint movement in an area of little interest.

Carl wouldn't have boarded until the last minute anyway,

regardless of police admonitions to get to a sleeping unit and stay there. So, he decides to follow the slender man through the crowded terminal. He catches up with him easily enough. The man's strolling casually toward the platform and the train Carl himself should be boarding.

It's amazing how many people travel at night. Almost all are men; it must be a good business strategy. A few families herd children on board, and Carl makes note of cars to avoid. He loses track of the man briefly, glimpses him again, and then loses him all together.

Carl wants to see the police put Will on a car, probably at the last minute, and Carl can jump on the nearest Pullman then. Sure enough, as he gets close to the baggage cars, he sees McElroy talking to one of the bulls standing about and making sure no one's bumming a ride—except William.

McElroy sees Carl, too, and heads his way, also strolling. When he gets close, he holds out a hand, as if he and Carl are friends who happened to meet on a winter's night by this particular rail.

"That went right well," is McElroy's greeting. "There was a gunshot, ours, took out Gill, got McConnell in our car before anyone got there. We've got us a dead body, and all anyone heard was a single shot. We can stall this whole thing, say McConnell's missing, for quite a while."

Carl nods and tries to look casual himself. "Will's O.K., ready to board?"

"Oh, yeah, and you should, too, Schroeder." McElroy sticks out his hand again. "It's been a pleasure. Take care of yourself."

Carl smiles, relieved, but not ready to turn his back. "I'm going to stretch a bit more. Don't worry, I won't get left behind." McElroy shrugs, and Carl can sense him shaking his head, as he moves toward the passenger cars.

It's only another fifteen yards or so to where O'Brien has joined the bull to lean against an open door. Unless they're talking to a suitcase, Carl's going to be able to look in and check on Will. As he passes, he looks left and picks up a motion in the dim interior, a salute maybe.

Carl's smiling, therefore, and looking about more confidently, when he sees another motion, off to his right, between two cars of the train holding down the adjacent track. He doesn't slow, just goes to take up a post of his own in the next opening.

O'Brien starts down the platform but ducks between cars to patrol the other side. Carl would like to call to him but doesn't dare. They hope the scene at the Park convinced a second assassin to call the job done. But if there's another assassin in the terminal, the problem's not getting away from him. It's drawing him out. With Will as bait. Maybe that's why the door's still open to Will's baggage car. And why the bull is moving in the other direction.

The conductor makes his first call. At this hour of the night, few farewells are being said, and the platform empties of all but rail employees. They close all the cargo doors except Will's. The police have been thorough.

Carl sees movement in the car, as if Will's checking the platform for himself, checking to see what's happening, offering someone a target.

And the suspicious someone rises to the bait. The thin man moves out, a car down from Carl, tosses a cigarette to the deck in front of his foot, and grinds out the lit end in a practiced move. The next moment he's reaching under his coat. Carl swallows hard and moves out himself. What he's going to do against a man who probably carries a lethal blade, he doesn't know. What he should be doing is calling for help, but he still isn't sure of the timing. The cops could oblige and reappear anytime now.

William apparently sees the man coming as well. He jumps from the door, and stands sideways, reaching back into the car. Will has a gun, but the timing would be a problem there, too.

The thin man draws the knife maybe eight paces from Will. Will responds by tossing a hard-sided case at the man, who simply dodges it, takes two more steps and lunges. Will falls against the car hard, his head snapping against the door's edge. The man pulls back, looking down at his blade, and Carl sees his opportunity.

Carl rarely uses his size except to push through crowds on occasion. Now, both concern and anger fuel his speed as he picks up the tossed suitcase and swings at the man's head.

Carl's shoulder all but cracks, and then his whole arm is stinging. But it works. The assassin collapses, rolling under the car and onto the tracks. The blade clatters further under the car, out of sight.

Carl drops the suitcase from a numb hand and reaches for Will. Who clutches his side and moans as he falls into Carl's arms.

Carl barely has room to lower Will to the platform as O'Brien pulls the thin man from the tracks. McElroy says, "That's Cutter Deem, sure enough." Then both police captains are leaning over Carl's shoulders. They're almost as eager as Carl to know if their plan has worked. Carl considers the blood on his coat sleeve and calls Will's name.

Will can cooperate by letting them know about the plan's success any moment now.

35

*From **The St. Louis Globe-Democrat**, Tuesday, November 1, 1910*

> *Word has been received from Rhode Island of the death from pneumonia of Julia Ward Howe, philanthropist and author of the "Battle Hymn of the Republic." Mrs. Howe, aged 91, was a champion of many causes including abolition, Greek independence, pure milk for infants, and the ballot for women.*

I was miserable, physically and emotionally, last night. In between attempts to get me to sit still for hot cloths on my back, Red and Aaron tried to assure me Chief Wright had gotten word to the Chicago police, and they'd be taking care of William. And Carl. When I insisted the guys should've telephoned the Congress Hotel themselves—instead of letting Jack Forest do it— Aaron went back to Headquarters and begged a long-distance call. A man at the hotel desk said William McConnell had checked out that evening, and he had no further information. Police asking or not.

I finally fell into bed out of exhaustion, said a few more prayers, and slept fitfully.

Morning is early and gray today, and I'm too anxious to talk, to the guys or anyone at work.

We all get to sit down. Farrell, the foreladies, Renke himself, urges us to make up for the slow day yesterday. As if it was our fault.

I think Renke's anxious, too. He keeps the office door open and goes to stand in it a couple of times, staring at the phone, willing it to ring, maybe. The only times he smiles, I'm the target. Esther notes his gaze and looks worried, looks angry even. I don't think she's angry at me, but I'm not at my best. Thoughts of William drift through my mind, like a cloud overhead, and I realize I've slowed to almost nothing.

We sit back down from our afternoon break just as Dexter and Mallory join Renke in the glass office. The break felt good because my back's still aching. I'm not the only woman who stretched the whole ten minutes. I think the cutters must be taking a break as well: huge stacks of bodice pieces wobble at the end of our table.

The telephone rings. It sounds much louder than usual, and I drop the piece I just ran a seam on. I glance up, and so do women near me. We're wary of telephone calls, particularly ones Renke seems to be waiting for.

The men close the door, so my only sense of what they're doing is quick glances. It's like a stereopticon dropping images in front of my eyes. Renke listening, the cutters straining to hear. Renke talking. Mallory with a hand on Dexter's back, maybe in congratulations. Renke hanging up the earpiece with a smile that makes me shiver. All three congratulating each other, the general sound coming through the glass.

I can't look anymore. My hands are moving, but I've dropped the silk piece, so I pick it up and the motion takes forever. Now the stereopticon in my mind drops images even faster, images of William, coming back again and again to the moment he got shot back in June. I had trouble breathing then with fear for him. Now I don't seem to be getting any air at all.

They're still congratulating each other when they emerge from the office. I'm afraid to look up. I hear Mallory tell someone, Farrell, surely, "We got our man."

"Job well done. Keep the waists moving." Renke sounds so damn happy. As long as I don't look at him, I can maybe keep going through the motions.

Why hadn't I tried to contact William last week? As if that would have made a difference. And the only difference I can make now is to nail Renke for something. Maybe murder. Not Meredith's murder. Not the white slave trade. The murder by hire of William McConnell. Or maybe I can simply kill the bastard myself. And if I hang for murder, so be it.

I'm trembling, but my eyes are strangely dry. They must be huge, unfocussed. Because I certainly can't see my work.

I've also lost track of Renke. When he pulls me to my feet, I scream. Not loudly. I don't have the breath. He turns me toward him, and the bastard's laughing. "Time to celebrate." He actually says that, and I respond, "No."

He must think I mean, "No, don't strap me to the table." But I don't care about that. At first. Sometime during the process, with my back already aware the nightmare has returned, I realize that if I'm the only one, it probably means he intends to fire me, maybe proposition me. Why would it be a celebration otherwise? Fine. I can struggle, bobble the work, let him fire me, let him take me to a sporting house, and see him go to jail.

Still, his hand on my back burns, and I can imagine how angry William would be if he could only see me.

I struggle indeed. The tears finally come, but everyone seems to think it's pain that makes me cry. Esther appears to wipe the work area, take a wet piece of silk away from me. She gives me something cotton to work on, and I have no idea what to do with it. She knows I'm gone, tomorrow if not today.

Quitting time happens. The room clears except for Esther and Farrell. They stand talking quietly, off to the side, and I prop myself on my hands. My back feels like it did yesterday afternoon, but today there's no desperation. Only despair. All in all, yesterday was better.

Esther finally leaves, but Farrell stays. The cutters and Renke must have finished checking women out before they come upstairs. I'm busy wondering how much blame for William's death is mine. And praying that Carl escaped.

The three of them crowd around, going through the motions of checking me for stolen items. I want to whimper, but on the chance William's watching, I clinch my teeth instead.

It takes all three to release me and help me down the stairs, assuring me that they'll be watching to see how much work I can do tomorrow, if I can redeem my performance of the last two days. Bastards. Dexter helps me on with my coat by pulling back on my arms. I'd collapse to the floor but he catches me. Renke laughs and keeps taunting me with threats of firing as I make my way out.

I tell myself I should be pleased. Renke will fire me, proposition me, take me off somewhere, and we'll have not only Meredith's murderer, but Will's. But the truth is, I can't imagine anything ever pleasing me again.

I can't say my back hurts much worse than yesterday. The hurt's different and deeper. The mist and haze are the same. And so's the tug on my arm, and Red saying, "What the hell have you done now, gal?"

I have to stay in character to get Renke. I whine. "It wasn't my fault, Enos. Don't hurt me no more."

"Hurt you? I ain't hurting you. But you got to get yourself straight. You can't spend another night whining. I got a job for you tonight."

I whine louder. "A job? Tonight? No, Enos, I can't. My back hurts like crazy, Enos. Just let me go home, Enos."

By now he's dragging me to a streetcar stop, once again in the opposite direction from the flat. I hear the trio laughing behind me. Good. They need to think Enos is a bully. Like them.

Unfortunately, Red stays in character. "What it is, Nance, is Mrs. Edwards. She's got some company and needs some help tonight, and we told her you'd help out. You can do that, now, you can. Her husband thinks maybe he can get Aaron a job with the city, and you need to be nice and help out."

I'm whispering, "No," and it gets louder as we near the car. People are staring again. Enos gives me a shake and tells me to behave myself. It's a wonder there's a seat, and I moan as I drop into it. Red stands in front of me, repeating the situation to the top of my head. I can't get his attention and don't see much point in telling his waistcoat how bad the news of the day is.

When we get off the second car, after a frantic and painful rush to transfer, it looks like we are indeed headed for the Edwards' house. So someone can tell me the news, no doubt. Maybe Chief Wright.

Red says, without much trace of Enos, "What the hell happened? Did he tie up more women?"

"Just me."

"Just you, Jule—Nance? Why?"

Red's unintentional use of my new nickname does it. The tears start flowing, and they won't stop anytime soon. Damn, I hate crying in front of cops. I once told William I'd never do that.

We're almost to the house, and Red struggles to move me along and stay in character and find out what's wrong.

I manage to tell him. "Renke was celebrating. He got word of William's death."

Red jerks my arm and says, "Julia, no!" I don't think he's trying to be obnoxious. "When? How long were you tied?"

I tell him, and he sighs loudly. And then the next moment, he says, "Where are you going, Nance? We go in the side door, not the front. You're hired help tonight. Aaron and me'll pick up some supper, she said we could eat in the kitchen, and then come back and get you later. It'll be fine now. Stop that crying. Aaron should be here already."

I can't figure out why he's suddenly Enos-the-bad or what he's talking about. It's unlikely there's any one around to tell tales to Renke, but Red must think we've been followed. That's surely the only reason he'd ignore my news about William. Unless he already knows it.

He knocks, murmuring, "It'll be O.K., Nance. Buck up, girl," and other nonsense and pushes me in the door when Marta Edwards opens it. I look around for the chief. Not in sight.

"Is she hurt too?" Marta says. I search her face, but she simply looks sympathetic. Red says, "Tied to a damn table again," and then has to apologize for his language.

He takes my arm but gently this time. All Red; no Enos. His blue eyes are huge. "I'm sorry, Julia. I was afraid someone would follow us." He turns me toward the hallway, asking Marta, "Back bedroom?"

"Yes, but knock first."

Strange. I'll take a bed. And a stack of handkerchiefs. But why knock first?

Red puts an arm around my shoulders. "I didn't want to chance anything now. Not now. I was afraid to tell you, didn't know how you'd react. He's here, Julia. He's not dead. They set up a run-in with an assassin and smuggled him out of Chicago, put out word he's missing. But he's here."

I've turned by the time he finishes. His face goes in and out of focus while tears puddle in my eyes and overflow.

"William's alive? Is that what you're saying, Red?"

"I'm sorry I couldn't tell you, Julia. There's even more reason to get Renke after this, and you might be in danger if we're not careful."

I take such a deep breath that I can't seem to exhale. Red reaches for me as I dash to the back bedroom door and open it. Without knocking.

William's sitting on the edge of the bed, his bare back to me. A nasty bruise, parallel to his waist, is boldest on the muscles to either side of the indentation along his spine. A bandage is taped into the thick hair on the back of his head. I finally exhale and try to say his name but not much comes out because now my throat has filled.

Will stands with a groan and turns, bumping into Mike Messerton, who's standing in front of him with a small bowl of something smelly, some homemade liniment involving vinegar, a calm voice in my head says.

"Julia!" William breaks into an honest-to-God, tooth-revealing smile. An even worse bruise shows around a cloth he clutches to his ribs. The cloth with the smelly liniment. I try to smile back.

Mike Messerton says, "Really, Miss Nye, you could give us a minute." He's frowning at me, and the same calm part of my mind finds prudery funny coming from the captain of the Eighth.

William's bending over slowly to pick up a towel and saying, "It's

O.K., Mike," when Red takes my arm one more time. He pulls me backwards and then pushes me toward the door, saying, "She can wait in the hall for a minute." William's still smiling at me.

I smile back as Red hands me out to Aaron. I can wait. For a minute. It will take me that long to get my breath, compose myself a bit. I'll watch the door, and he won't get away. Marta appears beyond Aaron with a wet towel in her hands.

But the door's still open, and I hear Messerton say, "Is she hurt again? Or still?"

William says, "Hurt? At the factory?"

Red's voice is jerky with anger. "She got to spend another several hours standing, tied to the damned sewing table—and listening to Renke brag he'd gotten rid of McConnell."

Messerton says, "Oh, shit." And then, "Take it easy, Mac."

I pull away from Aaron and turn back because I hear movement. The three men jam up in the doorway, as if the cops are trying to slow William down. Maybe because he isn't really dressed.

Behind me, Marta says, "Mr. McConnell!"

He's managed to pull up suspenders and is shrugging a shirt on over them, but he clearly isn't going to take time to button it. Given other circumstances, I'd like to stare, but just now I can't look away from Will's face. He's hurting. For me. I hold out a hand and hope he'll take it.

He does. He folds it in both of his and kisses my knuckles. It's a sentimental gesture for us. I'd done that when he'd been shot earlier this year, and I was trying to keep him alive and figure out how I could care so much about a man I'd only known for a few days. I hadn't understood my reaction or the kiss then. I understand them now. All I have to do is convince William.

Messerton asks, "Does she need to sit down?"

Red says, "Why don't you two sit in front of the fire? Mac was thawing out there earlier, and I bet that heat'd feel good on Julia's back."

That leads Marta to insist I lie down instead so she can put the hot towel on my back. And some of the liniment. Red scores again when he says, "Let's go think all this through, Captain," and pushes everyone ahead of him to the kitchen, Marta sputtering.

William and I scarcely look away from each other as we hold hands and make our way to the fireplace. Concern and relief play across his expressive eyebrows. We groan as we try to help each other down to the stone hearth and laugh lightly at our clumsiness.

William's immediately more serious as we settle in, and it feels like he's going to let go of my hand. I tighten my grip.

"William, I thought you were dead."

"I heard. Christ, Julia, I'm sorry about that. We couldn't think of a way to get word to you without exposing your ruse." He takes a deep breath and winces as it must hurt his bruised rib.

"Julia, I have to apologize. I let the cops think we're still seeing each other." He looks down at my hand, squeezes it, and lays it in my lap. When he looks up, there's a knot between his eyebrows, not so much a frown as an expression I've never seen. "I know I have no standing—"

"You have any standing you want, William." I grab his hand back and whisper fiercely.

The knot between his eyebrows loosens a bit. "I admit I hoped to see you. That was my plan, to get back into town, make some excuse to get word to you, ask if we could talk." He glances at our hands and then looks directly at me. "I came home determined to convince you I'm not . . . overly protective . . . not going to try to control you. I want the chance to explain to you that . . . I'm not like other men."

He's working so hard that it hurts to hear. I lean in and kiss him lightly on the mouth. My back twinges, but I hardly care.

"William, I know that, and I've wanted to tell you since I saw you that day in the factory." I offer a small smile. "I've practiced what I'd say if I only got to see you for a moment. Do you want to hear it?"

Will opens and closes his mouth and leaves it to his eyebrows to say, "Of course."

Now that the moment's at hand, I take a deep and careful breath. "I don't think my causes and the vote and my . . . concerns . . . are any less important than they were three weeks ago, William. But nothing is more important to me than you."

He offers another real smile. And a happier deep breath. Then he slides off the hearth to his knees and pulls me to him. Carefully. "Don't let me hurt you," he says.

"You're hurt worse." I put my arms around him, under the open shirt, trying to keep one hand above and one below the bruise on his back, shifting to his right to avoid the bruise in front. His first reaction says he's shocked. His second says he likes it.

He runs one hand up my neck, pushing his fingers into the thick strands of hair. He nudges the back of my head gently and presses his mouth to my forehead. Then he whispers, "I've been kicking myself. What kind of fool loves a woman so much and walks off without telling her?"

I hug him tighter and find his mouth with mine.

I should've figured Marta Edwards wouldn't stay in her kitchen, although I'm not sure whether it's prudery, medical concern, or curiosity that makes her nags at both of us. "Mr. McConnell, Miss Nye! Really! You're hurt. And you're not . . . well, the two of you . . . you're not even dressed, Mr. McConnell."

Because her concerns are directed at William, I let him answer her. I give him a bit of help, whispered in his ear. "Marry me, please, William."

He gives me another look I've never seen before, eyes wide, eyebrows tilted up. I think—hope—it's pleased surprise.

He stands slowly, helping me up to the hearth in the same move. Beyond him, we have an audience in the doorway across the hall.

"Mrs. Edwards, I appreciate your concern, but please understand. Julia and I are engaged to marry. We haven't seen each other, or been able to write, in a fortnight, and we've both been in danger. We've been worried sick about each other, Mrs. Edwards. If you're concerned we're going to do something unseemly on your living room floor . . . well, I don't think either of us could manage it right now. But if you want to find a justice of the peace, go ahead. Although . . . I'd pictured a wedding where we both could stand up straight."

The kitchen erupts in laughter—and applause. Marta Edwards' hands fly to her mouth, and then she goes right to the point. "Oh, I didn't know you're engaged. I'm sorry." And turns to flee. Seeing her audience across the hall, she stops and redirects her steps. "I'll get some more wood for that fire." She heads down the hallway.

I try not to laugh out loud. William turns awkwardly to sit by me. He's groaning and laughing at the same time and trying to stifle both.

I whisper. "Was that a 'yes'?"

"Absolutely." He runs a hand over my cheek. "It was a serious proposal, wasn't it?"

"Absolutely!"

I need to be closer. I also need to tell him I'm sorry I hurt him with my stubbornness. And, I'll do that. Soon. Right now, I want to run my hands over bare skin, broad shoulders, taut tummy, but I'm afraid I'll touch the yellow and purple bruise. And I worry about his head wound. So, I scoot toward him, gesture at the bruise, and say, "How did this all happen, Will?"

He sighs. "We had a plan. We thought one of the men after me would have a knife, and he did. But I was wearing a vest under my shirt, made of twisted metal leaves and backed with tight silk. The cops in Chicago came up with it—the ones who patrol the nasty neighborhoods. Messerton's fascinated with it. The metal caused the bruise, bent in by the force of the blow. And when the man attacked, I fell back against the door edge of a baggage car, hit my head, bruised my back."

My tears start again, and Will seems to reach for a handkerchief in a pocket he doesn't have. He wipes my cheek with his hand before he continues.

"The plan was to have a cop close to take the assassin out, but it turned out to be Schroeder who delivered the blow."

"Carl was there?"

"Naturally. He hit the man on the head with a suitcase. Knocked him out cold. When the guy came to, the cops told him he'd killed me. They also told a couple of papers a reporter from St. Louis has gone missing. The idea is to confuse matters for a while."

William seems pleased with the tale. But then he gets more serious. "I'm so sorry you had to hear it that way, Julia. A lot of people are going to read the premature news of my death, and I hope some of them are saddened. But not you."

Lordy. And this man thinks I take chances. I crawl into his lap and hold him as tight as I can. I don't care if I hurt him. He deserves it.

36

Carl wakes late in the afternoon from his nap. Music, bad music, filters in from the parlor, and that must mean his sister Lenna is giving a piano lesson. It's why he insists his sisters give lessons only when he's normally at work.

The morning was difficult. He'd had to explain every detail to Evelyn Kinkade, Will's sister, in Bowling Green. When he got back to his office, Zimmerman was happy enough with the German stories and Carl's edge on this new one about McConnell going missing. On the other hand, he isn't even sure Jack Forrest believed him. He'd finally had to say he'd see if the police can get Forrest word from William, wherever Will's holed up.

Normally, Carl would be covering election news. Demonstrations and fisticuffs proliferate over the prohibition vote coming up on Tuesday. Two weeks ago, he would've said there's no issue he feels more strongly about than the defeat of that stupid prohibition amendment. And, he still cares about the election, in principle. Covering it isn't his priority right now.

Having gotten through the morning, he faces a difficult evening. Cops are going to have all sorts of questions, and he isn't sure how much Chief Wright has told anyone. Worse yet, he has to do his job and still find time to get to Arnold Bauer. The faster he finds Bauer and gets those damn books, the faster the whole nightmare will end.

In fact, he'll look up Bauer first, starting with beer gardens close to his home, and move north, toward work.

The evening's chilly for November in St. Louis, and a cold rain has started. That makes it balmy by Chicago standards. Carl's warm enough, still using the heavy coat, gloves and muffler he'd taken to Chicago, and it's a good thing, because he's on his fifth beer garden when he finds Bauer.

Luckily, Carl's losing patience and getting aggressive. His attitude moves other patrons out of his way, and there's Bauer, sitting by himself in a back corner. When Arnold sees him, the little man turns and seems to look for an opening in the wall.

Carl picks up a chair without breaking stride and puts it down with a thud at Bauer's table. "Sit back down." He isn't sure if Bauer stood to greet him or to flee.

"What's wrong, Mr. Schroeder?" Bauer's whispering, probably because he can't get his breath.

"What do you think's wrong, Bauer? What's going on with your Mr. Renke?"

"Nothing." Bauer stares at Carl for a few beats and looks into his beer. The half-full one. Two empties sit on Carl's side of the table.

Carl leans closer. "What's going on at Renke's factory?"

"I don't know what you mean."

"Has Renke mentioned William McConnell?"

Bauer looks up, swallows, and can't seem to answer.

"Do you know what's happened to McConnell?"

Bauer shakes his head, jerking it back and forth.

"Well, I'll tell you something, Arnold. I don't either. But he's missing. He was leaving a hotel in Chicago and disappeared. I don't think that sounds too good, do you?"

Bauer jerks his head a few more times.

"And I happen to know he was asking about the accounting books, maybe the ones you said Renke brought from Chicago. Let me explain this clearly, Arnold: William McConnell is my best friend. If anything has happened to him because of those damn books, I will at least have them myself. That means you need to get them for me."

Carl sits back with a thump. A waiter appears cautiously, and Carl shoots him a look that sends him running back to the bar. Bauer's simply sitting there, trying to breathe. Damn it all, this whole thing is uncivil, and Carl wants it to end now.

He glares. He doesn't glare often, but it's worth a try. Bauer swallows repeatedly and finally says, "What books?"

Carl slams both hands on the table, and an empty stein topples and rolls off the table edge. Carl doesn't listen to hear if it breaks. "Come on now, Arnold."

Bauer moves back in his chair. Carl can see him trembling, can see his mouth working. Finally, the man says, "I can't tell you. Renke would kill me."

"Kill you? Has Renke said something to you about the books already?" Carl jumps to his feet. "Tell me, Arnold."

Bauer looks around and tries to motion Carl to be quiet. Carl sits to hear Bauer whisper, "I'm sorry Mr. McConnell is . . . missing. I liked him. But there's no sense in me being dead, too. I don't know where the books are. Renke's taken them someplace."

Damn. The man's likely telling the truth. Bauer obviously knows Renke targeted Will. Maybe that will be useful if the most they can come up with is attempted murder-for-hire. Meanwhile, Bauer's scared and probably should be and probably doesn't know where the books are.

Arnold's trying to stand very slowly. Carl looks him into his seat.

"What was in those books, Arnold? You can't tell me you hadn't looked in them."

Bauer's eager to answer that question. "I did look in them. It was just journal entries. Single-entry stuff. About fabric and salaries, and so on. I didn't see anything suspicious, Mr. Schroeder." Carl eases back, and he can see that makes Arnold more confident.

"You know, Mr. Schroeder, I don't think there's anything in those books that's . . . bad. What would there be? I think someone just asked about them, and Mr. Renke got all stubborn. People do that, you know?"

Bauer's bobbing his head now and urging Carl to agree.

Carl sighs and leans forward again. Arnold doesn't move. Damn.

"One last thing, Arnold. A number of people know I'm talking to you." Carl can't quite think who knows, at the moment, but that doesn't matter. "If anything happens to me, if I go missing like Mr. McConnell, you'll be the one the police will be after. If I were you, I wouldn't talk to Mr. Renke about me."

"Oh, yes sir, Mr. Schroeder. I wouldn't have to mention anything about it."

Carl stands to leave without thanking the man or saying good-bye. Arnold keeps blithering, "I mean, no sir, you just happened to stop by. I wouldn't mention that."

Carl keeps walking and hopes Arnold Bauer won't talk. And that Julia will keep her ears open for mention of his own name at her work. He certainly hasn't managed to move the case along any, so she might as well continue at the factory. Although Carl wants badly to see her, wants badly to see Will for that matter. Instead, he heads out to look for police news, worrying over what he might find.

37

*From **The St. Louis Globe-Democrat**, Wednesday, November 2, 1910*

> *Voters will go to the polls in less than a week to decide whether or not the sale and consumption of alcohol will continue to be allowed in the State. Proponents of prohibition and their opponents have a week of demonstrations scheduled in venues from Forest Park to the Courthouse steps.*

I know what's coming. I try to remember how I acted yesterday afternoon, letting the pain roll off me with my sorrow. But there's no sorrow now. There's a smile I fight to keep off my face as I walk into the factory. This is going to take acting skill, and I'm not sure I have it.

My back really does feel better. The hot towels and the liniment helped. When Red insisted I tear myself away from William and get home to bed, I was so tired it almost didn't distress me to leave. I have a long list of wonderful things to think about: wedding plans, where we'll live, holding Will again, how I'll continue to work for women's rights as a married woman. And why I'd thought that would be a problem. I can't quite remember.

There are darker thoughts, of course. William didn't take time to tell me all he'd found out about Oscar Renke, but I know he's angry about what Renke did in Chicago and concerned about what he might yet do here. And today will not be pleasant. Renke and company made that plain yesterday. We took time last night to form a plan for after work today.

Sure enough, Renke and his cutters are waiting downstairs when I appear. At the last minute, I wipe the grin off my face outside, and realize immediately I won't have to act. Reacting will do fine.

The two cutters stand on either side of me, Dexter actually holding my arm as if I might bolt, as Renke sits on the edge of one of the lunch tables and explains my "predicament." He obviously will have to punish me today because I've done such bad work lately. In fact, Mr. Mallory has been so kind as to cut some cotton for me to work on, but if I can't get the stack done by the end of the day, it will be my last day drawing twenty-two cents an hour for Justice Waists. In case I fail, I should have my cousin come talk to Mr. Renke first thing in the morning. I suppose he says that in case I'm too befuddled by evening to hear him.

Mallory takes my lunch and bag, and Dexter once again enjoys helping me with my coat. Roughly. I'm relieved to hear what Renke has to say and angry at the same time. Despite the fact I need the bastard to fire me and then talk to my bully of a cousin, I resent the implication that I can't do the work. How silly. When what really makes me tremble is the touch of Dexter's hands.

He pulls me up the stairs. Everyone has settled in to work already. Farrell sighs when he sees me, and Esther looks distressed. Women who can, stare.

There's no stool in sight for me. There's a stack of cheap cotton bodices and one already made up. It has lots of pleats and will be hard to duplicate, if not as tricky as the silk. Mallory stands by the door of the office, smiling, while Dexter and Renke do the honors with the apron and the strap. I clinch my fists on the table until Renke puts a hand on my neck, pulls me back as far as I can go, and says, "Try it, my dear."

By morning break, my back muscles have used up all the relief provided by liniment and hot towels. Other women stand while I lean on my hands and tell myself this is such a waste of everyone's energy.

By lunch time, I hurt badly enough I'm not sure I could eat. I'm hungry, but the thought of going down the stairs makes my stomach clench.

By the afternoon break, I fight not to call out for William. I'm doing no more than pushing fabric around. I haven't touched the machine for half an hour. I'm telling myself I will not collapse until the bell signals quitting time and sweet relief. Esther comes over to me, probably because Renke's downstairs and the cutters upstairs. She says, "I'm sorry, my dear. You really are a very good seamstress."

Then she whispers in my ear, "Say no to them. Have your menfolk say no."

I'm distracted for a while, thinking that if we can close down the operation, she might testify. Farrell even looks sympathetic. Surely they can testify that the same thing happened to Meredith and Hannah.

Then the women start work again, and I'm not thinking about anything but the burning in my back, the numbness down my legs, the tingling in my arms, the pounding in my head.

When quitting time happens, I topple onto the machine. I really don't care. I only care that I stayed upright as long as I have. Whatever Renke and Mallory are saying is lost.

I worried about getting down the stairs, but in the event I'm not aware of it. I'm on the floor under the rack and whimpering when Dexter uses his best technique for helping me into my coat.

And then I'm outside, sitting in what has become a steady rain, sitting in front of Justice Waists on the sidewalk and crying. Red comes to drag me to a streetcar, and it occurs to me how frantic I'd be if I really depended on this job.

I limp and groan most of the way from the streetcar, and then Red carries me. I try to relax in his arms and not think about much except the jolt of his steps, particularly going up the stairs. I must be getting heavy, and he's moving slowly from one step to another.

My bed hurts me. I try to call for William, and it's Aaron's hand on my mouth, shushing me. "Just wait."

Red has laid me on my back, and the damn corset makes it hurt worse. I can't seem to turn to either side, so I decide not to move. Aaron has put two blankets over me, and I'm trying to unbutton my coat under the covers. My hands aren't working well. Shaking too hard.

The voices in the kitchen are suddenly loud, something about a boarder. Lordy, Red has finally found his boarder. Tonight? What in tarnation is he thinking? I sob, loudly, and then the new boarder is the one trying to quiet me. Oh, yes, the plan.

Red and Aaron are in the living room, talking loudly enough for me to hear and, therefore, loudly enough to inform the neighbors in the hall that the new boarder can set up a bed in this room because we don't use it anyway.

I stare at William's dark hair. Disguises everywhere, this one thanks to dark henna, I think. Then he's pulling me into his arms and kissing his favorite place on my forehead, and I can smell the pomade he's used to slick his hair back instead of letting it fall in its natural part. Not that I care. I bury my face in his cold coat and sob.

38

*From **The St. Louis Globe-Democrat**, Friday, November 4, 1910*

> *Two suffragettes from Chicago, who are conducting an auto tour headed for St. Louis, were ordered off the streets last night by the Chief of Police of Greenville, Ill., when the Mayor of that town came to their rescue and allowed them to continue their pronouncements. In addition to calling for votes for women, the two are attacking Illinois state officials for not enforcing child labor laws.*

By Friday morning, my back's better. I might smell permanently of turpentine and apple vinegar, but I manage to get into the corset.

William and Aaron go out to look for work shortly after that, and Red drags me along to the Edwards. We're having a serious meeting and all arriving at different times and through different ruses. Chief Wright and Alexander Reed, a senior assistant district attorney, are supposed to arrive for breakfast. We chose this morning instead of yesterday evening because William insisted Carl attend. William went out late last night and telephoned to tell him about the meeting, tell him about our engagement. Carl's taking credit for saving our courtship. Maybe he did.

William and I have had lots of time to talk in a day and two nights. At first, I let him hold me and tell me stories of skyscrapers and police stations, Paul Rosenblatt's rooms, and Minna Everleigh's brothel. It will be wonderful if Carl can get Arnold Bauer to cough up the books. But a small part of me is bothered. I want Renke to be found guilty of Meredith Magruder's death. Maybe Hannah's as well.

Even if that doesn't happen, I want it to be a St. Louis offense, not the Chicago investigation, that gets Renke. And that seems likely, because we think Carl would've let us know immediately if he'd found the books.

On the other hand, we probably can't get Renke for hiring two men to murder William. I was unfortunately honest in telling Red I hadn't heard William's name. Even though events proved me right, a good defense attorney would destroy the link between the assassins and Renke.

Before we turned in last night, I managed an apology.

"Will, I'm sorry I was so angry . . . that night."

Will slid his arm off my shoulders and looked at me a moment. "You were angry from the get-go. What was the problem?"

I replayed what the chief had said, and Will barely let me finish.

"Wright let you believe I'd said that? Christ, Julia, no wonder you were angry. You know I wouldn't say that behind your back . . . don't you?"

I choked up again, nodded hard, and put my arms around him. He muttered while he caressed my hair, back in its braid for the night. I finally managed to say, "And then I was angry at the Castella, and I know you were right to be protective. Whoever it was."

After a kiss that lasted a satisfying few minutes, Will said, "Bauer. Wouldn't you know? I assume you didn't see him at the factory. And I hope he didn't see you there—or at the Castella."

I assured him I hadn't been anywhere near the office to see a bookkeeper, and we returned to my nonverbal apology.

This morning I find I'm anxious being away from Will, given the threats all around, and I'm relieved to see him arrive with Aaron at the Edwards's. And then Carl arrives. I give him a big smile and start to jump to my feet when my back catches. I recover quickly, but not before William grabs my arm, and Red says, "Be careful." So, Carl has to hear what the problem is, and he's upset. And is going to be more upset with what's likely to happen next.

Oscar Renke explained to Enos yesterday that I clearly can't handle the pressure of working for a sophisticated operation like Justice Waists, and that he won't recommend me for work any place else in the city. He knows it'll be hard on the family, and so he's come up with a job he thinks I can handle.

I'm fuming as Red plays all this back for Carl's benefit and for Alexander Reed. Aaron and Red and William are amused at my reaction, but everyone gets serious as Red explains the proposition.

Renke's offering me a job as seamstress in one of his "operations" in Kansas City. He'll pay Enos and Aaron a lump sum payment of $250 for my services. That's almost half a year's salary at my new wage given that work isn't steady in the garment industry. I'll get room and board and some spending money if "everything works out."

Chief Wright, who greeted me in fatherly mode, groans and says, "We just can't put you in any more danger, my dear. What operation could he have except a sporting house?"

"A pornography operation. Photography." William speaks quietly, looking at Carl, not me.

Carl must be in brotherly mode. He leans forward to get my attention.

"Julia, we know, from the Chicago cops, all that Renke and those two goons are capable of. You don't want to spend even a few hours, let alone a night, in their keeping."

Messerton says, "So, Schroeder. Did you get the books?"

Carl thuds back in his chair and glares. I don't like this new, tense personality. I miss the sunlit smile and the breezy busyness.

"Bauer won't give us the books because he says Renke will kill him." Carl mutters into a coffee cup. "He claims not to know where they are, that Renke has put them someplace. That line isn't going to work."

"Well, then, we get a warrant to look for the books," Reed says.

Irwin Edwards speaks up. "But if we can't find them, if he's destroyed them, then we've spooked him, let him know we're after him. He won't do anything illegal until he thinks we're not watching. And that could be a long time."

Carl says, "Isn't that good? Don't we want him to stop abusing women?"

"We could just drive him deeper underground if we spook him. And Mac and Julia would be in danger. He'll figure out he didn't get Mac and come after them." Red's so serious when he answers, his voice shakes.

"I see your point," Reed says. "So, if we can get him on anything, we can put him away and then go looking for the books."

"Maybe if we arrest him for something, Bauer will talk," William adds.

Chief Wright has been strangely quiet. "We can't get him on anything, Mac, without Julia taking the offer. Do you want her to do that?"

"That's her call, Chief, not mine."

Carl groans, and the chief snorts. "I hear you're engaged."

Will smiles at him. "That's right, Chief. Congratulate me."

The chief slaps the table. "Be serious, Mac. It's your wife we're talking about."

"And if you hadn't heard about the engagement, you'd think she's my girlfriend. Either way, it's her call, Chief. I want to take every precaution we can think of, but we can't get Renke on the Chicago charges without the books, and we can't get the books without arresting Renke for something here. If Julia doesn't want to do it, we wait for Renke to incriminate himself some other way. I don't doubt he'll do that—the question is how soon."

Messerton looks from William to me. "If we don't get Renke soon, what's Mac going to do? Stay dead for six months?"

Will's quick to say, "That's not a consideration, Mike."

But I can honestly say, "I've considered that, Captain."

And that puts all the cards on the table. William and I've talked, of course, but I haven't made up my mind. I want to hear what the plans might be. At least, that's what I've told myself, what I've told Will.

I ask, "When does he want me to go—and what would we do? Are we trying to get him on kidnapping? Or just enticement?"

Little smiles on the men's faces say, "Isn't it cute how she throws those words around?" I sigh, and all of them get serious.

Red sighs, too, and explains. "He wants you to show up in the morning at a quarter 'til eight, after the shift starts, at the factory." He adds, "He says he needs to know today, Julia. To make plans, have the cash ready."

I judge Carl and the chief want me to say no by the way they twist in their seats. Messerton and Edwards want me to try it. Reed probably falls into that camp: he's nodding as they are. Red and William are really leaving it up to me. I can't read Aaron, who's leaning against a doorframe, silent and frowning. Marta Edwards is clutching a towel.

"How far would he have to get me for it to be kidnapping? That's the most serious charge we can hope for, isn't it?" I ask Reed. It occurs to me rape would carry a longer sentence. It likely occurs to everyone, but no one wants to say it.

"If he told Witherspoon he was going to take you to Kansas City, and then he took you against your will as far as the train station, I'd say we could convince a jury." Reed's fiddling with a pen and pad, making notes. He looks up. "You'd have to resist somehow. It would be his word against yours unless you object in public. Or unless he manages to restrain you somehow and still walk through the Station."

Lordy.

Reed wiggles the pen and says, "Of course, there'd be charges of operating a brothel if you get that far and see evidence of him appearing to be in charge. And enticement if we can prove it's clear that he intends to confine you. The pornography hardly carries enough to bother with except it would give us an excuse to go after the books. All in all, about twenty to thirty if we can get a sympathetic jury."

I nod.

Messerton glances at the chief and turns back to me. "We can have people watching the factory. If he takes you to the Station and you resist, that should get you witnesses, and we can arrest him there."

Carl flounces again in his seat. "And what if she doesn't appear for a while? What do you suppose could happen in that factory, in a back room or a basement? What about Mallory and Dexter? All three of them have bad reputations in the Levee."

You could conjure with the word "Levee," and Carl has used it to good effect. And he's right: I'm as afraid of the two cutters as of Renke himself.

"And"— Carl lowers his voice, and looks at Will, not me—"what if it's a trap? What if he's known all along who she is?"

I take a second to glance around the table. Everyone knows how serious that question is.

I shake my head. "First of all, he's had his eye on me from the beginning." Yes, he has, I now realize, although I'm still not sure why. "And secondly, he wouldn't have given me the raise."

"Not that you've gotten any of that money yet," Red says.

"No." I agree with a nod to him. "But it seems a nudge to get you—to get my family—to agree when the time came. He didn't know he wouldn't have to actually pay me. He wasn't planning to celebrate so soon."

That evokes groans and a German curse from Carl.

"So. Red would take me to the factory, get paid, and Renke presumably would take me to the Station. We're not sure how he'd restrain me and still get me to move in public. I'd have to be sure to object enough." This time all the men are silent and staring while I think. "But we don't have to know the details. He'll have a plan for getting me there. I just have to fight back."

There are more groans at that. But Red needs an answer, and I'm ready. I'm looking at Will when I say, "I think we have to chance it."

There are nods and mutters, and Messerton says, "Let's think of all that can go wrong."

◆　◆　◆

By evening, William and I have gone through the whole list. We sit at the table in the front room of the flat and assign odds. We think there's little chance, say one in fifty, that Renke knows I work for the police. We think there's about a one in four chance that the cops will somehow lose me and I'll end up in Renke's custody. Given that option, we think there's something like a one in five chance that I'll be raped or otherwise molested before the police can find me, and a one in three chance I'll suffer some lesser damage. Our heads tell us this is a reasonable risk for the chance to nab Renke. Our hearts aren't so sure.

William is having trouble talking through jaws that clench every few minutes. He must be fighting the urge to tell me to call it off. But he won't do that, no matter what the odds. I feel bad for him and move my chair closer to his. We manage to embrace, and the kissing and caressing go on for a while. Finally, William draws back to look at me, a look that tells me what he's thinking, asking. I don't know if it will make the morning better or worse, but the night will certainly be more comforting.

He heads to the kitchen to have a word with Red and Aaron and, soon enough, they're on their way to the Green Parrot, announcing loudly that they're going to celebrate coming into some money in the morning. I don't know what they're thinking, but they're probably as worried about the morning as we are and happy to have us take our pleasure.

Many of the women in my circle assert that men care only about their own pleasures in bed. Of course, I'd have said William was likely to be pleasantly different. To say I underestimated him along those lines is an understatement itself.

Still, the morning looms, and we alternate between delight and worry.

39

*From **The St. Louis Globe-Democrat**, Saturday, November 5, 1910*

> *Headquarters for betting on election outcomes Tuesday is the Rozier Hotel, where the odds are on the size of the vote against prohibition. One St. Louis banker who dabbles in politics, is said to have placed $10,000 in various small bets ranging from 100,000 to 200,000 vote majorities.*

The easy part is acting terrified. The hard part is leaving William at the flat, his eyebrows stark lines saying he's terrified as well.

After all the talk and the loving, we'd gotten down to the nitty-gritty: the implications for our relationship. Finally, William said, "There's nothing anyone can do to you that will make me love you any less." This morning, he simply took my hands and looked me in the eye. "Remember what I said."

As Red pulls me and steadies me through the streets, the weather suddenly sunny and crisp, it occurs to me Renke might think of things that will make me love myself less. I vow I won't let that happen. If William McConnell can watch his wife-to-be walk into sexual slavery for a cause, I can at least keep my focus on that cause as well.

Brave talk. I'm clutching Red's arm when we enter the office door of Justice Waists. Renke smiles briefly, and Red almost calls it off right there, judging from his face. But Renke doesn't give him time. He pulls me away and hands Red an envelope thick with bills.

"Count it," he says, and when Red starts to do that, Renke drags me into the lunchroom. I look back, and Red is clenching the wad of bills in a fist, clenching his jaw against saying anything.

The lunchroom's empty, and Renke says, "Hurry up, Nance. We got a tight schedule here. Take off your hat."

Good, I tell myself. We should move things along. Carl's with the cops in the building across the street. More cops are at Union Station. Chief Wright, William, Alexander Reed, and Red will gather in a meeting room in the Harvey Restaurant.

Renke takes my hat from me and drags me down the back stairs to a basement. I see a ramp that must lead up to the alley. And big flat carts for moving boxes up and down the incline. And there're stacks of boxes, some of which have labels indicating fabric, some of which probably hold parts for machines, and some of which are empty, waiting for the cardboard boxes of waists being assembled upstairs. I picture Esther and wish I could talk to her.

Instead, we come to a stop and I'm looking at another woman. Maybe Renke has bought two women in celebration. This one's wearing a chemise and petticoats over her underthings and stamping with the cold that comes down the ramp from the street. She's talking—or maybe trying not to talk—to Dexter and Mallory. I stare at her, and she stares back. She's tall, shapely, dark-haired. And she looks familiar, but I can't remember where I've seen her. That alone would be worrisome if I had any more capacity to worry.

The cutters must have put in time early to get waists done so they can help out. Arrangements indeed. It's obvious they have this planned down to the minute.

They walk toward me, and I try to pull away. Mallory grabs my other arm. I scream, "No," and think how pleased Reed will be. Provided, of course, the other woman can or will testify. I'm getting ready to repeat it, explain that I want to leave, when Dexter shoves a braided piece of cloth into my open mouth. Mallory puts a hand in my hair to hold my head still while Dexter ties the braided strip behind my head. So much for protesting, verbally at least.

Carl predicted this, with his warnings of what he'd heard of the three. They have this down to an art. One of them moves behind me and pulls off the sweater I wore in place of a heavier coat. I can't tell who's holding my arms tight behind me while Renke unbuttons my waist, and then undoes my belt and the waistband of my skirt.

You can't really say I fight them. I gasp and struggle, but they have my waist and skirt off in no time. I watch them toss the garments to the waiting woman, and I hardly realize it when they move me into position under a ring, like the one that holds the curtains upstairs. They strap my wrists to the device and turn their attention to "Delilah." She seems relieved to have something to wear. This isn't going to go as we planned.

Sure enough, as soon as she slips on my sweater and pins on my hat, Renke hurries her off, toward the stairs. They rush past me and Renke says, "Just in case your cousin changes his mind." I twist to watch them leave and see the woman glance back at me. Will the cops across the street follow, thinking it's me? What if they try to arrest Renke at the Station and find a willing partner on his arm? Where will I be by then? Which thought makes me turn back to Dexter and Mallory.

They're close and laughing, no doubt at the look on my face.

Maybe they need to get back to work, but more likely they enjoy wielding their knives as quickly as they can, cutting the rest of my clothes off and tossing the scraps into a pile. They have a good laugh, while they work, over the corset cover, and I tell myself I'm glad to see it go. Not that my eyes are open.

I open them after a bit but don't look up. Those are Mallory's hands, going through the motions of feeling for contraband, out of habit perhaps. Dexter comes rushing over and says, "Here, stop feeling her and use the tape."

The word tape scares me because I suppose they mean a tape that will bind. But Dexter hands Mallory a seamstress's measuring tape, and Mallory uses it in all the standard places. I struggle for a moment, but Dexter grabs my chin, looks me in the eye, and says, "Stop it." I do. In fact, I almost stop breathing for fear of what I see.

It probably takes Mallory five minutes to call off numbers to Dexter, who's making notes in a small memo book. The length from neck to waist, the measurement around my waist, around my bust, the distance from waist to mid-hip and waist to ankle, the measure from shoulder to wrist. Mallory has to stretch for that one. Everything down to the quarter inch. "Got it," Dexter says, jamming the book in a coat pocket. "Let's get her dressed."

They start with boots, heavy and too big, men's I would guess. Without thinking I start to kick, and Mallory sees it coming. He grabs a breast, and I'm too busy trying to scream again to pay any attention to Dexter. I'm frantic when Mallory steps away from me. I try to get my feet back under me and look down to see that the boots are held on by the irons around my ankles. There's maybe half a foot of chain slack on the floor.

Mallory is fastening a skirt around my waist, made of coarse gray fabric and buttoned down the front. The skirt reminds me of prison garb, and with good reason, I realize a moment later.

The top is a tunic. It has a large neck and is going to show more than an appropriate prison outfit ought. They have to release my wrists to get it on me, of course, but I can't run. Dexter holds my arms while Mallory takes the predictable wrist cuffs out of a box and secures them. Dexter chuckles in my ear while Mallory pulls a chain tight around my waist. It's long. He threads it through the metal links between my wrists and connects it to the chain between my feet. And I'd panicked when they strapped me to a table.

They step back to admire their work. I stand there helpless and twitching. The prison garb smells bad, as if it's been wadded up damp and then mildewed. The smell makes it harder to breathe. They look pleased.

Dexter motions me to walk toward him. He laughs as I struggle. I have to lean forward to make enough slack to walk.

He keeps backing up and motioning. When he gets to one of the flat carts, he motions me onto it. I stand there, gasping for air through my nose. Mallory growls and lifts me. I intend to stand, but he pushes me to my knees. I land on a sturdy, long rope draped across the cart. Mallory ties another strip of cloth over my mouth, for good measure, I guess. Then he starts on my hair.

He tosses pins on the floor and pulls it all down. He ties it at the nape and then starts braiding it loosely. How ironic. Corsetless, hair braided down my back. Maybe it'll be easier for the cops to recognize me.

Dexter steps up and ceremoniously slips a small chain over my head, to lie on top of the braid in back. The key that dangles from it looks like the key that will unlock the irons and the cuffs. I've seen keys like that in Dad's jail. I start crying about then. Dexter pulls out the front of the tunic and drops the key in. It's cold between my breasts. He runs a hand over my face and catches a tear.

Then there's the veil. Dexter slaps the small brim on my head, pins it on, and drapes the veil front and back. It's just past my breasts and dark enough I can barely see through it. Damn.

Mallory arranges my feet so I can sit back on them. The rope comes up over my legs and under my hands and he yanks it tight. I groan, but I can't hear that I've made much noise, and that's as bad as the pains. Then he pushes me forward. The long ends of the rope come up over my back, and I'm folded as tight as my arms allow. I can move my head, and that's all. But I can't look up to see the men. So, Dexter handily kneels down and puts a fist under my chin.

"You're just property, Nance. Worth a little more than a good knife, a little less than a mediocre machine. Mr. Renke will treat you like valuable property unless you give him trouble. The more your worth goes down, the less fun it will be."

He reaches up and Mallory must hand him another strip of cloth, which he uses to pull my head down, catching the cloth around the cuffs. Mallory drapes something heavy, a tarp maybe, over me, and we're moving. A minute later the cold and the angle tell me we're headed up the ramp. One of them keeps a hand on my back.

We must be outside when they lift me roughly onto a surface and push me away from them. Their voices fade. Can the cops see me from where they are? They're supposed to be across the street. I tremble and strain, but I doubt I'm moving the tarp. Voices come close again, and something hits the surface next to me. A box of waists, I suspect. I likely made some of them. From the sound and vibration, a gate of some sort closes then, and my best guess is a motor truck with a gate to keep things—property—from sliding out.

I can hear their voices but can't make out much. I recognize cranking and the truck starts. Mallory's closer when he says, "Hurry back." So, I'm riding somewhere with Dexter, somewhere I'm sure I don't want to go.

40

Captain Mike Messerton is ready to dispatch Nelson, a cop from the Eighth, to trail Renke and Julia. Even though Carl insists to the captain that it isn't Julia.

Messerton's listening, but Carl struggles to explain that the walk is wrong, the body too voluptuous, the hair too dark. He knows Messerton's considering his observations about another man's fiancée. And Carl doesn't care. Messerton just needs to listen and believe.

The captain decides to telephone Chief Wright, let him know in case the pair show up in the Station. He tells Nelson to return to the old office building where they're waiting or to find the chief at Union Station, whichever's close and quick to the pair's destination. Meanwhile, he and Carl and Irwin Edwards return to watching Justice Waists from a window of the building one door south across Locust.

Carl can hardly stand still at the window for the need to pace. He turns to the glass with an oath when, probably a quarter of an hour after Renke left, an auto-truck pulls out. There're boxes on back and something covered by a tarp.

"Could be legitimate. They have to ship out the waists they make." Messerton's frowning at the vehicle, then craning to see it, as it turns west, away from them.

Irwin Edwards asks, "Why not more boxes? And what do you suppose is under that tarp?"

"A sewing machine?" Messerton suggests.

Carl presses the side of his face against the window. "He's turning."

Edwards tries to get a window up while Messerton imitates Carl. By which time the truck is gone.

"He turned north?" Messerton asks.

Carl whirls to face the officers. "Meaning he isn't taking cargo to the Station." He take a moment to finger a sense of dread he can't explain. "We should follow the truck, not Renke."

"With what? We don't have an auto." Edwards sounds worried for the first time. Good. His aplomb is irritating Carl.

Messerton reaches for the telephone again. Chief Wright's waiting for any word of movement.

Apparently, the chief's saying he'll send someone out to look for the unusual vehicle. Probably too late. And then the chief gets distracted when Nelson walks in. Renke and the woman have gone in Ellie's brothel on Twenty-first. Messerton repeats that for Edwards and Carl's benefit and rings off.

Nelson hadn't stayed to watch for any other movement, it seems, and Messerton decides he's the man to go in and check out the situation. He leaves, on the run, for Ellie's place.

Carl frets over the truck, frets over the silent telephone, frets over what might be happening inside Justice Waists. He would be relieved if Irwin Edwards thought his fretting silly.

When the machine does ring, it's Chief Wright. Messerton's back from the brothel and has chilling news: the woman wearing Julia's clothes was one of Ellie's harlots. Renke left in an auto waiting behind the brothel. Ellie was willing to say all this because her girl

Delilah recognized Julia from the raid that freed Meredith and is very worried about "the police woman."

Furthermore, Ellie's puzzled about a man Renke brought in the night before. He appears to be a Kansas City cop. And he left with Renke, in the auto.

The open question is whether Delilah told Renke that Julia works for the police. Delilah denies it and Ellie vouches for her, but Messerton repeats that they're terrified of Renke. Chief Wright wants Nelson, who's returned to Locust Street, to stay put and stay close to the telephone in case anything happens at the factory, but he wants Edwards to join the men at the Station. And Carl, if he so chooses. As if he'll stay and stare at this cursed building.

When he and Edwards break into the meeting room, behind the stylish dining room of Harvey's, Carl looks immediately for Will. It takes a second. Lord, Carl hates the dark hair.

Will's sitting at one end of a longish table covered in white linen. It would be the head table if the room were hosting a civic meeting. Chief Wright and Alexander Reed sit close by on the far side. Messerton has one hip on the near edge of the table and stops in mid-gesture when they come in. Red Witherspoon is leaning over a table to Carl's right, looking closely at a map.

Messerton keeps talking. "So, Schroeder. You think she must have been in—or on—that truck. Right?"

"It makes sense. The woman with Renke was a decoy. It's either the truck or he's keeping Julia in the factory."

Red looks up. "You know, I could go in there, the factory, and say I've changed my mind."

The chief snorts. "And someone would say she was gone, whether she was or not. That won't do any good."

Messerton says, "Maybe we should send a man down that alley, see what can be seen from those windows, maybe check an open door."

"It would have to be open," Reed says. "Otherwise, I need to get a warrant from a judge."

In response to a look from Chief Wright, he adds, "Judge Seymour knows what's going on today. I could do that."

"And we could be wasting time." Edwards is playing with a cigar as he talks. "And tipping off his men. He's not there, and one of them was maybe driving the truck, but that'd leave one of the cutters, right?"

Red nods.

"Let's think about the truck just a minute." Chief Wright's making notes. Or nervous circles. "Where would he take her on a truck? Surely he isn't driving to KC. If that's really the destination, he's going to get on a train someplace. Renke, that is. He'll have to meet up with the truck driver at a depot."

Carl asks the obvious. "You've checked the trains here, right?"

"They weren't on the 9:05 to KC. That was the reasonable connection for early morning—since he wanted her before eight. The next connection is the 12:10 Wabash." The chief appears to be writing it as he speaks. Carl wants him to look up, look somebody, Will maybe, in the eye.

William speaks up anyway. "We know they didn't get on the passenger cars. We didn't check cargo. Where was she, Carl? On the seat in the truck? Or on the platform?"

Damn. Carl doesn't want to say what he's thinking. Which is a silly and dangerous concern. "I didn't see anyone up front with the driver, but it's possible. I suppose she could have been on the floor in the front." Carl takes a breath and says it. "My guess is she was on the back of the truck, under the tarp."

Reed leans forward. "Why the truck, instead of being in the building?"

William answers. "Because there's no point in keeping her there. I've been in that basement, part of the tour I got. There's no photography studio, nothing like the set-up in Chicago."

Carl holds his breath for a second, remembering the place in Chicago. Thank God the telephone rings.

It's Aaron Jamison, who's watching traffic downstairs. That isn't an easy job because the Station is chaos today. There're dueling prohibition demonstrations outside, and the participants are using the shops of the Station as refueling and nursing venues. Carl would have been in the middle of it.

Jamison has recognized the cutter named Dexter, from seeing him outside the factory. The man has just made it to the head of the line at the telegraph window.

Everyone jumps to their feet, but it isn't clear what they should do. The chief turns to Reed. "We need the message." Into the phone he says, "Have someone down there . . . who's there? . . . Laidlaw? . . . follow him . . . maybe two of you so one can phone back."

Messerton's moving as he says, "I can get the message. It's probably Jordan, the manager, down there. He'll give it to me."

Carl realizes there isn't that much difference between Chicago cops and St. Louis officers. Messerton, at least, is one of the same breed.

Will undoubtedly wants to go downstairs, and that would be a very bad idea. Red's looking anxious as well, and the cutter would recognize him before Aaron. Carl grabs his hat and follows Messerton and Edwards. He glances back at Will, who nods him on.

Downstairs, Messerton pounds away on the side door of the telegraph office. Carl intends to stay right behind him. Aaron

Jamison is telling Messerton what Dexter looks like: tallish, more slender than not, long hair. Really, that's his only distinguishing characteristic. Long hair and the look on his face. Messerton snorts.

Jordan's busy, but he takes time to sigh as he lets Messerton in. The captain pushes within inches of the taller man. Carl figures lots of men are taller than Messerton, and that's why the captain's so aggressive. He has a way of going up on the balls of feet and vibrating in a man's face.

Messerton doesn't wait for Jordan to ask how he can help the police. "A man was just in here, a suspect in a kidnapping. We need the message he sent."

A frown settles on Jordan's face. "Now Captain Messerton, you know we can't give you people's telegrams without a court order. People send telegrams like letters. You wouldn't tell the post office to open a letter for you."

Messerton's vibrating visibly. He lowers his voice. "Look, Jordan, this isn't some old case we're working on. That man just tied a woman up and sent her away to a brothel, probably in KC. We need to know what's happening right now. Do you understand? We can wait for your damn order and sit around while she's raped somewhere. I don't think you want to deal with us if you let that happen."

Jordan swallows hard and says, "What man? Are you going to go through all the messages?"

Aaron Jamison crowds closer. "It's been in the last five minutes, and we could see which were sent by men matching the description and if any went to Kansas City."

Jordan seems to think it will be best to get it over with. He gets the description from Jamison and asks his clerks, one by one, if they've seen such a person in the last few minutes. The clerk on the far left has. He smiles to stall a fuming patron and immediately turns and frowns at his boss. They talk briefly, and the man pulls out the second message from the top in his "sent" pile, shaking his head.

Jordan walks over to the cops and Carl, shaking his head as well.

"This one fits your bill, but I sure hope you know what it means."

Carl cranes his head over the captain's shoulder and sees a series of letters and numbers. No words at all.

"You're sure this is the one?" he asks.

Jordan looks at him closely, no doubt not recognizing an officer from either district that borders the Station. But he answers. "The man fits your description. Freddie says he took it slow to get the numbers right. It's harder to send something like this than words that make sense. The man was urging him to hurry it up. Said he'd been out to Ferguson with a delivery, and the line wasn't working there. Seems possible." Jordan looks disgusted suddenly. "They've been having a problem out there, and we've routed around it. Meant he had to stop here, he said, and couldn't hardly get parked for the demonstrations. Freddie remembers because it's that much harder to send something when the customer keeps yammering at you."

Messerton offers as much charm as he ever musters. "Great work, Jordan. You've given us a place to start."

Messerton walks out with the message in hand. Jordan starts to protest and then gives up.

The four men stop when Thomas Donaldson, a sergeant from Central District, runs up to them. "We followed the man Aaron pointed out." He glances at Carl and goes on, probably figuring Messerton would have kicked a reporter out by now if he shouldn't hear this.

"Our man sending the telegraph was driving a truck, fair-sized platform on back. I heard the chief mention a truck leaving the waist factory, so I sent Laidlaw to try and follow it. The kid's fast and the traffic's so bad out there, he can keep up with it on foot. For a while. At least over to Locust.

Carl sighs as they all troop up the stairs. The thought of Julia as cargo is causing the muscles of his stomach to tighten, but this is the kind of break they have to have. On the other hand, from Ferguson the train will be headed to KC with at least a three-hour head-start. If they can verify all this.

41

Messerton bursts into the big dining room shouting, "Ferguson. The captain rushes toward the head table. "He turned north off Locust, could have been heading to Ferguson."

Carl watches everyone react. Even Will rises. Red's immediately back to his map.

"What's the connection with Ferguson?" Chief Wright's leaning across the table, demanding an answer.

"Did you walk off with the telegram message?" Reed's pointing to the paper in Messerton's hand and shaking his head.

"Yeah," Messerton answers the prosecutor. "Want to see what you make of it? The only thing I get there is the address. In KC."

Red leaves his map and crowds around the table to read the message, such as it is. "Are you sure this is Dexter's message?" he asks Aaron.

"Sure as we can be."

Everyone shakes their heads, and Will's the one who takes the paper and continues to study it, while Messerton explains the Ferguson connection.

Red says, "The Wabash that leaves at 9:05, the one we thought they'd missed . . . it could have gotten up to Ferguson at about the right time. Maybe Renke and the driver met up there, and Renke's got Julia on that rail after all."

Will looks up, and everyone else stares at the sergeant with the strange hair. It's a theory that fit the facts, and everyone knows it.

The chief grabs the telephone and asks for a connection to the Ferguson depot. When he gets it, he asks to speak to any constable or St. Louis County deputy who might be on patrol. The room gets quiet as he says, "Officer Simmons. Chief Wright in St. Louis here. I've got a question for you."

The chief nods and ahas and looks up at Messerton. Then at Will, who's gone still. "I see, that's a big help, and I'm glad you phoned. I hadn't gotten the word yet, but that was smart of you. Good work, Simmons. We're on it."

The chief has been smiling as if the man on the other end can see him. The smile disappears immediately, and the chief slams the base to the table. The earpiece falls off, and he knocks the whole thing over in response. Reed quietly rights it.

"Sure enough. God dammit, god dammit, Mike, I told you this was . . ." The chief picks his note pad up and throws it against the wall. "O.K. County deputy's already phoned Four Courts, who's probably looking for you, Sergeant." He nods at Donaldson. "Thought it was real suspicious when two businessmen and a Kansas City cop dragged a female prisoner onto the KC run at the last minute. It was one of the businessmen doing the talking. Said he was helping the Kansas City police transfer a prisoner because the woman had worked for him, and he certainly did feel bad about that and was headed to KC anyway, and they'd take a compartment. Didn't want the traveling public to have to see such a sight."

Red's cursing as he reaches for the train schedule beside his map. "Timing's right. Should be at Kinloch in half an hour." Carl can tell everyone's ready to move out, to ride in rescue to Kinloch. Will's the only one not moving.

"We can't drive it by then, certainly not with this traffic. And we can't leave by train until noon." Will's tone freezes everyone in the room.

The chief turns toward him, stricken. Will says, "You could have them hold the train at Kinloch. But unless you have someone you trust there to get her off immediately, Renke will get suspicious, maybe take her hostage if he sees police approaching. Same's true all the way to KC."

Carl gets in front of William. "KC when? There're lots of stops on a Saturday. It'll be late afternoon. You think she's safe riding for seven hours in a compartment with Oscar Renke?"

"I think she's better off in the train with him thinking he's safely away than with someone storming the compartment. It's the three-hour head start I'm worried about. She'll be in KC for three hours before we get there."

"And what if he's figured out who she is?" Carl slams a fist on the table in front of Will.

"Then she's dead already," Reed says quietly.

"No, no, no," Wright's yelling now. "If we thought that were the case, we'd never have started this."

Messerton nods as he looked from one to another. "Why would you go to all that trouble to kill her on the train? This is pretty good proof he thinks everything is going as he planned it. If he thought there was anything fishy going on, he's probably convinced his little deception with Delilah took care of cousin Enos and everything else. The one thing he doesn't know is that Jamison saw Dexter downstairs." He's still nodding. "This is good, really."

"What did the men look like? Did you get a description, Chief?" Will's voice is more clipped than usual.

"Just that one did all the talking, and the other was a small man who kept quiet."

Will draws in a ragged breath.

"What is it, Mac?" Messerton asks. "Do you think it's not Renke?"

"I don't doubt it's Renke. It's the small, quiet man I'm worried about." Will looks at Carl. "It could be Bauer."

"The one who wouldn't give Schroeder the books. Well could be," Messerton says. "Does that make anything worse?"

Will swallows hard. "The night before you all moved to the northside"—he nods to Red—"Julia and I went to eat at the Castella. Bauer was at a table near the door. I immediately pushed Julia behind me and ordered her out of the building. She left, and I went to speak to Bauer, said hello, said I was supposed to meet someone who should have been there. I said goodnight and left." Will turns the telegram over in his hand. "Bauer looked surprised but didn't mention seeing my companion."

When Will looks up, everyone's staring. "I wasn't worried that Renke knew who she was this morning. I'm worried he's finding out about now—at least that Julia has a connection to me."

No one has an answer to that. Maybe, like Carl, they can't breathe sufficiently to say anything. Finally, Messerton says, "Well, we can't control that. We've got to think what we can do."

Red Witherspoon takes two tries and finally says, "I agree about the county officers in Kinloch or wherever, but what about the KC police? The problem with letting him take her off the train there is that he could rape her first thing when they get to wherever they're going."

Chief Wright runs a hand over his face, and Carl can read all the regret in his face. "Well, Red, we don't know that KC will help. It depends on how much Renke's paid the Pendergasts." The chief lets out a huge sigh and then moves into action.

"We're going to assume Bauer is smart enough not to say anything—or that he didn't see her—or that Julia can talk him out of it. I'll get hold of Chief Benson in KC and feel him out. I think Renke will toy with her for a while, maybe take some of his photographs. Thomas, I want Jimmy Parson with us, for the photography angle. I won't know what I'm looking at. Get him over here. I'm going to get us a private car so we can plan on the way." The chief bustles out of the room, and Reed hurries to catch up with him. Donaldson grabs the telephone.

Red and Aaron join Carl at Will's end of the table. Red has the guts to say, "It's hell not being able to do anything."

Will nods. He has the message in his right hand and something he's fingering in the left. Is that a lock of hair? A braided lock? No, it can't be. Neither of them would be that sentimental. Or old-fashioned. Carl has a lump in his throat that leaves him silent, and Will smiles briefly to see it.

Aaron says, "But at least we know where she is. That's better than running all over town looking for her." He adds, "What we need is one of your aeroplanes, Mac. Just fly right over that train and be waiting in KC." He smiles weakly. Will looks up and stares at him and then turns his gaze on Carl.

"Do you suppose we could locate a pilot? And an aeroplane? Maybe we could contact Al Lambert and ask."

Carl swallows and tries to think. "I don't know. But if there were a pilot and a machine out there, could it make it all the way to KC? I think it would have to stop for fuel. Where would it land in KC? If it's as far from a landing spot to the KC depot as it is from Kinloch to Union Station, you'd have to have a car as fast as TR's to meet the train."

Red shifts. "I think there's another possible problem. You'd be by yourself. And we don't know if we can count on help from the KC police."

Carl shudders. He doesn't envy Micah Wright the call to KC, where the police take orders from the Pendergast family.

Red's looking at Will with regret. "Not that you can't handle yourself, Mac, but I'd be more comfortable if there were a lot of us on the ground at that address." He nods toward the paper in Will's hand.

Carl watches the hope fade from Will's face, watches the eyebrows fall, watches his friend rearrange his features in their usual cool pattern.

"You're right," William says, nodding to Red. "We need a full complement of men to deal with whatever we find—whether the KC cops help or not." He gives Aaron a nod, too. Probably to make Aaron feel better. Witherspoon looks like he's biting back more curses; he twists in his seat.

The telephone rings again, and Donaldson, who's just put it down, grabs it. "Right. That's what we thought. Good work, Laidlaw. Sounds like you're out of breath. Stay up there with Nelson. I think we've got her located on a train, but just in case, stay put."

Donaldson looks at the group at the end of the table and then to Messerton and Edwards, who're talking over by the door.

"Truck's back to the factory. Empty. Nothing at all on the back. The man Jamison saw downstairs went in a back door, off the alley. In a hurry."

Carl leaves off muttering, "Dammit, Bauer" under his breath and finally finds a voice. "At least we've got an address in KC off that telegram. What is it, Will?"

William doesn't even look down. He's memorized it already. "816 Mulberry. I think that's near the Depot. In the red-light district." Everyone reacts. And Carl tries to still his shudder: the address makes sense, a sick, gut-tightening sense.

42

There's a roaring in his head. It comes, that sound, when he's excited or scared. Or once, really angry. Hig isn't angry now, though. He's excited. He's going to see her any minute.

The boss seems excited, too. But Hig thinks that's because the train's leaving in ten minutes. The boss talked to the conductor and arranged for a compartment for the four of them. The boss and the little man who works for him in St. Louis and Hig and his new woman. Hig doesn't know exactly what a compartment is, but he's too busy looking for the auto-truck to ask.

It seems like ages ago the boss telephoned. It was Wednesday night, and the boss must have known he'd be at Anna's. The boss said he thought he'd secured the woman, the live one to replace Hig's dead woman, and the boss needed his help to get her to Kansas City. Said he'd let Hig know for sure at the last minute.

Hig hadn't imagined it would be so hard. He'd thought the boss would just get the woman on the train, and he'd meet them at Union Depot. But the boss had to do it his way. One of the boss's men brought her to the depot at this town called Ferguson just outside St. Louis—under wraps, the boss said with a laugh—and Hig could see her and ride back to Kansas City with her.

Hig hopes that will make the trip a lot quicker because he'd thought the train would never get to St. Louis yesterday. Hig has never traveled so long or so far in his life.

And he'd been scared silly when he got off the train. He knew he was indoors, but he could barely see the ceiling of the train shed. And then he walked into the big midway. It would be bigger, of course, than the little depots along the route, but he couldn't imagine a station bigger than the Union Depot he sometimes patrolled at home.

There could've been a thousand people, Hig thought, all hurrying to be somewhere, and stairways like he'd seen in a book about castles, leading up to a big wall of a building. A building inside a building yet. People were selling everything imaginable and holding up signs about the liquor vote and yelling at each other.

Hig had gotten distracted watching some of the hated St. Louis cops trying to keep order. He wondered if the ones who killed his woman were here. His first woman.

And then the boss had appeared and the roaring in Hig's head had gone almost away, and the crowd was still loud. The boss had taken him upstairs to a grand hall with a huge curved ceiling and polished wood and sparkling tiles and deep soft chairs. And wonderful paintings of women in gauzy little gowns that showed their necks and shoulders and arms. Dressed like Greek women, the boss said. When they'd left, Hig had looked back, through the crowds and their signs, to see that the station really was a castle on the street side.

Now the house where he spent the night was more like home. The madam, Ellie, was prettier than Anna, but you could see she wasn't used to him. She'd looked angry when the boss told her Hig could have a woman "on the house," but she'd done it, of course. The one he got was the one who got up early to go with the boss and came back with him in different clothes. That was just before they got in the boss's auto again, and the boss had clapped him on the back, and said, "We got her. It worked, Hig."

Hig doesn't care about the woman he had last night. He's only interested in the one the boss has chosen to take to Kansas City. The boss is going to take photos of the new woman, and Hig can't wait to see that. And help the boss make art.

Hig doesn't see her at all at first. The truck has stopped behind the depot, and they have to go 'round back and help the driver move a box out of the way. Hig stands back while the driver and the boss pull a bundle off the truck bed. The bundle, covered in a tarp, is awkward somehow, and they put it on the ground and kneel between Hig and the truck to work on it.

The boss throws the tarp back and says, "Nance, my dear." Hig's busy thinking, "Nance." Her name is Nance. Hattie, and now Nance, a voice in his head says.

The boss and the driver are working fast, untying a rope. Hig tries to peer around the boss and can see a gray mass moving. The boss has explained he was going to dress the woman like a prisoner. Hig thinks that's clever. He's helped move lots of prisoners, and he knows what to do. He's wearing the uniform the boss suggested, everything that can be polished shining. Except for the missing button. No one will think anything about an officer moving a prisoner.

The woman is taller than Hig had imagined. She's almost as tall as the boss. In fact, she's only a bit shorter than Hig himself. Her hands are chained in front of her, and there're irons around her ankles. Hig takes a deep breath and is smiling when he takes her arm from the driver, who's smiling as well.

Hig can't tell exactly why the woman is so hard to handle. Maybe she has pins and needles from being folded up like that. Maybe she's trying to get away. But she can't, not with the irons. Maybe that's the problem. It doesn't look like she has much slack.

When they get to the steps at the end of the platform, he and the boss lift her up, and Hig thinks he can hear her moan. The little man who works for the boss, the one they picked up on the way here, is staring, and the conductor is telling them to wait a minute, they can get on last, and use the compartment at this end of the car.

Hig takes the opportunity to try to see her. The boss said that she'd be wearing a veil, and that Hig can see most of her on the train and her face when they get to Anna's. But he can't resist trying to see through the dark, tight mesh. The boss smiles and says, "Hig, this is Nance. Nance, meet Sergeant Higginbotham."

The woman jerks and tries to look at Hig. Maybe she's afraid of police, being from St. Louis. When she turns, the wide neck of her prison tunic shifts, and Hig can see a lot of shoulder through the veil. Like the Greek women.

He looks at the boss and says, "Thank you."

43

Renke and Dexter drag me to my feet, and all I can think about are the various pains, nothing permanent, not even anything that will last the hour. And then I'm distracted from those.

It's immediately obvious we're at a small depot somewhere and that Renke avoided my rescue at Union Station. And it's clear we're indeed headed west, presumably to Kansas City. I check the sun to the south of the locomotive. And the name Ferguson on the depot. I hear the conductor refer to me as a prisoner. So, I know where I am and where I'm headed and the ruse that accompanies me.

The problem is the company. Renke I expect. But his companions scare me as well. Bauer's one of them, I'm pretty sure. Carl described him to all of us. He scares me because he's scared. Scared of Renke. God only knows what he'll do or let Renke do. I can only pray he didn't see me with William at the Castella or will be decent enough not to mention it. At least I have some time on that, because he can't see me through the veil, isn't trying to see me through the veil, like the other man is.

That man is scarier yet because he's so strange. Once they sit me down on a seat in a closed compartment, Bauer's afraid to look at me. Renke settles in to light a cigar. But the man dressed in a police uniform sits across from me and stares. Does he really think I'm a dangerous prisoner? Then why is he smiling? The man bothers me for reasons I can't figure out immediately. I look closely enough to see that the badge says "Kansas City Missouri" on it, and I wonder if it's really his.

"Are you comfortable, my dear?" Renke asks. I look at him beside me and can't decide my best strategy.

"Well, let's try this," he says. He turns me slightly, lifts the veil by draping it over my shoulder, unclasps the chain, and removes the key. He unfastens one wrist cuff, and I hope that's good. Then he pulls and turns me and refastens my arms behind me. And tells me to stand.

I do, but I'm fighting to keep my balance on the accelerating train, and it's harder with my hands behind me. Then he tells me to walk to the end of the compartment. It's only a few steps, but they're hard. The man's such a bastard, I tell myself, as if that's news. I turn as he directs, and he nods to the officer. Higginbotham, he'd said.

Higginbotham slides to the end of the seat, right next to me. He looks back at Renke, who nods again.

The officer lifts my skirt.

I try to shuffle away but, of course, there's no place to go, and the officer pulls me back closer. He tucks the skirt in the chain around my waist and proceeds to caress my legs. I glance at Bauer, who's managed to scoot even further away and has his eyes closed. Renke's angled back into the corner of his seat, smoking, enjoying the show.

It goes on for hours. Higginbotham makes no move to take me and no move to see my face more clearly. He gets around to pulling up the tunic, of course, and I shiver with the cold and the humiliation.

I have plenty of time to think about it, and I decide

Higginbotham is like a child who's never had a pet animal—and has suddenly been given one. He's curious about everything and has no sense about what will hurt. He pinches and pokes, and I grit my teeth and repeat William's parting remarks in my head. Lordy, William must be frantic. Does he even know where I am?

By late afternoon, according to my best guess, we're surely getting close to KC. I'm freezing and hungry and thirsty, and my hands are numb and my shoulders ache. Hig, as Renke calls him, has me in his lap. He doesn't smell too good, but then neither do I. He doesn't seem to mind.

He looks behind me and whispers in my ear, "They're asleep." Not necessarily a good thing for me.

He lifts the veil enough to pull the damn tunic to one side. It leaves the shoulder closer to him bare, and he starts kissing it. I swear to God he says, "You're my Greek woman."

I've been trying not to look at him, but I turn my face to him in surprise. What I see, through the haze of the veil, is incredible sincerity in the bright blue eyes. He smiles, and it's indeed childlike. Except for a rotting tooth. The thought of being his pet chills me even more.

"I'm glad you're safe, away from St. Louis." He kisses the shoulder again. "You know, the cops there killed my other woman."

I jerk against his arm, and he seems to take that for disbelief. Which I suppose it is.

"That's right, Nance. They killed her. They thought she was a whore, the boss said, and they killed her. The boss gave me photographs of her." He pauses and smiles again, checks to see that Renke's asleep and says, even more quietly, "Do you want to see her?"

I nod, and he reaches into an inside pocket. He pulls out a

leather photo case and opens it to reveal two pictures, facing each other behind thin glass.

The photographs are maybe two by three inches. One of them shows a tall, slender, dark-haired woman posed as . . . a statue, maybe. A naked statue. Her hands are pressed to columns on each side, and her head's turned to be in perfect profile. One long strand of hair hangs between her breasts. The background's murky. I wonder if it's Messerton's Hannah—although it could have been taken anywhere and Renke lied about the St. Louis connection.

The other photo's a close-up, a bust shot and the bust is once again bare. But strips of lace cross between her breasts and press on her forehead. Maybe she was restrained that way.

Hig's looking at the pictures with reverence. He turns to me and surely can't see me well between the veil and the growing darkness. He whispers, "Do you want to know her name?" I nod again, and he puts his mouth against my ear to whisper, "Hattie," through the veil.

Hattie. Could that be Hannah, and we messed up a name again?

I forget about the questions as Hig has more to whisper. "We're going to take photographs of you, and when we're through, the boss will give you to me. And I'll have a live woman."

I try to shrink, to pull away from him. He doesn't seem to realize it. His response is to run a finger over the first photo, close the case, return it to his pocket, and play with my hair. He pulls up the back of the tunic and starts running the tail of my braid up and down my spine. I want to scream. Instead, the tears are flowing again, and I try to keep from moving with the sobs. I certainly don't want his sympathy.

The train halts, yet again, and there's a knock on the door. The porter hasn't inquired about us the entire time, and I hope his presence will make Hig stop deviling me. Sure enough, Renke's on his feet immediately, pulling my tunic down and pushing me back into the opposite seat. Hig's smiling and doesn't seem to mind. Bauer comes awake with a gasp.

Renke opens the door, and the porter says, "We're at the Depot, sir. We can pause for a moment before we move in."

Oh glorious. We aren't going to make an appearance in the Kansas City station either.

Renke grabs my arm and doesn't wait for Hig to help. I can't move as fast as he wants, and he's cursing. Things come to a halt when we hit tracks we have to cross, and Renke asks Hig to carry me. He doesn't pick me up in his arms; he throws me over his shoulder. I almost manage a noise.

44

We struggle to a waiting auto, and Bauer cranks it to life. Hig tosses me in the back seat and goes around to the other side. I twist to get situated, and Renke growls at me to sit still.

It's a chilly dusk, suggesting a cold night. I don't want to go wherever we're headed, but indoors will be an improvement. I look around, in case I have to retrace these steps. The smell of the stockyards helps, but it gets fainter and the river smell stronger, and I get lost on streets full of old houses—looking suspiciously like the Mill Creek Valley in St. Louis.

Renke drags me from the auto and tells Hig to return it. Hig obviously doesn't want to. Bauer, on the other hand, looks like he doesn't want to get out of the vehicle. Renke yells at them to return it now, and Bauer slides over to drive. Hig folds his arms and pouts.

Renke runs his forearm under my arms from behind and drags me up on the porch backwards. I'm ready to roll back down the steps if I can get away, but he doesn't give me the chance. A worried-looking, dark-haired woman opens the door and says, "We're busy tonight. Can I help you get her upstairs?"

Renke doesn't answer her, just pulls me through the parlor toward the back of the house. At least two women and one man are staring. The first woman tries to pick me up by the other arm, and they drag me some more. In the wonderfully warm kitchen, Renke sits me down, tosses the veil, retrieves the key from my bosom, and unlocks the ankle irons. Unfortunately, that only leaves me free to walk where he wants me to go.

He pulls me up and says, "Is the dress ready, Anna?"

She has her hands on her hips, and I know she's debating the wisdom of defying him. I can read it in her eyes, even if he can't. I try to communicate with her, to ask for her help. She has dark slanted eyes and is pretty in a stern sort of way. Stand up to him, I beg, silently.

"It's upstairs." She says it to him, but she's looking at me. He misinterprets the tone. "I'm sure it'll look good, Anna. Give me a quarter of an hour with her, and then come up and help."

Anna nods at me, not him. And Renke heads me for the back stairs.

A quarter of an hour. The going's awkward in the loose boots, and my heart is thumping. I don't want to go into a room with him. I tell myself that I have him, not the other way around. I have him on kidnapping. Probably enticement.

The minute he unlocks the door at the top of the stairs and pushes me through, I know I can add pornography to the charges. The room's amazing, and its purpose is obvious.

We've come up the back side of the building and enter next to a large fireplace. The fire in it lights the end of a long hall. It looks like someone has taken out walls up here and left pillars. Which have rings and chains. There're props sitting around: a swing, an archway, steps that lead nowhere, even a painting of a cottage garden. Electric lamps and lanterns sit about, and there're two large cameras on tripods. And a bed, high and luxuriously dressed.

At the other end of the hall, there's a couple of doors. They must open to fairly small rooms. On the other side of the fireplace, there's a single door. The faint smell of chemicals probably comes from that direction. I've smelled the same odd odors in Jimmy Parson's photography and fingerprint workroom at Headquarters. Across the hall, toward the street side, a front stair must be behind a wall filled with picture frames. I don't want to see those pictures.

The most unusual thing—apart from the chains—is the windows. Windows in one wall must face the alley; I see a nearby roof. But when I look up to see where the dim light's coming from, I'm amazed to see three more windows in the ceiling. They follow the slant of the roof and look to be fixed. As if you would open windows on a roof.

The whole thing reminds me of a barn loft with windows. An odd image. And disturbing. I always used my Dad's barn loft to get away from everyone. I felt safe there. There's nothing of safety here.

Renke's laughing softly. He's let me look around, I realize, as if he's proud of the set-up. He turns me toward the fireplace and tells me to kneel. From behind me, he takes the cloth off my mouth, but leaves the gag. Then he takes the chain from my neck and uses the key to remove the wrist cuffs. I groan with the pain in my shoulders and fall forward. I stay still while he takes the boots off. Good. They hurt. And the fire feels good as I scoot around with my back to it. Renke pulls a chair over, sitting close, looking at me huddled on the floor. I try to pull the skirt over my feet.

"O.K., Nance. Let me explain what's going to happen. Both doors are locked. You can't get out of this room. There's a toilet back there," he gestures toward the small rooms behind him, "and Anna will bring food up. I'm going to be taking photographs of you for several days or longer. It depends. You don't have many choices, but one of them is whether you cooperate or not. If you do what I say, no back talk, it will be that much longer before you join the ranks of the whores downstairs."

I'm not surprised, of course, but I try to act like it. I waggle my head and make as much noise as I can. Which isn't much, given that I'm smart enough not to remove the gag myself.

Renke shakes that off. "You have no choice in that. You owe me money, the money I had to pay your cousin, and you have to work to pay it back. I choose how you'll work. I'll get Dexter and Mallory over here, maybe next Sunday. Maybe ask Hig to help. And when we're through, you'll be convinced. You'll be a whore because no one else will have you. And you'll be available whenever I want you for the pictures."

He starts pacing in front of me, touching my hair, my shoulder, as he passes.

"I've had my eye on you for some time. You're different somehow. Not at all conventional. You wear simple clothes, do a bit of make-up, but you move with energy, confidence. I can capture that. Bind it." He pulls the tunic off my shoulder as he says that. Then he pulls me to my feet.

"Nice hair. Skinny, but I can use that. And my friend Hig wanted tall."

I jerk, and Renke laughs again. "Does Hig scare you?"

He doesn't seem to want an answer. In fact, he's turning my head, looking at my profile. He runs a finger down my nose. I grip the skirt in my fists so I won't fight him.

"Hig's useful. You'd have to be a considerable disappointment for me to give you to him. But he's useful." Renke turns me and starts unbuttoning the skirt. I'm still holding it when he finishes, and he freezes, glaring at me. I let go of the cloth immediately.

"He's the reason you won't have any cops looking for you, even if your cousin changes his mind. Stupid Hig is, like a wall. A wall that will keep you safe here with us." He smiles at me, and I must look as panicked as I feel. He means Hig has connections, almost undoubtedly with the Pendergasts, that will block a police investigation. Or police assistance to their brothers from St. Louis. Renke loves the look on my face. His laugh bounces off the windows in the ceiling.

"Raise your arms." I do. There's no use fighting him because I'll lose. And be beaten silly by the time William gets here. William will get past the Pendergast wall somehow. He and Red and Chief Wright. Renke pulls the tunic off, and I'm naked again.

"Come over here, Nance. Let me show you my work."

He uses the standard handle. My upper arms are sore from men dragging me around.

I know I'll see women in poses strained and sexual. But I'm amazed. I wouldn't have thought there're so many ways to show off the female body. Some of the women are naked, some are draped, some wear sheer dresses. They're in every setting imaginable, and the photography itself is beautiful. If it weren't for the subject matter, it would be art.

We move down the wall of photographs, some large, some small, all in ornate frames, Renke pointing out details. I'm shaking from more than cold. When we turn the corner onto the far wall, though, it gets worse. The women in the first section showed glimpses of chains, worn as part of the motif of bondage. These women, on this wall, are chained in place, held still by force. Who would buy these?

Renke's talking very quietly now, holding my arm more tightly. And answering my question. "This is the hard way to do it, Nance. I will hurt you, during the sittings, and when I punish you, and I'll make sure the rest of it is unpleasant as well. But we can do it this way if you want. I have clients who would love to see you struggle forever on their wall."

I look at him. He looks at me, and I wonder what it must take for women to defy this bastard. I'm thinking about Meredith when I respond to his silent command to turn, and I scream, a strangled thing, when I see her looking at me.

How long did he wait to get her to open those beautiful blue eyes and look desperate? It's a close shot, and it seems like her arms are stretched to either side. She's wearing the white gown I found her in, open past sight and not yet filthy. Was this taken at Ellie's, in the basement? And had he broken a lamp moving his equipment out? Moving fast because he knew Mike Messerton was coming?

The equipment must've been more valuable than Meredith. Lordy. Her beautiful face is etched with pain and anger.

He must think I'm frightened by the photo. He can't know what I know. And I don't want to know what he knows he's done.

"See what I mean, Nance? I think, if you don't cooperate, I'd have to withhold food for a while. You're thin enough, I could make you up like a beautiful skeleton. Now see, this woman was thin, and I could have done that with her."

He doesn't explain how his plans were interrupted, but I can guess. There're two photos of Hig's woman. Hattie. She fits the description and the location. One photo's an enlargement of the statue pose that Hig showed me. Renke looks at it for a second and then at me.

"Make your decision, Nance." He turns me to head back to the fireplace, and I see the dress, on a dressmaker's dummy. Which will have my exact measurements, no doubt.

He can tell I see it. "Anna's a good seamstress. Maybe if you make it to her age, you can retire to sewing, too." He chuckles. "Let's try it on."

But before he does that, he takes the cloth out of my mouth. I gag.

I hear the door unlock, open. A witness. It's worth a try to say something.

"Mr. Renke, please. My cousin will give the money back. He didn't know, didn't know what you—"

Renke doesn't find out how I'll describe his plan. He grabs my throat with one hand and winds his other hand in my hair and shakes me. I grab at his arms and try to scream. I don't hear her come up behind us.

Renke's saying, "Don't talk back to me or I'll make sure you don't say anything ever again."

Anna says, "She probably won't make the mistake twice. Shall we work on the dress?"

Renke throws me to the floor. I can tell he wants to kick me and is holding back. Bruises probably ruin the aesthetic he has planned. I crawl toward Anna, just in case. "Get her ready," he orders. He fumes his way into the darkroom, and I collapse, still gasping.

Anna helps me up and motions me to be quiet. In a normal voice, she says, "Let's see if those measurements were good." As if we planned to work on a new tea gown this evening. But her eyes are full of warning.

She pushes me gently toward the fireplace, probably seeing me tremble, and brings the dress over. I stare at it and shake my head. She mouths, "You have to. Or he'll hurt you."

I close my eyes. Would I rather William and the cops find me naked? I suppose not. Although there isn't much difference.

The dress is done in as sheer a fabric as I've ever seen. It has a poet collar, starched, designed to stand up and slightly away from my neck, and a wide facing that outlines the front opening. Which opens to my waist. There're no buttons, no closure at all that I can see. It's pinned at the moment, but it looks like a dressing gown with no overlap.

Anna unpins the waistband and holds the shoulders for me. I feel terrible slipping into it. I'm not fighting this at all. I have good reason not to. I'm not Hattie or Meredith. Rescue's coming even if Hig slows them down somehow. But by putting on the dress, I'm making it easy for Renke, and that goes against my nature. If I'd been one of the women who thought my fate had been sealed, Renke would be beating me senseless right now.

I shrug into the dress and stand there trembling so hard that Anna's having trouble not sticking me with the needle. She's sewing me into it with a few hidden stitches at the waist. Lordy. It's almost as bad as ropes and cuffs.

The skirt barely wraps. A step will show bare leg. Breasts show through the fabric, bare skin between. Everything else shows as well. It's a sheer, white skin. The measurements were good indeed.

The sleeves are long and narrow and bunch at the wrists. Renke can hide thin ropes there.

Anna pulls a brush out of a chest of drawers on the other side of the fireplace and starts in on my hair. I haven't done much to tangle it, except suffer Hig to play with it. She murmurs, "Very nice. Do what he says, Nance, put off getting hurt as long as possible."

She's right. I vow to be as cooperative as possible and let him touch me as little as possible. That's a kind of courage, I tell myself.

Anna keeps at it, washing away tear marks, applying make-up. When Renke emerges from the dark-room, I'm ready to face his camera. *Kidnapping, enticement, pornography*, I recite to myself. *I've got you, Mr. Renke.*

45

The one good thing Carl can say about this trip: at least he isn't the only one fidgeting.

Chief Wright has gotten them a coach of their own, complete with food and beer, and at any given moment, half of the ten men aboard are moving. Changing seats to share their thoughts with someone else. Moving from the optimist's chair to the pessimist's. Trying to avoid Will, then seeking him out because they've thought of something positive to say. Worrying about him for the obvious reasons and for a new one: soon now the train will stop in Mexico, Missouri, and pick up Will's father-in-law-to-be.

The Wabash line cuts north of Callaway County and Sheriff Nye will have had one train ride already since getting the call from the chief. Edwards and Donaldson have a bet going as to who Nye will be more angry with, Will or Chief Wright.

Carl has heard Will's story of Julia proposing. In detail. Because Will enjoys to tell it. Carl's appalled. Julia actually said she'd give up some of her notions of freedom to marry Will? And he'd said she didn't need to? Good Lord. And the remarkable thing is that William doesn't seem to see the connection between his intellectual position and Julia's current physical distress.

"Lord, Will, I don't want to make you feel worse, but if she was willing to . . . to say that you're more important to her than this freedom nonsense, why didn't you take her up on it? And stop this whole thing?"

The look on Will's face shakes Carl, a look that conveys all Will's immediate concerns and his underlying calm at the same time. "Freedom isn't nonsense, Carl. I'd never thought about it from a woman's perspective, not until I met Julia. But if we're free to decide to take risks, she should be as well. I'm worried about her physical safety, Carl, not about her political stance. Nor mine."

"O.K. Freedom isn't nonsense. I get that. I get that you have a new kind of relationship, and I can respect that. But this whole scheme, this putting herself in Renke's grasp—you could have said no to that."

"Not and keep the new kind of relationship."

Carl winces at his own thought. "Something like you'll defend to the death her right to try this—even if she dies trying?"

Will doesn't break eye contact. "That's unlikely."

Carl shakes his head, to disagree and to lose the images that keep flitting behind his eyes. He can only whisper. "She could be raped on that train."

"Unlikely."

Carl slams back into the seat. "Are you going to tell her father all this?"

"If he asks."

"Lord, Will, he'll never let you marry her."

"She's twenty-one now. And she asked me, remember?" Will smiles with the memory, and Carl groans. "Go have another beer, Carl."

Carl sighs and stands, but as he turns away, he sees Will reach into the bag near his feet. Julia packed it, against an emergency, and Jamison ran back to "their" flat to get it. Lord.

Messerton wavers through the smoke from God knows how many cigars they've all consumed, sitting across a table from Red Witherspoon—who's back in uniform—and fiddling with the damn bulletproof vest. Carl hefted it before Will first donned it in Chicago and been impressed with its weight and construction. Messerton almost has the dent worked out, the dent put there by Cutter Deem's blade. The metal leaves interlock, and it looks like Messerton's gotten them all back in place.

Red is silent, watching his captain work, but thinking about Julia, surely. It must be hard on him, too, handing her over. The sergeant's helmet is on the chair beside him; hair that's trying to return to its natural color down the center part and at his temples catches light. Red manages a small smile and moves the helmet for Carl.

Messerton asks Carl about the Levee, about the Bloody Maxwell, about the Chicago cops. It's a good distraction for a while.

They get quiet, and Carl lapses into worrying about Bauer. It has to be him, from the description. What might he say to Renke—to make things worse?

Carl doesn't find out who won the bet. Sheriff Nye's angry at every one on the train. He starts with his old friend, demanding to know why Micah Wright let this get started or let it continue beyond the damn factory job. Messerton tries to step in with justifications, and Nye replies that he can't see that his daughter's life is worth less than some prostitute Messerton's trying to avenge. Carl glances at Will at that one and gets only a raised eyebrow in return.

Alexander Reed tries, and Carl judges that the man's prestige in St. Louis legal circles is lost on the country Sheriff. Reed tries saying it was all a good idea that has gone wrong, but some good might come out of it yet, and that we'll know soon how much cooperation we're going to get.

That's the other concern. They're waiting for word from KC Chief Benson. Carl shudders thinking what will happen if the KC police get involved and won't hold Renke for any time. Having Renke back out on the street because he paid protection to the Pendergasts will be a disaster. Will and Julia can't burrow deep enough if Renke and his hooligans are on the prowl.

Chief Wright explains that he told Benson he'll call again when the train stops in Centralia. The implication is that Benson will have had time to check with his own legal staff—that being the politicos who march to the Pendergast music—to find out Renke's status there. Reed tries to impress Nye with the importance of that and, of course, the Sheriff understands it clearly. He's all the more angry that Julia's headed to Kansas City.

Reed interrupts, maybe to try to distract Nye from glaring at Wright. "It's the Kansas City problem, you see. Wouldn't be so bad if we didn't have the Pendergast—"

"Of course," John Nye ignores Reed. "Good God, Micah. You knew this Renke might be headed for Kansas City when you let this get started."

Chief Wright levels his look at the man who used to be his patrol buddy and says what Carl's been trying to get straight in his own head. "Julia thought it was important to get the man. And we agreed."

Nye snorts and shakes his head. Likely because he knows his daughter. Then he puts his fists on his hips and looks at Carl for a moment, cocking an eyebrow. Before Carl can think what to say, Nye turns to Will. Will's standing, balanced against the side of a seat, waiting. Nye's likely seeking Will because Julia's told her father of their frequent dates. As to the engagement, Will will have to break that news. If he dares. And he probably does.

"McConnell. I'm glad to see you're breathing after all." The sheriff doesn't sound glad about anything, but those are the words that come out of his mouth.

Will nods. "I'm glad to be breathing. And I'd like to have a word with you, sir." Carl sighs and hears Chief Wright do the same.

Will and Sheriff Nye sit in the far end of the car, and everyone else moves off. Carl stays as close as anyone, although he doesn't know that he really can send moral support down the row of club chairs. Or which man to send it to.

The sheriff doesn't look any happier when he gets up and heads for the beer, and Will's looking out the window again. Although it's too dark to see much. Clouds have moved in as they've rushed west.

At the Centralia stop, Chief Wright hurries off and then bounces back on just as the conductor is getting frantic.

"Good news," Messerton mutters. Carl agrees: the chief has been uncharacteristically quiet and now he's back in control.

He speaks to the car at large, smiling at Will, smiling at John Nye. "Just what I wanted to hear. Benson was waiting for my call. He says the KC officer with them is for real. He's a simpleton who stays on the force because his brother works for Tom Pendergast. Benson thinks he's harmless, doesn't think he'd hurt Julia. Here's the really good part: apparently Renke thought the officer's connection with Pendergast was all he needed. So Renke's been too cheap to pay whatever the going price is in KC"—groans and snickers all around—"and the Pendergasts think it would be good publicity if Benson goes in and cleans out . . . whatever the operation is."

Men collapse back in their seats. William nods coolly. Edwards claps Red Witherspoon on the back, and Messerton stares at the vest in his hand, seeing something else, most likely. Someday Carl will write all this down, not news, just a damn good story.

"Therefore, Chief Benson will meet us with a squad of men at the Depot, and we'll head over to this address on Mulberry." Wright is all but bouncing. "Benson says it's a brothel his men thought was owned by Anna Henry, this A. Henry on the telegram. She always paid, but Renke's probably bought it up, like the ones in St. Loo. Anyway, they'll have some ideas if it's not the right place. I told them about the numbers. They're mulling over that as well."

"I think I know what they are," Will says. All eyes swivel his way. He has the telegram in his hand again.

"I think they're measurements, body measurements like you'd take to make a dress. A dress to model for a photographer."

Will nods to the chief, leans back, and looks into the darkness again.

46

Hig and the little man have to hike back to Anna's from the auto garage, and the little man can't keep up. Hig wants to see Nance's face and see what's happening, and finally, he pulls the man along, more roughly than he moved Nance, for sure.

He leaves the little man downstairs and knocks on the door at the top of the front stairs. Footsteps say the boss is hurrying to open it. The boss smiles at him like he knows Hig's going to enjoy what he sees.

The boss has hung the long black drape in front of the back wall and positioned the steps and the arch painted to look fancy like marble in front of it. Nance is standing on the top step, wearing the most incredible dress Hig has ever seen. It's a white cloud floating close around her, barely touching her. Hig gets closer to look. To look at her face as well.

She's beautiful. She looks at him out of the corner of her eye, and Hig realizes the boss must have told her not to move. She stands in the same pose as his old woman, legs close together, hands on either side of the door frame, head turned to one side. But she isn't tied that way like Hattie was. She looks like she belongs there.

There're lanterns behind her and lights shining in front. The lanterns in the back, Hig figures out, are what make it so easy to see through the dress. The lights in front make it easy to see her beautiful complexion and hazel eyes. Hig wants to run a hand over her cheek, but he knows his hands are dirty, and the boss would be mad. He also shouldn't touch her hair, the hair he'd played with in its braid. One strand hangs down, brushing the side of a breast, waving with its natural curl and the curves left by the braiding. She's a better version of his old woman. And alive. Hig can hardly stand still. She's trembling herself, and Hig tries smiling at her.

The boss says, "Move, Hig." He's been fiddling with the camera and now he's ready. He orders Nance to keep still with her eyes open. He takes the photo, no need for the light to flash because the whole end of the room is lit like daylight. Hig thinks it's the most exciting thing he's ever seen. The voices in his head are excited, too.

Now the boss wants a different photo, one of Nance turned sideways to the camera. He goes over to move her according to his vision, as if she's a statue made of pliable flesh instead of stone. Hig watches every move and can see Nance doesn't want the boss to touch her like that. Hig shifts, uneasy. Maybe he should ask if he can move her next time. He doesn't know why she should be scared about a photograph, but she is, and that makes Hig want to help.

He tries smiling again, and Nance stares at him. When she can look his way. The boss is muttering and changing her hair, working it so that part of it is up and part of it hangs away from her back. Like the Greek women. Hig has to hand it to the boss: it's art again when he has her arranged. Her and the lanterns. You can see every line of her body, her bosom, her long waist, her graceful back and slender buttocks, and those long legs, caught in the light of the lanterns through the sheer white dress. Hig has to remind himself to breathe.

The boss finally gets all the photos he wants of Nance standing that way and nods to Hig. Hig hurries over to pull her down the steps. Tears are running down her face, but she seems to be afraid to take his hand. Hig takes her face in his hands, the first close look he's had. The boss laughs and says, "It's after seven. Anna's gonna get some food up here, and then we'll go back to work."

Hig pulls her over to the small table in the far corner of the room, but the boss says, "Don't let her sit. She'll wrinkle the dress."

Nance moans. She's barefoot, and Hig wonders how long she's been standing.

"Can she lean against something?" Hig asks.

The boss says, "Oh, O.K. Don't get the dress dirty." Hig pulls her back across the room to lean close to the fireplace, making sure the wall is clean first. Nance looks grateful, and Hig feels good.

Anna and the little man come up the back stairs, Anna unlocking the door and the little man carrying the food. They set it on the back table and pull the unmatched chairs around it, the three of them. The boss says Hig can join them but Nance can't. He wants her to look thin. She can maybe eat a little bit when he's through with her for the night. Nance doesn't moan this time, just looks at Hig strangely when he says he'll stay with her. Hig wonders if the boss has told her not to talk. Because she doesn't say a word. Hig plays with her hair a bit while the three others eat.

The boss finishes fast, like he always does, and starts working with his camera. Anna comes over to them, looking closely at Nance. It occurs to Hig that maybe Anna will let him stay up here, stay with Nance. He'll ask. Later.

The little man trails after Anna, looking around, looking up at the ceiling where you can see clouds blowing across the night sky, lit by the city lights. As he gets nearer, he starts looking at Nance closely, too.

"You know," the little man says to Anna, "I've seen her before."

47

Nance has moved somehow. Hig can't say how, but she's closer to him, even though it doesn't seem like she's taken a step. Hig looks at her and smiles. She's frowning.

The little man gets closer still, and Hig frowns too.

"I think I saw her with . . . in St. Louis . . . with a reporter I knew. He's dead now, but—"

The boss hears. He rushes over and grabs the little man's arm. "Bauer, what the hell are you talking about? What reporter?"

The little man gasps and says, "Well, I'm not sure. Not sure if she's the one. I saw a woman with McConnell, you know the reporter from the *Globe*—"

The boss shoves the man in Anna's direction, and they both stagger. Hig says, "What is it, boss?" and tries to get Nance behind him. That gives her time to whisper, "I don't know what he's talking about, Mr. Renke," but the boss reaches for her and pulls Nance around so that Hig's behind him and can't see her.

He hears her scream, though. Not loud. She's on the floor, and the boss pulls her to her feet and hits her again. And she hits the floor again.

Hig thinks she's trying to explain that the little man is wrong, but the boss isn't listening. He's screaming, and he's louder. He calls Nance a bitch and says he wishes he hadn't killed McConnell so he could kill her first and send her body back to him. Hig wants very much to know who McConnell was.

The boss is trying to kick her while he talks, but she scoots behind one of the pillars. The boss catches her anyway, of course, and pulls her to her feet against the support.

Hig's afraid for her, and he decides it's the little man's fault. The little man is backing across the room, and Hig goes after him.

People are sometimes afraid of Hig, and he likes it, although he really doesn't know why it is. He's strong, real strong, he thinks, but he doesn't see how people know that. Right now he wants to scare the little man. Behind him, Nance is trying to scream, he can tell. He hears a thud and knows she's hit the floor again.

Hig doesn't even have to say anything to the man. The man stops looking scared and looks past him. That makes Hig look too, and say, "No!"

Nance is on the floor, doubled up and gasping for breath. Hig thinks the boss hit her in the stomach. He's reaching down for her again.

The little man rushes over and actually puts his hand on the boss' arm. He says, "Mr. Renke, please. When you pulled her up against the pillar, I can see how tall she is."

The boss is barely listening. He's trying to get Nance up, and she's trying to scoot again. The lovely dress is getting dirty.

"Really, Mr. Renke, she's way too tall. She sort of looks like McConnell's woman in the face. I hadn't seen her face before. But she's too tall. I should have remembered that from the train."

The boss kicks Nance in the leg, and Hig rushes over himself. He goes to his knees to help her, but the boss kneels down, too, and pulls Nance up to a sitting position by her hair. "Who the hell are you, bitch?"

Hig doesn't like the question. The boss should know who his woman is. Hig knows. Voices in his head are chanting her name. Most of them. Some are still talking about Hattie.

Nance is panting and can barely make a noise, but she says, "Nance Armstrong. I don't have a boyfriend, Mr. Renke. I had one, back home, sort of, but Enos said I couldn't stay there, I had to come to the city and help."

The boss finds that funny, for some reason. Nance looks at the little man, and she's maybe angry at him. Or some other look Hig doesn't understand. The boss laughs some more and lets go of her. Hig catches her.

The little man keeps saying, "She's a lot taller."

"Mr. Renke." The voice is Anna's, and it seems to come from a long way off. They all look for her. She's facing the back windows, looking out like she's trying to see what's moving on the side street, on Ninth.

"We've got a problem, Mr. Renke," Anna's voice is soft, and the boss stands and moves toward her.

"It's the church people. They patrol on Saturday nights, you know. I'll try to get rid of them."

Anna turns and starts for the door that leads down the back stairs. "It wouldn't hurt," she says, over her shoulder, "if I had a man down there with me."

The boss is angry again. Hig and Anna told him about the church people that patrol the neighborhood, stopping in front of the houses and singing hymns, embarrassing customers, talking about the liquor vote.

The boss starts cussing and says, "Bauer, get down there with her and take care of it."

The little man looks surprised, but he runs after Anna. The boss strides over and locks the door after them. He looks out the window and shrugs.

Hig is trying to help Nance stand. She wants to stay bent over, even when she gets to her feet. The boss comes over and pushes her shoulders against the pillar. There's a ring screwed in there, and she puts her hands behind her to protect her back. Hig runs a hand over her shoulder, but she's staring at the boss. She's pretty smart, Hig thinks.

The boss is looking her over, looking at the damage to her dress. It's dirty where she crawled on the floor, and the boss dusts it off with his hand. It doesn't look too bad. Except, where the boss kicked her, his boot left a mark.

But her mouth and nose are bleeding, and Hig knows she'll have bruises soon now. The boss pulls out a handkerchief and blots her mouth, holds it against her nose. She winces, and he growls at her.

Finally, the boss says, "We can do some other kinds of shots."

He hurries over to start moving the camera away from the steps. Hig caresses Nance's face, and she slowly moves one arm around front and holds her waist and bends over a bit. Hig lets her and starts patting her hair.

"Take that hair down," the boss says while he's moving the camera toward the bed, and Hig doesn't know where to start, but he tries. He's feeling better again, and the voices are chattering away.

Only one of them is saying what his mother always said, "You're aiming for trouble, young man."

$$48$$

fter the longest day of his life, Carl glimpses some hope. Chief Benson seems delighted to cooperate. The man probably is relieved he doesn't have to tell Micah Wright he can't help arrest a kidnapper because Thomas Pendergast said so.

Chief Benson is all hustle and bustle, although he isn't as good at it as Micah Wright. The KC chief does read correctly that none of the St. Louis crowd think there's a moment to spare. He's also impressed that a senior prosecutor is along for the ride. And a sheriff. And then he figures out who the sheriff is.

He invites Reed and Sheriff Nye to join him and Chief Wright in the lead car. Chief Wright says he'd like for William to crowd in, and Chief Benson is taken aback.

Carl joins officers from both cities who crowd onto parallel seats in the back of a wagon. Both vehicles, the old and the new, make their way to a three-story house on Mulberry Street.

Carl can't see how it's come about, but by the time the two chiefs hit the front porch, a woman is already outside.

She's standing on the steps, motioning the crew to get onto the front porch, glancing up as if someone might be looking out an upstairs window.

"Mrs. Henry." Chief Benson might be guessing, or maybe he knows her and is putting a good face on the situation. It doesn't sound like a question.

"Are some of you from St. Louis?" she asks in reply. Without waiting for an answer, she says, "Because if you are, there's a woman upstairs who needs your help."

Chief Wright steps up to the plate. "She's our employee." The Henry woman's eyes widen.

Will starts moving, and Mike Messerton grabs his arm. Messerton and Chief Wright start talking at the same time. "Is Oscar Renke up there?" is the gist of their questions.

The woman nods. She looked at Will, who says, "We need to get her now."

Mrs. Henry nods again and says, "What we need is to get Renke downstairs first. I can do that." She turns for the door, and Messerton is pulling back on Will's arm again.

The woman stops when about half the group has made it in the door. "Are you going to arrest him?" Curious women and nervous patrons are appearing.

Reed speaks up, "He kidnapped her. Isn't that how you read it?"

The woman looks at him a split second. "No doubt about it. Will you arrest him for it?"

"Of course. We'll throw everything at him we can find. He's probably responsible for several deaths we can't prove yet, and we intend to put him away."

The woman smiles and says, "Good. I want my house back. I'll get him down here, and it would be best if he only sees people he doesn't know as he comes down the stairs. I told him a religious group was in the street, and now I can say they've pushed their way in. Once you've got him, you can go up. The third floor." She looks at Chief Benson. "Higginbotham's up there, too."

The Kansas City chief sighs, but the woman starts for the stairs at a jog. That worries Carl, and he can tell it worries Will. Will has his hat off and is doing serious damage to the brim with one hand. He's carrying Julia's bag in the other.

Chief Wright directs the scene, suggesting Messerton, Edwards, John Nye, Alexander Reed, Chief Benson, and Carl himself wouldn't be known to Renke. Carl asks about Bauer, and Chief Wright curses and orders William and Carl into a nook under the stairs. Carl has to pull Will with him. All the Kansas City cops swear off any knowledge of the man, and Chief Benson ordered the ones not in uniform to join the "church group."

◆   ◆   ◆

Hig hears a knock, at the front stairs this time, and it's Anna's voice saying, "Mr. Renke" and sounding desperate.

The boss is cussing again when he jerks the door open. "What the hell is it, Anna?" Hig can hear voices that aren't in his head, that are coming from the first floor.

"I need your help. That dammed Bauer ran off, and the church folk have come into the parlor and say they're going to pay for girls and preach in the bedrooms. Customers are running for the street. You've got to stop this, Mr. Renke, they won't listen to me."

The boss slams the side of his fist against the wall. "Goddamn those people."

He turns to Hig. "Get her on the bed, Hig, and chain her there. Use the ankle irons. Here." He hurries back across the room and hands Hig a key.

The boss goes out the door, and Anna follows. Hig notices she left it mostly open behind her. He thinks he should go close it, but Nance speaks, startling him.

"Help me, please, Sergeant."

Hig smiles at her and starts moving her toward the box that sits by the fireplace. "Now, Nance, you just have to do what he says. He's stopped hurting you."

Nance doesn't want to move. Instead, she takes a deep breath, turns toward the door, and screams.

Hig stands stock still for a second and then starts shaking her because he thinks she might scream again. "Nance, stop it. The boss will hear you."

She isn't going to stop it. She moans with the shaking but is trying for another deep breath. If he lets go of her to close the door, she'll get lots of screams off, maybe follow him and try to run down the stairs. So, he puts his hand over her mouth and pulls her along, over to the box. He sits her on the floor next to it and fights her as she tries to crawl away, ending up by the box with her between his legs. He pulls a handkerchief out and ties it through her mouth.

She gags, and Hig wonders if the handkerchief is dirty. He wants to get the iron on her, close the door, and take the dirty handkerchief out of her mouth before the boss comes back. He has to reach around her tight to hold her arms down and get the iron on her ankle. She grabs at his hand while he turns the key, but she can't stop him. She digs her fingernails in, and Hig says, "Stop that," and shakes her again.

♦   ♦   ♦

Carl's shaking his head over Edwards and a KC officer making obvious comments about the not-so-religious nature of the enterprise. Messerton glares at them and turns to Chief Wright.

"You know the St. Louis madams are terrified of him. They'd as likely warn him as help us."

Chief Benson says, "No, no, Anna won't cross us with the . . . uh . . . organization wanting her back in the fold."

The St. Louis contingent stares, but the answer to Messerton's concern comes barreling down the stairs.

Oscar Renke pivots on the newel post on the first landing, and says, "You people can turn right around and get out of here now." The man's face is red, and his eyes bulge, and he doesn't really give anyone time to move if they intend to. He charges into the group demanding to know, "Who's in charge here?"

The scream from above stops everyone, including Renke, for a second. Everyone in middle of the room looks up, but Messerton manages to say, "Oh, do you own this brothel now, Mr. Renke?" Renke yells, "I do, and I want you out of here. Who the hell are you anyway?"

Carl has a fight on his hands, trying to hold Will. Will breaks Carl's hands off his shoulders and pushes past him for the stairs just as Messerton and Edwards pounce on Renke. That puts Will beside Benson, Reed, and Sheriff Nye, who have dodged around the struggling mass in the middle of the room. Kansas City officers are helping cuff Renke's hands behind his back.

Chief Wright steps into the picture on his way to the stairs and says, "You're under arrest for kidnapping, Renke."

Carl is half afraid to know what's happening up the stairs. He watches Renke who's saying, "Chief Wright, I just happened to visit—" when Renke sees William.

"McConnell?" Renke shouts.

The hair only stops him for a second. Renke breaks loose, puts his head down and charges up the stairs, shrieking, "McConnell" even as he struggles with the handicap of cuffed hands.

Will disappears around the first landing, and Renke's next shout is directed up the stairs, "Hig! Kill that bitch!"

Carl's behind the crowd of officers chasing Renke up the steps, but he can see Will return to meet Renke—and bring a fist up under his chin.

Renke staggers then regains his footing.

Will's next punch catches Renke just below the ribs and drives him back toward Mike Messerton. Renke's gasping, "Kill her," when Messerton catches him, wrestles him flat on his face on the steps, and puts a foot in his back, saying, "I've got him, Mac."

Not that Will likely hears him. Carl can feel Will's footsteps pound up the stairs.

◆　◆　◆

Hig's bothered by Nance fighting him and by the dirty handkerchief, and he doesn't want to see if she'll walk to the bed. He picks her up around the waist, the empty end of the iron dragging the floor, goes to the far side of the bed, and throws her on it. She lands in a sprawl, and the dress is open from the waist.

Hig takes a moment to look, the key in his hand. She struggles to sit up, and Hig starts working the iron around the foot rail of the bed. He locks it just as she manages to get upright. Nance grabs the key from him.

Hig gets hold of her wrist, but her hand is clenched in a fist. With her other hand, she reaches behind her head to undo the gag, and Hig doesn't know what to do next. He's getting angry, and the voices are roaring. One of them chants, "Kill the bitch, kill the bitch."

49

The next thing Hig hears is a sort-of familiar voice telling him to stop it. But it isn't Nance, and it isn't in his head. It's Chief Benson.

Hig only sees Chief Benson once a year, sometimes twice. But now the chief is striding across the room from the front stairs, followed by several other men, and saying, "Stop that, Higginbotham. Let go of her."

Hig lets Nance's hand drop. The chief says, "I guess this is your woman, Micah," looking at a shorter man with gleaming dark eyes standing beside him. The man says, "Julia, are you all right, my dear?" and Hig looks down to see Nance nodding her head and unfastening the iron on her ankle. He bats at her hands, and she says, "Dammit, Hig."

Hig is shocked. He takes a deep breath and says, "You can't do that. The boss said . . ." But there's no talking to a woman. He looks to the men and says, "She can't do that. She's my woman, and she works for the boss."

"She works for me," the stranger says. Hig looks closer and can see a badge. Like the one Chief Benson wears. The tall man behind him is wearing a badge, too, on his suit coat. Both of them are frowning at him.

"Hig, this is Chief Wright, from St. Louis. The woman works for him. They've been trying to get this Renke, and they just arrested him downstairs."

Hig says, "No, they can't do that," but he's distracted watching the tall man move around the bed to come up beside Nance. "Do you want me to get that, Julie?"

Julie? Julia? One of the voices starts screaming, "Julie, Julie" over the other voices murmuring about "Nance" and "Hattie" and "killing the bitch."

Hig watches carefully. He takes in the dirty handkerchief on the bed beside her and her slender hands working the iron loose. She shakes her head and whispers, "I can get it, Dad." And then Hig stares at the man. Maybe. But he thought Nance's father was dead. It was a cousin that sold her to the boss. So she could be his woman.

Another man, dressed in a good suit, no badge, appears and says, "Miss Nye?"

"Kidnapping, enticement, pornography," Nance says. Her voice cracks. "Assault."

The man says, "Good work, Miss Nye."

Hig tries again, turning now to Chief Benson, who's put a hand on his shoulder, trying to pull him away. "Her name is Nance, and she works for the boss."

"No, Hig, she works for the St. Louis police. She's an . . . officer. They've been trying to arrest Renke, and they've got him for kidnapping. He brought her here in chains, didn't he?"

Hig remembers the truck and Nance folded up under a tarp, under wraps, the boss said. And his own part, acting like she was a prisoner. But the chief said she's an officer. He must be wrong. The voices are screaming that is wrong.

There're loud footsteps on the stairs, and a dark-haired man rushes across the room, looking right at Nance. Nance begins crawling across the bed. Hig forgets about everything else, watching her. The sheer dress reveals every movement. The tall man who might be her father says, "For Pete's sake, Julie."

She straightens up at the edge of the bed and reaches for this new man, and he lifts her to the floor. She grabs hold of one lapel of his suit jacket, while the man shrugs out of his overcoat and wraps it around her. They look at each other for a moment, and Hig turns to Chief Benson to protest. He's going to explain how she left her boyfriend behind when she moved to St. Louis, but he's interrupted by even more people crowding into the big room. Hig recognizes Detective Nesbitt from his district, and Nesbitt comes to stand close to him. And he realizes the other men are probably St. Louis police. The voices in his head get louder, and he forgets what he wanted to say to Chief Benson.

The dark-haired man looks like . . . an eagle maybe, with brows that point to his nose and make him look angry and stern. But he kisses Nance on the forehead, and Hig can tell she likes it. In fact, she runs an arm under his coat, and Hig can feel his anger rising.

Then the man holding her looks up at him, stares right at Hig, and says, "If this officer is working for Renke and has a gun, I'd like to see someone take it away from him."

Hig gasps. He's never even thought about his pistol. Why would he use one now? Who would he shoot?

Detective Nesbitt says, "Give me the gun, Hig. For a little while."

Hig turns to stare at him, and Nesbitt holds out his hand. Then he moves around Hig and slips the gun from its holster. One of the voices howls, and Hig flinches.

The dark-haired man nods, and Nance looks up and says, "Is the captain here?" and a medium-height, middle-aged man with close-set eyes steps up, almost blocking Hig's view of her.

"Captain." She's breathless. "Check the wall. Meredith's picture is there, and maybe . . . Hannah's."

The St. Louis captain and a taller officer turn and rush to the wall where the pictures Hig cared for, the picture of his first woman, hang.

Hig's aware of several things happening: Chief Benson and the St. Louis chief talking with the tall man Nance called father, an officer in a St. Louis uniform heading into the boss's dark-room, a tall red-haired man not in uniform crowding close to Nance and talking to her.

But mostly Hig's watching the two officers over by the wall. The taller one, who's maybe a sergeant judging from his uniform, takes down the picture of the blonde-haired woman. Hig had done that, too, because the boss had written their names on the back, in his most elegant hand. Hig liked to look at the names.

They point to the back and immediately look to Hattie's picture. The shorter man takes it down, and Hig hears him say, "Hattie. Not Hannah. Hattie Elliott."

The voices scream, reminding Hig these could be the very cops who killed his Hattie. The voices urge Hig to do something about it. He's across the room before he can make the decision, pulling his knife as he runs. Above his voices, he hears Nance scream, "Hig!" and someone else yell, "Mike!"

The shorter man turns, and Hig can't stop himself. He drives the knife into the photograph the man holds up. The glass shatters, and Hig knows it's his blood that splatters over Hattie's image. What's left of it.

Hig screams along with his voices, and he turns on the taller man who's grabbed at his arm. They wrestle, and Hig tries to drive the knife into the man's ribs. And does. But the knife seems to bounce back in his hand. One voice says to drop it and run. Another says, "Try again, harder. He probably killed Hattie."

Hig's confused, but he hears footsteps at his back and turns, twists the knife and his hand, holds the sergeant as a shield against the filthy cops that line up in front of him.

Nance is one of them. She's lost the man's overcoat and is holding the front of the dress together, saying, "Red, are you hurt?"

Hig doesn't know who Red is, but Nance looks downright frantic. Maybe the man he's holding is Red, but he isn't the one with red hair. And Hig can't hear an answer for the voices. Of course, the man might not be able to speak. Hig's knife is surely pressing into his ribs.

Then Nance starts talking to him. "Hig," she says. "Please listen to me, Hig."

Hig stares at her, and she really looks at him in return, like she looked at him on the train, through the veil. When they'd been talking about Hattie.

Hig pants as he says, "They made me tear up her picture."

"You have the other ones, Hig. And I'll bet the boss kept negatives in the darkroom. You can get more."

Hig doesn't want to tell her he has a big one at home. She might be jealous. Then he remembers she won't be his woman. His woman is dead.

Just then the sergeant tries to push forward, and Hig's hand slides onto the blade, and blood spurts. Hig gasps and stares at the blood that reached Nance. The bright red spots on her cheek and on the sheer fabric over her right breast make Hig think of the wax seal.

She puts out a hand, gentle, on the chest of the man Hig still holds. She says, "They didn't kill her, Hig. Is that what you think, that they killed Hattie?"

He nods, and tears come to his eyes.

"Oh, Hig, no. That's not right." She gets even closer. "Hig, he lied to you. The boss lied to you."

Nance is looking him in the eye. She's tall enough to do that.

"No, he wouldn't lie to me, Nance. It was man to man. He wouldn't lie to me."

"Hig, he did. The cops didn't kill Hattie. She killed herself, trying to get away from the boss. He killed Meredith, the blonde one. He suffocated her in a hospital, Hig."

Nance lets the dress fall open and puts a hand on his hand, the one holding the knife. She pulls at his wrist, and he lets go of the man. Hig takes her hand with his bloody one and stares at the red smears on her beautiful skin. The St. Louis sergeant stumbles past her, saying something. But Nance is the only one close enough for him to hear through the chorus of his voices.

"Hig, he lied to you about me. I wasn't going to be your woman. He told me . . ." Nance stops, like she doesn't want to say anymore, doesn't want to hurt his feelings. He runs his other hand over the blood on her cheek.

And then she screams. She looks over his shoulder and screams, "No!" and his voices scream louder. They're louder than they've ever been, so loud he can't hear what else Nance is saying. Hig wants to get away from them, from the voices, wants to hide in Nance's arms. He tries to get closer and stumbles. Thank God she catches him.

EPILOGUE

*From **The St. Louis Globe-Democrat**, Friday, November 18, 1910*

> *Police Chief Micah Wright confirmed today that the three men now extradited to Chicago in the white slavery scandal are suspected in the death of a young woman at City Hospital in October. Miss Meredith Magruder, who was rescued from a brothel owned by Oscar Renke, was found suffocated in a hospital room.*
>
> *Apparently, one of the men managed to slip into the room because the hospital staff was busy dealing with injuries among the crowd that had gathered to see Colonel Theodore Roosevelt.*

I managed to lower Hig to the floor. Of course, it wouldn't have been a problem in the first place if Mike Messerton hadn't used his billy club. A Kansas City cop stepped in to rouse Hig and leave me free to worry about Red. It took a split second to realize I didn't need to.

When I turned, William was struggling to get Red's uniform coat off his arms—struggling in part because neither could stop laughing. The knife hung from a hole through Red's shirt. Chief Wright was explaining about the knife-proof vest to Chief Benson. Messerton was chuckling and trying to help. Carl was wheezing and wiping his face.

I understood the nervous laughter. The men were tense because their plans had gone awry. But they'd found me in one piece, and Renke was under arrest, and it was Red Witherspoon in danger.

Except that he wasn't, really.

I left them laughing and limped off to get clean with Anna Henry's help. I tried not to say much to anyone, even Will. But it caught up with me on the private train car where Will and I had some space to ourselves. I worried about Renke getting free. I worried about Bauer's absence. Renke had managed to tell any number of bystanders to kill me, to kill William. I ached where Renke had slapped me and where I'd hit the floor, and I couldn't stop shivering.

I cried, finally, and then apologized for crying. And for not being able to let go. Will assured me that he had no desire for me to let go of him, that he didn't want to let go of me either, and that he wouldn't mind the privacy to shed a few tears himself. I knew how worried he must have been. It hadn't been that long since I'd agonized over assassins in Chicago.

When Dad thought we'd held each other long enough, he said, "Micah thinks you should stay with me in Fulton a while, Julie, until he's got Renke in St. Louis and the two other men arrested."

"Not without William."

Dad looked at William, and William returned the look, making me wonder what the two had said to each other on the way to Kansas City. Dad sighed and said, "Of course. McConnell's welcome."

As we left the train, I asked Red to make my excuses to my housemates when he returned my things—and noted he was glad to do so. And then William and Dad and I made our way to Fulton. That night and the next week deputies watched the house and the train station. Apparently Renke was making threats, in jail and in court when he was arraigned, but we assumed assassins had gotten scarce for a man who seemed likely to be behind bars for a long while. Reed had decided that my testimony was enough to arrest Dexter and Mallory on kidnapping charges as well, and the chief had telephoned from Anna's to tell the Eighth District cops to pick them up, guessing correctly that they were at Ellie's, harassing Delilah.

William got a story in Monday's paper, as did Carl. I sat shivering in Dad's parlor and listened to William's words, marveling that they were about me. The reports probably got lost in the election hoopla. By the end of the week, though, St. Louis was once again safe for the consumption of liquor, and the story of a female police agent going into a factory to nab a white slaver had the city buzzing. William's resurrection from the dead made it that much more exciting. I was glad we were out of town.

We convinced Dad there was no reason to wait. Carl arrived on Saturday morning, swearing he'd never take a train anywhere again and declaring—in what we hoped was humor—that we were barely worth another trip. And Saturday afternoon, a scant week after the adventure had ended in Kansas City, a Fulton judge married me and William McConnell.

We arrived back in St. Louis to find that Arnold Bauer had indeed surfaced. He'd walked into the police Station on the Sunday before we returned and managed to leave a package on my desk. We discovered it on Monday, sitting atop the mess that had accumulated. Inside were accounting books, along with a note saying Bauer wanted to give them to me by way of apology that he couldn't help me when I needed it. Messerton, Reed, and Chief Wright called Carl and William in, and they crowded around the two volumes. They found sizeable sums next to women's names, tucked in among legitimate transactions—and larger sums dated a few days later next to the names of brothels Carl and William recognized. Purchases of photographic supplies showed up. William pointed out a missing page corner and explained its importance. Messerton and Edwards scooted off to Chicago that afternoon.

One of my concerns, strangely enough, was Hig. I never wanted to see him again. I didn't want to think about him, really, but I was waiting to hear that he'd recovered. On Wednesday, a call from the Kansas City police confirmed my fears: Elias Higginbotham had died without coming to. The KC doctors said it was an apoplexy. What a sad man.

Three days later, Messerton reappeared with Alexander Reed in tow. The two stood in front of my desk, ill at-ease.

"What's the problem?" I looked from one to the other, and that seemed to make them more nervous. "No one's escaped, have they?"

"No, ma'am," Reed insisted. "Actually, we have good news."

Messerton nodded vigorously. "We're going to hang the son-of-a-bitch, Julia."

"Hang him? On kidnapping charges?"

Reed fingered his watch chain. "On murder charges. The Chicago prosecutors have all they need. And we're going to extradite all three of the bastards."

They could surely tell I'm less than happy; they escaped my desk and hurried on in to talk to Chief Wright.

Word spread, and folks came by to congratulate me. It's great news, everyone said. We've driven a white slaver out of St. Louis. An untold number of women are safer. Women we know of and those we don't know about are avenged. There's talk of a group of businessmen buying Justice Waists and continuing to pay good salaries, trying to duplicate Renke's profits. There'll be less pornography on the market, with all that implies for public morals.

I should be proud of myself, everyone said.

I tried to smile about it in public, but I sat in bed that night, on top of the covers, with my arms locked around my legs and rocked, trying to keep from crying. Will put an arm around me and said, "I'm sorry." It used to bother me that he can read me so well.

"It's only that I want Renke to pay for Meredith's death. Not a man's. Not some old leech he sold pornography to." I rock some more. "A jury will convict him because he killed an upstanding member of the community. A male member of the community. All the women he harassed and mutilated and sold into prostitution . . . where's the justice for them?"

"In the publicity you generated, Jule. Chicago wouldn't have him if the lady in St. Louis hadn't had the courage to go after him."

I snorted and started crying after all. When I finished, I said, "Well, there was the courage of the St. Louis reporter who went digging up his past."

And then, we were under the covers and holding each other, and William let me know he appreciated the compliment.

A month later, the trials ended. Dexter and Mallory were each convicted of attempted murder for hire, to wit, the attempts on one William McConnell, as well as assorted assault, kidnapping, and rape charges. I provided a deposition, and Cutter Deem added the clincher. It's enough to keep them in jail for years. Renke was indeed found guilty of Rosenblatt's murder—apparently Renke and Rosenblatt each had threatened to blackmail the other—and sentenced to hang in Cook County Jail. In three weeks.

Today.

William and I take Carl with us to Castella's to mark the occasion. I don't drink very often, and I've never made a toast before, but I lift a wine glass. "Here's to Meredith and Hattie. Here's to Anna Henry and Esther-the-forelady . . . and working girls everywhere."

We drink to that. But after a moment of looking at the two of us, Carl raises his glass again and says, "Here's to good from evil."

We drink to that, too.

AFTERWORD

Historical Note

One of the pleasures of research is looking at old books in flea markets. Most often I pick up novels from the period around 1910 to get a sense of the language. Occasionally, I find a book that speaks to a situation I should address. Early in my writing, I found *The Social Evil in Chicago*, the report of the city's vice commission that investigated "white slavery." The report noted that the "white" in "white slavery" was a misnomer because women of all races were involved, but the phrase had official standing in national legislation. The Commission defined a white slaver as "a man who employs men or women or goes out himself to secure girls upon some false pretense or misrepresentation, or when the girl, intoxicated or drugged, and not in possession of her senses, is conveyed to any place for immoral purposes."

The Commission began its work in 1910 and finished up in 1911, having interviewed hundreds of prostitutes, sporting house, saloon and dance club owners, police, medical officials, and more.

It's difficult to read about prostitution in Chicago during the early years of the 20th century and not hear the names of the Everleigh sisters, Ada and Minna. You can search the internet for the Everleigh Club and find pictures of the interior and exterior of the luxurious brothel on Dearborn Street.

As it turns out, the sisters had about another year after the events of this story to operate the Club. As a result of the vice commission's inquiries and a particularly hostile mayor's action, the club was closed down in October of 1911. The sisters clearly had enough more than enough money to live on and moved away from Chicago to enjoy life elsewhere.

Oscar Renke's scheme to procure factory girls is not recorded in any of the documents I read. His idea of paying well is a perverted example of efficiency wages—for those economists among you who know the term.

And what about Teddy Roosevelt's historic flight? It was pretty much as I describe it, and you can see it on YouTube. Before that convenience, I happened onto the film in a small room in the history of flight section of the National Air and Space Museum in Washington D.C. When I saw the date, I couldn't resist. And did the promoters offer a flight to a lucky reporter? I find no record of that in St. Louis although it would have been a good idea. When my husband and I were reporters a good number of years later, he managed a flight with the Navy's Blue Angels in the same kind of promotion. Like William, he had a great experience and landed safely.

Book Titles and Music Titles

The books in the Julia Nye Mystery series are named for popular music of the day. "Heaven Will Protect the Working Girl" has a great title for this book, but the original song might sour a little if you take seriously concerns about sexual slavery. The original was a burlesque/vaudeville number that parodied the stereotype of the young woman moving in from the countryside and being taken advantage of. The song was written by Alfred Baldwin Sloane for Marie Dressler—whose exaggerated style made comedy of a serious issue.

You can find the same title for an early comedy "short" and for other productions, including a documentary about working immigrant women. Ironically, that is the situation that leads Julia into trouble in the fourth book of the series.

Preview of the next Julia Nye Mystery: *Bread and Roses*

After Julia's time at Justice Waists, she becomes interested in safety issues for factory women and joins the St. Louis chapter of the Women's Trade Union League. That organization was famously composed of working women along with their upper-class, society "allies." Julia is working closely with an immigrant union woman and a Central West End society activist when *Bread and Roses* opens—and within hours the society activist is dead.

Julia's usual license to investigate her friend's death is sharply revoked by the new Chief of Detectives who is itching to fire her while Chief Wright vacations. Julia's troubles mount as she deals with his opposition and—ironically—with her happy marriage. It is a temptation to withdraw from investigating, particularly after William announces that he can no longer join her and Carl in detection. But if Julia lets the case go, the immigrant woman's brother will likely hang for the crime. As Julia looks for other suspects, the murderer begins to look at her.

And more on the Julia Nye Mystery Series

Please check out my website at joallisonauthor.com. On it, you will see synopses for all the current books in the series. You will also find the description of a collection of short stories and vignettes that take place before and between the novels. The site announces a publication in October of 2021 by Globe Pequot Press, a nonfiction work that owes my authorship to the mystery series. It is named *Storied and Scandalous St. Louis: A History of Breweries, Baseball, Prejudice, and Protest.*

I hope you have enjoyed *Heaven Will Protect the Working Girl.* If you have, please leave a positive review on Amazon or other sites. If you have issues or questions, please contact me through my website.

ABOUT THE AUTHOR

Jo Allison is the award-winning author of historical fiction and nonfiction, set in 1910s St. Louis and beyond.

Jo drives librarians and family crazy with the depth of her research, but delights readers who like good, solid history with their stories.

You can read about Jo and reach her at joallisonauthor.com. Find out more about the time period at 1910-stlouis-by-jallison.com.